Praise for *The Farm*

"Equal parts *Resident Evil* and *Hunger Games*—and just as thrilling . . . A gripping dystopian tale . . . a web of vampires, love, sacrifice, and survival."
  —Chloe Neill, *New York Times* bestselling author of *Biting Cold*

"A gritty, white-knuckle ride . . . fresh, fraught, and super scary."
  —Veronica Wolff, national bestselling author of *Sierra Falls*

"An intense read . . . the kind of book you can't put down."
  —C. C. Hunter, *New York Times* bestselling author of
Taken at Dusk

"Be prepared to stay up all night."
  —Marie V. Snyder, *New York Times* bestselling author of
Touch of Power

"McKay's phenomenally crafted characters—the true highlight of the book—will keep you waiting for the sequel."
  —*RT Book Reviews*

"*The Farm* is a tightly wound atmospheric thriller . . . A very solid read that leaves you wanting more."
  —*Fiction State of Mind*

D0011151

THE LAIR

Emily McKay

BERKLEY BOOKS, NEW YORK

THE BERKLEY PUBLISHING GROUP
Published by the Penguin Group
Penguin Group (USA) LLC
375 Hudson Street, New York, New York 10014

USA • Canada • UK • Ireland • Australia • New Zealand • India • South Africa • China

penguin.com.

A Penguin Random House Company

This book is an original publication of The Berkley Publishing Group.

Copyright © 2013 by Emily McKay
Penguin supports copyright. Copyright fuels creativity, encourages diverse voices,
promotes free speech, and creates a vibrant culture. Thank you for buying an authorized
edition of this book and for complying with copyright laws by not reproducing, scanning,
or distributing any part of it in any form without permission. You are supporting writers
and allowing Penguin to continue to publish books for every reader.

BERKLEY® is a registered trademark of Penguin Group (USA) LLC.
The "B" design is a trademark of Penguin Group (USA) LLC.

Library of Congress Cataloging-in-Publication Data

McKay, Emily.
The lair / Emily McKay.
p.   cm
Sequel to: The Farm.
ISBN 978-0-425-26412-6 (pbk.)
1. Vampires—Fiction.   2. Survival—Fiction.   3. Sisters—Fiction.   4. Twins—Fiction.
5. Horror stories.   I. Title.
PZ7.M47865735Lai 2013
[Fic]—dc23
2013025495

PUBLISHING HISTORY
Berkley trade paperback edition / November 2013

PRINTED IN THE UNITED STATES OF AMERICA

10   9   8   7   6   5   4   3   2   1

Cover photo by Nikki Smith / Arcangel
Cover design by Leslie Worrell
Book design by Laura K. Corless
Title page art © iStockphoto.com/VallariE

This is a work of fiction. Names, characters, places, and incidents either are the product
of the author's imagination or are used fictitiously, and any resemblance to actual persons,
living or dead, business establishments, events, or locales is entirely coincidental.
The publisher does not have any control over and does not assume any
responsibility for author or third-party websites or their content.

*For all the people who've loved Mel like I love her
and to all the folks on the autism spectrum
who've helped with research and answered questions
and given me the insight to write Mel.*

And, as always, for my wonderful husband and kids.

ACKNOWLEDGMENTS

I always choke when it comes to this part. So many people make a book possible. I could not have written this book (or any book, really) without the help of my fabulous critique partner, Robyn DeHart, and my wonderful writer friends, Tracy Wolff, Shellee Roberts, Hattie Ratliff, Sherry Thomas, Skylar White, Karen MacInerney, and Jax Garren. Thank you for giving me hope, keeping me sane, promising me I can quit right after I finish this book and never laughing at me when I get a new idea five minutes later.

Thanks to my fabulous agent, Jessica Faust, for believing in these characters and being the best agent ever!

Thanks to my editor, Michelle Vega, for letting me stretch the story to the limits and always being there to pull me back when I go too far. And to all the people at Penguin who've worked on the book: Erica Horisk, the copyeditor; the fantastic people in the art department who created this great cover for Mel; and of course the people at Penguin UK, Claire Pelly and Kim Atkins.

Thanks to all the people who helped with research for this book: my in-laws—who took me out to the country and let me fire all kinds of guns and bows, Cynthia Peterson—who answered all my questions about antibiotics and gunshot wounds, and finally, the wonderful staff at Barton Creek Pediatrics—who didn't call CPS when I asked how long a newborn could survive without food or water.

A really big thanks to my two Beta readers, Kaitlyn and Kathy. Kaitlyn, you really helped keep the voice consistent and I loved reading your notes about the story. Your positive feedback kept my morale up through the final stages of getting the book to press. Kathy, you caught so many of my typos—things even the copyeditor didn't find. I'm amazed by your keen eye. Thank you both so much!!!!

And, finally, my deepest apologies to the people of Sweetwater, Texas. It is not nearly as small as I made it seem in the book. I've just always loved the name and couldn't resist using it. I drove through Sweetwater back in June and am happy to report they do have a Walmart. So if you ever need to seek sanctuary from Ticks, it's a good place to be.

PROLOGUE

MEL

I wake to a thirst unlike any I've ever known. My body is a violin string plucked by hunger. I throb with it. Pulse with it. Vibrate with it. Sing with it.

I am a Slinky knotted over on myself. My beautiful coils twisted out of shape. The song my body sings is of agony and anguish.

Then the breeze shifts and my nose twitches. Food is nearby. Not fresh baked bread like Nanna's. Not garden grown. But food.

Flashlike, my body isn't a Slinky, it's a spring. I poise and pounce. I fly through the air on the thrum of hunger.

I land beside the body of a Tick. The food I smelled.

My mind recoils as my body lunges. I can't feed on that. I can't not feed on that, either. The beat of my need is louder than my revulsion. Louder than bombs. I must feed. Feed or die.

Before I can think my way out of doing the unthinkable, something slams into me. I am flat on my back and pressed into the pavement. Flat like a flower pressed between the pages of the annotated dictionary. Not a pretty posy, but a beastly belladonna.

The force knocks me breathless. It's him: the silent shark. Sebastian. My murderer. My maker. My mentor.

"Don't," he growls. If sharks can growl. Maybe only tiger sharks can.

But he's all iron muscle, instead of limber cartilage. All gruff anger, instead of lithe irony.

I thrash against him, helpless and small like a pilot fish caught in the wake of a shark. A pilot fish drowning in air. Drowning in hunger.

"I can't let you feed on a Tick," the tiger shark growls in my ear.

I know there's a logic there. A reason he's letting me drown. But stomach trumps brain and I fight him. Unfortunately, shark trumps fish. All I know is hunger. All I feel is pain.

"I'll let you up, but you must swear to obey my every command."

I snap and bite. I growl.

His hand jams up under my jaw, jamming it closed.

"Swear it and I'll feed you."

I recoil and I fight. I can't swear to obey him. I won't.

It's not in my makeup to obey. Girls are supposed to be sugar and spice and everything nice, but I'm no malleable cookie dough, to be rolled flat and cut to shreds.

Even Mary, Mary wasn't this contrary.

"Swear it."

The breeze shifts and I smell it again. Food. Need roars through me. Floodwaters sweeping away the last of me. Of who I was. The girl who can't obey is gone. All that's left is thirst. Need. Anger.

I nod.

I am free.

Free from the small, tight skin of the pilot fish.

Slowly, the weight of the tiger shark lifts from my body. Testing my obedience by increments. I'm too desperate to hate his caution like I should. I can't breathe past the hunger eating me.

Then I am up and Sebastian thrusts something at me. Now more nurse than tiger, he puts a straw between my lips and I drink.

The first drop of it hits like water on an oil-hot pan. It sparks and fizzles on my tongue. It is hot and sweet and heady, like the cocoa Nanna made for us on icy Nebraska days.

I drink and drink. I gulp and consume and devour until the fire of my thirst is extinguished and all that's left are the red coals. Still hot enough to flame, but banked to embers.

And still Sebastian brings me more to drink.

The world is shifting back into focus. Silent and still around me. Silent as night. Still as death. Noiseless. Music-less. Sated now, I feel that loss keenly.

How can I live in a world without music? But I know this is no proper life and my drink is no warm cocoa. Nurse or not, this is nothing Nanna would feed me.

I look up at Sebastian, who stands ready with another straw, another steaming mug of silent death.

He is talking again. Maybe he never stopped. Maybe I couldn't hear him past my roaring need.

"You can't feed from Ticks. Ever. You can drink their blood, but you can't drink directly from them. They all have the regenerative gene. If you pass the vampire virus to them, they will regenerate. Do you understand?"

I do, but only barely. I have always been music and math. Genetics has never been my strong suit.

CHAPTER ONE

CARTER

No one starts a rebellion expecting to fail. No one leads the charge into battle thinking their troops will be massacred. And no one falls in love knowing their girl will die horribly.

I thought I'd trained myself to expect the worst life had to offer. Being ignored by my mother, beaten by my father, kicked out of countless schools, and arrested when I was sixteen did that to a guy. And that's all the good stuff. The stuff that happened in the Before. Before two percent of the population mutated into bloodsucking monsters that devoured every human in their path, especially the teenagers with yummy hormones. Before the U.S. government sold us all out by rounding teenagers up and keeping them penned on Farms to feed the monsters we'd all taken to calling Ticks.

Hey, this is life, right?

Don't bitch about things unless you're willing to get off your ass and change them.

But that's the attitude that got me into this mess to begin with. I never planned on being the leader of the rebellion. I just didn't want to be farmed for my blood. Not when I knew the Ticks could be defeated. Not when I knew there was one bad-ass vampire behind the fall of civilization and if we could stop him, we could defeat the Ticks.

I never thought it would be easy to rescue teens off Farms and form a rebellion. To track down and kill Roberto, the vampire behind it all. To find and rescue Lily and keep her safe. I didn't expect it to be easy, but I thought it would be possible. I thought I could do it.

I hate it when I'm wrong.

I didn't know how wrong I was until Lily, McKenna, and I finally made it to Base Camp after what had to be the worst road trip since the Donner party. A little over a week ago, Sebastian and I had rescued Lily; her twin sister, Mel; and McKenna and her boyfriend, Joe, from a Farm in north Texas. And, yeah, only three of us were left by the time we made it to Base Camp.

Base Camp was located in an abandoned underground storage facility snuggled up under the mountains in Utah. The human rebellion operated out of Base Camp. There were less than two hundred of us: the forty-three guys I'd fought with when the Ticks attacked Elite Military Academy, plus another sixty or so kids we'd since rescued from Farms. Sometimes Sebastian was with us; sometimes not. But he didn't really count as a human anyway.

Getting to Base Camp was hell. Not just the part where Ticks were trying to rip out our hearts or even the part where the deranged Dean had tracked us across the country. Once all the bad shit was over, the actual driving sucked, too. Even though it was unseasonably warm, there was still ice on the roads. Very little, thank God, or we wouldn't have been able to drive, even in the Hummer we'd picked up in Nebraska.

Since I knew the way, I did all the driving myself, letting McKenna rest in the back, while Lily curled in the front seat beside me. It was peaceful, somehow, but I knew it wouldn't last.

Base Camp was supposed to be safe.

We rolled into Base Camp around mid-afternoon. Normally, the fenced parking lot outside the old storage facility was bustling with activity during the day. When you live inside a mountain with minimal electricity, you spent as much time as possible outside, even when it's cold.

I knew something was wrong as soon as I saw what was left of the fence. When I'd left to go find Lily, the fence had encased the entire parking lot. It wasn't electrified—we didn't have the solar panels to operate that kind of thing anyway—but it was topped with razor wire and nothing had gotten through it in the time we'd lived there. Now, a swath big enough to drive a semi through was torn out and peeled back. Like someone had sliced open a sardine can. Something had gotten past Base Camp's first layer of defense.

I stopped the Hummer about twenty feet shy of the gate and left the keys in the ignition. "I'm going to go in first. See what's going on." I shot Lily a look. She was frowning as she looked through the front windshield. It didn't take a genius to figure out this wasn't exactly the safe haven I'd led her to expect.

She cocked her head. "Maybe everyone's just inside?"

"On a warm day like this? Everyone should be outside. We don't have the electricity to power the lights during the day. At the very least, everyone with KP duty should be out in the yard, cooking." I pointed to the two oversized garage doors set in to the mountain-side. They led into the loading dock and were big enough to drive a train through. The tracks went a hundred yards into the storage area. Beside the two bay doors was a simple steel door, which led in to the office area of Underground United, the storage company from the Before. "At the very least, those doors should be open. Besides, when I left, this fence was intact."

I didn't mention the stretch of dirt on the far southern side of the parking lot. Just outside the fence, but away from the tree line was a round spot where the snow had been cleared. Or where a funeral pyre had melted it.

Even though I didn't say this aloud, Lily's gaze seemed to follow my own.

She looked back at me. "I don't like this. I'll wake up McKenna. We should all go in together."

McKenna had been asleep in the backseat for the past several hours. No one would have blamed her for bailing on the rebellion. She was six months' pregnant. But even though I'd offered—over and over again—to drive her up to Canada in search of some last outpost of civilization, she'd refused. She wanted to come to Base Camp. If her boyfriend, Joe, was alive out there somewhere, he would be heading for Utah, so that's where she wanted to be. Which was all well and good, but that didn't mean I wanted to put a pregnant girl at risk.

"No," I whispered. "I should go in by myself. I can move faster on my own if things go bad." Then, because Lily didn't like being ordered around, and I didn't blame her, I asked, "Do you mind staying here?"

She seemed to think about it for a minute. I sure as hell wouldn't wait in the car while she went in. Lily could take care of herself, but I was hoping she'd want to stay to take care of McKenna. Finally she nodded.

"I'll stay here." Then she looked up at me with real fear in her eyes. "But, Carter, if things do go bad, I'm driving straight through the fence and coming after you."

And this . . . this was why I loved her.

Lily had never backed away from a fight in her life. She

scared the hell out of me, but there was no one I wanted on my side more.

She leaned forward, and I couldn't resist slipping my hand behind her neck to pull her in for a kiss. Her hair was soft against the back of my hand and her breath warm on my mouth. She tasted like cinnamon and hope. And fear. Yeah, there was always a hint of fear mixed in there. That was the world we lived in, but here in the car, with the craziness locked outside, I could almost block out everything else. I could almost believe that it was going to be okay. That I would be able to keep her safe and that we'd be able to make a difference. Almost.

A moment later, I was out of the car, slipping between the jagged edges of the chain-link fence to walk across the vast, open space of the yard with only a hunting knife in the sheath at my boot and a Glock pressing into the small of my back.

I skirted around the edge of the yard and approached the door to the office. Just outside the door, I pressed the sole of my boot to the rock, so I could pull out the knife without bending over or taking my eyes off the woods. I left the gun where it was. Unless you had enough bullets to take down a bull elephant, guns didn't do a lot of good against Ticks. I couldn't hear anything from my side of the door. I raised my hand to the steel and tapped out the first five beats of "Shave and a Hair Cut." I held my breath, waiting for the next two beats. Nothing.

For one endlessly long moment, there was zilch.

What if that was it? What if Base Camp was just gone? What if I'd rescued Lily, dragged her halfway across the country, and got her sister turned into a vampire all on the promise that there was a rebellion to join, only to find out that it had been wiped out?

I was good at talking my way out of almost anything. At bluffing. But even I couldn't bluff my way through this. If Base Camp was gone, we were screwed.

I returned my knife to its sheath and pulled out my lock picks. A voice from behind me said, "I wouldn't do that if I were you."

A voice I recognized. Thank God.

I slowly turned around to see Eddie Mercado, one of the guys I'd gone to the Elite Military Academy with, pointing a rifle at my chest. I nearly laughed. "What are you going to do, Merc? Shoot me?"

Merc studied me cautiously. He didn't look pissed off or angry. Not the way you'd expect from a guy who wasn't lowering his rifle. Instead he looked nervous. Maybe even a little afraid, something I'd never seen before. He'd told me once that his mother was black and his father was Cuban, but I'd always suspected there was a little rino in there somewhere, too. The guy was just that tough. I could fight him, but there was no way I could win. Certainly not when he was the one with the rifle.

But instead of lowering the nose of his weapon, he said, "No. I'm not going to shoot you. I'm going to escort you and the two ladies in the van into quarantine. And if you try to rip my heart out anytime in the next three days, then I'm going to shoot you."

I looked from Merc to the locked door and then out toward the charred patch of grass just outside the mangled fence. Suddenly, this all made sense.

I nodded and slipped my knife back into its sheath. "Sounds like a plan."

* *

After that, I shut down my emotions. As I listened to Merc's story, my mind whirled, trying to fill in the missing gaps, to formulate a plan. Find a solution. All my anger, my fear, my panic—I just shut it all down.

Sebastian—my "mentor"—would have been so proud. When you're fighting for survival, there's no room for emotion; only strategy, action, and reaction.

Then again, Sebastian had been a bloodsucking monster for the past two thousand years and he wouldn't know a human emotion if it threw him to the ground and beat the crap out of him. So maybe he wasn't the best role model, but in this situation, he was all I had. I listened dispassionately. I planned. And when Merc was done talking, I gave him a nod that probably looked like agreement, and I walked back to the Hummer.

By the time I reached the driver's-side door, I was done keeping the anger in check. I wanted to rip the Hummer apart. I wanted to peel the damn thing like an orange and leave it in pieces. I might have actually done it, too, but we'd need it to drive away in.

Lily slid over as I climbed into the driver's seat.

"What's going on? What happened?"

I immediately reached for the ignition, but realized she still held the keys. "Give me the keys. We're getting out of here."

She looked down like she was surprised to see them in her hand. She hesitated, and I could feel her looking from Merc—who had followed me up to the gate and was now opening it—to my hand gripping the steering wheel so tightly I was surprised it didn't crack.

She was too damn smart not to figure out something was very wrong. "Can you first tell me what's going on?"

I didn't want to tell her, but figured she had the right to know how badly I'd screwed this up. "Right after I left for Texas to find you, a group went out on a food raid and got attacked by a Tick. There were four survivors. No one realized that one of them had been exposed to the virus. He disappeared into the catacombs deep inside the mountain. Thank God someone figured out what had happened before he killed anyone else. . . ."

"Damn." She muttered the word on a soft exhale.

"That's why Base Camp is all shut down. They're hiding in there. They're too terrified to come out and risk infection again. Merc said he'll let us in, but only if we spend time in quarantine."

I looked over at Lily to see her staring straight out the front windshield. Her chin had that stubborn jut to it and I could tell her mind was racing through the story she'd just heard. She twisted in her seat to look at me, but she kept the keys clutched in her hand. "Okay. So what's the problem? Why are we leaving?"

"Lily, when I got you and Mel out of that Farm, I promised to keep you safe. But I didn't. Our trip here was one screw-up after another. But I thought that at least once we got here, everything would work out. But now—" My throat closed over the word as I imagined Lily trapped there in that mountain with a killer. Panic hit me again and all I could do was curse.

I looked over at Lily, expecting to see horror on her face. Or fear. Panic, like mine. But she was frowning, head tipped a little to the side.

"So you think we should go?"

"Yes. Hell, yes."

"Just drive off and leave them? I don't understand. Why would we—"

"Because I thought it was safe here and it's not. If Base Camp isn't safe, if we can't even go out looking for food without getting attacked by Ticks, then we're all screwed. We can't survive like this. I can't protect you—"

"Maybe it's not your job to protect me. No, wait. Hear me out, okay?" She waited until I nodded before she continued. "When you rescued me, you thought I was an *abductura*, you thought I had this amazing power to lead the human resistance and sway people's opinions. Whatever. If I had been an *abductura*, then, yes, keeping me alive would have been more important than anything else. But I'm not that person. Which means you don't have to work so hard to protect me."

"Lily, that's not the only reason I want to keep you safe." The thought of her hurt, in pain . . . it drove me crazy.

But she waved aside my comment. "Maybe I can't lead the rebellion, but I still want to fight. We've made it this far. I'm not going to turn around now."

"Don't you get it? If you're not the *abductura*, then there's no one to lead the rebellion. We don't have a leader. We don't have security. We don't have shit. There is no human rebellion. Which is why you need to hand over the keys so we can just get out of here."

"No." Lily clung tightly to those keys. "As far as you and I know, this is the last outpost of free humans on the planet. Maybe there are still pockets of humanity in Canada or Beijing or Brazil or wherever, but as far as we know, for certain, this is it. Maybe the rebellion doesn't have an *abductura* who can magically brain-wash other humans into joining, but the rebellion still has a leader and that leader is you. It always has been. And you can't just turn your back on these people. Not for me. Not for anyone. They need you."

When Lily talked like that—like I was some kind of friggin' hero—I couldn't even look at her. The weight of her expectations was too damn heavy on my shoulders. All I wanted was to keep her safe. To just bury my face in her hair and hold her close and maybe forget for a few hours how completely screwed up everything was. But instead, I had to go save the world.

"Exactly how excited do you think they're all going to be when they realize that after everything we've done to find to you, I was wrong?" She didn't answer, just stared blankly out the front window. I followed her gaze and realized that up ahead, Merc had opened the gate and stood waiting. Watching us talk in the car. "Think about it, Lil. Those kids are terrified. They expect a leader. When they find out you're not that person, they are going to freak out. There might not be a rebellion left to lead. The only thing holding Base Camp together is the hope that we can fight the Ticks. That we'll be able to get more and more kids out of Farms and that someday we'll be able to fight back. I think the Greens believe it because the guys from Elite believe it. The guys from Elite believe it because I've told them we could. Because I believed you would be able to lead us."

"I'm sorry," she said softly.

"Why are you sorry?"

She glanced at me from under her lashes. "Because I'm not what you thought I was. Because you thought I could be this great leader and instead I'm just . . . me."

I reached across the console for her and cupped my hand around the back of her head so she looked at me.

Lily was crazy smart and determined. And she fought like a demon to protect the people she cared about. And I was crazy about her. Just the way she was. "You have never disappointed me," I told her. "I don't care that you're not an *abductura*. Hell, in some ways I'm glad you're not. But it's my fault we're in this situation. I'm the one who told them you could lead us. It's my mistake. Not yours."

She looked at me wordlessly, and I watched her swallow as she nodded. "Okay, then. We have to lie."

"What?"

"If they expect an *abductura* and if Base Camp is going to fall apart without one, then we'll have to lie and pretend I'm an *abductura*."

"I'm not going to lie to them."

"You may not have a choice. The reason civilization collapsed in the first place is because Roberto used an *abductura* to convince everyone the Ticks couldn't be killed. If he can lie to destroy humanity, then we can lie to save it."

I turned over her logic in my mind, trying to find the flaw. I didn't want to lie to anyone. When had that ever worked out well? I'd lied to Lily when I came to rescue her from the Farm, and it had led to one screw-up after another.

"I don't know," I admitted. "People are going to wonder. They'll have doubts. And I don't see how a lie like this can stand up to the questions."

"Yeah, if it was just the one lie, it wouldn't stand. But maybe lies are like cards. You can't ever get one to stand up alone, but you balance them against each other and they'll prop each other up." Her lush mouth twisted into a wry, sad smile. "Didn't you ever build a house of cards when you were a kid?"

"No. All I know is that they're destined to fall down." My childhood had been spent in the back wing of the house, playing video games and hiding from my parents, because if they forgot I was there, they were less likely to give me a hard time.

"Yeah. But we don't need to convince everyone forever. We just need them to believe it long enough to come up with a better plan. Or find another *abductura*. Something. And the Elites are used to following you. If you say I'm the *abductura*, they'll believe you. I don't like it, but it's better than driving off and leaving them here with no leader. Even if we could find safety—and there's no guarantee for that, but even if we could—we can't just walk away from this."

"Lily—"

"She's right," McKenna said from the backseat.

Lily and I both whirled around to see her slowly stretching as she sat up. Hell, I'd forgotten she was even back there.

"We have to stay here," she said.

Lily's mouth twisted a little, like she wanted to smile but was too sad to really do it. "You just want to stay here because you think Joe might show up."

"Duh. This is where he'll go. So, I'm staying no matter what. But I agree with Lily. You need to stay, too. You're their leader. You—"

"I can't lead these people," I protested.

"You've led them this far," Lily said gently.

"Yeah, but that was the easy part. I had a plan: find you. Let you convince the rest of humanity to fight. Let Sebastian do the rest. I could do all of that. I can't do this."

"Sure you can," Lily said. "All you need is a new plan."

"A plan to lead these kids, who are terrified and starving? In the middle of winter, when we can hardly leave the mountain?"

"Okay, so that's the first step in the plan: find more food. Stay close to the mountain. And then when spring hits, we go get more recruits from Farms. That's what you were doing before, right? So that's what we'll keep doing."

When she broke it down like that, it seemed doable.

All my life, everyone had treated me like I was a screw-up.

My parents, my teachers, even Sebastian. They'd all expected me to fail, miserably. And all my life, that had pissed me off. Now, here I was, ready to finally live down to everyone's expectations of me and along came Lily. And she didn't expect me to fail. In fact, she expected me to save the world.

When she looked at me like that, I almost believed I could.

CHAPTER TWO

LILY

Lily's stomach turned over as she climbed out of the passenger side of the Hummer. Carter had parked it right in the middle of the otherwise empty parking lot. The parking lot was separated from the surrounding forest by a tall, chain-link fence, and it butted right up against the side of the mountain. Set into the mountain was a door under a sign reading "United Underground." Beside that was a pair of huge garage doors, one of which was slowly rising. Carter had told her that nearly a hundred people lived at Base Camp, but the collection of kids huddled just inside the door didn't seem close to that number—maybe because they were all so thin. Or maybe they were just small compared to the huge, open space inside the mountain.

Lily rounded the Hummer to help McKenna climb out. They'd been cramped in the SUV for a long time. Even though it was big in there, she needed a minute to get her legs under her and suspected McKenna would, too.

She automatically put her hand under McKenna's elbow. Not that she knew what it was like to be pregnant, but if her legs were stiff, she could only imagine how McKenna must feel. Besides, it gave her something to think about other than the hundred people staring at her. The guy with the gun—Merc, Carter had called him—led them through the open doorway without getting too close. Or lowering his weapon.

The doors opened directly into a huge loading bay, a cavern carved out of the mountain. The ceiling was twenty feet up and made of smoothed stone, like the floor. Columns, maybe five feet across, dotted the floor every forty feet. Though the area near the doors was lit by overhead fluorescent lights, she couldn't tell how far back it went. The cave just slipped away in the darkness.

"What's with all the RVs?" she asked in a whisper.

A row of maybe twenty vehicles lined the communal area at the front of the cavern. They were fanned out in a semicircle below the last row of fluorescent lights.

"This used to be a mine in the Before, a long time ago," Carter said. "When the ore played out, United Underground took over. They used the space for climate controlled storage. They stored everything from legal documents to RVs and boats. When we first moved in here, the guys and I stayed up near the front, in United's offices, but when we started bringing Greens back, we brought RVs up from the deeps for people to live in."

"The deeps?"

Carter's steps slowed and he pointed off toward the darkness. "Deep storage, farther in. There are hundreds of storage units we haven't even broken into yet. Once we get out of quarantine, stay up here, where there's light. You don't want to get lost until you know your way around more."

When that guy whom Merc told him about had started to become a Tick, that's probably where he'd hidden while he was transforming. He'd slipped away into the darkness, which Ticks loved best. What had it been like for that guy? Had he known his humanity was slowly slipping away? Had the craving for blood been so strong he hadn't cared that he was becoming a monster?

Lily suppressed a shudder and pushed aside her thoughts, concentrating on taking in her surroundings. When Carter had first told her about Base Camp, that there was a place where kids were banding together to fight against the Farm system and the Ticks, it had all seemed very romantic. Not glamorous, but noble at least. And better than life on the Farm.

But the other teens seemed worn and suspicious. Hungry. And this cave they lived in—it may be safe, generally, when there wasn't a Tick trapped inside with them, but it wasn't hospitable. It was dark and even though it was warmer in here than it had been out in the Hummer, the air was cool and damp so that it already seemed to be seeping through her clothes.

Still better than a Farm. Still better than "donating" blood to feed the Ticks.

Carter led her and McKenna over to a portion of a cave, which had been walled off, and through a door. This must have been United Underground's business offices. There was a large reception area and then a hall with closed doors on either side. Merc came in behind them, his grip on his rifle relaxed.

"Where are you going to keep us in quarantine?" Carter asked.

Merc nodded down the hall. "Thought we'd use your old office. No one moved in while you were gone, so it's still empty."

"How long will we be there?" McKenna asked, following Carter down the hall.

She was wiggling a little as she walked, so Lily asked, "Is there a bathroom in there? Or can we go first? We were in the car a long time." McKenna wasn't the kind to bring that sort of thing up, and even though Lily didn't have to go right now, she had no idea how long they'd be in quarantine.

"There's a bathroom back there in reception—" Carter pointed down the hall. "But we can't flush it without water, which we don't have set up yet. There's another office next to the one I stayed in. We'll set it up with a bucket. Someone will come and empty it twice a day." He paused to rap his knuckles on a door. "Merc will get it set up, right? And we'll be here."

Carter held open the next door so that Lily and McKenna could go in. A desk was pushed against the wall. A punching bag hung in the corner. It was windowless, of course, since it was underground. The walls were lined with bookshelves, most of which were empty except for a bunch of bobbleheads on the shelves right at eye level. There was a leather sofa, three chairs, a useless desktop computer. No sign, however, that Carter actually lived here— when he wasn't out rescuing girls from Farms.

McKenna wrapped her arms around her chest and sat on the edge of the sofa, bouncing a little, like she was excited or really had to pee.

"Can you let us know as soon as you get the bucket set up?" Lily asked just as Merc was starting to close the door behind them.

She wasn't used to feeling so protective of McKenna. She'd known her in the Before, although they hadn't been friends. Not by a long shot. But she no longer had Mel to take care of, and watching out for McKenna gave her something to focus on. Something to think about besides the fact that there were a hundred people out there who expected her to lead them to greatness.

A few minutes later, Merc came back to tell them the bucket was ready. A few minutes after that, they were all back in the office, the next few days stretching out before them.

McKenna flopped back on the sofa. "Quarantine? This sucks. How long do you think they're going to keep us here like this?"

Lily found herself looking at Carter, wondering the same question. "If it was me," he said now, "I'd keep us in here for three days at least, watching for symptoms."

McKenna groaned a little. "That's obnoxious. None of us are sick. Besides, I thought you were their leader."

"No. It's smart," Lily said quickly. She didn't know for sure if Merc or anyone else was listening at the door. If he was, she didn't want to rehash the whole issue of whether or not Carter was the leader—particularly the part about her not being an *abductura*. The longer they kept that under wraps, the better.

"But none of us has been exposed," McKenna groused.

"We don't know that," Lily said gently. Funny, just a few days ago, she would have been annoyed by McKenna's whining. Now, she knew this was just how McKenna acted when she was afraid. Under the circumstances—McKenna must be terrified. She was pregnant and alone. Joe was probably dead. Frankly, it was a miracle she could function at all. "We were all really close to Ticks not that long ago."

"It's not airborne," Carter said quietly. "It's passed from one victim to the next by bodily fluids. Like the vampire virus. A Tick has to bite you or—I don't know—swap blood somehow. We should all be safe."

But his voice sounded desperate rather than confident. That's when Lily knew he'd figured out the same thing she had.

But McKenna obviously hadn't figured it out yet, because she said, "So, what? If one of us does show symptoms, they just leave us in here to die?" McKenna broke off mid-rant; she must have noticed both Lily and Carter staring at her. "What? Get sick and die, right? That's how it goes."

"Yeah, for most people." Lily pushed herself to her feet and moved to stand over by the shelf. Right at eye level was a bobble-head of a superhero—one of the ones she didn't recognize. She reached out and gave his head a nudge and then watched it bob for a second before turning around, but she still couldn't make herself look at either of her friends. "But if I show signs—I mean, any signs, any fever at all—you've got to take me out right away, okay?"

"What?" McKenna gaped.

"Lily—" Carter took a step toward her, but she held out a hand to stop him.

"You know I'm right. So we might as well get it all out on the table."

McKenna wobbled to her feet. "What are you guys talking about?"

Lily opened her mouth, but couldn't make herself say it aloud. Instead she turned back to the bobbleheads, trusting Carter to fill in the blanks for McKenna.

"She's talking about the regenerative gene. There's some rare gene that only about one to two percent of the population has. If you have that gene and you're exposed to the Tick virus, you turn into a Tick."

"Yeah, I know that. Just because I was a cheerleader in the Before doesn't mean I didn't watch the news."

"According to Sebastian, when Genexome Corporation did the research that created the Tick virus, they started with Roberto's genes, with his DNA. They created a virus that mimicked some of the characteristics of the vampire virus. Roberto was trying to create an army of monsters that he could control. So he made a virus that also affected the victims' mental capabilities and he did away with the territorial thing all vampires have going for them, but he still started with the same gene."

"So?" she asked.

"So, if Mel didn't have the regenerative gene, when Sebastian fed off her she would have just died. Instead she turned into a vampire. That means she has the gene. And Lily and Mel are identical twins. Genetically identical. So she has it, too."

"Oh."

For a second, no one seemed to even breathe. Finally Lily gave the bobblehead one last nudge and turned around. No superhero was going to save her. "So there it is. That's why it's a good idea for me to be held in quarantine. And probably why you guys should stay in a separate room."

Damn, she should have thought of that before now. She made a move toward the door to go talk to Merc, but Carter stepped in her way.

"No. Don't go borrowing trouble. We know you weren't exposed."

"No, we—"

"Yes. We know. I was with you the whole time. You weren't bitten. Besides, it took us two days to drive here. I've been watching for symptoms that whole time and haven't seen any. And I know you haven't, either."

"How do you know—"

"The way you kept asking McKenna if she was cold, too? And the way you kept holding my hand to your cheek? You've been watching for signs of a fever. Not very subtly, either." He brought his hand up to her face and cupped her jaw. His other hand slipped to her waist. For just a moment, her heart pounded with something other than fear. "You're fine. Don't worry."

The anguish in his voice as he said it matched the way she felt. Then he dropped his forehead to hers, and she had to close her eyes against her tears. It was all she could do not to press her body against his and just lose herself in his touch. But it seemed wrong under the circumstances with McKenna there. Especially since McKenna had just lost Joe. So instead, Lily swallowed hard and stepped back. Carter trailed his fingers down her arm and clasped her hand.

"Did you really think I hadn't noticed?" he asked.

Lily gave a shrug. "You're the one who's always talking about how smart I am. I guess I just hoped I'd figured it out before you. I didn't want to freak anyone out unless—" She couldn't even bring herself to say it.

"Well, we don't have to worry about that," he said brusquely. "You're fine."

Okay, time to get past her squeamishness. She didn't want to say it aloud, but she couldn't afford not to say it, either. "Look, about that. If something does happen—"

"Nothing's going to happen. We're here now. We're safe. That's not something we have to worry about."

"Sure. Right now. But if I am exposed, I want you to promise me—"

"It's not ever going to happen." Carter's voice was like steel.

Lily dropped his hand, wanting to throw up her own hands in exasperation. "Fine. We'll pretend it's not a possibility. But just so we're clear, if I ever am exposed to the virus, if I ever do start to turn, I want you to take me out before I can hurt anyone else."

"Jesus, Lily, you can't ask me to kill you."

"I'm only asking you to do what you would do for anyone else."

"But you aren't anyone else. You're you."

"If I'm exposed to the Tick virus, I won't be *me* anymore. I'm asking you to do the right thing. I'm asking you to protect the people I care about if I'm not in a position to do it myself." Just to be sure, she turned and looked at McKenna, too. "Got it?"

McKenna gave a queasy nod. "Got it."

Carter didn't respond, but just stood there, his jaw clenched so tight she thought he might crack a molar. She stepped closer to him and looked him in the eye. This close, his eyes were startlingly blue. She thought of all the things they'd been through together. She thought of the boy she'd met in the Before two years ago—

that impossibly handsome, recklessly charming guy. That guy she'd crushed on and then made herself forget. And then she thought of the guy who showed up at her Farm to rescue her and Mel just over a week ago. She knew now that he was so much more than just that hot guy she'd crushed on. He was a hero. A guy who'd put his life on the line to save her and to lead this ragtag band of human teenagers. And he claimed to love her.

"Look," she said bluntly, "I'm not going to just hide here in this cave. I didn't escape from that Farm and come all this way so I could cower. I came here so I could make a difference. So I could fight. You have to accept that."

Carter pulled her back into his arms and tipped her jaw up so she met his gaze. "Fine. And you have to accept that I'm not gonna let you get exposed. Ever. I'm going to do everything in my power to keep you safe. No matter what."

He didn't give her a chance to answer. Which was probably just as well, because she didn't know what she'd say. She was used to taking care of others, not having anyone take care of her. Having Carter in her life was going to take some getting used to. Just like the cold of the cave. Just like the knowledge that she had the Tick gene, that she had the potential to become a bloodthirsty monster.

That was okay, she was adaptable.

CHAPTER THREE

CARTER

Six weeks later

I knew I was in trouble when I walked out the bay door and saw Lily waiting for me by the Hummer.

Spring had come early to the mountain—thank God—and the last deadly ice that had covered the parking lot had finally melted. Which meant we were doing more food raids and sending out patrols nearly every day. It also meant that the ice and snow farther up the mountain was melting as well. Which was why Taylor Tech and I were going up the mountain to the solar array he'd installed last fall. Taylor had landed at Elite for stealing, hacking, and reselling five hundred iPads from his old school district. If it had wires and a circuit board, he could hack it. And thank God for that, because if it hadn't been for the solar panels he'd scavenged and then set up, we wouldn't have any electricity at Base Camp. Living in the caves without light would be difficult, but without the air filtration system, it would be impossible. Just up the mountain from camp, the solar panels had been inaccessible for most of the winter. Which was why Taylor and I needed to check on them today, make sure they were in good shape, and hopefully have time to install a few of the new ones that had been scavenged in the last food raid.

While I couldn't blame Lily for wanting to be outside now that the temperature was finally above freezing, I didn't like it. Even though she was still inside the fence line. Even though I was right here. Even though there was no way a Tick could get at her, it still made my skin crawl having her out in the open like this.

"What's up?" I asked.

She had her hands shoved into her pockets, and rolled up onto the balls of her feet. She grinned, tipping her face toward the weak spring sunlight. "Merc said you were driving up the mountain today. I thought maybe I'd tag along."

"Are you kidding?" But her good mood was infectious and I couldn't help smiling.

She sidled closer to me, stopping just a few inches away. Her fingers tiptoed up the front of my shirt and she looked up at me with her head tilted to the side, an impish smile on her face. "A solid two to three hours alone? Out in the sunshine? Away from Base Camp? No way I'd joke about that."

My head swam in response to her words. Base Camp was safe, but it was almost impossible to be alone. Yeah, we could catch a minute here and there. Like this, this moment out in the sunshine, with the chaos of Base Camp a whole twenty yards away. But two to three hours? I hadn't had that with Lily . . . well, since that night we'd slept side by side for a few hours on the Farm, right before we'd escaped. And, oh man, I wanted her alone.

I trailed my fingers up her arm. She had on a couple of layers of clothing, but, hell, layers could be peeled off. Her smile widened, like she knew just what I was thinking. And that combination— the smile, the hint of intimacy, the lure of time alone with her—it was like a mind wipe. There was some reason this was a bad idea, but for the life of me I couldn't think of why.

"Hey," a voice called from behind me. "We heading out soon or do I have time to grab some food first?"

I turned around to see Taylor walking toward the Hummer. He did a little double take when he saw Lily peeking out from behind my shoulder.

"Oh, sorry, man. Didn't realize you were . . . occupied. I'll just grab a bite to eat and be back in a minute, okay? Then we can head out. 'Cause we should get started soon. I mean, if you still want to . . ."

No. I didn't still want to. I didn't want to drive up the freakin' mountain to install more solar panels. I wanted just five freakin' minutes alone with Lily.

"Fine. Be back in five minutes."

Taylor trotted off and I looked back at Lily. She smiled sheepishly. "I guess that means no three hours alone."

"Yeah, I guess not." I blew out a breath and stepped away from her. "Just as well."

She frowned. "What's that supposed to mean?"

"Come on, it's not like I'm going to let you go traipsing around on the mountain with me."

She took a step back herself and did a double take. "Not going to *let* me go?"

"You know what I mean."

"Maybe you better tell me." She propped her hands on her hips. "Because it sounded to me like you think I need your permission to leave Base Camp."

"Of course I don't think that."

"Good."

But that stubborn look in her eyes sent fear dripping down the back of my neck. "But just to be clear, you're not leaving Base Camp."

She arched an eyebrow.

"I have to leave Base Camp eventually."

"No, you don't."

"Yes, I do." She stepped closer and dropped her voice, so that even if someone was out in the parking lot with us, they'd have a hard time hearing our conversation. "Have you noticed the way people treat me here?"

"Yeah. Everybody loves you. They think you're great."

"Right. I don't know if it's because they think I'm an *abductura* or just because I'm your girlfriend or what, but the Elites all treat me like I'm a friggin' China doll and the Greens act like I'm Joan of Arc or something."

"So?" She'd had a hell of a time on the Farm. And she'd lost Mel. If anyone deserved an easy time of it now, it was Lily.

"So, I need to be doing something."

"You do plenty. You do KP duty nearly every day and—"

"I need to be doing something important. Whether I should be or not, I'm in a position of power here." She gave me a small, sheepish smile. "I need to—you know—use my powers for good. Not evil."

"Fine. But that doesn't mean putting yourself in danger."

"I'm not planning on being reckless, but I need to help. To do something concrete. Besides, I think seeing me do things will help morale. In case you haven't noticed, things in the cave are getting tense."

"Yeah, I noticed. I'm not an idiot."

Her lips twitched just a little. "So then you noticed how skittish all the Greens are. I don't think I've seen a single Green leave camp since we got here. Since that guy was exposed just before we arrived."

I knew she was right; I just didn't know what to do about it. I pushed a hand through my hair.

"They're scared," Lily said.

"Wouldn't you be?" Hell, I knew the answer to that question. Of course Lily would be scared, but that wouldn't stop her from doing something, not if she thought it was important. "Look, it's going to take a while for people to get over it, that's all. I'm not going to force anybody out of the caves."

"Of course not; I'm not saying you should. But if the Greens see me outside, going on food raids or helping with the solar panels, it'll help them get over their fears."

"Their fears are totally rational." Too bad Lily didn't have rational fears to balance out her sheer guts. "It's dangerous out there."

"So what? We should all just hide in the caves and starve?"

"Obviously not. But I'm not going to send a bunch of untrained Greens into danger just because they have cabin fever."

"So train them!" Lily threw up her hands in exasperation.

"The Elites—"

"The Elites are overextended. Right now, the Elites do all the food raids, they do all the patrols. It's not so noticeable now, because there aren't enough warm days for you to send people out every day, but spring is here. And there are only forty-three of you. And nearly a hundred Greens. We Greens have to pull our weight."

She was right about the Elites being overextended, but I didn't want to admit it because I didn't have any clue how to fix it. "Look, right now I need to focus on getting these solar panels installed. When I get back, I'll try to think of some way to encourage the Greens to do more."

I turned and walked to the other side of the Hummer, hoping that if I looked busy, she'd take the hint and head back inside. But she followed me to the driver's side instead.

"That's the beauty of my plan," she said, her voice eager. "You don't have to encourage anybody to do anything they don't want. Just send me out on the next food raid—"

A bark of hysterical laughter burst out of me. Lily on a food raid? Fifty-plus miles from the safety of Base Camp? Wandering around an unknown city searching for supplies she could pillage? What a nightmare. "Tell me you're joking."

"It's the perfect solution. You know I can handle myself out there. And if the other Greens see me doing these things, some of them will want to do them, too. I know they will."

"No," I said automatically. "Absolutely not."

"You need us to go find food, damn it."

"No, Lily. Right now, the only thing I need is for you to be safe. For you to get your ass back in to Base Camp."

"Carter, I can't—"

"Lily, you have the Tick gene. If you get exposed, it's all over. And I can't live with that."

"Well, *I* can't live by hiding in a cave." She stepped closer to me, her eyes blazing. "I can't stand by and do nothing. I have to have some purpose here. And I know I'm right about the Greens. There is no way Base Camp can continue to function like this."

I stayed silent and prayed like hell that she would back down. Instead, she bumped up her chin again and said, "And *I* can't spend the rest of my life hiding from danger. I have to be doing something. I have to be working toward *something*, otherwise I might as well have stayed on the Farm."

I could almost see the logic of her point. Almost. But this was *Lily*, and logic had nothing to do with it.

Over by the bay doors, I could see Taylor walking toward us, moving with exaggerated slowness and trying so hard not to stare it was a miracle he didn't fall on his ass.

"Look, Taylor and I need to get up the mountain and KP needs the parking lot to start lunch. You and I can talk later." I didn't wait for her to answer, but instead raised my hand to gesture to Taylor. "Yo, Techy, let's go."

He took the hint, jogging the rest of the way to the Hummer and sliding into the passenger seat. A moment later, I drove off, leaving Lily standing alone in the parking lot. I didn't really focus on driving until I saw the Elite at the gate lock her in.

CHAPTER FOUR

LILY

Lily's blood boiled as she watched Carter drive off.

Damn it! She was right about this. She knew she was, and he wasn't even going to consider her opinions because of the risk.

The risk to her was no greater than it was to anyone else. Yes, if she was exposed, the consequences were greater, but the risk? The risk was the same. Almost everyone who caught the virus died. Less than two percent of the population would turn. And, yes, she was one of those.

She knew the consequences better than most. She'd been face-to-face with a Tick, close enough to smell the Tick's fetid breath. She'd seen the dull stupidity in its eyes. The inhuman thirst for blood. It haunted her nightmares. Not the thought of dying, but of becoming . . . that.

Of course it terrified her. She had a monster buried in her genes waiting to come out. The knowledge of what she could become, of her horrible potential—it was forever just below the surface of her consciousness, like a layer of muck at the bottom of a crystal-clear pond. Every time she dipped below the surface, it sucked at her, threatening to pull her down.

But living on the Farm had terrified her, too. Of course, she'd feared for her life and for Mel's. She'd feared the predators outside the fence as well as those within. But even more, she'd feared the dark places in her own heart. She'd been afraid of losing herself to the regimented class system of the Farm—a world where bullies became Collab leaders and where fertile girls got pregnant and bartered their babies' lives for their own. Without an autistic sister to take care of, would she have had the strength to fight the system? To plan and make an escape? Or would she have just given up? She didn't know.

She'd been lucky, though. She'd had Mel to focus on. Protecting Mel had brought her outside of herself. It had given her purpose and meaning. Something her life here at Base Camp lacked.

And she wasn't the only one. Walking back through the main cave toward KP, she had to force herself to look at the gaunt faces, at the scared, shifting eyes. It wasn't long before Shelby—a girl from a Farm in Oklahoma—slipped over to her. Shelby was small and light, with the build of a gymnast. She had arrived at Base Camp just before McKenna and Lily. Though she was naturally cautious, she didn't yet have that trapped, glazy-eyed look that some of the Greens had. Shelby was the kind of girl everyone liked.

"How's the weather out there?" Shelby asked.

Sometimes Shelby seemed so damn young. In reality, she was probably only a couple years younger than Lily. Everyone at the Farms was under eighteen because when they'd first created the Farm facilities, teenagers had been the most vulnerable. At eighteen, people aged out of the program. No one knew for sure what happened to those people. No one assumed it was good.

Carter had gotten them out right before their birthday, which made Lily one of the older girls at Base Camp. But it wasn't age that made Lily feel older.

"It's great," she told Shelby. "Okay, not great, but sunny. You should go out."

"Nah. I don't have KP duty until later in the week."

The Greens with KP duty were just beginning to gather up the cooking supplies. None of them had ventured out yet, so they were still hovering by the bay doors. Not far off, a group of Elites were strapping on gear, ready to head out on a food raid—the first in a couple of days.

"Well, I'm going to go check on McKenna. I'll see you later, Shelby."

"Wait, Lily. I actually—" Shelby sent an awkward glance over her shoulder toward a cluster of girls hovering and whispering by the KP station. "I need to talk to you about something."

"Okay . . . What's up?"

Shelby sent her a strained smile. "We're almost out of supplies."

"Yeah. The shelves are pretty bare. That's why Stu and those guys are going out on a food raid."

"Not those kinds of supplies," Shelby said with an exaggerated wince.

"Oh." Lily had the urge to slap her own forehead. Of course. Not food. Not even basic hygiene stuff, like soap and toothpaste . . . because the Elites who went on food raids thought of all that. But there was one thing no group of seventeen- and eighteen-year-old guys was going to think about: feminine hygiene. "How bad is it?"

"We're down to one box of panty liners and twenty Always pads."

Great. That, and nearly fifty teenage girls. Perfect.

True, many of them were so damn thin that they'd stopped menstruating. You needed body fat for that. But there were still plenty of girls for whom this was a huge issue. It was bad enough living in these cramped quarters, without having to go through this crap in a tampon-less world.

"Okay, I'll handle it. I'll go talk to Stu."

Shelby relaxed. "Thanks."

"No problem." She didn't dare complain when the Greens practically worshipped her. Still, she'd bet Joan of Arc never had to do this crap.

Stu was almost to the bay when she reached him.

She didn't know him that well—certainly not well enough to discuss this with him without dying of humiliation—and she could feel her cheeks burning as she described the problem. It was almost gratifying to see his cocky smirk fade as soon as she started talking.

He gave an awkward shrug and sent a desperate look toward the bay through which the other Elites had already disappeared, like he was looking for rescue. "You can't be out already. We just brought a bunch of that stuff back."

Which she knew couldn't be true, because she'd helped sort the supplies brought in from every food raid the Elites had done since she'd arrived. "When?"

"I don't know." He scratched his head, which didn't make him look any smarter. "Back in December, maybe."

"In December?" She shook her head. Boys. "That was like, five months ago."

"So?"

"So. We need more. Do you need a biology lesson? There are nearly fifty of us." And because his awkwardness was starting to annoy her, she spelled it out. "Always pads, Kotex, tampons, even freakin' Depends—whatever you can find, bring it back for us."

"Fine," he grumbled, edging toward the door. "Make me a list. I'll get it the next time we go out."

"Next time won't cut it. We need stuff now."

"Okay. Fine."

"I'm serious, Stu. We need—"

"What do you want to do, come with me to make sure I get the right kind?"

She broke off, eyeing the bay door that he was already edging his way toward. And, just like that, inspiration struck. "Sure. Sounds great."

Stu stopped dead in his tracks. "What?"

She glanced down at her clothes. She was already dressed warmly, in case she'd been able to talk Carter into letting her go with him up the mountain. She had on her most comfortable sneakers and several layers of clothes in case it got warmer later in the day. The bow and quiver of arrows she'd been practicing with was in the armory, but that was right beside the door. She could walk out of here right now.

"I'll just tag along on the food raid. It's a great idea."

Stu's gaze shifted nervously. "I'm not sure about this."

Which was fine, because the more she thought about it, the more sure *she* was. The girls at Base Camp needed supplies— things they couldn't count on the Elites to get. And they needed them now. More to the point, that desperate and squeamish group of girls needed a role model. They needed her to stand up to the Elites and go on a food raid. They needed to see that someone—a Green like them—could do it.

"It's just a simple food raid down the mountain, right?"

"Um . . . yeah, I guess."

"Come on, Stu. I'm sure you could use the extra help." Elites pulled patrol duty, guard duty, and food raid duty. And they all did physical training to stay in shape. They barely had time to sleep.

"And Carter's okay with this?" Stu asked.

Here was the tricky part. "We talked about it just this morning."

Which was technically true. "I've been out there," she reminded him. "I've fought and killed Ticks. Besides, I've been doing PT with the Elites every morning since I got here. I'm in great shape."

All of that was totally true.

"Why do I feel like I'm going to regret this?" he grumbled, but in the end, he held open the door and gestured for her to head out with him.

She smiled and for the first time in months felt excited about something—about something *she* was doing. Not just about being Carter's girlfriend. "Just let me get my bow and arrow."

And she ran to get it, just to make sure they didn't leave without her.

CHAPTER FIVE

LILY

Recon, sit rep, retrieval, extraction.

Lily chanted the words in her head over and over again as she approached the house.

That's what Stu had drilled into her ever since he'd agreed to let her come along. You get into the building and do a quick reconnaissance to secure the location. You report in to the raid commander so the rest of the raid team knows what's going down where. You locate any valuable supplies. You retreat to the extraction point.

It all seemed simple enough when they were driving down the mountain. Now, as Jacks, Stu, and Lily approached the empty house, it seemed much less cut-and-dry. Maybe it was the adrenaline pumping through her veins or the sweat pouring off her palms. Or maybe, she'd just gotten used to the relative comfort and safety of Base Camp. Maybe the six weeks in Utah had made her soft.

As she walked up to the house, Lily scanned the area. They were on the outskirts of a tiny town tucked right up against the mountain range in a neighborhood too rural to be suburban. The lots were big and hilly and a creek flowed behind the houses because there was a dense tree line that ran parallel to the street. There were only three houses on this block and no signs that anything living had been here recently. The other team had been dropped on a different street.

There was absolutely no sign that this town had seen any Tick activity. You could always tell when a town had been hit hard by Ticks. They destroyed everything they touched. The houses on this block looked abandoned but not ravaged. Hopefully Lily and the rest of the team could load up the truck on this one block alone and head back up the mountain.

So Lily gritted her teeth and swallowed her anxiety. She wasn't really a newbie. She knew the threats, but she also knew how to fight them. She patted the bow slung over her shoulder. She'd been practicing with it every chance she got. She had this.

They paused about twenty feet from the house. Lily swung her bow off her shoulder and wiped her palm on her jeans before pulling an arrow from her quiver. She notched it, but kept it low to the ground. Better safe than sorry on all counts. When Carter found out she'd gone on the food raid, he was going to be pissed, even if things went well. If she accidentally shot Stu, it would all be over.

"We ready?" Stu asked.

As they approached the house, Stu took point. He tried the knob on the door first, just in case. When it didn't easily open, he moved down the wraparound porch to the nearest window. Jacks moved in the opposite direction, toward the south side of the house and Lily followed him. Jacks found a window open just a crack. While he worked to pry it open, Lily scanned the woods beside the house, paranoia dancing along the back of her neck, her fear whispering to her:

Don't screw this up. You mess this up, you mess it up for everyone. For every Green who's going stir-crazy in the caves. For every Elite who needs one less thing to do. Worst of all, you screw this up, Carter will never trust you again. It's bad enough that you came in the first place, if you screw it up, it's all over.

Her nerves were rattling so badly, her vision blurred around the edges. Worse still, she couldn't trust herself, because her nerves were groundless.

Everything she saw, every car parked silently on the street, every tree in every pristine yard, told her that Ticks had not been through this area—at least not recently. There were no overturned vehicles. No broken windows. No deep gouges in the lawns where the long claws of Ticks' feet might have gained purchase before they leaped for the kill. No lingering stench of rotting flesh. No smeared bloodstains on the porch. There was no destruction. Anywhere.

It was like Sleeping Beauty's castle. Like the people who'd lived here had simply walked away from their lives.

She'd once heard a rumor on the Farm that when things went bad, all the Mormons had retreated to some vast underground fortification beneath Salt Lake City. Maybe that's what had happened here. Maybe they'd all just left. And maybe without the scent of fresh human blood to lure them here, the Ticks had simply stayed away.

It was the only explanation Lily could think of.

Jacks jimmied the window open then pulled his radio off his belt and brought it up to his mouth. "We found an open window. South side. We're going in."

"Copy that," Stu's voice buzzed through the radio. "I'm working my way over there. I'll be around in a second."

Jacks brushed the curtain aside and stuck his head through the window. Then he nodded back toward Lily. "Lights are off, so you'll need your flashlight."

Lily slid the arrow back into her quiver and slung the bow over her shoulder before pulling her flashlight out of her pocket.

"I'm going in." The window came down low enough that Jacks was able to just swing his leg over the ledge, duck his head, and step inside. Lily waited a moment before following.

The windows opened into the dining nook in the house's kitchen. A table was positioned right beside the windows; the seven chairs around the table were askance, as though a family had sat there just this morning. At one end of the table, there was a high chair. A lone Cheerio on the high chair's tray was the only sign the house had ever been lived in.

She thought of the houses they had searched for supplies on their way north. At each one, she'd had this same sick feeling in her gut, like this was a horrible invasion of the homeowner's privacy. Mixed with that was a kind of sorrow. A mourning for the lives that had been lost.

Both of those emotions flooded her now, as well as something else. Something she couldn't quite put her finger on. An ineffable sense that something wasn't right.

And that was what guilt felt like, she supposed. *Yeah, you dumbass. Something's not right. You lied to Stu to come on this food raid and Carter's going to be pissed as hell. That's what's not right.*

Too late to do anything about that now. She was here. She should find what she needed and get out.

Jacks's radio buzzed, making Lily jump. "Can I have a sit rep?"

Jacks raised the radio to his mouth. "We're in the kitchen. I'm searching the cabinets."

"Okay," Stu answered through the radio. "I haven't found another open window yet. I'll be there in a second. Start looking for a stash of supplies."

"I'm going to go search upstairs," Lily told him.

Jacks hesitated, but finally nodded. "Don't leave this house."

"Right. I'll be careful."

Shining her light ahead of her, she made her way down the hall. She moved the light across the open doorway of a laundry room and moved past to the stairway going up to the second floor.

There was no point in creeping around, so she took the stairs two at a time. At the top was a narrow hall, the door to a bathroom open at one end, and a pair of open doors on either side. Bedrooms, presumably.

She looked through the bathroom first and found what she was looking for under the sink. She swung her backpack off her shoulder and quickly filled it with two boxes of tampons and a package of maxi pads. Not much, but it would help. And there were surely other bathrooms in the house. Still, what they needed to do was hit a store. She found no other useful toiletries. No toothpaste, no soap, no first aid kit. Sure signs that the family had made it out, but her initial sense of unease didn't dissipate.

The house looked too pristine. But she wasn't sure why that bothered her. In the next bathroom she found a stash of toilet paper. Even as she loaded the rolls into her backpack, it bugged her. Why bring everything, down to the last Band-Aid, but leave five rolls of toilet paper?

Crap. This wasn't right.

Skipping the rest of the rooms, she turned to head back downstairs. Somewhere down below, she heard Stu's sat phone ring and then him answer. And a second later, she heard a noise from one of the bedrooms. Probably a rat. But if it wasn't a rat, she didn't want to turn her back on the sound to blithely walk down the stairs. If there was something in this room, she wanted to face it head on and well armed. She slung her bow off her shoulder and pulled an arrow from her quiver before nudging the door open with her toe.

Heart pounding, she pushed open the door to the bedroom the rest of the way. It had once been a child's room. A pair of bunk beds lined one wall. A low bookcase stretched the length of the window. There was a toy box beside the door, the lid ajar with the arm of some stuffed animal dangling out. The kid's books, the toys, the cheerfully yellow bed linens. The innocence of the room did little to banish her terror, it only made her heart twist and squirm in her chest.

Food raids were the worst job. Ever.

Another faint sound emanated from what must have been the closet—a sound that was neither as innocent as rats nor as ominous as Ticks. A human sound.

If the person in the closet was a crazy, survivalist gun nut, wouldn't they have already come out, guns blazing?

Unless, and the thought stopped Lily in her tracks, the person in the closet was a kid.

CHAPTER SIX

CARTER

My eyes were heavy as I drove down the mountain. The road was sharp and winding, the pavement slick. Driving should have taken my full attention. Instead, I was damn near nodding off. Maybe Lily was right. If I couldn't stay awake behind the wheel maybe the Elites were doing too much. But what was the alternative? Send untrained, untested Greens out to gather supplies and do patrols? Christ, it'd be like sending lambs to the slaughter. And if I wouldn't send Lily out into the field—and she at least had combat experience—then I sure as hell couldn't ask anyone else to go.

I briefly considered pulling over on the side of the road and taking a combat nap, but Taylor was still up on the mountain fiddling with the Romex wire and his solar panels. I'd left a couple of other Elites up there with him, so at least someone had his back, but I knew Taylor. He'd stay up there working away until I either brought him what he needed or he ran out of food. Either way, I figured I needed to do it quickly.

I was headed down the mountain, past Base Camp, toward Elderton. Since I didn't want to surprise anyone, I picked up the satellite phone and buzzed Stu, who was heading up the supply raid in Elderton.

"Yo," Stu said.

"How's the raid going?" I asked.

There was a moment's hesitation on his end. "It's great. It's going great. I can totally handle this."

Maybe sleep deprivation was making me punchy, but he sounded a touch paranoid. I rubbed at my eyes, which were starting to feel like they were lined with sand paper. "Yeah. I'm sure you can."

"Excellent. 'Cause I got this. Nothing's going to happen."

"Right." Nothing happened on most food raids. They were pretty routine. The thing with the Tick attacking the guy before Lily, McKenna, and I arrived, that was the outlier. You had to be cautious, sure, but it was nothing a group of Elites couldn't handle. "No, I'm sure you're doing great. I just wanted to let you know I'm heading into town, too. I didn't want to surprise anyone."

"You don't have to come check up on me. I've got this."

"I'm not checking up on you. Taylor realized we're going to need another inverter on the solar panels. He says he saw at least a dozen houses with solar panels when we did that first sweep of the town back in the fall. I know there are a lot of other towns where I could pick one up, but I figured I could get in and out of Elderton quickly, since you guys have already done a sweep today."

"Oh, okay." Stu sounded relieved. "I just didn't want you to think I couldn't take care of her."

"Take care of who?"

Suddenly I was wide awake. Instinctively, I slammed on the brake and the car started skidding across the road. It spun to a stop just as Stu answered. I knew what he was going to say before he even spoke.

"Lily. She's doing great, by the way. A little jumpy, but she's handling it."

I sat there for a moment, heart thundering in my chest, vision darkening around the edges, sucking in one breath after another.

Finally, my voice was calm enough to ask, "Lily came on the supply raid with you?"

"Yeah." Despite my attempt to sound calm, something in my tone must have tipped my hand because Stu sounded nervous. "She said you guys had talked about it. I never would have let her come if I'd known you hadn't approved it." Then Stu muttered a string of curses.

And now I looked like an idiot who'd been duped by his girl-friend, Lily looked like the bitch who went behind my back, and Stu felt like he'd betrayed me. Damn it!

"No, it's fine," I lied. Goddamn it! What the hell was she think-ing? "We did talk about it. I just—" Jesus, I hated lying, but what choice did I have? "I didn't think we'd settled it."

"You sure this is okay?" Stu asked.

No. It wasn't okay. It was pretty effin' far from okay. Because Lily was in danger. Far more danger than Stu knew. "Just keep an eye on her, okay?"

"Yeah. Of course."

I slipped the Hummer back into gear and eased my foot onto the gas. I glanced down at the paper map open on the seat next to me and did some quick calculations. "I'll be there in less than twenty. Give me the address again." I wrote it right on the map as I drove. "Probably more like fifteen minutes. And don't let her out of your sight until I'm there."

CHAPTER SEVEN

LILY

Lily crept across the floor and pressed her back to the wall. She stood there for a long moment debating what to do, her heart pounding so loudly she was sure whoever was in the closet could hear. Was this crazy? Part of her screamed that she should tiptoe back downstairs, grab Stu and Jacks, and get the hell out of there. But she couldn't leave a kid alone here in this house. She just couldn't.

"I'm going to open this door," she said loudly. "I don't mean you any harm. I'm here to help."

Then she twisted the knob and yanked the door so it swung out opposite her. There was nothing. Just clothes hanging on the rods. Shoes scattered across the ground.

She flicked the light over the interior and that's when she saw it. One of the shoes inched back. There was someone there. A kid in scuffed black Mary Janes.

"I know you're there. I—" and then she broke off. What had this kid been through since the Before? How had she even survived? Lily used her most soothing voice, the one she used to use to talk to Mel when her sister was freaking out about something. "I know you're frightened. I can help you."

Nothing.

No more movement from the shoe. No rustling of clothes. Hell, as far as she could tell, the kid wasn't even breathing.

On impulse, Lily added, "I have a younger sister." Which wasn't true. Mel's autism always made her seem like the younger one. The one who needed to be taken care of.

"I would do anything to protect her." Which was true. There just hadn't been anything she *could* do. Lily felt a surge of anguish rise up inside of her. How was it possible that Mel was gone? Maybe forever. How had she let that happen?

"I know there are a lot of things to be afraid of, but I can help you. I can keep you safe." Again, a lie. In the world they lived in now, no one could keep anyone safe. No matter how you tried to protect them. Wasn't that what she'd told Carter just this morning?

"I can help you, but only if you come out. You can trust me."

Gently, the row of clothes stirred. Fingers crept around the arm of a coat and then the girl stepped forward, out from between the clothes, into the beam from Lily's flashlight. She blinked and held out a hand to shield her face.

Lily lowered the flashlight and flicked it off.

The girl was maybe six or seven and dressed in a faded cotton dress and leggings. Her dark hair fell in fat, messy ringlets, but it was her eyes that surprised Lily. She'd expected to see fear and caution; instead, they were bright with curiosity.

Lily crouched down to her level and held out her hand. "Hi, I'm Lily. What's your name?"

A sickening thought occurred to her. What if the girl didn't know her name? What if she'd been here alone so long she'd forgotten it?

Then she reached out her hand and pressed her palm to Lily's, quick as a bird, then tucked her hand behind her back. "I'm Danielle," she whispered, her eyes huge. "Can you really help us?"

Lily's insides turned to ice. "Us?"

"Did you come here to help us?"

Us?

Shit.

Lily mentally backpedaled through all the tiny bits of evidence that proved just how screwed she was. All these little snapshots that hadn't made sense until that instant: the open window, the Cheerio on the high-chair tray. That was all new. It had been from today.

This wasn't some kid scraping by waiting to be rescued. This was a kid with older siblings or even parents. This was a kid with defenses.

Crap.

All of this flashed through her brain, but she didn't have time to flee or shout out a warning to Stu and Jacks. In the distance, from downstairs, she heard Stu's sat phone ringing again. Her breath caught in her chest as she waited, hoping she'd hear Stu's response. But the silence was only broken by the ringing phone. No Stu. No Jacks.

She glanced back over her shoulder toward the hall. The door was open. If she strained to listen, she could hear the faintest hint of footsteps on the floor below.

She turned back to the girl. To Danielle.

"Honey, go back in the closet. Hide, okay?"

Because someone was downstairs and it probably wasn't Jacks. Whoever had kept Danielle alive all this time, they hadn't done it by letting strangers wander through their house.

Danielle cocked her head to the side and scrunched her mouth into a frown. Then she shook her head.

"Go," Lily urged. "Hide!"

A moment later a man's voice called, "You might as well come out. I know you're up there."

She waved at Danielle to go back into the closet one more time. As she crossed the bedroom, she tucked her flashlight into the back of her pants and pulled an arrow from the quiver. Sweat made her fingers slick as she notched it. Her hands were shaking. She wouldn't be able to aim for crap. Probably for the best anyway.

The bow and arrow were just for show this time. There was no way she would shoot this man in his own home, but maybe—maybe—if he saw she was armed, he'd at least hesitate long enough for her to talk her way out of this.

She kicked the bedroom door open and then spun out into the hall, facing the stairs and pulling the bow taut as she moved.

She aimed down the staircase, toward the voice. The dark, hulking shape of a man blocked out most of the light. She couldn't distinguish any of his features or guess at his age, but he was bulky. A grown adult. He held Jacks in front of him. Jacks clawed helplessly at his grip and at the gun the man held to Jacks's throat.

She had no idea where Stu was, only that she hadn't heard any gunshots yet. She assumed he'd been taken out. Disabled. Knocked out, but probably not shot. Yet.

Her mind raced, trying to think of a resolution to the standoff that wouldn't involve Jacks's brains being splattered all over the wall. Or hers. Or possibly both.

Maybe she could stall him. Maybe the cavalry would show up.

Yeah, right.

The cavalry was Carter, up on the mountain somewhere. Miles away.

With a show of bravado she so didn't feel, she called out, "Let him go!"

He ignored her and called back, "You okay, Danielle?"

"She's fine," she yelled before Danielle could answer. However this went down, it wouldn't be good. Someone would die—her or Jacks or the man. Maybe all three. Jesus, she wished Danielle would go back to hiding in the closet.

"She's just fine," Lily called again, trying for the soothing tone she failed at so miserably. "If you let my friend go, I'll send her down."

The guy let out a guttural sound that was part growl, part sneer. "You think I'm going to just let you and your little friends walk out of my house?"

"We didn't do anything wrong."

"'Round here, we shoot thieves like you."

"We're not thieves." But the line between thieves and scavengers was a thin one. "We didn't know anyone lived here. You let us go and we'll never bother you again."

"I let you walk now and you'll come back and murder us all in our sleep."

"We don't want to hurt you." She could feel her anxiety rising as her voice rose in pitch. Her arm quivered with fatigue from holding her bow. "We have plenty of supplies without yours."

"What sort of Pollyanna bullshit is that? Where've you been living, missy, that you think there are plenty of supplies anywhere?"

She automatically tensed at the aggression in his voice and instinct caused her to pull the bow even more taut. Her eyes were starting to adjust to the dark and she could see more of him now: gray, shaggy hair, worn plaid shirt, work boots. Jacks's feet dangled above his. Oh God, were his kicks getting weaker? He was about to pass out. He was going to die. For all Lily knew, Stu was already dead.

She had two options: put down her weapon and let him kill her or shoot him herself. Jacks wasn't a small guy, but this guy was huge. She might hit his shoulder or arm, if her aim was steady.

But she'd never shot anyone. Not anyone human anyway. She'd shot targets at Girl Scout camp. A rabbit once at her uncle Rodney's. She'd thrown up after that. And then Ticks. She'd shot lots of Ticks. She'd thrown up then, too.

That had been horrific enough.

Could she shoot a human? A sentient, normal human? A guy who was just protecting his kid?

Before Lily could lower her bow, Danielle pushed her way past and into the hall. She threw herself in front of Lily, arms outspread.

"Don't shoot her, Daddy! She's here to help."

"Get down, Danielle!" her father shouted.

"Get back," Lily yelled at the same time.

She could tell she'd surprised him. He expected her to use his daughter against him.

On impulse, Lily lowered her bow, releasing the tension until the arrow clattered to the ground. It slid down a couple of steps before the fletching caught on the step.

"What game are you playing, missy?"

"My name is Lily," she called back. "I'm not playing a game. I don't want anyone to get hurt. Danielle, go down to your father."

Lily looked back at the girl. Her eyes were wide and panicked. How much violence had she seen in her short life? No child should be so afraid. Lily handed her the bow, hoping that her father would understand what that meant. She was defenseless now.

"Go on," she urged. "Take this to your daddy."

"You said you were here to help."

"I was. I still am, if your Daddy lets me." More promises she probably couldn't keep. She looked back up at him. "Let my friend go. Please."

She imagined she could see the hesitation on his face. The flickering of doubt. She thought his muscles loosened and he started to let Jacks go.

Then a savage cry came from somewhere off near the kitchen. The cavalry had arrived after all.

CHAPTER EIGHT

CARTER

I crept across the side porch of the house, my heart pounding from my flat-out run from the truck. And, yeah, my terror. What would I do if I was too late? If something had already happened to her?

During the crazy drive down the mountain, I tried to tell myself that I was overreacting. Okay, so Lily had left on a supply raid without telling me. Yeah, I was pissed. But just because I was paranoid, that didn't mean she was in immediate danger. But then I'd called Stu a second time. And no one answered. Not Stu, not Jacks, not Lily. On a three-person team, someone should be able to answer the damn phone. Unless they were in serious trouble.

Using two hands, I held my Glock extended out in front of me as I moved down the porch, constantly scanning the yard and the interior of the house for signs of movement. The house looked innocent enough. A white farmhouse with a deep porch wrapped around the first floor. An open yard with a detached garage a hundred feet away. The grass in the yard had gone wild and long even though it was only early spring. The grass shifting in the breeze was the lone sign of movement.

In this crazy world, there was one thing—one goddamned

thing—that actually mattered to me. Keeping Lily safe. Why the hell couldn't I do that one thing?

I rounded the corner onto the west side of the house and saw Stu laying in a crumpled hump on the porch. Swallowing a curse, I crossed to Stu's side, crouched, and pressed a couple of fingers to his neck, searching for a pulse without ever lowering my weapon or diverting my gaze. I found his pulse, which was weak but steady. A quick glance and pat-down assured me that Stu had been knocked out but not stabbed or shot. The absence of a gaping hole in his chest meant we weren't dealing with Ticks.

A flicker of movement caught my attention when I stood. Someone, a huge guy, had Jacks in a stranglehold and was dragging him through the kitchen. But where the hell was Lily?

Rage coursed through my veins, along with a healthy dose of panic as my instincts warred with my training. I knew what Sebastian would say. I had to assess the situation. Before I acted. Before I charged in there and made things worse.

But if this guy had laid so much as a finger on Lily, I was going to kill him.

I sucked in a deep breath and blew it out slowly, trying to calm down enough to think. I didn't have a clear shot. I needed to get in the house and sneak up on the guy.

He was standing at the foot of the stairs, yelling up the stairs at someone. Probably Lily.

Who else could it be, right? He'd already taken out Stu. It must be Lily.

I sucked in another deep breath and weighed my options.

If I tackled the guy, the gun could go off. If I just shot him in the back, the bullet would go straight through Jacks.

I moved around the corner and found the door. I yanked

my picks from my pocket, tucked the gun back in its holster at the back of my waist, and crouched down to get started on the lock. I was normally pretty fast with the lock pick, but there was more than one dead bolt and I had to keep pausing to shake the tremors out of my hands. I opened the door just in time to hear Lily call down an answer to something the guy had said. Relief flooded me.

I crept around the corner just in time to see her hand her bow over to a little girl and I knew she was ass deep in trouble. The guy moved the gun away from Jacks's neck. He was gonna shoot Lily. Right here in front of me. He was going to shoot her unless I did something to stop it.

After all this time. After all the things I'd done to protect her and keep her safe. She was going to get shot.

Anger washed through me as I charged the guy. Barreling into him was like plowing head first into a brick wall, but I was fast enough and mad enough that I knocked him back a step. The gun fired a rapid spray of bullets as all three of us flew through the air and slammed into the ground.

The impact rattled my bones and my head. My ears were ringing from the gunshot. I pushed myself to my knees, shaking my head to clear my ears. For a long second, I was disoriented, the lack of hearing throwing me off balance. Then I looked up the stairs to where I expected Lily to be. She stood at the second-floor landing. For the briefest second, I was overjoyed. She was alive. I'd made it in time.

But her skin had gone a ghostly white. Her mouth was wide and gaping. Her eyes panicked. Her lips bright as blood.

I called her name. At least, I thought I did. Though her mouth was moving, I couldn't hear her. I couldn't even reach her in time.

All I could do was watch as she sagged against the wall. Her eyes rolled back in her head as her feet slipped out from under her. Lily had been shot. That single stray bullet had hit her. She tumbled down the stairs, leaving a smear of crimson on the wall.

And in that moment, I knew what it was like to be killed by a Tick. To have my chest ripped open and my heart torn out. It was beyond pain. Beyond imagining. Shock and anguish roared through me.

The ringing mingled with the screams coming from several different places. And with my own blood pounding through my head, blocking out reason and logic and caution.

There are a lot of things I could have done to eliminate this guy as a threat.

A fist to the guy's jaw. Over and over again. Followed quickly by solid punches to both kidneys. My forearm pressed into his windpipe to cut off his oxygen supply along with jabs to the ribs. A solid knee in the nuts.

Any one of those things would have disarmed the guy. Hell, I might have done all of them.

I don't know. Because when I saw Lily go down, pure, blinding rage overtook me. Hot and intense. Next thing I knew, I was being pulled off the guy and pounded myself. Someone was holding me and someone else was jabbing me in the stomach. I kicked up my legs trying to break free and take out the guy using me like a punching bag, but a third guy's fist slammed into my jaw so hard it made my teeth clatter.

The three of them together, they were going to tear me limb from limb. And I welcomed it, because if Lily was gone, then what was left?

Then I heard the unmistakable click-clack of a shotgun being primed.

Everyone froze.

The two guys who'd been hammering on me slowly turned to face the gunman, edging out of the way so that I could see him. Or rather, her.

The person holding the shotgun was a little girl. She was maybe six. Seven, at most. With long, dark hair and a thin face that looked underfed but stubborn as hell.

I looked from the man on the ground at my feet to the guys who'd pulled me off him. The gun-toting asshole had a couple of bruises already forming on his cheeks and his lip had been spilt open, but I hadn't done any permanent damage. The three boys who'd pulled me off him ranged from about my age to a year or so younger. The guy who was holding me didn't let go, but the other two held up their hands as though ready to surrender. Then I looked back up the stairs to the little girl.

Hell, how could she even hold the shotgun? The damn thing looked like it weighed more than she did, but she held it tight to her shoulder, like someone who'd been using it her whole life. And, well, if this family was tough enough to survive the Ticks, then maybe she had.

"Are you here to kill my daddy?" she asked.

It took me a heartbeat to realize she was talking to me. The haze of my rage was clearing along with my ears.

But Lily had been shot. I could still see her crumpled body lying on the stairs. Blood still stained her lips, which meant internal bleeding. Which usually meant death, even in the Before, in a world with ER surgeons and ambulances.

If I told this girl yes, would she shoot me?

But even I wasn't enough of an asshole to force a little girl to execute me.

"No," I said.

I glanced down at the other man, who was only now starting to sit up. With his legs stretched out in front of him, he rubbed his hand over his stubble-covered jaw. He glanced down at the blood on his hand.

The oldest of the boys wiped his palm on the leg of his jeans and said, "Now Danielle, you hand that shotgun over to me before someone gets hurt."

But the girl just narrowed her eyes. When she spoke her voice was strong, but small. "I'm not putting the gun down until you go get Dawn so she can tend to Lily."

Wait. Tend to Lily? Was she still alive? I kept my gaze pinned on her chest until I saw it rise and fall. I surged forward toward the stairs, but the guys holding me tightened their grips and I couldn't break free.

"Danielle, you are going to be in a mountain of trouble," her father muttered at her. He started to walk toward her, but she shifted the gun.

"Not you, Daddy, him. I'm sorry, but I know if I let any of you out of my sight, you'll just go grab more guns and we'll be back in trouble again." She shifted her gaze to me. "Walk over here and set your gun down halfway between us. Then go out back to the bunker and find my sister, Dawn. And—"

"Danielle, you can't tell him—"

"Daddy, I'm sorry, but I'm not going to let her bleed out because you're being stubborn and mean. Besides, she said they can help us. What if they can? What if you just shot the only lady who can help us?"

I had no idea what fairy tales Lily had told this girl. But it didn't take a genius to know that we couldn't help her. If she was going to send me to get help for Lily, I damn sure wasn't going to tell her she was wrong.

Slowly, begrudgingly, Danielle's father nodded. Somehow, when he looked at his daughter, his gaze full of equal parts exasperation and love, he looked less like a psychopath and more like a man who would do anything to protect his family. I couldn't hate him for that. But if Lily died, I would damn sure kill him for it.

CHAPTER NINE

MEL

My nursery rhymes rhyme less than they used to.

I can feel myself changing. The Mel I was is nearly lost to memory. The Mel I am now is becoming lost *in* memories. They are all I have left of myself. I have too much time to heal, even as my body changes. I sleep endlessly, except for when I'm feeding, though Sebastian still doesn't let me feed or hunt. He keeps me locked away, safe as a newborn kitten. He feeds me the blood of Ticks he hunts alone. I am as dependent on him as I ever was on Lily.

Lily, Lily. My sister, myself. The thousand stings of sisterhood don't sting any less. Her betrayal is a flash of alcohol skimming across the surface of my vampire newness. I cannot think of her without resenting the choice she made for me when I was too weak to make it for myself. So instead I linger on other memories.

We had a cat named Trickster when I was little. A real prince of Siam. Trickster's favorite trick was catching bunnies in the yard. He gifted us each spring. Their blood on our welcome mat chilled my blood colder than April.

I'd screamed for hours after that first Thumper.

Lily puked. Mom shoveled. Dad babbled. He babbled a lot. Even my screams didn't block the echo of Thumper's dying thumpity, thumpity. Tiny hearts beat fast, and I can't forget the glazed-eyed horror on Thumper's face. Or the praise Trickster thought he'd earned.

Even the fiercest killer kills for love as well as food. Not just the love of food, but the love of sharing.

How now could I drink like that?

Dr. Seuss's Brown Cow never prepared me for that How.

Other hows haunt me as well. How do we forgive the people we love? How can I forgive Lily for her betrayal? I gave her a gift greater than any of Trickster's Thumpers. I gave her the gift of my life and she turned that gift on me. She turned me just as much as Sebastian did. I learned to forgive Trickster. Can I learn to forgive Lily now that I'm a trickster myself?

I still loved Trickster after Thumper number one. And learned to close my screams each spring and to let Lily leave the house first in the morning. There were other Thumpers, I know, but the Trickster's lullaby purr and steady heartbeat lulled my senses and let me forget.

It's easy to forgive a predator. As long as we're not the prey.

CHAPTER TEN

LILY

Lily woke up slowly, lingering in that odd, half sleep where she didn't know where she was. Her mind befuddled by fuzz and too-real dreams, which she drifted in and out of.

Then, suddenly, she was awake. Her eyes flew open and she tried to sit up, but pain lashed through her, seeming to hit from everywhere at once. She groaned without meaning to.

Her head ached, but even worse was the agony throbbing through her shoulder. Every heartbeat seemed to pump more pain throughout her body.

Where was she?

And why the hell did she feel like someone had beaten the crap out of her?

Wherever she was, it was nearly pitch-black. She tried to rise again, blowing out a slow breath to manage the pain, but before she could sit up, a hand touched her right shoulder, pressing her back.

"Lie back," a female voice murmured.

"Who," Lily croaked, her throat so parched, even just that one word barely made it out.

"I'm Dawn Armadale. This is our house."

"Wh . . ." She tried again to ask where she was.

"Water? Would you like some water?"

Before Lily could answer, the woman disappeared only to return a moment later with a plastic cup that had a straw sticking out.

"Can you turn your head?" she asked.

Lily nodded and the action sent a new burst of pain radiating through her shoulder. Rather than try to talk, she focused on turning her head enough for Dawn to slip the straw between her lips. It was cool, but had the funny aftertaste of the chlorine they'd used to sterilize it. She'd gotten used to the taste now, but she still wrinkled her nose against the smell of bleach.

Her head pounded, like her brain was suddenly too big for her skull. Despite that, her eyes were starting to adjust to the dark as she looked around. The room was roughly semicircular, with the walls sloping up toward the ceiling. There were two sets of bunk beds crowding the space, and when she looked straight up, she realized she must be lying on the bottom bunk of another set. The woman beside her was sitting on a stool. She wore a simple T-shirt and jeans with her hair pulled up into a ponytail on the back of her head. Without more light, it was impossible to guess her age, but there was something familiar about her face. Something about the set of her wide eyes.

"Where . . ." Again she couldn't get out another word and Dawn raised the bottle to her lips.

"We brought you down to the bunker. We haven't seen Ticks around here for a couple of months, but after you got shot, we all thought it was best to get out of the open. No point in luring them here, right?" She reached down and pulled out a flashlight. "I cleaned your arm and stitched you up while you were still out. Now that you're awake, I need to check your pupils and ask a few questions, okay? If it seems like you don't have a concussion, then I can give you a shot for the pain."

That was all the warning she gave Lily before flicking the flash-light on. Lily automatically cringed away from the light, but Dawn held open her eyelids, then moved the light from one eye to the other and back again.

The light made her head throb even more, but it gave her some-thing to think about besides her damn shoulder. As she breathed slowly and didn't move, she could disconnect from the pain. Man-age it. Sort of.

"Do you remember what happened?" Dawn asked. "Do you have any confusion?"

Lily frowned. She didn't remember exactly what happened. Which was odd. Bits of the food raid came back to her, but nothing solid. The question marks in her mind made her twitchy. She swallowed and found that she could talk now that her tongue had rehydrated. "I don't know where the hell I am or what's going on. That confused enough for you?"

Dawn rolled her eyes. "Whatever. Your pupils are responding. I think you'll have a nasty bump on your head, but no concussion."

With that, Dawn stood. She set the light on the edge of the bed, but didn't turn it off. She moved around the tiny room as she started talking. "You're in our bunker. My father shot you. Since you were looting our stuff, you can't blame him."

Suddenly the events of the morning came rushing back to her. Holy crap.

She tried to sit up again, this time ignoring the burst of pain in her arm. The sudden movement made her head spin and her gut churn, but she shoved aside the sensation and swung her feet over the side of the bed. She wasn't wearing her own clothes. At least not her jacket anyway. She had on a green hoodie, which was zipped up only partially so her wounded arm hung out. She kept her left arm tucked close to her side and her head ducked because of the upper bunk. "What happened after I went down?" She clutched at Dawn's arm. "What happened to the others? Is Jacks okay? What about Stu?" For an instant, she thought her heart might actually have stopped beating. "Carter? Is he all right?"

Dawn gave her a reassuring smile. "Slow down. And calm down. Panic isn't going to help you heal."

She forced herself to speak slowly. Not because she gave a damn about whether or not her gunshot wound healed, but to appease Dawn. "Are they okay?"

Was he okay?

Carter wasn't in here being treated, which either meant he didn't need medical attention or was past the point of needing it.

"I don't know everyone's names, but the two guys you were with are both embarrassed that a man in his fifties was able to take them out without a sound. They'll get over it. As for the guy who came to rescue you . . ."

"Carter."

She shook her head, smiling ruefully. "After you fell on the stairs, he kind of lost it. It took three of my brothers to pull him off my father. And he didn't calm down until I showed up to check you over and promised him you were okay."

"Oh." Lily breathed out a sigh of relief, but her heart was still racing. She didn't think a straight-up hit of oxygen would calm her down.

"And he's okay now?" she asked again.

"Yeah." Dawn nodded and she set the flashlight down on a small chest beside the beds. She pointed the light up toward the ceiling so it cast enough of a glow for Lily to see more of the room. "Things calmed down once I showed up. The two guys you showed up with headed back up the mountain as soon as they came to. But your guy—Carter?—was going to wait for you to get stitched up.

My brother Darren offered to drive you back up the mountain but
Carter said he'd wait. That's Darren for you. He's been itching to
get out of town for months now. To see what else is out there, but
Dad won't let him."

"I know this probably shouldn't matter, but what happened to
my clothes?"

Dawn cringed. "I had to cut your shirt off of you. Saved the
jacket, though. You should be able to patch the . . . um . . ." She
gestured toward the spot on her own bicep where Lily had been
shot.

Lily nodded. Well, at least there was that. She really liked that
jacket.

"Your backpack is by the door. I hope you don't mind, but I kept
my stuff that you were stealing."

Dawn's voice was sarcastic, but not hard-edged.

Yeah, she should probably be glad Dawn wasn't being more of
a bitch about the whole stealing thing, but really all Lily could
do was shake her head at the irony. After all this, she hadn't even
been able to bring home the one thing she'd come for. She'd come
here hoping to solve one small problem and instead she'd created
a huge one.

"Sorry," she said to Dawn. "About everything."

Dawn shrugged. "Hey, no hard feelings. Just don't be surprised
if my dad isn't as forgiving."

While Dawn continued to fiddle with the medical supplies,
Lily's mind flooded with questions. Before she could stop herself,
they poured out. "So your whole family made it? How many are
there of you?"

"We've been lucky." Dawn moved as she talked. She had a storage box, sort of like a tackle box that a fisherman might use. Instead of lures and hooks, Dawn's was full of medical supplies. Like

a first-aid kit on steroids. She opened one compartment after another, looking for things and pulling out what she found. "I was back from school when the first outbreak hit. Darren, too. Of course, Dad's been preparing for this kind of thing for years. As soon as the virus hit Utah, we moved into the shelter. You met Danielle, who should know better than to play in the house by herself. Then there's Darren, Derek, and Dex. Donald, my eldest brother, was on mission in Colombia when it hit." She shrugged, and Lily didn't press her for more information. "But there are a couple more of us now. Micah and Noah moved in early on. They're twins who played soccer with Dex and lived up in Logan. Logan got hit pretty hard."

"Yeah, I know." Logan was just north of here. It was closer to Base Camp so they'd done a lot of food raids there. In fact, they'd about picked the town clean. Almost all the supplies they had had come from Logan and they hadn't seen any sign that people had survived at all.

"Are there more families here in town?"

Dawn slanted Lily an odd look as she ripped open an alcohol pad and swiped at a spot on Lily's arm. "Yeah. Of course. It helps that we're up in the mountains. Ticks don't seem to like it up here."

"How many people live here?"

"Oh, close to two thousand."

"Wow," Lily murmured, hardly knowing what to say. Then she winced when Dawn jabbed a needle into her arm. "What the—"

"Antibiotic. Intravenous would be better, but I don't have the setup for it. Still, this should go a long way. I've got an oral you can take home with you, too. As well as some painkillers."

"You have antibiotics?" Lily asked, baffled. Of course, they'd looked for them on food raids. They just hadn't found any.

Justin, one of the Greens who'd been at camp the longest, had nominated himself camp medic. He was busy reading every book he could find on medicine. "We have a guy, Justin, who is kind of a medic. He's always hassling people to look for antibiotics, but we've never found any."

Dawn gave a shrug that looked a little self-conscious. "Yeah, my dad used to take trips down to Mexico to stock up on stuff like that. Even in the Before we had random medicine on hand all the time." She ripped open a second alcohol wipe and prepped Lily's other arm for another shot. "This one is morphine for the pain; it'll make you a little woozy, but—"

Lily pulled her arm away. "No. I'm good."

Dawn frowned. "Your arm has to be killing you."

"I don't want to be woozy." In this world, woozy got you killed. Maybe not if you were down in an underground bunker, like she was right now, but eventually, it got you killed. And she didn't plan on staying down here for long.

"If you won't take the morphine, at least let me get you an oral painkiller." Dawn must have seen the hesitation in Lily's eyes because she added, "You can bring it with you and take it when you get back to your camp."

Lily held out her palm and Dawn handed over a bottle of the antibiotics. She put the painkillers in a tiny Ziploc bag.

For the first time, it occurred to Lily that although she had a ton of questions for Dawn, Dawn didn't seem at all interested in hearing about Base Camp. Did that mean she just wasn't interested? Or did she already know about the camp?

Lily hoped she'd have the chance to ask her later. But for now, she wanted to see Carter.

"Are we done here? Where are the others?"

"Up at the house. I can take you there." She placed a gentle hand on Lily's other arm. "Easy now. Let's get a sling on your arm. It'll help with the pain."

"Okay. Why are you cringing?"

"For you to wear the sling, we have to get your arm through the sleeve of the sweatshirt. It's going to hurt like a bitch."

And she was right. It did end up being cringe worthy. If Lily hadn't been trying so hard to be tough in front of Dawn, she probably would have cried.

By the time Dawn had the sling adjusted, Lily's arm throbbed so badly it made her head spin.

"How is that?" Dawn asked as she adjusted the last strap.

With the sling in place, Lily relaxed and let the fabric accept the weight of her arm. "Better," she admitted. "Much better."

"Well, it's no morphine shot, but it should help."

A moment later, she swung open the door to the sleeping area and led Lily into another room shaped just like the first. This room had a kitchenette off to one side, with a table and chair and a small sitting area on the other side. Straight ahead was an open door, which led to a flight of stairs. Her uncle Rodney had an underground bunker like this, but his was smaller. More of a hidey-hole, as opposed to this, which seemed to be a full home buried underground.

By the time they made it up the stairs and through the final door, Lily was nearly shaking from exhaustion. Sweat poured down the back of her neck. Dawn opened the hatch door, flooding the passageway with light.

Blinking, she walked out into the sunlight. At least it was still day.

CHAPTER ELEVEN

LILY

Carter looked up when Lily entered the house, but his expression—dark and closely guarded—was impossible for her to read. Which was strange, because she'd gotten to know him pretty well in the past six weeks.

He sat, one of several men, at a table, but was the only one who held her attention for long. Dawn's father, Mr. Armadale, was at the head of the table. There were a couple of younger versions of him—Dawn's brothers, most likely—and a couple of men Armadale's age who must have been neighbors or fellow townspeople.

She barely noticed any of them. Carter studied her for a minute and she felt very self-conscious. Strangely aware of how she looked. Aware of the borrowed hoodie she had on and the fact that she wore nothing underneath it, not even a bra. Aware of the sweat beading on her hairline, despite the cool weather. Aware, too, of the fact that she'd lost blood and her skin would look too pale, almost bluish, which she knew from the months on the Farm—where it was common to be down a couple of pints.

Just when she was starting to fidget and to feel faint, Carter stood and crossed to the door. Only then did she look around the rest of the room again. And felt faint for a whole 'nother reason. Every male at the table—except Carter—had a weapon laid out in front of him. They were mostly handguns. A few she recognized, like the Glock and the Smith & Wesson, as well as several she didn't. Nasty-looking, little snub-nosed guns. A guy who looked enough like Dawn to probably be her brother had a rifle sitting across his lap. Armadale had two guns: the automatic handgun he'd shot her with and something with a sizable clip to it. Only the dark wood of the table had kept her from noticing the guns right off. They nearly blended in with the wood.

No one looked particularly happy to see her and unless she was mistaken, several hands were creeping closer to their weapons.

Carter stopped beside her, subtly putting himself between her and the others. He didn't even look at the other men but kept his gaze focused on Armadale.

"We can go now."

It was both a question and not a question. He was telling her and Armadale. Not asking permission exactly but letting Armadale know if he was going to stop them peacefully, now was the time to do it.

Armadale gave a tight nod and stood slowly. He angled his jaw to the side, scraping the backs of his nail across the stubble on his cheek.

"You kids keep to yourselves and I don't see as we'll ever meet up after this."

Carter nodded. He didn't move for the door, but Lily felt his hand on the small of her back exerting a little pressure, letting her know they'd soon be moving in that direction. Probably the second he knew for sure that Armadale wasn't going to shoot them where they stood.

"You won't see us again."

Armadale nodded. "You stick to the towns north of here. There's nothing for you south of Logan."

They were almost to the door when Dawn stepped forward and gave Lily a quick hug. "One of each pill, twice a day, with food," she whispered. "Keep the wound clean. If it looks bad, you find a way to get back here, okay?"

Surprised, Lily nodded.

More quickly than she could have thought, Carter was helping her climb into the truck's cab. His jaw looked tense, but it was the fatigue around his eyes that tore at her heart. He didn't look anything like the guy who'd come to rescue her from the Farm nearly two months ago. He looked . . . worn. Older.

She'd known, of course, the toll stress took on people. She'd seen it in her mother when her father had walked out on them. So, yeah, she knew. But she'd never seen it on someone her age. Never seen it this up close. She reached across her chest, trying to maneuver the seat buckle into place without jarring her arm too much then straightened to watch as he rounded the hood of the car.

She was hoping that once he calmed down and assured himself she was okay, he would pull her into his arms and hold her tight. Even though she was okay. Even though she was physically going to be fine, she wouldn't feel okay, until that moment.

But that comfort never came. Instead, there was only a long stretch of awkward silence in which Carter drove and Lily waited. And waited. His silence stung so deep, she felt like she couldn't breathe all over again.

Finally, not sure what else to say, she said, "Carter, I—"

But he didn't let her get out more than that. "Jesus, Lily, what the hell were you doing on that supply raid?"

"There were things we needed."

"You knew I didn't want you going!"

"And you knew I wanted to go anyway. This shouldn't be that surprising."

"I shouldn't be surprised that my girlfriend snuck around behind my back doing something that could have gotten her killed?"

"I never said I wouldn't go out. The opportunity came up. I took it. And in my defense, I was watching for Ticks. There were no Ticks there at all."

"Oh, I feel so much better now, knowing you were almost murdered by a human."

"I'm the one who got shot. Why are you so mad at me?"

"I'm the one who had to watch you get shot. Jesus, do you have any idea what it was like for me watching you go down? It nearly killed me."

"It did?" she asked softly.

Instantly, his posture relaxed. "Yeah," he muttered. "It did."

Just like that, despite the trauma of the day, despite her pain and the grief and the fear, despite all that, she felt better. Yeah, Carter had told her he loved her before, but it wasn't something he talked about often.

She scooted closer to him and put a hand on his arm. "Well, now you know how I feel every time you go out on a supply raid." He didn't say anything and as the silence stretched taut between them, she changed the subject. "Well, they seemed . . ." But then she didn't know what else to say so she tacked on a weak ". . . nice?"

Carter didn't take his eyes off the road, but he cursed. "Jesus, Lily, are you kidding me?"

"Okay," she admitted. "They don't seem nice. They seem . . . prepared."

"If that's the polite way of saying they're effing crazy, then yes, they're *prepared*."

"I'm not trying to pick a fight here."

"Then what's your point?"

"Obviously this wasn't an ideal situation, but it's not all bad, right? We can use all the allies we can get."

"Allies? Is that what you think? These gun-toting wack jobs are going to be our allies?"

"They're within easy driving distance. Surely there's someone in town with a satellite phone. We should have given them our number."

"I'm not giving our number to the guy who shot you."

"Yeah, he shot me. But it's barely a scratch."

"You were lucky. Eight inches to the right and you'd be dead."

"Yes, I was lucky, but think about it from his point of view. He thought his kid was in danger. Can you honestly say you wouldn't do the same to protect your family?"

"He shot you with a handgun, Lily. Have you thought about what that means? Anyone who's lived this long knows that a pistol isn't going to do jack to a Tick. A half-dozen bullets won't do more than piss a Tick off. So if he had a pistol, it's because he intended to shoot people. Humans, Lily. That's the only thing a handgun is good for shooting. Think about that for a few minutes before you tell me you think we should make these people our allies."

"He was protecting his family."

"Jesus, Lily! Would you listen to yourself? Just for a minute? He *shot* you. Stop taking his goddamn side."

Lily blew out a slow breath. "You're right. Everything you've said about him is right. But just hear me out, okay? I'm not saying we need to start a book club or anything. But think about the bigger picture. Just for a second. There's a whole town there. A town that was hard hit, but a town, Carter. An honest-to-God town with close to two thousand people living in it, from what Dawn said. That's the first sign we've had that there's anything left other than Farms and Ticks. This is huge! This is good news!"

"Seriously?"

"Let's forget for a moment that he shot me. For the first time, in, like, forever, you get to go back to Base Camp with good news. With hope. With potential allies. Just forget for a second whether or not these allies are ones we actually want. They're human. That's . . . a miracle."

Carter let out a curse and slowed the Hummer to a stop before turning to face her.

"You're right. I should be thrilled." His voice was anguished. "And maybe, soon, I will be. But for now, I'm still a bit freaked that you nearly died out there today. And you know what's worse than that? You getting shot wasn't his fault, it was mine. I'm the one who charged in. I spooked him. If I hadn't panicked, you wouldn't have been shot."

She sat back against the door of the cab, all her anger slipping away. "Carter, I don't blame you."

"*I* blame me."

For a moment Lily just stared at him in shock. Then she said, "Carter, I—"

He whirled on her. "Damn it, Lily, don't you get it? All this time I haven't been keeping you at Base Camp because you haven't been ready to go on food raids, I've been keeping you there because *I* haven't been ready."

"But I—"

"People get hurt on food raids."

"Yeah, sometimes they do, but that doesn't mean I'm going to hide back in the caves. People look up to me. They see me as a leader, and a leader has to be out in the field."

"Bullshit."

"*You're* out in the field. The Elites will follow you anywhere because they know you'll lead the charge. Generals in ancient Rome did the same thing. They were always the first onto the battlefield. That's what made the Romans the fiercest warriors of their day, and I—"

"I don't give a crap about ancient Rome. I care about *you*. I care about keeping you safe."

Carter looked away from her and glared straight ahead, even though he wasn't driving and had no excuse to pay attention to the road. Even though there was no traffic or other cars or any reason to even look at the road.

Suddenly that expression she couldn't read earlier became perfectly clear. Beneath that outward show of bravado was fear. Fear for her.

"People get hurt in food raids. You got hurt. When you were shot, when I thought you might be dead, I—"

His voice broke on the next word. Carter—who was so tough, tougher than anyone she knew. Carter—who had killed more Ticks than anyone. Carter—who had argued with Sebastian and refused to back down. But despite being that tough, whatever he'd been about to say, he couldn't get it out.

He just shook his head, hands still twisting on the steering wheel, eyes straight ahead. He was giving her nothing, showing her no emotion. Her breath caught in her chest. Because she suddenly, desperately, wanted to know what he'd been about to say.

"What?" she prodded.

He turned to look at her. He gave his head another little shake, his mouth turned down in self-disgust, his eyes hard.

"I care about you too much."

"Too much?" she asked, and then wished she hadn't. Nothing about this was going the way she'd hoped.

"When I thought you were hurt, I didn't handle it well." This time he said the words in a rush and seemed to have no trouble at all getting them out. "I wanted to kill that guy."

"Armadale?"

"Yes. I beat the shit out of him. I nearly didn't stop."

"Well, you didn't kill him. So, it's all okay, right?"

"No, it's not okay." His voice was hard. "If I'm the leader of this rebellion, then I'm making decisions for everyone. Right now, my gut reaction is always to put you first. To protect you. And that's not right. That's not fair to everyone else. I can't be the leader of the rebellion and be with you."

Her heart slammed inside her ribs. Suddenly, she knew what was worse than getting shot: this. This was worse than being shot. Carter was breaking up with her.

"Look, I messed all of this up when we were leaving the Farm. I didn't trust you when I should have. I wasn't honest when I should have been. I lied to you. I tried to do the right thing over and over again, but everything I did ended up not being the right thing and—"

She interrupted him. "Carter, what happened at the Farm, with Mel, it wasn't your fault. If it was anyone's fault, it was mine."

"No. It wasn't. Think about it. If I'd been honest from the start. If I'd told you everything up front. About Sebastian. About how I felt about you. About my plan to get you out of there. Things would have been different. I wouldn't have tranqed you and brought you to the Dean's office. The Dean never would have seen you. He wouldn't have come after you. He wouldn't have grabbed Mel. Everything would have gone down differently."

She wanted to argue with him, even though there was logic to his words. And it wasn't like she hadn't been playing those same mind games herself. How often had she laid awake at night playing "what if"? Wondering what she might have done to prevent Mel from ending up dead in a parking lot with her begging a vampire to turn her.

It was something of an obsession of hers, so she didn't know why it surprised her to find out that Carter felt the same way. Carter had an almost painful sense of responsibility; of course he was doing the same thing. Even though they'd never talked about it.

Funny how all this time had passed and Carter and she hadn't really talked. Oh, they'd made it through their day-to-day lives. They functioned. They certainly functioned on a physical level. Whenever he held her body close to his, whenever he kissed her and made the world fall away, it was easy to lose herself. It was easy to pretend life was normal. This was the way it was supposed to be. That it was okay. That this huge thing hadn't happened between them—her sister dying, Mel's influence over them vanishing. Maybe they could both pretend when they touched. Maybe there were just some things that were too difficult to say aloud.

Or maybe she was a coward.

Either way, she had this sick feeling in her gut that had nothing to do with the shot Dawn had given her.

"I don't blame you," she told him. And she didn't. She blamed herself.

His mouth twisted into an ironic smile. "That's not my point. My point is, if I'd been more honest, maybe things would have shaken out differently. Six weeks from now, I don't want to be having this same conversation with myself. I'm done keeping things from you because I'm trying to protect you."

He paused like he was waiting for her to say something.

So she nodded, even though her gut told her she wouldn't like where this was going. "Okay."

"This isn't working."

That queasy feeling in her gut coalesced into dread. "Okay," she repeated numbly, even though it was not okay.

"I don't see how I can do this anymore. I can't—" He broke off, turning away from her so she couldn't read his expression at all. "Look, I know you expect me to be this great leader of the rebellion or something. But I can't do that. I can't be that guy and be your guy. I can't do both. It's not fair. Not to anyone. I'm fundamentally not okay sending you into dangerous situations."

"Carter, I can take—"

"Don't tell me you can take care of yourself. I know that." He plowed his hand through his hair. "Jesus, you think I don't know that? You handled yourself better than Jacks or Stu. You took care of it. I'm not saying you didn't. You handled things a hell of a lot better than I did. That's the problem. Don't you get it?"

"No," she answered honestly. Because she didn't get what he was saying at all. "What's the problem?"

"I fucked up."

She wanted to disagree. He hadn't messed up. He'd made a tough call in a tough situation. He'd done the best he could. No one would ask more than that.

"I will continue to eff up anytime you're in danger. It's that simple. You said it yourself. I effed up big time with Armadale. If his kid hadn't been there . . ." Carter broke off, shaking his head. "When I saw that he'd shot you, I lost it. If his kid hadn't been there, I might have beaten him senseless."

"But his kid was there."

"You think that makes me feel better?"

Her throat tightened. There were a hundred things she wanted to say but none of them were right. So she just sat there, swallowing her fear and her yearning, just like she swallowed the nausea churning in her stomach.

He must have realized she didn't have an answer, because he stopped waiting for one. "That's what kills me about this, Lily. Everybody expects me to be the leader of this rebellion, but I don't have the head for it. When it comes to shit like this, I'm never going to make the right decision. When you're in danger, I'm never going to be able to think rationally about whether or not the guy holding a gun on you is a potential ally. I'm never going to be able to stop and think it through."

She turned to face him in the cab of the truck. "That's only because you're thinking about it wrong. You just haven't gotten used to the idea that I'm not an *abductura*. You spent so long thinking that I was special. That I was important. More important than anyone else. You just haven't adjusted yet to the idea that I'm not."

He gave her a look hot enough to steam the windows in the cab. "Is that what you think? That you're not important now? Just because you're not an *abductura*?"

"I'm not important—at least, no more than anyone else. I'm just another Green."

"You will *always* be important to me."

"No, Carter, you just think that because—"

"Damn it, Lily, when are you going to get it? I care about *you*. Not because of what you can do for the rebellion. Not because of what Mel may or may not have made me feel. But because you're *you*. Because I need *you*. Because you're smart and you make me think about things I would never think about on my own. Like using Armadale to our advantage instead of beating the shit out of him. I never would have thought of that on my own."

"On your own, you wouldn't have been in that position in the first place."

Even though he didn't agree with her, she knew she was right. She just didn't know what to say about it, let alone what to do.

But no. She did know. There was an obvious solution. She just didn't like it. "I think maybe we should break up."

To her surprise, Carter tipped back his head and laughed. The sound was amused and pained and bitter. It made her ache and broke her heart all at the same time.

"You think that would do any good? You think some label is going to make me not care about you?"

Good point. She didn't want him in danger any more than he wanted her in danger. That would never change.

She hated this feeling of helplessness. Hated knowing that she was bad for him. No matter what else he thought or said, the rebellion needed him. He was the only person everyone trusted enough to lead. And the simple truth was that she was in his way. She made his job harder. Her being here made everything worse.

CHAPTER TWELVE

CARTER

We drove for a while in total silence. I stared mindlessly out the front window. Lily stared out the side window. I could tell from the way she toyed with the fabric of her hoodie's sleeve that her arm was bugging her. She wouldn't want me to notice, but I'd had plenty of wounds myself. With a close call like that, you were tempted to poke at it. To reassure yourself that it wasn't as bad as it might have been.

Hell, it was all I could do not to demand she rip off the bandage and show me Dawn's sutures. I had been in the room when Dawn had cleaned the wound and started stitching it up. Hell, I knew it wasn't bad. But I wanted to see it. To assure myself.

But I didn't touch her. I didn't even talk to her.

What was left to say?

We might have driven all the way back to Base Camp in silence, except the satellite phone rang.

The sat phone ringing wasn't anything to take lightly. Only a handful of people even had phones, let alone the number to this one. Sebastian had a phone. Base Camp had five others: two that stayed at camp, two that went out with teams that worked the Farms, and one that was used on food raids. The phones were a luxury item. No one would use one if it wasn't an emergency.

When it started ringing, Lily just looked mutely at the duffle bag holding all the food-raid supplies—the sat phone included.

"Pick it up," I told her.

She dug through the bag with her good arm, and found the phone only to stare at it for a second before fumbling to answer it. She pressed the phone to her ear. "Hello?"

The expression on her face as she listened said it all. Hell, the fact that anyone had called at all said it all.

I slowed the truck to a stop and set the brake, anxiety churning in my gut. Lily met my gaze as she handed me the phone. For just a second, she cradled my hand in hers.

"Tell me." Hearing it from her would buy me at least a few seconds to process whatever happened before I had to talk to whoever was on the other end of the line.

Her eyes were wide with shock and fear made her voice tremble. "Base Camp was hit."

"Gun-toting psychopaths?" I didn't really believe that's who it was, but at least if the attackers where human, Base Camp might have had a chance.

But Lily shook her head. "Ticks. They attacked an hour ago."

"During the daylight?"

"It wasn't a full pack. Just three."

"Casualties?"

"Thirteen. Two Elites and eleven Greens. They were cooking lunch out in the yard. The Ticks got nearly everyone who—"

Lily broke off, squeezing her eyes closed. I took the phone from her, and braced myself to hear the rest from whoever was on the other end of the line. From whoever had lived to tell the tale.

I started driving again as I listened to Merc's sit rep. Merc described the attack in terse, emotionless sentences.

Jesus, it had been a bloodbath.

I drove fast and hard to get back to Base Camp as quickly as I could. So that I could get there and assess the damage myself. So that if other Ticks attacked, I would friggin' be there this time. And so that I wouldn't have to be here in the truck with Lily any longer than necessary. Because I couldn't stand to see the disappointment in her eyes any more than I could stand to hear her quiet tears.

* *

Lily threw herself from the cab of the truck as soon as it stopped in the parking lot outside of Base Camp. I hadn't even set the brake yet and she was already running for the cave.

She hadn't said a word after the phone call, but I knew she'd want to get to McKenna as quickly as possible. She'd need to verify with her own eyes that the girl was okay. It didn't have anything to do with needing to get as far away from me as possible. Probably.

Still, it took everything in me to let her go.

Maybe she hated me right now. I could live with that. What I couldn't live with was how many things had gone wrong today. I was still reeling from the sight of Lily being shot. And I couldn't even begin to process the attack on Base Camp.

I climbed out of the cab more slowly than Lily.

I tucked the keys into my pocket and tried to tamp down my nausea as I surveyed the damage. When I'd left that morning, there had still been patches of snow and ice around the parking lot. Drifts of bright white near the tree line, piles of gray slush that softened during the day and refroze each night.

Now, there was blood everywhere. The bright splatter of red, hot enough to burn holes in the snow. The rivulets of pink, where the slush had melted and washed away carnage like a grisly river delta. The stench of blood and death and panic hung in the air, suffocating me.

Thirteen people. The loss was unthinkable. Unimaginable. This was the carnage of defeat. Of disaster. It smothered me.

Someone had covered the bodies with sheets, trying to mask the horror, but the result was ghastly. On TV when someone covers a corpse, the body is laid out like an Egyptian mummy. The shape beneath the cloth still looks human. Like someone tucked into bed with the sheets drawn up too high.

This looked nothing like that. Blood had seeped through the cloth, mimicking the appearance of the blood-splattered snow. The bodies beneath the sheets were twisted, broken, and misshapen. The bodies of the Ticks had been covered, also. They were set apart slightly—out of respect for the dead, I guess. But I would have recognized them anyway. There was nothing human about them, just a pile of hacked-up limbs. The survivors here hadn't taken any chances that the Ticks might regenerate.

And they hadn't yet thought far enough ahead to realize we would have to take that same precaution with the fallen on our side.

We had no way of knowing who—if any of them—would have the regenerative gene. We had to be sure that the people who died today, stayed dead.

I would do it myself. Every cell in my body rebelled at the thought. It made my stomach wrench and my skin crawl, but I would do it. Because I couldn't ask anyone else to do it for me. Because I had to be sure. And because I was the leader.

This job—this horrific job—fell to me and no one else.

Besides, the deaths of those thirteen people . . . their blood was on my hands. If I'd been here, I wouldn't have been able to stop it, but I damn sure could have fought. I couldn't have saved all these lives, but I could have saved some of them.

Yeah, the girl I loved was safe, but at what price? Even worse, part of me was glad Lily had been shot.

If she hadn't been shot then she would have been here this afternoon when the Ticks attacked and I knew how she would have reacted. She would have jumped right into the fight.

It was one of the things I loved about her—her complete refusal to back down from a fight, even one she had little hope of winning. What if she'd been one of these Greens who had died senselessly? The thought literally made it impossible to breathe. It crushed me.

"You okay?"

I turned to see Merc walking out of the caves. "Should I be?"

Merc didn't meet my gaze. "No."

"You and Taylor didn't run into any trouble?"

"We only got here about ten minutes ago. Taylor's fine."

I nodded, but didn't comment. Thank God Taylor was alive. As horrible and unthinkable as this was, Base Camp couldn't function without Taylor. This attack might break us. I knew that, but without someone to keep what little electricity we had up and running, we would all be dead.

Merc nodded toward the bodies. "I figured . . ." He gestured and only then did I realize he held an ax in each hand. The blades gleamed in the weak afternoon sun. He'd just sharpened them.

"Yeah," I said, because I couldn't say anything else aloud. I held out my hand, palm up. "I'll do it. Just keep the parking lot clear for a while. But I'll prepare the bodies for disposal myself." Besides, if I did the work alone, no one would notice when I puked my guts out midway and cried like a friggin' baby afterward. "You go on in, Merc."

Merc slanted me a wtf look and handed me one of the axes on his way to the bodies.

Merc wasn't the kind of guy who talked a lot, but he followed orders and never hesitated to step up. Even to do what had to be the crappiest job on earth.

Back in the Before, before this whole nightmare began, I never would have conceived that my job description would have included chopping the heads off my murdered friends.

I'd sworn to protect these people. Some of them were just kids. Kids I'd personally rescued out of Farms. And now, they were dead and it was my job to defile their bodies. I couldn't even bury them afterward.

As cold, hard, and rocky as the land was up here, it would take days to dig enough graves and there were too many bodies for a funeral pyre. We couldn't afford to burn that many trees. The absolute best we could do was load all the bodies into the back of one of the trucks and drive up to a nearby ravine and drop them over. Even though I would never have asked Merc to help, I was glad he was there.

All those times I'd played "Assassin's Creed"—all the times I'd thought how badass it was to swing a sword—all those points I'd racked up, none of that could have prepared me for the first swing of the ax. This wasn't the first time I'd done this, but it never got any easier.

We worked in silence. It was gruesome, terrible work. No matter how many times or how many ways I told myself that it had to be done, that it was honoring the human this body had been, I still hated it. It made me feel like a goddamn serial killer and I just freaking hated it.

It helped, somehow, knowing Merc hated it, too. We both

threw up more than once, but we worked quickly and were finished loading the bodies into the back of the truck within an hour.

Afterward we cleaned up the best we could. Out by the tree line, the dirt was sandy and there were a few dry patches. We used that to scrub off most of the blood so that we wouldn't waste precious soap. We had both worked barefoot—shoes were too difficult to clean and too hard to come by if they were ruined by blood splatter—and despite the cool weather, we both stripped off our shirts and scrubbed them in the dirt, too. Sand absorbs a lot of blood.

A little bit off in the woods, we had set up a primitive bathroom. Water, which we pumped up from Bear Lake, was stored in a tank. There were tubs for washing up and a gravity-fed shower. There was very little privacy, which didn't matter much because it was too miserably cold for anyone to linger out there. Usually, people signed up for time in the bathroom weeks in advance. Today it was predictably empty. I washed out all my clothes myself and Merc did the same. I put my jeans back on wet.

The last thing we did before going in was shovel buckets of sand across the stains in the parking lot. It helped. A little. The stains would fade slowly, from the concrete and from people's minds, but covering up the blood made it possible to pretend today hadn't happened.

I couldn't look anyone in the eyes as we walked back into the caves. I thought about what Lily had said about the Roman generals who led the charge into battle, who were the first to kill and, if need be, the first to die.

After today, that didn't seem like bravery or even stupidity. Charging into battle seemed smart, because the general who died in battle never had to bury his own men.

Because this was the stuff you never got over. This was the stuff that haunted you until the day you died. The stuff you never thought you could do but did anyway, because if you didn't do it, who would?

But through it all, through the horror and anguish, through the bitter cold and aching muscles, I felt this awful relief, because at least Lily hadn't been there. Because as hard as *this* was, there was nothing on earth, no fear great enough, no horror bad enough, no promise binding enough that would have given me the strength to do this to her.

CHAPTER THIRTEEN

LILY

Carter might have called after her, but she didn't stop. If she had, she would have lost it. She couldn't have stopped to look at a single body. She just couldn't. Because none of them would have been just bodies. All of them would have been Mel.

She would have been back in that church parking lot where her sister had had her heart ripped out of her body while Lily stood by, unable to do a damn thing.

If she had stopped for even a moment, she never would have recovered. And the last thing Carter needed was for her to go completely catatonic on him. Especially when she'd just spent the last several hours trying to convince him that she could handle herself and whatever was outside base camp.

So she bolted for the cavern, each step making her more nauseated. Her head spun and so did her stomach. Whatever drugs Dawn had given her had messed with her system, but still she ran.

She thought she'd be okay once she made it inside, but there was more blood there. Not on the ground like outside, but on the people. Those thirteen were not the only victims. The Ticks had caused a lot of damage before they'd been brought down.

That's when the panic set in. When it hit her that those bodies out there weren't Mel, but real people. People she knew. People like Shelby. People like McKenna.

Oh, God. *McKenna.*

Heart beating wildly, she scanned the crowd for McKenna's distinctive, swollen belly. She didn't see McKenna among the victims in the triage area, but she hadn't looked at any of the bodies outside. She hadn't stopped to make sure none of the victims were pregnant.

She ran for the door, only stopping to brace herself against the wall when she reached the exit. One of the Elites—some guy whose name she couldn't remember—stood by the door. She sucked air into her lungs, trying to stop her head from swimming. Damn it, she hated feeling weak. Too out of breath to talk, she waved a hand at the door, gesturing for the Elite to let her out.

"Sorry, Lily. No one goes in or out."

"What?"

"Carter's orders." The Elite's expression was grim. The guy didn't even look at her. "He's taking care of the bodies."

"But . . ." she stammered. He shook his head. *Oh God.* What if McKenna was out there? What if she was dead? What if she had died out there while Lily was off playing Joan of Arc? What if she never even saw the body, because she'd been too much of a coward to look at the victims?

She pushed herself away from the wall. "You have to let me out."

"Can't do it."

"I'm looking for"—Her voice broke and a sob rose up. It took everything she had not to collapse right there—"for my friend McKenna. Maybe you've seen her, she's—"

"Everybody knows McKenna." Finally he looked at her, a flash of sympathy in his gaze. "I helped cover the bodies. I didn't see her. I can't promise, but—"

"Thank you." She turned back around and surveyed the open cavern, looking one more time for McKenna's form. The cavern was packed. It looked like every Green and Elite was either out in the triage area or over by the KP station. No one wanted to be alone. But she still didn't see McKenna. That's when she really ran. Past the tables at KP where the uninjured clustered, past the pallets someone had laid out on the hard, stone floor, past the dozens of injured Greens and Elites. She practically flew through the cavern so that it passed in a blur of blood-soaked clothes, anguished cries, and fearful whimpers.

Lily's eyes moved frantically over the crowd, cataloging the wounded without really seeing them.

What would she do if McKenna was hurt?

But no. McKenna couldn't be hurt. She just couldn't be.

Fear pounded through Lily's veins as she wended her way through the honeycombed cavern. Anxiety, cramps, and pain all mingled in her gut so that by the time she reached their RV, an Itasca Sunrise with the double teal stripes, she had to bend over at the waist and spit a mouthful of bile onto the hard rock of the cavern floor. She pressed a palm to her side as she straightened, willing her stomach into obedience. Her stomach muscles were cramping from her burst of running, and the pain from her gunshot was so intense it was like fireworks bursting behind her eyelids, but she dragged herself up the three steps and threw open the door to the RV.

"McKenna?" she called.

"I'll be out in a minute!" came a voice from the RV's bedroom. *Oh, thank God.*

Lily's knees gave out and she slid to the floor, her back against the closed door. She was shaking. Not just a little tremble in her hands, but shaking all over. Every major muscle group quivered as wave after wave of adrenaline swept through her. She clutched her legs to her chest, desperate for warmth, and cursed the cold humidity of the cave, sure she would never be warm again. Not after the months of living under this damn mountain. Certainly not after seeing all those bodies. Not after fearing that someone else she loved might be dead.

She had no idea what McKenna was doing in the bedroom, but she was glad for this moment of solitude, this chance to pull it together before she had to face her friend. She needed to be strong. Not just for McKenna, but for herself, too. If she cracked now, she'd never be able to put the pieces of her shattered self together again.

She didn't know how long she sat, burying the tears and panic deep inside. When she felt a little steadier, she pushed to her feet and walked to the bedroom. She needed to make sure that McKenna was okay. She needed to see for herself that her friend was uninjured.

"Are you okay?" she called through the door.

She could hear McKenna moving around in there, but she didn't answer. Lily asked again.

"I'm fine!" she called back, her voice far too cheerful under the circumstances.

"Are you sure?" Lily asked.

Why would McKenna be hiding in the bedroom? Was she hurt? Crying? Possibly huddled in the corner, a broken emotional mess?

She swung open the door to find McKenna bustling about the tiny little room, grabbing things from the built-in storage and jamming them in a duffle bag.

"What are you doing?"

McKenna looked up, a towel clutched in her hand. She gave an exaggerated wince. "I'm packing to leave."

"I can see that." Lily didn't need to ask why. Probably everyone left at Base Camp was considering bailing. But where would they go? As dangerous as it was here, wasn't it more dangerous out there? "Are you hurt?"

"No."

"Not at all?"

McKenna stood, grabbed the bag she'd been packing, and managed to sweep past Lily, even though she was waddling and there was barely room to walk, much less sweep. "I'm fine. Not a scratch on me."

"But the Ticks—"

"Don't like pregnant blood, remember? They didn't even sniff in my direction."

Lily got another hit of adrenaline. "What the hell, McKenna? Why were you even out there? Why not just run in here and hide? It's what I would have done."

McKenna's gaze hardened. "No it's not. You're not a coward. You would have run into the battle and fought."

"No one expects you to fight, McKenna. You're pregnant. You're—"

She whirled on Lily. "I was right there by the door when the fight broke out. I just grabbed a stake and I ran out and I did it. And it didn't matter. The girl that thing was killing was already dead and the battle ended so quickly. And it had already killed so many; what I did barely made a difference. They're so much faster and stronger and—"

McKenna's voice broke and she sagged against the cheesy Formica counter. It was like all the energy just sapped out of her, and she crumpled to the ground. She brought her knees as close to her chest as she could and braced her elbows on them, hiding her head.

Not knowing what else to do, Lily went and sat beside her. She placed a hand on the back of McKenna's head. She could feel her taking in deep, ragged breaths.

"McKenna, I—"

"Joe couldn't have made it out of something like that."

"Huh?"

She twisted her head to look at Lily with tear-damp eyes. "All this time I've been telling myself he might still be out there, looking for me, and that all I had to do was stay alive and that he would find me. But I—"

Her voice broke again in a way that made Lily's heart ache. Nothing about today had prepared her for the yearning in McKenna's voice. For the open longing. The crushed hope. The burgeoning sorrow.

So she did the only thing she could think of to do. She continued to stroke McKenna's hair. "Oh, McKenna—"

"But if he got cornered by more than one, then there's no way. He'd be dead for sure. There's no way he could make it. He—" She broke off again and sucked in another deep breath.

"If he couldn't make it, then what makes you think you could? You can't go. You need to stay here, where it's safe."

"It's not safe here! Three Ticks, Lily! Just three Ticks and they decimated Base Camp."

"Look, let's think about this logically."

"I'm going to have a baby in a month! I can't do that living in a cave with a bunch of teenagers! There's no doctor here. No hospital. No—"

"Have you even thought this through? I mean, really thought it through? Where are you going to go? How are you going to get there? This is crazy!"

"It's not crazy." McKenna pushed herself to her feet, rubbing the bottom of her belly as she stood. "I'm going to head to Canada. That was always the plan, right? Head north and seek asylum?"

"But we don't even know for sure if Canada is still there. What if it's fallen to the Ticks, too?"

"I don't know." She was struggling to pull air into her lungs, like she was battling a full-on panic attack. "All I know is that I can't stay here. I just can't. I can't keep waiting for him. I can't. I—"

Lily could hear the panic rising in McKenna's voice again. That desperation and fear. The way she was sucking in air like she couldn't breathe.

"Hey, calm down." Lily rubbed a hand up and down McKenna's arm. When that didn't seem to help, she gently pulled her friend into her arms and just held her. "We'll figure something out. I promise."

"But—"

"Just give me a while to think about it, okay?" She could feel McKenna nod against her shoulder. "I'm not going to let anything happen to you or the baby. We'll figure it out."

McKenna started crying again, leaning so heavily into Lily that she had to brace herself against the wall of the RV to hold her friend. But the RV's walls were flimsy. They were no better at holding up her weight than they were at keeping out the cold, and Lily couldn't help but feel like the walls were going to collapse in on them.

Here at Base Camp, they didn't live in RVs, they lived in a

house of cards. Carter's leadership, Lily's ability as an *abductura*, McKenna's hopes, everyone's safety. They were all cards, each one leaning against the other. She'd always known the slightest jostle would send them tumbling down. Today, the attack from the Ticks hadn't been a tiny bump. It had been an earthquake.

CHAPTER FOURTEEN

CARTER

I couldn't wait to get back to my room, just to have a moment alone. To get out of these damn serial-killer clothes and to breathe in air that didn't smell like blood. When you do something like bury the dead, the stench of blood clings to your nose and the sight of it is seared on your retinas, so that every time you close your eyes, you see it again. For days. Weeks, sometimes.

I'd never paid much attention in English class, but ever since Sebastian first taught us how to prep bodies after we fought off the Ticks who overran the Elite Military Academy, I'd thought a lot about Lady MacBeth and how the sight of all that blood drove her crazy. After a few hours of hacking bodies to pieces, I knew how she felt. Like I'd never be clean again.

Normally, I couldn't walk through the main cavern without twenty different people stopping me. Not today.

The Elites all knew what Merc and I had done. They knew to steer clear of either of us. The Greens followed their lead. So Merc and I walked through the cavern in silence. At some point, he disappeared into his room and I walked on to mine, glad to be completely alone.

I shut the door behind me and immediately changed into clean clothes. None of our clothes were washing-machine clean, but anything was better than the jeans I'd had on. I wanted to burn the damn things, but who knew when I'd find another pair that fit. I pulled on socks, too, first rubbing my toes between my palms. They'd lost all sensation in the cold and now that they were warming up, they burned like hell.

What did frostbite look like? Would I know it if I had it? And what the hell would it matter if I did? Having all my toes wouldn't do shit to keep my people alive.

I pushed myself to my feet, my mind racing, my anger and despair threatening to pull me under. How the hell was I supposed to do this? How was I supposed to lead this rebellion against these crazy odds? Without even Sebastian around? He was badass in a fight, and all vampires had a sort of spidery sense that let them know when other vampires or Ticks were around. If he had been here today, things would have been different.

Sitting on the shelf right at eye level was that row of superhero bobbleheads. The damn things were taunting me, with their overly cheerful faces and silly bobbing heads. Superheroes in movies made it look so damn easy. Rally the forces, kill the bad guys, save the world. Why didn't movies or video games show how it really was? Why didn't they show the hopelessness, the failure? The grief? Or maybe it was just that I wasn't a superhero.

I felt another wave of anger at the injustice of it all and I swung out an arm, swiping all the bobbleheads off the shelf. They flew through the air to land in an arc on the floor. One of the superhero heads snapped off its head and rolled across the floor. The irony was the last straw. I stomped over to my punching bag. Violence may not solve everything, but it sure as hell cleared my head.

I don't know how long I pounded away on the bag, only that when I heard a noise behind me, I whirled around to see Ely Estaban standing in my doorway. Ely had been with us at Elite. He came by Base Camp occasionally, but he never stayed long.

Ely gave a head bob. *"Que passo, vato?"*

Ely tried to play it cool, but I threw my arms around him and gave him a hug, because it was damn good to see him. It had been months since he'd been back to Base Camp. I hadn't had any idea if he was even still alive. "Jesus, Ely, when did you get here?"

His arms tightened around me for only an instant before he pulled away. The lines of his face were hard with tension. And it was in his tone, too, when he spoke. "No one told you?"

"No." But I hadn't really talked to anyone.

"A few hours before the Ticks."

He didn't look at me when he said it, but shoved his hands deep in his pockets. Ely always kept to himself, but he had his reasons and he was one of the best guys I knew.

Most of the guys from Elite were troubled kids of rich parents who didn't know what to do with their pain-in-the-ass offspring. Ely and a few others had been different. They'd been scholarship kids at the academy by court mandate. Ely's parents hadn't shipped him off because they didn't know what to do with him. They'd sent him there because it was the last option they had that didn't involve him being tried as an adult and then serving a prison term. They would have done anything for him.

When he broke into a Farm, he was in and out quick, because all he cared about was whether or not his siblings were there. We only saw him every month or so and he'd hit multiple Farms between visits. I didn't ask if he'd found one of his sisters or his brother this time. If he had, he wouldn't look this grim and edgy. Ely had always been a badass. Today, he looked like a badass who wanted to rip something apart with his bare hands. Instead, I just gave his arm a squeeze.

"I'm glad you're here." Only then did I notice that he didn't have his dog with him. Right after the academy had fallen, Ely found a chow-mix mutt. The thing started following him around and he'd been traveling with it ever since. "Did you leave Chuy out in the cavern?"

Ely's expression hardened "Nah. Chuy . . ." He just shook his head and I knew enough to let it alone. "I picked up six Greens from the Farm in San Angelo."

Which should have been something to be happy about, but Ely didn't look thrilled.

He was shaking his head and at first I thought maybe he was going to circle back to his dog, but instead he said, "I'm sorry, man."

"For what?"

"I think the Ticks followed us here." Ely didn't quite meet my gaze as he pushed his hair back off his face. "We came up through the mountains north of here and worked our way back down. I thought we'd lost them." He sat down on the arm of the sofa, ducking his head. "If I'd known they were still back there, if I'd had any idea at all, we would have kept on driving."

I bit back a curse as I fought the urge to punch him. Even though it wasn't his fault. Even though this kind of shit could happen to anyone.

"When was the last time you were out there?" Ely asked.

"I've been on regular food raids, but it's been about six weeks since anyone from here went much beyond the valley. Why?"

"Things are bad out there."

"You think I don't know that things are bad? Trust me. I know."

My tone must have irritated him, because he stood up and his gaze sharpened.

"No. You know what things were like two months ago. They're worse now."

Worse than six weeks ago? Worse than when everyone I had sworn to protect, everyone who had trusted me to keep them safe, had been in mortal danger? I had promised Lily I would do anything to protect Mel. And I'd failed. Miserably.

Did I think things were worse out there than that? Hell, no.

"Look, I get it," I said, trying to shake off that crushing sense of failure. "Things are bad. They're going to be bad for a long time. I can't imagine them getting better. What do you want me to do about it?"

"That's your answer? 'What do you expect me to do about it?' Way to man up." Ely gave me a look filled with disgust.

I let his disappointment roll off me. I was used to that look. It was the one I saw every time I looked in the mirror. That was the one upside of the collapse of civilization: fewer mirrors.

I started to walk past Ely, but he gave my shoulder a hard shove. Surprised, I spun to face him.

"What the hell?" I demanded.

"You're supposed to be the leader of this rebellion."

"So?"

"So pull your shit together."

I smirked. "Thanks, that's helpful."

"I'm serious."

"I get it."

"No, you don't, or you would be out there right now pulling people out of Farms. Bad shit's going down and you—"

"You think I don't know that?" I snapped. "You think I don't know how bad it is out there? Because I do."

"Then stop having this pity party for yourself, get off your ass, and get out there and save some fucking lives."

"You think I don't want to save lives? I do. But let's be honest here. Let's look at the facts. Of the last four people I pulled out of a Farm, two of them didn't make it. I don't exactly have a brilliant track record right now. I'm not going to pull people out of Farms just so they can be slaughtered by the Ticks on the outside. Hell, I buried thirteen people today. People who were here, at Base Camp. Where they *should* have been safe. I can't rescue people I have no way to protect."

"What about the people who are about to age out? What about them?"

"We don't know, do we? Let's face it. There is so much we don't even have a way to learn. We know kids age out of the program. We know they leave the Farms sometime after they turn eighteen. But we don't know jack about what actually happens to them."

"Come on, Carter, you can't buy that bullshit. You don't honestly think those kids just get set free."

"No, I don't. But I don't know for sure, do I? No one does. For all we know, those kids get pulled out of the Farms and shipped off to Tahiti, where they lounge on the beach all day. For all we know, we're not rescuing them. We're pulling them from safety for no reason other than the fact that we don't want to be out here alone."

I stopped abruptly when I realized I was yelling. When I realized that Ely was looking at me like I'd lost my shit. Like I'd gone, officially, bat-crap crazy.

The seconds ticked by while I just stood there, sucking air into my lungs, trying to calm the hell down.

"Is that what you're waiting for? Some kind of proof of what goes down in the Farms? Some kind of guarantee that the Farms are evil?"

"Yes," I said. "That's exactly what I want. I want proof. I know it's irrational. I know it's impossible. But especially after what happened here today, that's what I want."

Ely just stared at me for a long moment in silence. Then he nodded. "Okay."

He turned and left the room.

Alone in my room, I swung another punch at the weighted bag. The bag was mounted in place to the ceiling and the floor; no matter how hard you hit it, the thing barely moved. It was exactly like this fight against the Ticks. No matter what I threw at it, no matter what angle I came at it from, the thing didn't budge. It hurt me like hell. My knuckles were bloody and bruised from hitting it, but the bag always settled back in to the same position. You could never win a fight against a punching bag. It just wasn't possible.

On the other hand, when you needed to hit something, you might as well take the punch.

Right now, I really wanted to punch Ely. Not because he was a good sparring partner, but because I absolutely wanted to beat the crap out of him.

I knew my need for proof was all kinds of wrong. I knew this situation was seriously effed up. I knew that without Ely pointing it out to me. I knew that without Ely walking away from me in disgust. Hell, I was disgusted with myself. I knew all that. Having him know it, too, sucked.

I didn't want to make any more mistakes. I didn't want to endanger any more innocent people. But beneath all that noble stuff was the crushing guilt. I had put Lily and Mel in danger. And no matter what I had told myself at the time about how noble my goals were, I had to live with the truth. I'd put them in danger for one simple reason: I wanted Lily with me.

Yes, I had believed she was the *abductura*. Yes, I had believed that together she and I could save the world. But underneath the noblest of intentions was the plain and simple fact that I didn't want to be alone. I wanted Lily to be safe. I wanted her where I could protect her.

And my need to protect her had gotten Joe killed. It had deprived McKenna's baby of a father. It had gotten Mel turned into a vampire. It was a screwup of massive and irreversible proportions. A screwup I didn't know how to undo.

CHAPTER FIFTEEN

CARTER

A few minutes later, Ely came back with another guy.

"This is Zeke," Ely said, giving the guy a little shove forward. "I pulled him out on that last raid."

"He came in with you today?"

Ely nodded.

I looked at Zeke again. He was Latino, like Ely, but built differently. Ely was built like a fire hydrant. He wasn't tall, but he was broad and muscled. This guy was almost as tall as I was, but he was lean.

But there was something I didn't like about the guy, something I couldn't quite put my finger on. Something about the belligerent set of his jaw and the angry gleam in his eyes. Something about how he stood.

Then it hit me. Why he seemed so familiar. Why he set my nerves on edge.

I gave the guy a tight smile and nodded toward the door. "Give us a minute?"

Zeke nodded.

"Shut the door on your way out," I told him. "But stay right there. I'll call you back in a second."

Ely smirked like he saw exactly where this was going.

I waited until Zeke was gone and the door had clicked closed behind him before I said, "You pulled out a Collab?"

Ely shrugged. "He's a solid guy."

"Out of all the thousands of Greens whose lives are at risk, you pull out a fucking Collab?" What the hell had he been thinking?

Ely didn't even flinch from my gaze. "I figured he'd know more than any damn Green. That he'd be able to tell us more about the defenses, about how the Farms work. About how to bring them down."

"Sebastian and I have been in and out of more than forty Farms. You've been in and out of even more. We know how Farms work. We don't need some damn sellout to tell us how to game the system."

Collabs were teenagers just like the rest of us, but they'd betrayed the other humans. They held positions of power at every Farm. They used power, weapons, and fear to keep the Breeders and Greens in line. They drew blood from humans to feed to the Ticks. And when a Green stepped out of line and was punished by being left chained outside the fence at night, it was the Collabs who did the chaining. In short, the Collabs betrayed the entire human race to save themselves.

In my eyes, Collabs were the real monsters.

"I don't care how solid you think he is," I shouted "He's still a Collab. This guy is used to having power no person should have. He's used to taking whatever the hell he wants. Do you have any idea what that kind of power does to someone? It messes with your head. It twists something inside of you and breaks you in a way that can't ever be repaired. This Collab that you've brought into my house is fucked up. Emotionally. Permanently."

"You don't know that about him." Ely got right in my face. "Zeke is a good guy and I trust him." Ely gave my shoulder another shove. "And I don't give a damn if you trust him or not."

"I—"

"Hell, I don't even care if you kick our asses out of here, but do yourself a favor and listen to what he has to say first."

Everything in me rebelled at the idea of hearing a Collab out.

"Just listen to him. Just calm down for a second and listen to him. In ten minutes, if you still want to kick him out, I'll go with him."

But I'd known Ely for close to two years. He was tough as hell, and he'd saved my life more than once. Looking at him now, I didn't see even a flicker of doubt in his gaze. He believed Zeke had some bit of information that I needed.

Finally, I gave a stiff nod. "I don't like it. But I trust you. You're the closest thing I have to family. If you say he's a good guy, I believe you."

Ely looked at me hard for a second, before giving a nod in return. Then he busted out laughing. "God, don't be such a wuss."

I laughed, too, because neither of us was comfortable with the sentimental crap.

"Whatever," I said. "Bring Zeke back in."

I made myself go lean against the wall opposite the door. If I was standing, I'd start pacing, and I didn't want either of them knowing how on edge I was.

A moment later, Zeke was standing in front of me.

"Why'd you leave the Farm?" I asked him.

"Because when Ely showed up, he said he could get me out. Said he knew somewhere that might be safe. I figured it was worth the risk."

"Sure, but why? You were a Collab. You weren't in any danger. You weren't about to age out. Collabs are like gods on a Farm. Why leave that behind?"

Zeke scowled. "Hey, it's not like you're making it sound."

"How am I making it sound?"

"Like we can just do anything we want," he said. "It's not like that."

"Close enough. I've been on Farms all over the country and it's the same story."

Zeke eyed me up and down, his face twisting into a frown. "Look, I don't need this shit. I didn't get out just so you could treat me like a freakin' narc. I didn't come here for that."

"Then why did you come here?"

"Because I didn't like the shit that was about to go down at that Farm."

"What shit? What's going down at your Farm?"

Zeke frowned. "Ely didn't tell you?"

"No." I shot Ely a glare.

He just smirked. "I thought you should hear it from him."

I looked from Ely to Zeke and back again. "Would one of you please just spit it out. What's going on?"

Zeke sent another look in Ely's direction and then said, "The Dean is trying to poison the Ticks."

"Oookay." I drew the word out. Zeke looked like he was about to say something else, but I held up a hand to stop him. "Back up a sec." I still had too many damn questions. Obviously the Ticks were a problem for everyone. Even if Roberto had engineered the Tick virus, they'd clearly gotten out of control. But I didn't see how this new twist—which should have been good news—was something Ely and Zeke were both worried about. "How's the Dean poisoning them?"

"Antifreeze. About a month ago, we were ordered to mix it into the blood before we brought it out to the feed stations."

It was a brilliant idea. Antifreeze was poisonous but sweet. Most animals would drink it if it was out. I'd seen some PSAs about it in the Before. "Did it work?"

"For a while it was great. Ticks were dropping dead all over. But they"—he gave a shrug that seemed part shiver of disgust—"they got smarter. Or maybe only the stupid ones ate the tainted blood. After a couple of weeks, they stopped coming to the feeding stations. Then for a while we rotated the clean blood and the poisoned blood, but they always seemed to know and pretty soon, they stopped coming altogether."

I looked at Ely. "Do you know if any other Farms are putting out tainted blood?"

Ely shrugged. "Hard to say for sure. My man Zeke here is the only Collab I've talked to about it. If I had to guess, I'd say there are four or five other Farms doing it. That's based only on the number of abandoned feeding stations I've seen."

"Any close to here?"

"At least one in Colorado."

"Shit. That explains why they've started hunting up here when they used to avoid the area." That meant things at Base Camp could get bad, fast.

"Exactly. And that's not even the worst." Ely nodded to Zeke again. "Tell him the rest."

"About a week ago, we heard there was a new plan."

"To get rid of the Ticks?" I asked.

"Yeah. But this time it's super hush-hush. Only the Dean and maybe three or four other guys know what's going on, but whatever it is, it's not good."

"Why do you say that?"

"For starters, the Dean shipped all the Breeders to another Farm."

"Where?"

"I don't know. They just loaded them all up in about twenty cargo vans and shipped them off. Then they shipped off about half the Greens. And most of the Collabs went with them. We used to have close to two thousand kids, now we got less than a thousand."

"It sounds like they're shutting down the Farm altogether."

"That's what I thought, too," Ely said.

But Zeke interrupted him. "But they're not, because last week, they stopped moving people around and they switched out the shots they give the Greens. They used to give them a daily shot of Procrit to help increase their red blood cell count, but, they stopped doing those. Instead, we started getting shipments of Diazepam."

"Valium? They're sedating Greens? Why?" Sure, I could see the advantage of having the Green population as calm as possible, but outright sedation seemed a bit extreme. "Are they just trying to calm everyone down?"

"At first I didn't get it either, but then they bought a huge shipment of tranq darts. I mean, huge: two thousand, three thousand of the things."

I frowned. "I thought the darts had a use-by date on them. That they were only good for a month or so."

Zeke nodded. "They do."

Which meant whatever the Dean was planning to do with all these tranq darts, he was going to do it soon.

"If you think you know what's going on, go ahead and tell me now. Stop beating around the bush."

Zeke blew out a breath. "Okay, I think they're planning on doping the Greens, then letting the fences drop. All the Collabs they've left on the Farm, we're all good shots. Once the Ticks get doped up on blood, we shoot them with the tranq rifles."

"And theoretically the combination of the Diazepam and the tranquilizer in the dart would be fatal to the Ticks."

"Exactly. It'd be like shooting fish in a barrel once they've consumed a heavy hit of Valium."

"Oh, it's a great plan," I muttered. "Unless you're the bait."

My mind was reeling from everything Zeke had told me. From the horror of what he'd described. From the crushing weight of responsibility. How the hell could I go save those people? How could I abandon the people here at Base Camp to go save the Greens in San Angelo?

With attacks from Ticks on the rise, the threat to Base Camp was very real and imminently dangerous. Leaving Base Camp now would leave nearly a hundred people vulnerable. But ignoring the threat in San Angelo could cost nearly a thousand lives.

It was an impossible choice.

Why the hell was I the one in charge of making it?

In what kind of screwed-up world was an eighteen-year-old kid responsible for the lives of thousands? And yet, I was undeniably the one in charge here, because Zeke was just standing there, waiting for me to . . . do what? Give him orders? Lead the charge into battle? What exactly did he expect from me?

Crap.

I needed time to think. To process what he had said without him and Ely standing there watching me.

I gave a stiff nod in Zeke's direction. "Thanks. You can go now."

He looked like maybe he was about to say something else. Like he wanted to ask a question or something, but that was one good thing about dealing with Collabs. They were good at taking orders. So Zeke just closed his mouth and left. Which left Ely standing there. Still waiting for some kind of response.

And here I was with no damn idea what to say, let alone what to do.

So I pushed myself away from the wall and walked over to the punching bag.

I threw a couple of punches before Ely asked, "So you're just going to ignore that? Just beat the shit out of that punching bag and pretend this will go away?"

I whirled around. "What the hell do you want me to do? It'll be a fucking bloodbath. None of those Greens will make it. I can't go rescue a thousand kids. Even if they were still alive when we got there, even if we could get them out, how the hell would we get them back here? How would we feed them when we did? How the hell do you transport a thousand kids across a thousand miles in the middle of winter, through Tick-infested middle America?"

Ely stormed forward and got right in my face. "That's why you don't want to go? Because it's going to be too hard?"

"We've got just over a hundred people here." I felt a burst of raw anger, hot and caustic in my chest. I realized I was yelling again. "And we're surviving. Do you have any idea what it takes to keep a hundred people alive? It's not too hard to rescue those thousand kids. It's impossible."

"Okay, so don't rescue them."

I just stared at Ely, but before I could ask what the hell he meant, he kept on talking.

"Go lead them so they can rescue themselves! Those kids are terrified. Or they would be, if they weren't drugged into not caring at all. They believe that outside those fences are unstoppable monsters they have no chance of killing. When those fences come down, they're not going to put up a fight at all. They are just going to roll over and die. But you know differently. You know how to kill the Ticks. And you found Lily, right? That's what the other Elites said".

Ely eyed me. "Is she the real deal?"

I didn't want to answer, but I'd told this lie so often, it came out easily now. "Yes."

"And it's just like Sebastian said? She can control what people feel? Fear, terror, courage, hope?"

"Yes." The power of the *abductura* had been exactly what Sebastian had described. The only problem was that Mel wielded the power, not Lily. "If Lily really is the *abductura*, then she could convince them of it. As long as she's there, she could make a difference. You don't want to rescue them? Fine. But at least bring her down there to Texas and let them know they can rescue themselves!"

Maybe it was the stress. Hell, maybe it was just straight-up terror at the thought of Lily down in San Angelo, facing down fifty armed Collabs and hundreds of bloodthirsty Ticks. Whatever the reason, I hauled off and punched Ely. He blocked my punch and swung back. I danced out of the way, but brought my fist up to his ribs. He moved fast enough that the punch barely grazed him. And, just like that, it was as if we were back at Elite Military Academy, in the boxing ring, with Edmunds, the PT coach, teaching us to fight. Edmunds had been a good teacher, but he'd bailed early in the Tick outbreak. All the teachers had. When the world was ending, no one gave a damn about a couple hundred troubled kids.

No one had fought for us except Sebastian, and even he had had ulterior motives.

And here was the thing: if I walked away from those kids in San Angelo, then I was no better than Edmunds.

We were at war. In the months since the Academy had fallen, I'd seen almost no signs that civilization existed beyond the Farms. I had no idea what was going on in other parts of the world or even other parts of the country, but right now, we were at war. And we were losing. Bad. The other Elites and I had joined this fight knowing we might have no chance of winning. We had joined the fight because fighting was better than rolling over and dying. We joined knowing that we might well die so that other people could live. But the Greens in San Angelo weren't soldiers who'd willingly joined the battle. They had no training. They had no choice. And they would be drugged. Even if they wanted to fight, could they?

By the time Ely backed away from me, panting, and held up a hand as a sign of concession, my hands were aching, my knuckles bloodied and bruised. It was an enormous effort just to pull air into my lungs. I dropped down to my knees and lowered my head.

"It's impossible," I panted.

"So you're just going to let all those kids die?"

"Kids are dying every day. I can't save them all."

"So what? You're not going to save *any* of them? You're just going to sit on your ass?"

"No," I admitted.

It was stupid. It was a suicide mission. It would be a bloodbath whether we were there or not. But it was a bloodbath I couldn't walk away from. Not if I wanted to live with myself.

Suddenly, resolve settled into my gut and my mind starting clicking the puzzle pieces together.

"Okay, if we're going to do this, we need five vehicles. Five kids in each one, loaded up with food and gas for the trip. I can't leave

Base Camp unguarded, so we'll be pulling equally from the Elites and the Greens. That should leave about twenty Elites to guard Base Camp.

"We're going to drive straight through the night to get there as quickly as we can. We'll go in, take out any Collab resistance, and get the Greens off the Diazepam and keep the electricity online so the fences don't go down. I'll have to make sure Taylor comes."

"Why?" Ely asked.

"Turns out he's damn good with electronics. He's the guy who set up our electrical system from solar panels we'd scavenged. If anyone can keep the grid from going down, he should be able to. The drugs and the grid are our top priorities. We'll worry about how to get everyone back here later. If we don't get there in time, that won't be a problem anyway."

Ely smiled, and for the first time I got the sense that he was actually enjoying himself. I didn't know if I could blame him. He'd always liked a good fight, but then, so did I.

"Anything else?" he asked.

Yes. I needed to find a way to keep Lily from coming with me. She wouldn't be happy about it. If there was a fight, she'd want to be in on it. But this time, that wasn't an option.

"Yeah." I pinned Ely with a stare. "This is top secret. I don't want you breathing a word of this to anyone. Especially not Lily. Got it?"

"Got it. But you are bringing her with you, right? That's the whole point."

"No. The point is saving lives. Lily stays here. As far away from the action as possible."

"But—"

I whirled on Ely. "Back off. She's not coming to Texas."

Ely raised his hands in the air and backed up a step. "Hey, no worries, *vato*. You don't want her in Texas, she won't go to Texas."

Maybe if everything lined up, if we got there in time, if we could keep the fences up and stay ahead of the Ticks and the Collabs. Maybe, just maybe, I could save some of those kids. Maybe.

But when it came to Lily, I wasn't willing to trust it to maybe. When it came to Lily, I wanted her safe. Which meant I had to keep her the hell away from me. I had to make damn sure she didn't even know about the trip to Texas.

CHAPTER SIXTEEN

LILY

By morning, the mood in Base Camp had shifted from fearful to angry. Lily sensed the change the second she stepped out of the RV to go empty the composting toilet, which had to be emptied every day. Most people rotated the duty between everyone who lived in their RV, but she certainly wasn't going to make McKenna do it. She could use the exercise anyway. Funny, she'd never been much for exercise in the Before. Being able to run had never seemed important until she had something to run from.

McKenna had already been out for food and back again by the time she got up. Lily had hoped that by morning, McKenna would be ready to see reason, but she wasn't. She was just as determined as ever. She woke Lily with perky descriptions of how they could steal a car from the nearby city of Logan.

Listening to McKenna's plans made her head spin, and for once she was actually glad to leave the RV in the morning. Even drop duty was better than trying to change McKenna's mind.

She watched her step as she made her way through the cavern. After twelve hours, a bucket of piss really starts to reek. The ammonia seems to worm its way into her nose and lodge there. The last thing she wanted was for any of it to slosh out. But worst of all was the wrenching pain from her shoulder. Pain was good, right? Her body's reminder to take it easy.

Besides, once she was up there, she planned to talk to Carter about McKenna's plans to leave Base Camp. If anyone could talk some sense into the girl, Carter could.

Early mornings were usually busy around Base Camp, but this morning everything seemed unusually still and quiet. People were staying in their RVs. The few people who were out and about kept their gaze down and skittered away from each other. She wanted to believe that this was a normal reaction to the Tick attack. That people just wanted to grieve in private, but what if she was wrong? What if people weren't grieving, but were hiding from her? Carter had been with her when the attack had happened. If he'd been here instead, maybe it wouldn't have been as bad. Maybe people blamed her for the attack. Maybe they were right.

As she made her way toward the receiving bay, she noticed the front doors were still closed. By this time there should be enough light to scare off the Ticks. The doors should be open. So why weren't they?

She skirted around the new triage area and made her way to the doors. The smell grew overwhelming as she got closer. A row of buckets lined the wall beside the doors that a pair of Elites was guarding.

Lily set her bucket down near the others and went over to Chris, one of the Elites standing guard. She gave a nod of greeting to Merc and then asked Chris, "What's up with the doors still being closed? I have drop duty."

Chris gave a sympathetic shrug of his shoulders. "Sorry, Lil. Can't let you out. We've been ordered to keep the doors closed this morning. We're going to have armed guards to go out with the group in about an hour. You can leave your bucket here until then."

"Okay, I'll be back."

Only then did Merc speak up. "Didn't you get shot yesterday?"
"I'm okay," she lied. "It's barely a scratch."

Merc just shook his head. His voice was deep and no-nonsense.
"Sorry, Lil. No way you're doing drop duty today."

She wanted to argue, but could tell it would be pointless so she
left the bucket and walked away. Great. Now she was making more
work for people.

The block of offices at the front of Base Camp where the Elites
lived was like a rabbit's warren, but she'd been back there enough
that she knew her way around. The door was partially open, so she
knocked on the frame and then let herself in but Carter wasn't
alone. There was another guy in there with him, someone Lily had
never seen before.

He was shorter than Carter, but broad through the chest, like
a pit bull. He had long, dark hair and enough tattoos to have had
his own reality TV show in the Before. Okay, so she didn't really
know how many tattoos he had. She was just extrapolating based
on the fact that he had tatts peeking past each sleeve cuff and his
collar. One sprawled up his neck. *Mi Familia.* This guy had "Latino
badass" written all over him. Literally.

The desk had been moved back to the center of the room and
had a map of the U.S. spread out across the surface with bobbleheads holding down the corners. Both of the guys looked up when
she walked in. Carter smiled when he saw her, but there was
something invasive about the way this new guy sized her up. It was
a look that simultaneously assessed her physical assets and dismissed her as useless.

That kind of good ol' boy bullshit annoyed the crap out of
her, so she walked up to him and stuck out her hand. "You must
be Ely."

His eyebrows inched up his forehead then slowly he smiled as he gave her another once-over. "I guess my reputation precedes me."

"Only forty-three Elites made it out of the Academy. I know forty-two of them already, so . . ." She thrust her hand forward again. "You're Ely, and I'm Lily Price."

He had already started reaching for her hand, but when he heard her name, he froze. "Lily?" He sent a look to Carter, before finally taking her hand in his. "Lily. You're Carter's Lily."

She firmed up her handshake a little. "Actually I'm *my* Lily."

Ely chuckled. "Yeah, you are."

Even Carter laughed a little and the sound made something inside of her quiver with longing. God, it had been so long since she'd heard him laugh. Only then did she notice that he had a nasty-looking black eye forming and that the skin on his cheek-bone was spilt open. The injury didn't look fresh, but she was sure it hadn't been there the day before when they'd left Armadales' house. Ely had a similar collection of scrapes. His lip was busted open. And those were just the wounds she could see. Obviously they'd beaten the crap out of each other sometime in the past twenty-four hours.

Funny, everything in the world had changed. The friggin' apocalypse had happened and she *still* didn't get guys. Go figure. If they had so much extra fighting energy, did they not have enough targets?

Carter gave her a nod and asked, "What's up?" She walked over to the desk but Carter rounded it quickly. "You need something?"

"Yeah, you got a second?" She tried to glance around him, but again he angled himself between her and the map. Which was definitely strange. Why the sudden secrecy?

"Sure." He took her arm and started steering her out the door.

He led her a few steps down the empty hall before turning toward her. "What do you need?"

She sucked in a deep breath and just spat it out. "I need you to talk to McKenna. She's freaked out about the Tick attack and about having the baby here. She's started talking about leaving. Trying to drive up to Canada. But she trusts you. If you tell her she can't go, she'll listen to you."

"Of course she can't go," he said stiffly, still not really looking at her.

He seemed distracted—which was fine, she didn't feel like she had to be the center of his universe. But there was a distant, dismissive quality to his voice that she'd never heard before and it tore at her heart.

So this was it. This was him distancing himself from her. This was going to be brutal. This was going to hurt. Not just now, but every day, it was going to hurt.

Half to herself she muttered aloud, "Maybe I should just go with her. Solve all our problems."

Carter's gaze cut to her. "What was that?"

She blinked. "What?"

"You're thinking about going with her?"

"Well, no. Not seriously." Until now. Maybe leaving now would be better than this. "I can't let her go alone. I can't force her to stay here. And what if she's right? What if we could find help in Canada? Maybe they have no idea there are still kids in the United States who need their help."

Carter looked at her like he couldn't decide if she was a genius or a crazy woman. "You can't be serious. You can't just take off for Canada on your own, when—" He broke off and spun away from her to plow his hand through his hair. "It's out of the question."

"What am I supposed to do? Base Camp is a sanctuary, not a prison. I can't lock her in the RV and force her to stay. And I can't let her go by herself."

Carter paced the hall, clearly frustrated. Which was no different than how she felt.

She had wanted his help convincing McKenna not to go, and now—inexplicably—she was arguing to leave with McKenna. How had that happened?

"Forget it," she said, turning to leave.

Except Ely was there in the hall, arms crossed over his chest, listening to their argument.

"She's right."

"What?" Both Carter and Lily asked at the same time.

"No one knows for sure if Canada is there, but it couldn't hurt to send them to check it out."

Carter's expression darkened. "No way." He took a menacing step closer to Ely. "There is no way in hell I'm sending two girls, unprotected and alone, to drive up to Canada just to 'check it out.'"

Ely held up his hands in a gesture of mock surrender. "Just saying. It's a short trip. Canada's, what, a two-day drive from here? They'd be gone, what? Four or five days. Tops."

"Did you miss the part where I said I wasn't sending two girls alone?"

"If you don't want them to go alone, no worries, I'll go with them."

"You?"

Ely flashed a smile that was more arrogance than charm. "Hey, you could do worse than me. I'm the best there is."

She looked at Carter, expecting him to slap down Ely's offer, but instead, he was looking from Ely to her, his expression calculating.

She held out her palm to Ely. "Give us a minute, okay?" She didn't wait for him to answer, but closed the distance between her and Carter and leaned in to whisper, "Is this what you really want? You want me to go with Ely?"

Carter looked at her. For the first time today, she felt like he was seeing her. Really seeing her. His expression softened and she felt that familiar pull. That aching yearning that she'd always felt around him.

"He'd keep you safe," he said simply.

"That's not what I'm asking."

How could he do this? How could he even think about sending her away?

His hand twitched, like maybe he was about to reach for her, but then he dropped it back to his side.

"McKenna isn't safe here. And you're right, we can't make her stay. How do you think people will react if she bolts?"

Lily hadn't thought of that yet. If McKenna made a run for it, other people would panic, too. They'd all want to go. It all came back to that house of cards. Yesterday was the earthquake that shook the foundation. McKenna bolting would be the tornado that knocked down the remains.

He dipped his head and kept talking, his voice low pitched and fervent. "But if you go with her, if Ely goes, if it really looks like a scouting mission, then it's better, right?"

"I don't know. Maybe," she answered honestly. She couldn't even think through this logically, because her mind was reeling and her emotions were raw. Carter was her protector. Her anchor. And now he was getting rid of her.

"You could go and be back in just a few days. If you find sanctuary in Canada, you could just stay there. Ely would come back for the rest of us." Carter sent a look down the hall to Ely. "He'll keep you safe. He's the best of the best."

"Do you trust him?"

Carter looked across the room at where Ely leaned insolently against the wall. "I do. I fought beside him at the school. He's tough and he's strong. The fact that he's lived on his own this long means he knows what he's doing out there. And Ely, he's"—Carter broke off and rubbed his hand across the back of his neck—"he's honorable. If that makes sense. If anyone can keep you safe, he can."

She looked down the hall to where Ely stood, looking just as arrogant as he had a minute ago. Carter was really going to do this? He was really going to send her off with another guy to go looking for sanctuary in Canada?

She couldn't believe what she was hearing. And she couldn't shake the feeling that there was something going on that she didn't understand. That more was at stake here than just McKenna wanting to leave. More even than them breaking up yesterday. But maybe this was just him distancing himself emotionally from her.

She grabbed Carter's arm and led him farther down the hall, away from Ely. "This is really what you want? You want me to go?"

She held her breath, waiting for his answer. He glanced at Ely and then his gaze flickered to the room where the mysterious map was spread out on the desk.

Finally he nodded. "Yes. This is what I want. There is bad shit about to go down. I can't take care of you here."

"You don't need to—"

He grabbed her arms, like he was going to shake her, but then he quickly let go and stepped back. "Don't tell me it's not my job to take care of you. Don't say that, because it doesn't matter. As long as you're here, it's my job. As long as you're here, I'm going to care about whether or not you're hurt or exposed to the virus or whatever. I can't not care about that."

"I'm not asking you not to care. You think I don't care whether or not you're hurt? We all have to care about each other. But that doesn't mean wrapping people up in bubble wrap and sending them away."

"I'm not wrapping you in bubble wrap."

"Then trust me to take care of myself!"

"It's not that I don't trust you. It's that if you fail and you're exposed to the Tick virus, then I'm the one who has to deal with the consequences. You've asked me to kill you if you get exposed. Have you thought about that? About what it would do to me to have to do that? Because I have. Because after what I did yesterday, after I had to deal with all those bodies, I can tell you right now, I can't do it."

The raw anguish in his voice tore at her, but it didn't convince her that this new plan was the right thing, either. "Look, I'm sorry. I'm sorry I have the gene and I'm sorry that you're in this position, but this isn't my fault. If you don't want to dig my grave, then don't do it, but—"

"Dig your grave?" he asked, shaking his head. "Lily, what is it you think we do with bodies that have been exposed?"

"I—" She broke off, thinking. Thinking hard. "I don't know." In all the time she'd been here, no one had talked about it. From the revulsion that flickered across Carter's expression, she could guess it was something horrible. "What do you do to the bodies?"

Carter turned, making his expression impossible to read. "It doesn't matter."

In other words, he was trying to protect her. Her mind raced along the path he wouldn't take her down. "You'd have to make sure the bodies wouldn't regenerate." Sebastian had said something about this once, after they'd escaped The Farm. Something about how a stake through the heart would slow them down but to really stop them— "You cut off their heads."

She sagged against the wall, rubbing her hand over her forehead.

"Jesus, Carter." She knew he was tough. She knew he was strong and determined. Dedicated to this cause like no one else. But, Jesus, that's what he had to do? Correction: that's what he'd been doing. Yesterday.

And that's what she'd asked him to do to her.

Was it any wonder he didn't want her to go outside? Any wonder he wanted to send her as far away as he could?

Now that she knew, now that she'd thought it through, she could never ask him to do that.

Leaving Carter would nearly kill her. It would . . . No. She drew in a shuddering breath.

She had watched her sister's death. This was nothing compared to that. If she could live through that, if she could walk away from the sister she loved more than her own life, then she could do this.

She shut down all her emotions. If she was going to cry, she'd do it later. No way would she beg Carter not to send her away. She'd get through this the same way she'd gotten through everything since the Before. With logic and sheer determination.

"Okay," she said, pushing herself away from the wall. "The three of us will go together."

She didn't particularly like Ely, and she wasn't entirely sure she trusted him. On the other hand, he could drive and he could fight.

And if Carter trusted him, then she could trust him to do what needed to be done. If it ever came to that.

If everything went as planned, by the end of the week McKenna could be tucked away in some Canadian hospital and Lily could be returning to Base Camp to guide everyone else to safety up north. Not a bad bargain.

CHAPTER SEVENTEEN

MEL

Vampires are not like in the movies. But I think I knew that, too. If someone tells my story someday, will they get it as wrong? No number of wrongs makes a right, but the more opinions you get, the closer you can triangulate the truth.

This truth I do know—if it is my emotions that make me human, then I am more human now than I ever was in life. Sometimes I stare at the remnants of the life I once had, awash in my loss. My pink backpack, my stuffed squirrels, my Slinky. I still possess these things but they no longer bring me peace.

I never knew anger until now. It is as keen and sharp as my hunger, and neither has been slaked by blood.

If Sebastian would let me hunt I wouldn't feel so twitchy, but he won't even let me out of the car.

There must be more power in words than I ever knew, because my word has bound me as tight as his will. Or maybe it is just fear. I can't forget what happened in that church parking lot. That I was near death, but that it was him who killed me, before he brought me back. Until I'm ready to kill him myself, I won't disobey.

Still, I won't wolf-cub to his alpha. Not entirely.

We are at the kitchen table in an empty house in a city whose name I don't know. I like this house though, because it smells like cinnamon and moth balls, like my Nanna's house used to.

Only Sebastian's presence destroys the illusion.

"Soon you can hunt for yourself, Kitten," he says one morning when he gets home. He hunts each night while I prowl the empty house mourning my music and the girl I once was.

I say nothing, but keep glugging the blood he's brought me in a plastic cup.

"You will need to be careful. The behavior of the Ticks is changing. They used to stay close to the Farms, to their food source. Now they wander farther astray. If they caught you alone . . ."

His voice trails off. I know what he's saying.

If they caught me alone, they might kill me. If they didn't, I would kill them. A tit for tat that's worse than tic-tac-toe. Another zero-sum game.

Still, I can't bring myself to admit he's right. So I say nothing. Stillness and nothing are what I do best these days.

Finally, he slams his hand down on the table. "Snap out of it, Melanie, stop pouting. It's been six weeks."

Six weeks? I'm shocked, because it doesn't feel that long.

I hide it behind a shrug.

"I don't remember the last time you spoke. Snap out of it."

I open my mouth and when I speak my voice sounds unused. "All work and no play make Jack a dull boy."

His lips twitch like maybe he's amused, but I can't hear it in his voice. "Nice try, Melanie. But I don't buy it."

He's right, of course. The rhymes don't come easily anymore. I have to work to find those words. That, too, has been stolen from me, along with my life and my death.

"Mary, Mary, quite contrary," I grumble.

"You don't need to do that anymore," he says, his voice as tone-less as my ears. "That's not who you are."

I leap up from the table. I can't listen to him anymore. I can't hear him past the fury blaring in my ears. He stands, just watching me.

"That's who you were," he says calmly, "when you were human. That's not who you are anymore."

I whirl back toward him. My voice comes out drenched in my fury. "That is who I'll *always* be!"

Instead of answering, he just stares at me. I hate the look in his eyes as much as I hate him.

Because I know he's right. I can feel it in my bones. In my every cell. I'm not Mel anymore. Not that human girl. Not that autistic girl. Not that living, breathing, music-savant, indigo girl. I'm not her.

She died in that parking lot. I have her memories. I have part of her body, but I have very little else from her. My stomach. My taste buds. My ears. My mind. They are all different. Unique. Inhuman.

Even my anger is my own.

She was never this angry.

Pouty, difficult, temper-tantrum throwing. Yes. Resentful. Yes. Indignant, prickly, fearful. Yes.

But this burning anger? This all-consuming fury? These are all Melanie. They are not what I want. I want hope and music and my sister. Instead I have this.

Perhaps this anger is what makes me a vampire. Maybe this fuels my thirst. Makes me a killer.

I still can't imagine killing another human to feed myself, but maybe the anger is what would push me over the edge. Maybe all vampires are this angry.

"Listen to yourself," Sebastian says, his voice as seductive as the gleaming coils of a Slinky. "Your rhymes are so slow and labored now, I can practically hear you struggling to come up with them. But when you're too angry to think before you speak that's not what comes out at all."

"I'm always angry."

He stands and walks over to me. "Of course you are. No one likes being helpless. No one likes having a sacrifice like the one you made for your sister thrown back in her face."

He runs a hand up and down my arm in a gesture that I guess is supposed to be soothing, but I can't stop looking at his hand. It's weird being touched. I used to hate being touched. By anyone. Now, I haven't been touched since that first day. The sensation is pleasant. Not needle pricks, like how being touched used to feel.

Still, I don't like *him* touching me. It's disingenuous. He doesn't want to touch me. Vampires, by nature, aren't touchers. There's no snuggling in vampirism. I wrench my arm out from under his hand and flick my hand to backslap him.

He grabs my wrist before my hand makes contact, a smile oozing across his face.

"Very good," he murmurs.

I don't know what surprises me more: the fact that I tried to slap him or that he anticipated it. That it pleased him.

I jerk my hand away and back up. I clasp my arm close to my body, shielding it from his touch with my other arm. "What do you want?"

"I want you to snap out of it. To be yourself. As you are, not this ridiculous shadow of yourself."

Again the hatred boils inside of me. "There's nothing ridiculous about who I was."

"The ridiculous thing is that you're still pretending to be her. She's dead. Why are you fighting me so hard on this?"

"I'm not fighting you. I'm fighting *this*."

"Why?" he demanded. "Why are you fighting what you've become?"

I just stare at him blankly, unable—or maybe unwilling—to force this into words.

"At the risk of overstating this, there are people who would give anything to have the kind of power you refuse to even acknowledge you have. You should be ecstatic to—"

"Why? Why should *I* be ecstatic? Because of what I was before? Because I was autistic? Turn the poor autistic girl, give her the ability to talk, and she'll be over the moon."

Sebastian rocks back. "Ah. I see."

His knowing look annoys me and I want to stop talking, to stop giving him the satisfaction, but now that I've started, I can't stop. The words are pouring out of me. "You think I should be grateful, just because I was autistic? That I should be thrilled with who I am now? But I'm not. Because I was fine before. That girl I was? She was just fine."

"And if you accept who you are now, that would mean admitting she, that girl you were, wasn't okay."

"I *was* okay," I say firmly

"I knew you then, when you were on the Farm. I saw how frustrated you were when people didn't listen to you. When they ignored you. Were you really okay then?"

"I was fine," I say again stubbornly.

"Yes, you were. You were smart and observant. You fought harder than most humans do. There's nothing wrong with who you were. But that's not who you've *always* been, is it?"

He doesn't wait for me to answer, which is okay, because I have nothing to say.

"Carter told me you used to be different. When he knew you in school, you functioned almost like a normal teenager. No nursery rhymes. No chanting. Is that right?"

"Yes," I admit reluctantly. "I'd had years of therapy to get there. I had routines that helped. Rituals that helped me express myself."

"So at some point, in the Before, you functioned. You'd worked hard, you'd made progress. For years. All so you could be more normal. For you to work that hard, that must have been something you wanted very badly."

"It was."

"So what's different now? Why work so hard in the Before to be heard and understood, and throw it away now?"

"Because it's not the same! The Mel I was when I was a child is the same Mel who functioned as a teenager. On the inside, I was the same—not less, just different."

"And that's what you think now? That you're less than she was?" He tipped back his head and laughed. "I turn you into a vampire. Into the top predator in the world. You are practically a god. And you think you're less?"

"I am less! I live in silence now. I have nothing. I contribute nothing. You say I'm an apex predator, but the only thing predators do is consume. In the Before, I created. Everything I did, everything I was, fed the world around me. Now that's gone. I am different *and* less."

"You are not less. You're a vampire," he says. "Act like one."

"Fine." I straighten my shoulders. "I'll start to act like a pompous ass. That's how the only vampire I know acts."

His lips twitch, but I can't tell if I've amused him or pissed him off. "Come on. We're going out."

"Out?" I look around the tiny kitchen. I don't remember how long we've been here. Days, at least; maybe weeks. If it's been six weeks since I was turned, then it's been nearly that long that I've stayed in this house. Sitting here at the table, or laying on the sofa. "Why?" I ask.

"Because Domino's doesn't deliver pints of blood, and I'm tired of bringing you food while you pout. It's time you learned to hunt. I'm not going to be around forever to act like your nursemaid."

His words sting, but I know they are true. Vampires are very territorial. They cannot stand to be near one another and they always live alone. Newborn vampires like me are the exception, but only for a short time. Sebastian and I will have six, maybe seven months before I am fully vampire. After that, I will live alone. Forever.

Sebastian has been honest about this from the start. He claims that when the time comes, I will want to leave him. This is both easy and hard for me to imagine. I hate Sebastian. Yet he is all I know of this world and the thought of being alone in it leaves me panicked.

"I thought you said I couldn't hunt Ticks," I point out.

"No, I said you couldn't feed off Ticks. When you were new and starving to death, I couldn't risk it. You're well fed now. And stronger. You need to learn how to feed yourself."

"I won't eat humans," I quip.

He smiles. Damn him. "If there were enough humans around to feed on, I'd be happy to test your resolve. But let's not eat the last of an endangered species, shall we?"

He turns and walks out without even glancing my way again. I follow. If Mel the human wasn't a quitter, then Melanie the vampire won't be one, either.

A moment later, we step out onto the unlit street. There are no lights anywhere, but there's low lying cloud cover, which casts the night sky in eerie, glowing grays, like it's been replaced with an abalone shell.

Wordlessly, Sebastian turns south.

I'm not much of a social talker. In the Before, I was grave silent.

I long for that now. For the comfort of silence. But there are things I can't learn through osmosis. If I'm ever going to be on my own, then I need to know the things only Sebastian can teach me.

As we walk, I ask, "You told Lily the scent of blood was no big deal."

"I did?"

"Yeah. Sort of. Back in the van. With McKenna and Joe and Lily. You said you could control yourself around the scent of blood. Were you lying?"

He barely glances at me. "No. I have plenty of control." He turns to look at me. "But I am not a newborn who is starving to death. You are another matter entirely."

"So you don't trust my control?" And here I'd thought I'd exhibited such tremendous restraint in not trying to murder him for being such an ass. "I've shown I can be trusted."

"So far, all you can be trusted to do is pout." He slants me a look as we walk down the street.

I still have no idea where we're going. I don't suppose it much matters in this sepia-toned world. I have nowhere I need to go. Nothing I need to do.

Funny, when I was human, I never thought about how ruled my life was by routine. How charted out everything was. Task charts, progress charts, timetables, and schedules. Printed out by Mom, administered by Lily. Our family worshiped at the altar of time management. That altar had been forever altered by my own altered state.

Vampires live in a timeless world. None of that matters. Routine had been my lifeboat. Now I am adrift in a sea of minutes.

I wander, barely aware of the empty houses on the block, as soulless as I am. One empty house ignoring the others.

We reach the corner of the block, where an unlit streetlight peers over the street.

I pause at the stop sign, instinct winning out over logic in a carless world.

Then Sebastian turns to me. "Let's see just what you can do."

I'm still gaping in confusion when he runs at the streetlight, grasps it and swings around with acrobatic grace. His legs kick out, aimed at my chest. Instinctively, I drop to the ground. I hit the sidewalk hard, but Sebastian misses me. He launches off the lamppost and lands maybe ten feet away.

"Not bad," he calls. "Good reaction time. But you still think like a human."

"How am I supposed to think?" I ask, standing.

"Like a vampire. Obviously."

He closes the distance between us in a flash and kicks my legs out from under me. I'm on the ground. Again. "What should I do, then? Rip your heart out of your chest and guzzle your blood?"

He smiles as he looms over me. Typical that he'd enjoy this. "I would like to see you try."

He reaches down a hand to help me up. I take it, but then kick my legs up at his chest and yank him over me. At least that's what I intended.

This doesn't go exactly as I imagined. I have no training. Girls on the spectrum don't exactly go out for wrestling.

Instead of flinging Sebastian, he flips neatly head over heels and lands by my shoulders, still holding my hand. He gives it a wicked twist and pain wrenches my shoulder.

"Better, but still not good enough."

Again, the heat of fury floods me in a wash of pain. "Let me go!" I scream.

He gives my arm another twist and I can feel it twisting out of its socket. "You're a vampire, Melanie. Make me let you go."

There's an audible pop as my shoulder dislocates. My whole body bucks off the sidewalk and a scream tears from my mouth. I look up at him from my spot on the ground. His face is distorted and upside down, a twisted Mardi Gras mask of pleasure. He's enjoying this. I pant out the words, "I will kill you for this, you sadistic bastard!"

"If you can get out of this, I may let you. From here, however, Melanie, my dear, it doesn't look like you'll be killing anyone."

"Let me go!" I yell again, but my words dissolve into a whimper. I can feel the tendons and connective tissue breaking loose. My fingers flop uselessly against his hand. I can't even control my own hand anymore.

He just laughs and presses his foot into my shoulder. "Perhaps I shouldn't have worried about you eating from a Tick. You couldn't go up against a Tick and walk away." He gives my arm a little tug and pain shoots through my body so intense that my stomach rebels and I wretch. But it's the helplessness that's the worst. He squats down then, much of his weight on my shoulder, his face close to mine. I reach out with my other hand trying to claw at his face, but he nabs my hand out of mid-air and holds it almost gently. "A Tick would beat you and rip your heart out. We already know you have the gene. You'd die. Again. And regenerate. Again. As a Tick."

That fury burning through me turns to something else. Not fear. Maybe shame. He was right. I couldn't defend myself against him. A group of Ticks would destroy me. I would be devoured and reborn.

I squeezed my eyes shut. Blocking out his voice and the pain. Shuttering my mind against my very existence.

Then I feel a hand on my face. A single finger tracing down my cheek. "Open your eyes, Melanie."

I pinch them more tightly closed to spite him.

"Come on, Melly. You gave me your word."

Melly. That surprises me. No one has ever called me that before. And I did promise to follow his orders. I open my eyes, surprised—again. He's so close that I can see the scalloped edges of his pupils. His voice is soft. His touch is whisper light.

"You are a vampire now," he says.

I cut him off, because I'm tired of hearing it. I speak through pain-clenched teeth. "So you keep telling me."

"And you have yet to hear me." He grasps my chin and makes me meet his gaze. "You are stronger and more flexible than almost any creature alive. Your autonomic nervous system is hardwired to pounce and fight. To kill and destroy. If you would stop thinking like a human, your body would do the work for you." He straightens, rocking forward so that even more of his weight rests on my shoulder. "Now stop acting like a child and fight back!"

Humiliation burns through me. It's not even that I don't believe him. I've seen him fight. His body in motion is a thing of beauty and grace. Hollywood special effects have nothing on him. Professional dancers look like clumsy puppets compared to him. But that isn't me.

He barks one insult after another.

"If you can't fight me, you might as well just give up now. You can't fight a Tick. You can't feed yourself. You're more helpless than a baby. No wonder Lily had to take care of you on the Farm. You never would have made it without her. It's a miracle you didn't get both of you killed."

That's it. Right there. My breaking point.

The excruciating pain in my arm is swept away in a wash of anger. A second ago, I thought I couldn't even control my hand, but now I twist it around and grab hold of his arm. I get my legs under me, arch up, and yank him forward over my head. With strength I didn't know I had, I fling his body to the ground, bounce up onto the balls of my feet, and launch myself legs first at his chest. He's up before I hit him. He grabs my feet, I twist in mid-air to plant my good palm on the ground and kick out of his grasp. I backflip away from him. By the time I'm standing upright again, I'm panting from the exertion. I give my shoulder a roll and it pops back into place, the too-stretched tendons springing like rubber bands. The pain is still there, but I can breathe through it and my cold fury has melted away.

I spin back to face him, bracing for an attack. But Sebastian doesn't so much as twitch in my direction. He's standing maybe six, seven feet away. He's smiling. Damn it. Smiling.

Not that irritating smirk he usually wears, but an actual smile. Like he's pleased. My breath comes in foggy bursts in the chilly night and adrenaline dances along my nerves. I've never felt so alive. Even when I was alive.

Despite all that, part of me is horrified. I used to have meltdowns in the Before, often when I was young, when the world was so at odds with my ability to process it. Biting, kicking, screaming meltdowns. But I never hurt anyone on purpose.

I wouldn't even know how to fight someone. And yet I did. I might as well be in a whole new body. Maybe this shouldn't surprise me. This bright, shiny new me needs getting used to.

I'm shaking and shaken and Sebastian is smiling.

He nods. "Good girl. That's better, isn't it? Better than moping about."

I suck air into my lungs and blow it out in a foggy puff. "I'm not a girl."

He smiles wider. "No. You're not. You're a vampire."

CHAPTER EIGHTEEN

LILY

"I'm coming with you," Lily said as soon as she made it back to the RV. No point in beating around the bush.

McKenna stopped still, staring at her in shock. "What do you mean, you'll come with me?"

"I'm not going to let you go by yourself." She moved to the tiny closet and pulled out her own backpack. The one she'd brought with her from the Farm.

"You and Carter need to be here. With the rebellion. I can't ask you guys to leave."

"You're not asking. And he's not coming," Lily said quietly. "I think . . . I think it's time for me to go."

"You're going to leave Carter?" McKenna asked doubtfully.

"I . . . yeah. I am." She paused, shaking her head. "Yesterday, if he hadn't stayed in Elderton with me, he would have been here. He could have protected those Greens." It was only one of the reasons. The only reason she would share with McKenna. McKenna didn't need to know about the whole head-chopping thing. That was an image no one needed in her brain.

"He's going to let you go?"

"It's not his choice. Besides"—she kept her voice impersonal, logical—"It's best for me to go. He sees that. Hell, he'll probably be relieved. If I'm here much longer, the Elites will start to question whether or not I'm really an *abductura*."

"They won't—"

"They're not idiots. They'll figure it out. My presence here is supposed to inspire a renewed sense of hope, right? A sense of calm and focus. That's the role of an *abductura*. To unite people, right? To inspire them to fight."

McKenna frowned as if worried she was being drawn into a verbal trap. Finally she nodded. "Yes, I guess. But you're not—"

"Exactly. I'm not an *abductura*. I can't do any of that. And the thing is, once the Elites realize that, they're going to question Carter. I can't let that happen."

"I still say he's not going to let you go. That boy loves you."

Lily wanted to protest. Love her or not, it didn't make it any easier to say good-bye.

"It's a done deal. He already agreed. Ely is going to take us. Have you met him?"

She babbled on about Ely while she packed. McKenna didn't interrupt again. McKenna's gut instinct to protect her baby would win out. By the time Lily had packed the last of her stuff, McKenna seemed convinced. Lily only wished convincing herself was that easy.

Once her bag was packed, she headed up to the food storage rooms to stock up on nonperishables. Carter was standing outside the RV when she stepped out.

She couldn't make herself look at him. The flickering fluorescents cast harsh light over his face, making him look like he'd aged about five years in the past couple of days. Or maybe having people die under your command just did that to someone.

Knowing how hard what happened yesterday had hit him, she almost felt bad about leaving. But it had been his idea.

"Hey," she said.

McKenna came out right after her, stopping short on the steps. Then she edged past Lily down the steps. "Why don't I go find those snacks and stuff. I'll just . . ." She didn't finish the sentence but trotted off toward food storage.

"Hey." Carter nodded back.

Lily opened the door and stepped back into the RV, holding the door open behind her so he would follow her in. When he stepped inside and shut the door behind him, she admitted, "I didn't think I'd see you again."

"You didn't think I'd come to say good-bye?" Carter was nearly a foot taller than she was and when he stood up straight in the RV, the top of his head brushed the ceiling. So in here, he always stood with his head ducked a little. It made him look bashful, maybe a little shy. It was charming, even if it was an illusion.

In this tiny space, he was awkward and off balance. Give him more room and he could kick anyone's ass. That was Carter all over: tough as hell until you got him up close.

"Is that what you're doing?" she asked. "Saying good-bye?"

He leaned his hips against the countertop, stretching his legs out in front of him. The stance bought him a little more head room and he was able to meet her gaze as he said, "I want you to be safe. When you're traveling."

That wasn't what she wanted to hear. Not at all. Her arm hurt like hell. She was tired and hungry. She felt miserable. Inexplicably, she wanted to curl up on the bed in back and just cry. She wanted someone to stroke her hair and tell her it was going to be all right. That was fair, right? To want that.

She distracted herself by sorting through the belongings she and McKenna didn't have room to bring. Everything they owned had been scavenged from somewhere else, and it would go back to the storage rooms. It would be sorted through and "owned" by other people after them. Somehow, packing up this stuff that hadn't really been hers brought her some peace. It gave her something to do while her heart was breaking.

She knew why he was doing this. At least, she could make a pretty good guess. It was all tied back to the conversation in the truck. To not wanting to be with her anymore.

Forget that he was doing it for the good of all mankind. Forget that this was best for humanity and for the rebellion and so that someday they could all live free again. Forget all that.

All that didn't make it any better. It just made it harder to hate him for this. No, it made it impossible to hate him. He was such a good guy. He was the best.

And it killed her that she wasn't good for him. He would never say it like that, but that's what it came down to, right? She wasn't good for him.

Carter watched her for a few minutes before saying, "So we're not even going to talk about it?"

"I don't think there's anything to talk about."

"Damn it, would you stop packing long enough to at least have a conversation with me?"

For a second, her hands clenched around a bath towel then she forced herself to let it go. She dropped it into a box and turned to face him, even if she couldn't make herself meet his gaze.

"About the conversation we had in the truck, listen, I . . ."

"I don't want to talk about it," she said automatically.

"Lily, I didn't want—"

"I know." She waved a hand, cutting him off. "McKenna needs me."

"Damn it, Lily—" Carter broke off and paced away and then

back again. His expression was hard and wounded all at the same time. "This is killing me. Do you know what it feels like, knowing you're going off with some other guy? Some guy who can protect you and who's willing to walk away from all of this."

She nearly laughed at that. "This was your idea and besides, you know it's not like that. Ely's a total ass."

Carter's lips curved and he looked a little relieved. "You think so?"

"Yeah." And then she did chuckle. "He's arrogant and annoying. I barely met him and I can already tell you that. I'm not going to fall for him. Certainly not in five days."

Carter reached out and grabbed her hand, giving it a gentle tug so that she stepped into the space between his legs. "You promise?"

"Yes."

"And promise you'll stay safe. That you won't take any stupid risks."

She had to swallow the lump in her throat before she could answer. "I wish I could—"

"I know," he said quickly.

"I could get hurt just as easily here."

"I know." He took her hand in his. His fingers were warm and strong where they grasped hers. She turned her hand to link her fingers through his.

"Jesus, Lily, I would do anything to protect you. Anything."

His tone was so fierce, she wanted to pretend it was enough.

That wasn't so much to ask, was it? For just a few minutes of clinging to the fantasy that there was someone in the world who would put her above all others?

She wanted to believe it so badly that when he gave her hand a tug, she stepped even closer to him, wedging her body against his. His hands clutched at her shoulders as he pressed his lips to hers. He tasted like cranberries and cinnamon. His mouth was warm and spicy. His hunger was palpable. His hands seemed to be everywhere at once, like he couldn't stop touching her. On her hips, her ribs, in her hair. Pulling her closer, like he could absorb her through his skin. She met him move for move, practically trying to crawl into his body. Everything else faded except the two of them.

He pushed away from the counter and backed her up a few steps until she felt the edge of the table bump against the back of her legs. His lips never left hers as he grasped her hips and lifted her onto the edge of the table. Her legs wrapped around him and she pulled him close, relishing the feel of his body against her, of his chest under her hands. Except he was too tall or the table was too short. The height issue must have frustrated him, too, because he lifted her up, turning around until she sat on the counter.

She didn't know how long he kissed her. Minutes, hours. Days. And it still wasn't enough. Even if she had a lifetime with him, she'd want more. But she didn't have a lifetime. All she had were these few minutes before they were ripped apart, maybe forever.

She wanted to believe that she would come back. That everything would be okay. That she, McKenna, and Ely would make it easily into Canada and that McKenna would get the care she needed. Then Lily could come back here, having done at least one thing right.

She wanted to believe all of that just as desperately as she wanted to pretend that when she came back, Carter would wel-

come her. That he wanted her—that he needed her—just as much
as she needed and wanted him.

The feel of his lips on hers and the urgency of his kisses let her
pretend. So she kept kissing him and she let herself get lost in his
touch.

So lost that she barely registered the pounding on the RV door.
Or the sound of it being flung open and rattling as it banged against
the cabinetry.

"Damn," a sarcastic voice drawled. "I can see why you're reluc-
tant to let this walk away."

Carter pulled his lips from hers. For a heartbeat, he just stared
into her eyes. Just when she thought her heart might break, he
stepped back, setting her on the floor as he did. Slowly they both
turned to face Ely, who was standing in the doorway.

"Did you need something?" Carter asked tightly.

Ely stepped farther into the RV and McKenna waddled in after
him.

She pulled a visible cringe. "Sorry! I didn't—"

"It's okay," Lily said, even though it wasn't. "What'd you need?"

Ely slanted her a smile. "You, sweetheart."

Carter took a half step toward him. Less than a half step. Given
the tiny space in the RV, it was tantamount to getting right in his
face. "What?"

Ely ignored his question, nodding in Lily's direction. "Grab your
stuff and let's go. It's time to head out."

"Now? We're not going to wait until morning?"

Ely faked looking at his watch. "It's only ten. Elite recon says
there are no Ticks in the immediate area. We should leave while
we can. We can be in Butte by nightfall."

As soon as he said it, Carter rocked back a step. Like the

words were a physical blow. That was how they felt to her, too. Even though she'd packed a bag, she wasn't ready.

But she didn't have a choice. This was best for everyone. Even though it broke her heart.

Again, she wanted to fall to her knees and cry. To wallow in sorrow and never get up again. But she couldn't. There wasn't time. Besides, in times like these, depression was for wusses.

CHAPTER NINETEEN

CARTER

I could hardly breathe as I stalked out of the RV and headed out to the deeps. I kept moving for one reason and one reason only. If I stopped moving, I would turn around, go back, and ask Lily to stay. I'd fucking beg her.

The idea of doing that terrified me. Because if I did, she would know just how much I loved her, how much I needed her. I couldn't ever let her know that because then she really wouldn't leave. She would stay with me. And eventually, she'd get hurt again. Something worse than being shot in the shoulder. Something more permanent. Something more horrible. Something I couldn't even consider.

Even the thought made the blood in my head pound. It was like I was in a fight with a Tick, the way my vision faded to black at the periphery.

Which was why I didn't even hear Ely approaching behind me until it was too late. Ely grabbed my arm and before I even realized what I was doing, I turned on him, slammed him into the next rock column, and held him, dangling there with my forearm wedged against his neck.

My vision cleared just enough for me to realize what I'd done. I lowered my friend to the ground. Ely just stood there for a moment with his hands raised and palm out in a gesture of innocence.

"What the hell, man?"

I didn't answer that question. Instead I jammed a finger in his face. "You keep her safe. Do you understand me?"

"Yeah. I got that."

"No. I mean, no matter what. You keep her safe."

"Of course."

"Like she was yours. That's how safe she needs to be. Like she was your sister, your whatever. You put her first. Above anything else. Got it?"

Ely dropped his hands to his side. He jutted out his jaw and bumped up his chin. "I'm insulted you even think you have to say it."

I studied him. The outrage in his expression, the anger.

Yeah, I was taking a huge risk in sending him with Lily instead of bringing him with me to San Angelo, but if I couldn't go with Lily myself, then I wanted Ely with her. No one had been on his own longer than he had. No one knew how to stay alive like he did. There was no one in the known world who could keep Lily safer than Ely could.

And when it came down to it, Ely would be able to protect her in a way I couldn't. If it came down to protecting Lily—not the body, not the life, but the person she was, Lily the *human*—Ely would do whatever was necessary. He would make the tough call in a way I knew I would never be able to.

She'd said it herself more than once. If she was exposed, she'd all but begged me to take the next step. To do what was necessary. Today, she'd realized exactly what that meant.

But would I do it? If it came down to it, would I be able to kill the girl I loved and mutilate her body? Probably not.

But Ely would do it.

I just hoped that it never came to that.

"Listen, if you make it up to Canada—"

"We're gonna make it," Ely interrupted.

"If you make it and there's still something there. If there's any kind of civilization, if there's any guarantee of safety at all, you make sure she stays."

Ely studied me for a second, like he was trying to figure out just how serious I was about this.

"I mean it. If you find someplace she can be safe, you leave her there. Got it?"

"What about coming back for everyone else? Isn't that what you said she should do?"

"Yeah, well, I lied. If you find safe haven for them, then that's where I want them to be. You can come back yourself, but you leave them there."

"You really think Lily's going to put up with that?"

"You say or do whatever you need to do. If you find a place she can be safe, then I never want to see her again."

I didn't wait around to see if Ely responded after that. He understood just what I meant.

Ely was the one person I trusted to keep Lily safe and to kill her himself if he didn't.

CHAPTER TWENTY

LILY

Lily waited for Ely and McKenna just outside Base Camp. She couldn't say good-bye to Carter more than once.

Ely had pulled the sleek SUV right up to the front gate. He hopped out as she walked toward him with her bag. They both stood there awkwardly while McKenna hugged the last few people who'd come to see her off.

After a minute, Lily said, "Nice car."

He nodded. "One of the perks of surviving the apocalypse: you get your choice of rides."

She cringed. She didn't like to think about the people whose stuff she was borrowing. Using. Whatever.

Ely must have noticed. "What? You squeamish about that kind of thing?"

"Yeah, I am."

"Why? You think the guy who drove this Porsche would have given a shit about you in the Before? 'Cause I can tell you right now that he never once thought about what your life on a Farm was like when he was parking this Porsche at the airport in Houston and taking that last flight out to LA or wherever the hell he went. All those people, all those so-called responsible adults, they bailed on us. They shoved their kids into Farms and just left."

"You don't know that," she argued. "You don't know that the guy who owned this Porsche left. Maybe he died trying to protect his kids. Maybe they all left together."

Ely snorted. "Yeah, right. And maybe the UN is rallying its forces right now, ready to swoop in and take the world back. Wahoo."

Okay, so Ely was a jerk. And he'd been alone a long time. He'd probably seen shit that was worse than anyone could even imagine, but his attitude still bugged her.

Maybe she wasn't as cynical as she'd once thought, but there was a tiny part of her that needed to believe that there were other people still out there, who were trying to fight against the Ticks and the Farm system. Maybe it was just a silly fantasy, but it was one she needed to believe in, just like she needed to believe that someday she might be reunited with her mother or her uncle Rodney. Until she had proof, she would continue to believe.

Because the truth was, they had no way of knowing. In a time without radio or TV, without even a postal service, all you had were the people in front of you. All you knew was what you saw with your own eyes. She couldn't help wondering if this would be the last time she saw Base Camp. The last time she saw Carter, standing off by the door, his hands crammed into his pockets, his shoulders sloped.

The thought brought such crushing grief she almost couldn't breathe.

Thankfully, Ely didn't seem to expect her to say anything else. A moment later he said, "Your girl's finally done." He slapped the roof of the SUV. "Load up."

Sure enough, McKenna was waddling over. Her smile was strained as she rubbed her hand over the side of the belly.

"You okay?" Lily asked.

"Yeah. Sure." She smiled at Ely. "Are we ready to go?"

"Been ready, sweetheart."

"You take the front seat," Lily told her.

Ely's Cayenne looked like he'd been living out of it, which he probably had. Candy wrappers littered the front floorboard, cans of food rolled around in the back, and a hand-crank can opener sat upright in one of the SUV's many cup holders. The floorboard on Lily's side held about a case of canned energy drinks. She shoved a pile of trash onto the floorboard to make room, then carefully laid her bow and quiver flat on the seat beside her. With her arm in a sling, she wouldn't be using it anytime soon, but she wasn't willing to leave it behind. Her backpack she kept on her lap. Most of the backseat was taken up by Ely's crap. The entire cargo hold of the SUV was filled with plants. Most of them looked like houseplants. Some she recognized. There was a pothos ivy, like her grandmother used to have in her living room, and a little bonsai plant. Some she'd never seen before.

Something striped and grasslike draped over the back of the seat, tickling her neck.

"What's with all the plants?" she asked, swatting away the leaf. "You taking up gardening?"

Ely met her gaze in the rearview mirror and smirked. "You'll see."

"You don't throw them at Ticks as you drive around, do you, hitting them like bowling pins?"

Ely just laughed.

Which was great. Nothing like putting your life in the hands of someone who was clearly bat-crap crazy.

CHAPTER TWENTY-ONE

LILY

They made it less than an hour north before the snow started falling. At first, Lily didn't even register what she was seeing. Yeah, she'd seen a lot of snow when they'd first gotten to Utah, but that had been almost two months ago. It was spring now.

She watched the gently drifting snow for several long minutes before saying, "It's snowing."

"Ya think?" Ely asked.

McKenna twisted in her seat to look back at Lily. "But we can still drive in this, right?"

How was she supposed to know? She was Texas born and bred. Just like McKenna. And Ely. How the hell were three kids from Texas supposed to drive in the snow?

"Let's see if it stops soon," she said to McKenna. And she ignored the snort of derision from Ely.

An hour later, the snow was still falling. Ely had slowed the Cayenne to a crawl. Finally, he pulled the SUV to a stop, the tires skidding on the slick road.

"This is bullshit."

She had to agree. Just watching the falling snow made her skin crawl with frustration. She had to get out of the car. Do something. Move.

But there was nothing to do but sit here and watch the road ahead slowly disappear.

Damn it.

"Okay, genius, what do you want to do now?" Ely asked from the driver's seat.

"I'm thinking." But they were out of options.

"You wanna turn around now or should we just wait here until a snow plow comes to dig us out?"

"Okay, smartass, what ideas do you have?" Lily demanded.

From the front seat, McKenna was just looking back and forth from Ely to Lily like she was waiting for a bomb to go off.

Ely held up his hands in the universal sign for hey-this-ain't-my-fault. "What do I look like, the world-renowned professor of making shit up?"

"No. You look like a guy who thinks he's smarter than everyone else, so he doesn't open his mouth unless he can prove it."

He gave a snort. "Hey, you're the chica who wanted to drive up to Canada. In the middle of winter."

"I'm a Texan. For me, winter is over after Valentine's Day."

"You wanna keep driving, I'll be sure to remind you of that when we're buried in a snowdrift in Montana."

"Okay, if you're worried about this, why mention it now?" McKenna asked. "Why didn't you bring this up back at Base Camp?"

Ely smirked. "I didn't think of it then."

Lily wanted to argue, but what could she say. *She* hadn't thought of it, either. "Okay, so what do we want to do? Turn around and go back?"

Ely muttered something she almost didn't catch. *"Gringa estupida."*

She leaned forward. "I had four years of Spanish in school."

"So?"

"So, if you're going to call me stupid, then don't mutter it under your breath in a language you think I can't understand. Say it to my face and be prepared to tell me why I'm being stupid."

He met her gaze in the rearview mirror and she saw something in his eyes that might have been a stirring of respect. Or maybe the sun was just blinding him.

"You wanna know what I really think of this *pendejada*? I think you're betting on the wrong dog."

"What do you mean?"

He gave another one of those shrugs. "Hey, you wanna go to Canada? Fine. White people trust other white people. I get that. But come on, the Canadians? You really think they were able to keep the Ticks out? They didn't even let people carry concealed there. There's no way they could stop the Ticks."

"Okay." But it wasn't okay, because her mind was racing. She hadn't thought about it like that. Not precisely. "So what? Are you saying you do think we should head back to Base Camp?"

"Nah. I say we should head to Mexico."

"Mexico?" both Lily and McKenna said at the same time.

Ely ratcheted up the smirk. "Yeah. Mexico."

"Oh, so you don't think the U.S. or the Canadian governments were able to stop the Ticks, but you think the Mexican government was able to stop them?"

"I didn't say the government. The drug cartels in Mexico are better armed than the *federales*. Besides, your dumbass government built that wall all along the border."

Lily's mind was racing. "Why bring this up now? Why not say all this back at camp?"

"You were the one rushing to get out of there."

Her gut twisted around the decision. It didn't feel right, abandoning the plan she'd clung to for so long. But that was just her gut speaking. She needed to think. To process.

And maybe she needed to trust other people more. Wasn't that the lesson she'd learned trying to get off the Farm? That she didn't always know everything? That sometimes you had to trust other people? How much easier would that whole experience have been if she'd trusted Carter from the beginning? But she'd fought him every step of the way and it had created half their problems. Maybe all of them.

Yes, she was smart and she was knowledgeable, but she didn't know everything.

And what were their options here, really? Either they could sit here in the snow, or they could go back to Base Camp, or they could head for Mexico.

McKenna turned to see Ely's expression better. "Have you been there? To Mexico, I mean? Do you know for sure that the Ticks haven't taken over?"

"No," he admitted. "But I've been down to the wall. It's still standing."

That would be the ultimate irony, wouldn't it? The American government had been so determined to control the flow of immigration. And now, instead of keeping the immigrants out, it was keeping the monsters in.

"I don't know," she muttered aloud. "The U.S. Army was the best supplied army in the world. I don't care what kinds of weapons the drug cartels had, they still couldn't match that kind of firepower."

But that argument made it simpler than it actually was. The Ticks hadn't won the war with weapons. The virus itself had done much of the damage, infecting and killing millions. But even that wasn't the real culprit. No, if Sebastian was to be believed, the real reason the United States had fallen so quickly to the Ticks was because Roberto had had *abducturae* spreading fear and paranoia.

So it wasn't about weapons or firepower. It was about what parts of the world Roberto wanted to control.

If he didn't want Mexico, then maybe Mexico was still standing.

"Okay," she said finally. "For the sake of argument, let's say Mexico is still standing. If they've held the border against the Ticks, then how do we know they'll let us through?"

"Guess we won't know until we get there."

"Great. That's very helpful," Lily said.

"What about medical care?" McKenna asked. "Will there be somewhere I can have the baby? Will they be able to take care of her?"

Ely muttered again, something about gringos. "A hundred million people. I think we've got childbirth covered."

Lily knew he was right. At least about that. Ms. Rivera, her Spanish teacher, had lectured all the time that Mexico City was a thriving, major city. So, yeah, if they could get there and if the border had held against the Ticks, then McKenna would be golden. It was a lot of ifs, but she'd faced worse.

Lily looked at McKenna in the rearview mirror. "What do you think?"

"Mexico is a lot farther away than Canada."

"Only four or five hours," Ely argued.

Four or five hours didn't seem like much. Maybe it wasn't. But it was a drastic change in plans. Lily didn't like change. But sometimes all the planning in the world wasn't enough. Sometimes you had to rely on other people's knowledge and experience.

She would never have made it off the Farm if she hadn't trusted Carter.

If Ely was right about Mexico, this could be the decision that saved all of their lives. Still, four or five hours was a long time. In this world, it only took a minute to die.

CHAPTER TWENTY-TWO

CARTER

I drove down the mountain into Elderton by myself. Generally no one went anywhere alone, but I guess if the responsibility of being in charge gave me any privileges at all, then the ability to break the rules was one of them.

If this trip down to San Angelo was going to work, I needed help. Supplies, if I could get them. Manpower would be even better. Yes, Armadale had pissed me off, but he obviously knew what he was doing.

Maybe I could talk him into helping us. Or maybe he'd shoot me on sight. No matter what happened, I didn't want any witnesses. Even if he didn't shoot me where I stood, I would probably have to beg him not to. And a good leader never lets his people see him grovel, right?

Thirty minutes after leaving Base Camp, I pulled into Elderton. I made one pass driving through town, heading right down Main Street before circling back to the outskirts of town where the Armadales lived. I saw only a few signs of life in town, but the people of Elderton hadn't stayed alive by sending out welcoming committees every time someone came through town. This time, I wanted people to know I was coming. No sneaking, no surprises.

I parked on the street in front of their house and sat in the car a while before climbing out. Then I leaned against the car door, legs stretched out in front of me, just waiting. I stood there in the cold until the wind burned my cheeks and my fingers started to go numb, even though they were shoved into my pockets. Then I pulled my hands out and held them up as I walked to the front door, like a prisoner about to surrender. I rang the bell. Then I knocked. Then I waited some more.

Finally, I called out, "Come on, Armadale, I know you're still there. I'm not here to steal from you or ask for any favors." That wasn't strictly true. "I just want to talk. I'm alone. I'm unarmed." And I was out of options. Time to grovel. "Mr. Armadale, please let me in."

Finally, I heard a door creak open somewhere around back. I purposely hadn't headed into the backyard. The last thing I wanted was Mr. Trigger-Happy thinking I was poaching.

He took his time meandering around the side of the house. He stood on the porch, his shotgun propped carelessly over his shoulder. His posture was casual enough that I knew he wasn't out here alone. Someone was watching his back.

Armadale gave me a smile that was more teeth than warmth. "I thought we settled this the other day. I'm not giving you any help, you're not asking for any, and that way we don't ever have to come to blows."

Just like during our previous meeting, Armadale talked with a backwoods drawl that made him sound ignorant. I wasn't fooled by it. No one who had survived the Ticks and kept their family alive was stupid. "That still stands," I called out. "But I have new information."

"Weren't you here just two days ago?"

I tried not to laugh—not because it was funny, but because it was ironic. A few days ago, the day Lily had been shot, seemed like a lifetime ago now. Now everything was different.

Armadale eyed me for a minute, like he was trying to figure out if I was lying to him. Then he swung around and headed back down the porch, saying, "Well, then, you'd better come on in."

I followed him around back, where he let me into the kitchen. I sat at the table, hands flat—and visible—on the scarred oak. He sat at the head of the table, his shotgun between us, his hand resting on the stock.

He just watched me. So I started talking. I told him about the Tick attack on Base Camp and about the dead we'd lost and about Ely and Zeke. But mostly I talked about the Farm in San Angelo and all the kids who were going to die.

Armadale didn't interrupt, not even to ask questions, but as I spoke his boys came to sit at the table. By the time I finished, even Dawn was standing in the doorway, her head cocked to one side so her hair fell over the side of her face, making her expression hard to read.

She was interested; I'd sensed that the other day. She might be willing to help. To fight, even. Maybe Armadale wasn't the only one I could convince.

When I finally finished explaining where I was going and what I needed help with, Armadale just sat there for a while, considering.

"That's all interesting, but I don't see that it has anything to do with me or my family."

"Look, I'm trying to do the right thing here."

Armadale nodded. "I can see that."

"I'm taking twenty-five guys halfway across the country to try to rescue what could be a thousand kids. And between us, we've got eleven handguns, five shotguns, and six tranq rifles." Armadale just kept staring at me, forcing me to ask outright. "If you have any weapons to spare, any ammunition you've stockpiled, we could damn sure use them."

"I got the impression you'd been scavenging for a long time now."

"We have. We've hit abandoned homes and stores all over the Midwest. We've been lucky when it came to finding food. We haven't been lucky about finding weapons." It baffled me, thinking that when people left their homes, they'd brought weapons with them but not food. "Plus, I can't leave Base Camp unprotected. I have to leave at least half of what I have there."

Actually, I'd planned to ask if he could help guard Base Camp, but now that seemed like pushing my luck.

He looked at me a long moment, then shook his head. "This trip you're taking down to Texas, this isn't my battle."

"With all due respect, this is everyone's battle."

"Nope. Not mine. My only goal here is to protect my family, and I don't see how outfitting your boys is in my family's best interest."

"Does it matter if your ammo kills Ticks here or in Texas? I'd think a dead Tick is a dead Tick, no matter where we kill it."

Armadale tilted his head to the side and scratched at the stubble on his jaw with the back of his fingernails. "Now, here I thought guns didn't kill Ticks anyway. Aren't they unstoppable?"

"They are not unstoppable." I aimed for logic and reason, because my gut told me a big show of emotion wasn't going to cut it with Armadale. This was a man devoted to keeping his family safe at all costs. No matter how sympathetic he was to our plight, I wasn't going to sway him unless I convinced him that an alliance with us would benefit him. And it would. We had knowledge he didn't. And once Sebastian came back, we'd have him, too. "A stake through the heart will stop one. You put enough bullets in a Tick, it'll go down just like any other animal. You can kill them.

I've done it. You don't believe me, then you come with me to Texas yourself and I'll let you watch while I do it."

For a second, Armadale seemed to be wavering. One of his sons, Darren I think, certainly was. Darren couldn't have been more than fifteen, but he was tall, like his father. He had the twitchy nerves of someone who'd been under the thumb of a strong parent. He'd been drumming a silent rhythm on the table with his fingers and he couldn't keep his eyes off his father's shotgun.

Armadale's lips twitched like he was amused. "Nice try, but I'm not buying it. Besides, the way I see it, if I hand guns and ammo over to you, I might as well be arming my enemy."

"Your enemy? Is that really what you think, that humans are your enemy? If I was your enemy, would I have walked back here to talk to you? Would I have just told you how to kill the Ticks?"

"Maybe not. Not yet, anyway. You've been able to find food so far. Well, you've been lucky. But how long before you start running out? Especially if you're talking about bringing another thousand people back? Let's say I loan you guns and ammo. What's to keep you from coming down here and stealing my food?"

"I don't need your food. I need a way to protect my people," I said.

"But what happens next winter, when you can't feed all those kids? You think your intentions will mean anything if you're all starving up there?"

"I think I'd rather help people now and find a way to feed everyone later. If I wanted to hurt your family, don't you think I would have done it three days ago when I had the chance?"

Armadale's smile tightened until his lips pulled back from his

teeth. His gaze hardened, and I knew I'd made a mistake by pointing out his vulnerability in front of his kids.

"Well, son," he said with a little sneer as he pushed back his
chair and stood, "you'd best go now."

But I couldn't go. I couldn't walk away. Not when I'd come all
this way and spent all this time. Not when we needed that ammo
so desperately.

I blew out a breath. Time to grovel again. "Mr. Armadale, I'm
begging you."

His gaze softened. "You may have the best intentions right now,
but that's not food in your belly five months from now."

"I give you my word—"

"It's not your word I'm worried about. It's your ability to control
all your people. I'm not trusting one boy, I'm trusting hundreds."
He shook his head.

I could feel the chance slipping away. Nothing I could say
would convince him. Not because he didn't believe it was the right
thing to do, but because of who I was. Because I wasn't old enough
or man enough to keep control of the people I led. Not because the
cause wasn't good, but because *I* wasn't good enough. I felt a fresh
wave of anger wash over me.

This trip, the half day I'd wasted, it was all for nothing.

I headed for the door, but then turned and stalked back to the
table. I planted my palms on the oak and leaned over so Armadale
had to look right at me.

"This is bullshit, and there will come a day when you will regret
this."

"Son, I think you better—"

I didn't give him a chance to finish, but kept talking over him.
"Someday. Someday soon. Because until now, Utah has had it
pretty easy. And I know you all think that's because of the grace of

God. You all think that it's ordained. Maybe I'm the one who's wrong, but I don't think so. Because there were a hell of a lot of believers in Texas, and Texas fell. Texas went down fast and hard. And you know why?"

I leaned forward, inches from Armadale's face. I gave him a solid beat to answer, but he didn't. He didn't blink. He didn't flinch. He didn't look away.

"Texas fell because of shit like this. It fell because more than half the damn state was armed and because none of them trusted each other. I watched it happen, city by city. I've been all over Texas since then. Places where so many people died so quickly there wasn't even anyone around to bury the bodies. I've seen more dead bodies than I can even count. And, yeah, there are plenty of people who had their hearts ripped out by Ticks. But there were way more people who died of gunshot wounds. And it's because of paranoid shit like this! Because as a race we can't just put aside our fear and paranoia long enough to fucking help each other out."

I didn't wait to see Armadale's reaction. It didn't matter anymore. I'd blown it. I'd screwed up. Again.

Not only did I not get the guns we needed, but I'd probably pissed Armadale off enough that I'd blown any uneasy alliance we might have had in the future.

On the bright side, I was leading the Elites into a bloodbath and we probably wouldn't be back. Maybe—maybe if we were extremely lucky—some of us would make it out. So maybe whoever took over after I left would have more luck with Armadale.

Yeah, that thought was real damn comforting.

I reached the car and yanked the keys out of my pocket. Then I slammed my hand down on the hood, cursing.

"He's just being stubborn," said a voice from behind me.

I spun around to see Darren standing maybe ten feet away from me.

The kid grinned. "He makes me want to hit things, too."

I nodded. "Good to know."

I didn't feel any better; that anger still burned inside of me. Hotter even than normal, because of the memories my little rant had pulled up. Stuff I'd seen that I'd done everything in my power to forget. Stuff that stayed with you forever. Because as much as I tried to bury the memories deep, there were things you couldn't un-see. There were things you couldn't ever wipe completely from your mind.

I pulled open the driver's-side door and slid into the car. I was jamming the key in the lock when the passenger door opened and Darren climbed in beside me.

"What the hell—"

"I'm coming with you. If you'll have me. I know it's not guns and ammo, but I can fight. And one more guy willing to fight is something, right?"

For a second, all I could do was stare at him in shock. "Absolutely not."

Because if I hadn't already pissed Armadale off, kidnapping his son would certainly do the trick.

"I'm strong and I'm fast. And I'm a damn good shot."

"And your dad would come up my mountain and kick my ass from here to Sunday if I take you away from him."

"I'm seventeen," Darren said. "I can make my own decisions."

Seventeen? Jesus when had I gotten so old that kids a year younger than I seemed like . . . well, kids?

I slanted him a look. "Seventeen? Really?"

Darren met my gaze steadily for a moment. Then his eyes

wavered and he looked away. "Okay, sixteen, but I'll be seventeen in four weeks."

"Oh. Four weeks. That'll be such comfort later today, when your father is beating the crap out of me." Shaking my head, I just said, "Get out of the car and get your butt back in your house."

Before I could say anything more, the passenger-side back door opened and Dawn slid in.

I spun around in the seat to look at her. "What the—"

"I'm coming, too."

"No. Abso-effing-lutely not."

Dawn grinned at me. "If Darren can come, then so can—"

"Darren can't come. Neither of you are coming. Get the hell out of my car."

Darren turned in his seat and held out his knuckles for a fist bump from his sister.

Dawn gave him the bump. She had several bags with her in addition to a bulky coat, and got situated while she talked. "If you're worried that Dad won't let us leave, you shouldn't be. He has to let us go."

"No, he doesn't. I have a handgun in the glove box, your father has a freakin' armory—I'm guessing here, so correct me if I'm wrong." I raised my eyebrows, waiting, but neither of the kids said anything, so I went on. "And we're on his turf. Just because I haven't seen anyone else in town, that doesn't mean there's not a dozen guys with rifles pointed at me right now. So would you please get your asses out of my car?"

"Hear us out," Dawn said.

"Yeah, give us a chance!"

Dawn gave Darren's head a little slap. "Let me do the talking."

Darren shrugged with a grin.

"He's not going to stop us," Dawn said. "If he was, he would have already."

Okay, so she had a point. Armadale could have blown me to bits by now.

I twisted in my seat to look out the front window, half expecting to see Armadale standing there, gun in his hand. Since he wasn't, I blew out a breath and strangled the steering wheel with my fists.

I looked back at Dawn. "I didn't come here to recruit you. I came here to convince your father to help."

Her mouth tilted up. "You did convince him. You think he'd have let us get this far if you hadn't?" She shrugged. "He has the littles to take care of. He can't come himself, but that doesn't mean you didn't make your point."

"Jesus," I muttered. I shot a look at Darren and Dawn. What the hell was I getting myself into?

As if she sensed I was swaying, Dawn leaned forward. "I'm assuming Darren told you what a good shot he is. He's really the best in the whole family. And you already know I have most of my nurses' training."

Which, I had to admit, would be useful as hell.

I fumed for a couple of seconds, considering. The last thing I wanted was responsibility for two more people.

But the flip side was, I needed them. I needed every good fighter I could find, and I sure as hell needed someone with medical training that didn't come out of a booklet from the American Heart Association. And if they had half the skills I thought they did, then I needed them.

"Okay," I said finally, slipping the car into gear. "Here's the deal. You can come with me to Base Camp. Dawn, we've got a guy who—"

"Justin, who does first aid. Lily told me about him."

"You can help Justin. And Darren, you can . . . I don't know. We'll find something for you to do. But you're not coming with me to Texas. And that's final."

Darren held his hand back for another fist bump from his sister. I could tell from their expressions that neither of them thought I was serious about keeping their asses in Utah.

And I was afraid they were right.

CHAPTER TWENTY-THREE

LILY

"That's the fourth church you've driven past," Lily said, leaning forward toward the front of the Cayenne as they drove through some town in the Midwest.

Ticks didn't always avoid churches, but it worked more often than not.

Ely smiled at her over his shoulder. "You don't honestly think I've survived this long on my own by relying on faith in God, do you?"

"So, what, you drive straight through?"

"When I have to."

No wonder he needed so many energy drinks. And no wonder he was such an ass. Apparently the guy hadn't slept in seven months.

"Well, you don't have to tonight. If we're driving straight through, pull over and I'll take a shift."

"Nah. We don't have enough gas for tonight. We'll find some to siphon in the morning. And I just found what I need." He nodded out the direction of the windshield.

Just ahead of them, on their right, a huge building hunkered down beside a mostly empty parking lot. A familiar blue-and-yellow sign hung crookedly from the front of the building. The sign in the parking lot had crashed to the ground.

"You can't be serious," Lily said. "A Wal-Mart?" she asked.

"Yep. There's one in almost every town in America."

"A Wal-Mart?" she repeated dumbly.

Ely pulled the Cayenne up to the front of the store and stopped in the fire lane. Not that it mattered. In case of an emergency, the EMS would not be coming to their rescue.

The Wal-Mart had obviously been looted. All of the front windows, however, had plywood installed over them. One of the panels had been ripped off. Another hung crooked. The glass behind both was broken. Still, someone—some employee or manager—had cared enough to try to preserve the store before it had finally fallen.

She looked out in the parking lot, where there were maybe a dozen cars parked. Some neatly in spots, others at angles as if they'd just been abandoned. On the far end was a dark smear of something that she didn't want to look at too closely. And she was thankful the dusk obscured the view.

Ely pushed his door open and she did the same, cringing when an icy wind cut right through her clothes. Wrapping her arms gingerly around her and hopping a little to generate body heat, she scanned the area, ignoring the pain radiating from her shoulder. Almost directly across the road was a small airport, its landing strip clearly visible from where she stood. "There's an airport. Lots of cars in that parking lot," she pointed out.

"Good catch." He winked at her. "We'll get some gas there in the morning."

She frowned, eyeing the Wal-Mart. McKenna's door swung open, and she levered herself out of the front seat. She arched her back, moaning faintly as she stretched. It was an achy sound, not a good one.

Lily rounded the back of the Cayenne and stepped close to Ely, hoping that McKenna wouldn't be able to hear her. "I don't like this. McKenna doesn't look good. And it's almost dark. What are we doing here, really?"

He met her gaze then and for the first time since she'd met him, she felt like he wasn't secretly laughing at her. "This is the best sanctuary I've found. Trust me."

She didn't want to trust him. But right now, he was all she had. "Okay. What do I do?"

He reached into the back of the Cayenne, moved aside a palm frond, and pulled out a shotgun. "First, we secure the building. Then we settle in for the night." He pulled out a pistol and handed it to her, butt first. "I assume you know how to use this?"

"And I assume you know that won't do shit against a Tick?" She pulled her bow out of the backseat. She didn't tell him she wasn't even sure she could notch an arrow with her arm like this. Why give him the satisfaction?

"Great. I'm bunking tonight with Katniss Everdeen. I'll let you know if we need that."

"She's really good with the bow," McKenna said from the other side of the car. Ely and Lily both looked over at her. "She can really shoot and it's more effective against Ticks than any gun, even a shotgun. That bow saved my life."

That might have been a stretch, but Lily appreciated her taking her side.

Ely gave her bow a suspicious look and added, "Just try not to shoot me."

"Yeah, I'll try," Lily said dryly. It would be easier if he didn't make it so damn tempting.

To McKenna, he said, "You can wait in the car until we're sure the building is clear. Keep it running; she's a bitch to start if she gets too cold and the last thing we want is to have to start her again. We'll be out in ten minutes to get you. Don't go anywhere."

Lily slung her quiver of arrows across her back and followed Ely up to the storefront, where one of the plywood panels hung lopsided. He swung the shotgun up to his shoulder and pulled a flashlight from the waistband of his jeans.

His flashlight wasn't a crank-powered lantern like hers but a Maglite with a bright beam, so that when he aimed it through the broken plate-glass window into the building the light panned across the front of the store. Things scurried away from the beam of light, but nothing looked sinister.

Ely took a step back then kicked the heel of his boot through the glass. Five quick kicks later, he'd expanded the opening enough to climb into the store.

She followed him in, stepping gingerly over the jagged shards of glass. What little merchandise that hadn't been sold or stolen lay in ruins on the ground. Even the shelves and racks had been knocked over. As they walked through the dry goods aisle, she paused by a pile of debris. She nudged the tip of her bow through the mound.

"Keep up."

She glanced up to see Ely ten steps ahead and scowling.

"I was just looking—"

"There's no point. There's nothing left here worth finding."

"But—"

"That's not why we're here. Keep moving."

Ely held his Maglite in his left hand, with his shotgun up, pressed to his shoulder with the barrel resting on his left wrist. He constantly panned the light over the floor, scanning for danger. He moved quickly and quietly through the store, straight toward the back.

He pushed through the door into the back storeroom. For a moment, she simply gaped. The storeroom hadn't been hit as hard. Apparently most people didn't think about all the stuff at the back of a Wal-Mart. All the things still in boxes that were waiting to be unpacked.

He glanced over his shoulder. "If we make it through the night, we'll search through here in the morning."

"If?" she asked.

But Ely had already reached a pair of massive metal doors.

"Are you kidding me?"

He flashed her a roguish smile. "What'd you expect?"

"This is where you seek sanctuary? In a freezer in Wal-Mart? You can't be serious."

"Serious as airtight, reinforced steel doors."

"Airtight, reinforced steel doors—" She paused to grab the handle and swing the door open. "That open from the outside."

He smirked. "Yeah. Handles on the inside, too. Besides, I haven't met a Tick yet who actually thinks to try that. They lose interest in what they can't see or smell. They're animals. Once you disappear into that box, you no longer exist to them."

She took a step closer to the door. A scent that was one part rotten meat and two parts mold assaulted her nose. "Holy crap, it stinks in there."

"Exactly." He nudged the door open with the nose of his rifle and stepped inside. He panned the beam of light from his flashlight around the interior of the room.

He didn't seem to notice the stench. Either he was used to doing this or his sense of smell had been obliterated already, because her nostrils were twitching in rebellion and she hadn't even walked inside.

A moment later, he walked out, his rifle slung up against his shoulder, his Maglite dangling from his hand. "Looks clear."

"Yippee."

"Here's the drill," he said, ignoring her sarcasm. "You stay here and clear out whatever's stinking up the inside of the box. If it still smells, leave it near the outside door. It'll cover our scent. Once we lock ourselves in, we'll be airtight. Any Ticks who come out after dusk will probably follow our scent to the store, but they won't be able to find us or get in. They'll lose interest before dawn and move on to other prey. Easy as pie."

"This is your big plan? Lock ourselves into an airtight room for the night? Doesn't that seem a bit . . . stifling?" Then it hit her. "That's what the plants are for, isn't it?"

"Bingo. Carter was right: you are smart."

"Smart enough to question the sanity of this plan. How do you know you have enough to generate enough oxygen for the three of us?"

He shrugged. "I don't. But I've been doing this for six months now, sometimes with more than five people. We haven't died yet."

"That's not super reassuring."

"Hey, if you want to be the one who sits outside the fridge and waits for the Ticks to come, that's fine by me."

"I just don't want to be the one who dies in the middle of the night from oxygen deprivation."

He ignored her. "I'll go get McKenna and start hauling stuff in. You clear out the fridge."

"Fine."

She glared at Ely's back as he stalked off through the store. She didn't bother to remind him that she was wounded and she couldn't really lift any of those boxes. She would kick the boxes out if she had to. He'd obviously given her the worst of the jobs. No big surprise there. Ely was so not her favorite person.

She set her bow and quiver down beside the open door and stepped into the room. Even breathing through her mouth, she could feel the mold spores invading her body.

She worked quickly, wanting to get all the stinky stuff out before McKenna came back. Moving the meat and other rotted food was a nightmare of squishy disgustingness. By the time she'd moved most of the big stuff, McKenna and Ely were back. He had most of the bags. She was carrying a potted plant. She smiled wanly but even that seemed forced as she rubbed her palm along the bottom of her belly.

Lily found a ratty desk chair from the staff room and moved it in for McKenna to sit on. It was the kind of thing no one would have bothered stealing when they were looting the store.

McKenna sat down awkwardly, still rubbing the side of her belly.

"It still stinks in here, but Ely says we'll be safe."

"It's fine." The corners of McKenna's mouth twitched, like she was trying to stifle her gag reflex.

Ely had disappeared back out to the car for another load of plants. Lily set the first one close to McKenna's chair, figuring she needed the fresh air more. Then she went out into the back room to look for anything else useful. By the time they were ready to lock themselves in, the air was better. She'd found some tattered blankets for McKenna to curl up on. The girl must have been exhausted, because once she stretched out, she fell asleep almost immediately. Lily situated herself on the opposite wall, her bow at her side. She wouldn't sleep, so she didn't bother to lie down.

Ely pulled off his jacket, rolled it up, and stretched out with his hands linked over his belly and his head on the jacket. A moment later, he was asleep.

She'd almost drifted off herself, when she heard a noise from outside: a long, slow scratch, like something running a claw over the floor.

The sound was distant and muffled, coming from somewhere either behind the back of the store or maybe out in the store itself. Her breath caught in her chest. For a long moment, she heard only the quiet snuffling of McKenna's snores. Then came a sound that chilled her to the bone—a sound she hadn't heard since the night her sister had been lost to her forever. The low, keening howl of a Tick.

One of them had caught their scent. Probably outside in the store. He—or she—had called the others. They traveled in packs, like wolves. They would tear the store apart looking for them. If Ely was right, they wouldn't find them.

In the absolute dark, Lily reached a hand out to the spot by her side where she'd put her bow.

"Don't bother," Ely said in the darkness.

Her heart about jumped out of her chest.

Crap.

She hadn't even realized he was awake. Past her thundering heart, she managed to ask, "What?"

"Don't even bother with the bow and arrow." His voice was soft without being a whisper.

"So, what? I shouldn't even bother to fight? If one of those things breaks in here—"

"None of them will. But if they do, we should have plenty of warning. A Tick couldn't get through quietly. It would make a ton of noise. We'll hear."

"Well, that makes me feel so much better."

"Anything comes through that door and I'll have the Maglite on it as soon as the door opens. The light will blind it. That should buy us twenty, thirty seconds to blow it away."

The brutal blood thirst in his voice should have terrified her. Instead she found it oddly reassuring. He had a plan. That was a good thing.

So she dropped her hand back into her lap, content knowing that her bow was nearby, if not actually in her hand, and that Ely had her back, at least for the night.

She fidgeted, trying to find a comfortable spot, but every way she twisted her body, it was all hard surfaces and cold seeping through her clothes. Plus, her shoulder ached, an angry throb that radiated across her chest and down her arm, as though she could feel every cell that had been torn apart by that bullet.

She wondered how the Ticks could do it. How they could take a hit and just keep coming. They must not feel any pain at all. Or maybe their hunger overpowered every other sensation.

Feeling even more uncomfortable, she eased away from the wall and rotated her shoulder, trying to work out the pain.

"Did you forget to take your painkillers?" Ely asked in the darkness.

"I—" Sitting in the dark, she wrinkled her nose. She wasn't a good liar, so she didn't answer directly. "It's no biggie. I'm fine."

"You're flopping around over there like a fish on land. You're in pain. If you need to take the meds, then take the meds."

"I'm all right."

"You're obviously in pain. Take something."

"I don't . . . I don't have anything."

"What?" She heard Ely shifting to sit up.

"I don't have any meds."

"Carter said that Mormon chick gave you meds."

"She did."

"If she gave you antibiotics but not painkillers, you should have said so back at Base Camp. They have pharmaceuticals, right?"

"Yeah, but . . ."

"But what? Why didn't you bring them with you?"

Suddenly, his tone of voice irritated her. Lily didn't need him talking to her like she was some idiot who didn't know jack and who needed a keeper to make sure she took her meds on time. She crossed her legs and sat up straighter, talking in a low hiss so as not to wake McKenna. "I'm not taking the meds because I gave them to Justin to give to one of the Greens before we left Base Camp."

Ely cursed softly then asked, "All your meds or just your painkillers?"

In for a penny, in for a pound. "All of them."

"Even your antibiotics?"

"Yeah."

He cursed again, and this time, not softly. "Of all the bone-headed, dumbass stunts—"

"Hey, those Greens needed them more than I did. There was a girl with a broken arm." There was so much disapproval in his voice, she automatically argued her case. "My injury was a clean shot. One bullet, in and out. I was stitched up by someone with actual medical training. And she gave me a shot of antibiotics before I left. I'll be fine. That girl—"

"That girl had an ugly gash and an arm broken in at least two places."

She sat back, surprised he knew which girl she'd meant. In the day and a half Ely had been at Base Camp, she'd gotten the impression he didn't mingle much with Greens, but apparently he'd at least checked out the medical ward. "Yeah. If you saw her, then you know she really needed those meds."

"No." Ely's voice was cold and hard. "That girl didn't need meds. She needed a bullet."

She flinched away from his words. "You can't mean—"

"Anyone with injuries like that is a drain on resources we don't have and is a liability the next time we get hit. Plus, she's in pain. She probably won't make it. And if she shows signs of the Tick virus, someone will have to take her out anyway. You should have kept the meds for yourself and gone for the pity kill."

"The pity—" She choked on her own words. "You don't really mean that."

"The hell I don't. What favors do you think you did for her?"

"I saved her life."

"You prolonged her death. That's all."

"Every life is precious."

"No," he cut her off. "Every able-bodied fighter is precious. Anyone else is just in our way."

"You don't believe that," she whispered, horrified. But the truth was, she didn't know Ely. She didn't know what he believed. All she knew about him was that Carter trusted him. She trusted Carter with her life. And she knew—she *knew*—that Carter would never suggest a pity kill. Not over something like a broken arm.

Ely didn't say anything else and she didn't, either. Instead, they just sat there in silence. She could still hear the noise of the Tick outside in the store. In her mind, she could picture him: his long arms would nearly drag along the ground. His sheer bulk would make him look stocky, no matter how tall or thin he used to be in real life. His jaw would be thick and powerful enough to snap bones. His brain would be small, maybe too small to operate a door handle.

She tried not to imagine him as he moved through the store, snuffling at the ground to follow their scent. Drool pouring from his mouth, which would already be watering. For her. The Tick could just as easily be a female. Male or female, it would be strong enough to kill her with a single blow. And then—

Another howl rent the air. The Tick was closer. So much for the freezer being soundproof. Another Tick joined the first. And then another. At least three then. More than enough to kill the three of them. If Ely was wrong about the door holding, they were dead.

Lily crawled closer to where Ely had laid down. "Hand me the flashlight," she whispered.

"Afraid of the dark?" he quipped.

"No." Geesh, couldn't he try to be less of a jerk, for even a few minutes? "I'm guessing you're a better shot than I am. If they get the door open—"

"They won't."

"If they do, I'll hold the light. That way you'll have both hands to fire and reload."

She expected Ely to argue, but an ominous thud came from the other side of the door, like something had thrown itself against the metal.

The Maglite flicked on, illuminating the cramped space. McKenna had rolled over so her back was facing them. Her chest moved in long inhalations. Somehow, she was sleeping through this. Lily felt like she was ready to squirm right out of her skin, she was so nervous. Ely slapped the Maglite into her outstretched palm. He may have seemed calm, but when he raised the shotgun to brace it against his shoulder, she noticed he already had five new shells lined up on the ground beside him.

"You sure this works?" She breathed out the words, terrified to make more noise than that.

"It has in the past." A few seconds later he added, "But usually, if there are Ticks in the area, I keep driving."

There was another screech of claws on metal. "So, you somehow magically know if there are Ticks around."

"Normally I have my dog with me."

"Your dog?"

"Yeah, I used to have a dog. Chuy. He'd let me know if there'd been Ticks in the area."

Terror clutched at her heart. "So basically, you have no idea if this will really work."

"It'll work," he muttered.

It sounded more like a prayer than a statement, but there wasn't much she could do about it now. Anger wouldn't help here. It was too late for that. It was too late to do anything except trust that Ely knew what he was doing.

All she could do was sit there, aiming the light at the door and pray. The flashlight shook in her hand, making the bright yellow circle dance across the door. She braced it with her other hand, breathing out slowly to steady her nerves.

Another howl tore through the night, followed by an answering howl, farther away. The scratch of nails against the door made her heart race with panic. Sitting here, opposite the door, was stupid. They should have braced something against it. Even their backs would be better than nothing. She lowered the light, ready to do it even if Ely wouldn't, but he stopped her with a hand on her arm before she could move. He gave a sharp shake of his head and made a shushing motion.

Her heart seemed to pause in her chest. This was it. Either the Tick would open that door and Ely would get the shot or . . . not.

But a moment later, the sounds from the hall outside the freezer faded. A series of howls echoed in the distance and then silence fell.

She didn't know how long she sat there in silence, holding her breath and the Maglite, waiting for the Tick to make it through, waiting for death to come. She didn't lower the Maglite until Ely pulled it from her hand and flipped it off.

Even then, she couldn't move. Adrenaline pumped through her blood, making her shaky and weak, but she couldn't move from her spot beside Ely, just opposite the door.

McKenna shifted in her sleep and made a snuffling noise. How the hell had she slept through that?. Ely stretched out beside her, not far from where he'd first sat down. His breathing evened out and Lily wondered if he was asleep.

"Ely?" she whispered.

"Yeah?" he asked, his voice sleepy.

"Did Carter tell you about my sister?" She had tried not to think about Mel and that damn gene, but this was her reality now. She couldn't hide from it anymore.

"Mel? The autistic one?"

Back in the Before, it had annoyed her when people narrowed their description of Mel to that one adjective. Now, hearing her described as autistic seemed better than what she was now: *a vampire*. "Yes."

"Yeah, sure." Ely sounded more alert now. Almost cautious. "He mentioned her."

"He told you what happened? With Sebastian?"

She heard the nearby rustling of Ely stretching and sitting up again. "Yeah. Sebastian turned her."

"Right." She swallowed, because it felt like her heart was going to pound its way up through her throat. And that pounding heart hid something other than fear. Shame, maybe. Dread, certainly. She spoke fast while she had the courage to. "The fact that he exposed her and she turned, it means she has the regenerative gene. She and I are twins. Identical. So I have it, too. That means if—"

"I thought you didn't believe in the pity kill."

"This is different," she said.

"Got it."

"If I get bit by a—"

"That's not gonna happen," he said, but there was no conviction in his voice. Only resignation. He knew as well as she did that he was making groundless reassurances.

"But—"

"If it does, you don't have to worry." She heard him sigh. When he spoke, his voice was serious and for the first time, she felt like she could actually trust him. "I'll do the right thing. I'll go for the pity kill."

CHAPTER TWENTY-FOUR

MEL

Things change after the night with abalone sky. Sebastian decided to teach me to hunt Ticks. I don't fight him anymore. I hardly need to talk—Sebastian talks enough for the both of us. He lets me keep my rhymes. Perhaps he knows how I need them.

However much I don't want to rely on him, I must. He is the kaleidoscope through which I must see the world. The view is fractured and confusing enough. Without him, I'd have no hope of making sense of it.

There is no cloud cover tonight. The abalone shell has been flipped over to reveal a sky so black it might have been painted in Indian ink, the stars just pricked in afterward like a child's art project. The icy air nips playfully at my skin. Used to be that I never felt the cold. Now I'm cold all the time.

I long to go back to the house. To curl up on the sofa in front of the TV that doesn't work. To stare at the blank screen. But he won't let me. Besides, the gravy train is gone. He won't feed me again and I must hunt or starve.

"What do you see?" he asks.

Everything.

Of course, I've always seen everything. In my Before, I saw so much more than anyone else. Dead screen pixels, freckles on the back of Ian Milan's neck, a cow's pores impressed in leather. Every

split end in my hair. Every dot in the acoustical tiles in the class-
room ceilings. I saw it all. Do I remember them so clearly because
I heard them all, or did I hear them all because I saw them?

Now, I see more but hear less. Nothing sings now. Nothing
even breathes. Except me and Sebastian. His music is louder every
day. I never heard it when I was moping, but now it rings in my
ears, almost making up for so much other silence. I had expected
something darkly complex, a never-ending Beethoven symphony.
The seventh, maybe. With layers and movements and emotional
connotations I barely understand. With passion and depth. Instead, he is an ancient tribal beat and I find myself dancing to his
rhythm.

Even now. Even when I don't want to. Even when I resist, I
dance.

"What do you see?" he asks again.

I make myself look again. It's not what I see; it's what I should
be looking at.

We are outside of town now. Which town, I don't know. The
houses are small and thin here. More Baltic Avenue purple than
Boardwalk blue.

This house, the door is ripped off and dangling. The frame
splintered, not just at the dead bolt, but like a cartoon doorway
a monster forced its way through. The weedy green has been
trampled—not all over, but from the woods behind the house to
the door. Like the path the neighbor's dog wore in their lawn from
food bowl to doghouse.

I look at Sebastian. "Birds of a feather nest together?"

He looks exasperated for only a second before smiling. "Yes. I
think so, Melly. They're out now, but they'll be back. We can wait
here for them or go out and hunt them. You choose."

Mel the girl would never choose to hunt anything. Mel the girl couldn't kill a cockroach because she couldn't stand the crunch or the tinny sound of its death.

But excitement dances along my nerves and I nod. "Hunt."

Sebastian's tribal beat picks up and he smiles. "Good girl."

I am already trotting off into the woods after them when he stops me.

"Not yet. First, how many are there?"

I look at the house. The yard. The dog path. Then the house again. I move toward the house, but he stops me.

"No. Don't go look in there for clues. Actually finding a nest like this—that was lucky. You won't be lucky next time. You can't rely on that. Figure it out on your own."

I'm supposed to just guess?

"Don't frown at me like that," he chides. "I'm not asking you to just pick a number at random. You should be able to tell, to sense it. What did Carter always call it?"

I hum a few bars of "The Itsy-Bitsy Spider" to help him out.

He nods. "That's right. My spidey sense. You have one, too. So use it."

This I don't believe at all. I'm not known for my sense. Common sense. Number sense, book sense. Sense of humor, least of all. Spidey sense seems too far-fetched for me to be fetching Ticks.

But I try.

I close my eyes and reach out through the moist, heavy air. Through the scent of honeysuckle and the musty, mold scent of decaying leaves in the underbrush. I wait for a new smell. A musky whiff of pheromones. Of the dogs that wore the path through the grass. It doesn't come.

I open my eyes growling in frustration.

He only laughs. "Giving up so soon? Poor, Kitten."

"I don't know what I'm supposed to do."

"Of course you don't. All your life people have done things for you. Now that something requires you to actually work, you're baffled."

His words sting, so I sting back. "You are useless as a teacher. This must be the real reason you don't turn vampires."

For an instant, his gaze hardens. Then he smiles, a grating smirk. "Very well, I'll talk you through it. I've told you before that vampires are territorial, yes? We can sense when we are near one another. Indeed, we cannot ignore it. We feel one another's presence. It's rather . . . annoying."

"Like you?" I ask.

He makes a low growling sound in his throat and his voice is suddenly serious. "No, Kitten, not merely like me. Like a berserker rage. Like a force so primal it takes every ounce of energy not to kill everything in sight."

I am grave silent at this. I have seen Sebastian kill. I have seen him hunt and destroy. I have never seen him lose control. The idea terrifies me.

"The Tick microbe was created from the blood of a vampire. The scientists at Genexome isolated the original vampire virus and worked off of that."

"Yes." This part I know. Carter had explained it to Lily and me. Roberto—the vampire who owned Genexome Corporation—created the virus based on his own blood. He wanted to create creatures like vampires, but more biddable. An army he could control to take over the world. Roberto was older even than Sebastian. He had once been worshipped as an Aztec god. Was it any wonder he was a power-hungry megalomaniac? "So the Ticks are related to vampires. That's why you can sense them."

"Exactly, but they are merely a faint buzzing."

"Not a berserker rage, then?"

"No, Melly. But I believe you might be able to hear them, even through you're not yet fully vampire. And it will be quite useful if you can, so be a good girl and concentrate, will you?"

I try again. And fail again. I pull away from Sebastian, but he pulls me back.

"Try again."

I want to stomp my foot, to temper tantrum my way out of trying, but Sebastian's not the type to tolerate that. So I try.

I close my eyes and breathe deep and reach.

Then it hits me: not a musky dog scent, but something else. The sound of them. Not the coyote yips and yaps they make out loud, but the sound of them that *I* hear.

It is a far cry from Sebastian's tribal beat, farther still from Lily's lilting melody.

A badly tuned piano playing in a distant room. Or two floors up. Or upside down and backward. Distinctly not right. Unforgettably wrong. Their music is as twisted as their genetics. As miserably out of tune as their bodies are. And, yet, together, they are a kind of rhythm.

I open my eyes. "Four."

"Good girl."

His praise rolls me to the balls of my feet. I am an eager beaver to win his shark approval and that's not the water mammal I want to be.

"How far away are they?"

"Close enough."

I can see from the gleam in his eyes that I've guessed right.

He eyes me and I know he's sizing me up for another test. "Do you want to wait here or go after them?"

I know, either from spidey sense or simple logic, that they will be back, probably before dawn. Waiting is the easy choice. The safe, Mel-ish choice, but it's not at all what I want.

"Let's hunt," I say and it's not until he smiles that I realize I forgot to search for a nursery rhyme. The fact that I have to search for nursery rhymes now disturbs me as much as my newfound thirst for blood.

The nursery rhymes used to be how I thought. Part of who I was. I don't know why I cling to them. Or maybe I do.

As I run through the woods, following the sounds of the Ticks' discordant notes, I wonder, do I have so much trouble letting go of the girl I was because I don't yet know the girl I'm going to be?

Is there anything left of that other Mel?

All my life I've been prey. Twitchy and nervous. Fearful and frightened. Only the music made it bearable.

People say kids can be cruel, but they aren't. They are natural predators. They are as proud as lions but more cackle than pride. Like hyenas, they hunt and scavenge. They pick off the weak, the strange, the affected. The girl I was, was perfect prey for a cackle of hyenas. Only my steady drumbeat, only my sister-flower, kept me strong. She was the rest of the herd that circles the frail and keeps them safe.

Now I live in bone-crushing darkness and soul-stealing silence, with a hunger so vast it is my everything. I miss the music, the wild cacophony that was my life in the Before. In my Before. In that other life. But for now, I am only hunger. I only feed. I am not prey, but predator.

CHAPTER TWENTY-FIVE

LILY

Ely didn't mention the close call with the Ticks the next day. Lily didn't, either. It seemed impossible that McKenna had slept through the attack, but if she had, who was Lily to tell her what a close call they'd had? Besides, the conversation with Ely had left her rattled. For all her tough talk, the idea of actually being exposed to the virus, of actually dying … well, it freaked her out. There was a big difference between talking about worst-case scenarios and meeting the gaze of someone who was willing to kill you. The fact that she wanted him to do it if it came to that didn't make the experience any less chilling.

So once morning came, she kept to herself as they searched the store and loaded up the car. They looked for food in the back and unfortunately found very little. Ely siphoned gas from the cars near the airport.

She tried not to look at the more recent signs of destruction. She kept her head and her mind focused. Which was probably why she hadn't noticed that McKenna wasn't feeling well until they were packing up the last of their stuff.

"How are you doing?" she whispered. She wanted to urge McKenna to move faster, but her every step seemed to be a struggle.

McKenna's eyes were wide. Her skin pale and blotchy. The hollows of her cheeks even more pronounced than usual. Her steps faltered and Lily grabbed her elbow with her free hand, wedging her forearm under her friend's to support her. "How bad is it?"

She opened her mouth then pinched her lips together again. Her whole face quivered as if it was all she could do not to cry. Finally she said, "I'm okay."

"McKenna—"

"Just those Barton Hicks things."

"What?"

She pulled her arm from Lily's hand and rubbed her palm down the side of her belly, taking a determined step toward the front of the store. "I read about them in my book. The one Justin found for me. They feel like contractions, but they're really not."

Lily fell into step beside her. She wedged the plant she was carrying into the crook of her elbow so her hands would be free to grab McKenna if needed. "And they're common? These Hicks things?"

"Yeah." Again she breathed out through her pursed lips. "Every woman has them."

"Do they have this many?"

McKenna stopped, sucking in a sharp breath. At first, Lily thought something she'd said had freaked her out. Then McKenna hunched over, clutching her belly.

Lily dropped the plant and grabbed her arm. McKenna's weight sagged against her. Panic seized Lily. "McKenna!"

Her fingers dug into Lily's arm.

"Are you okay?" Lily asked. Which had to be the stupidest question in the world. Clearly she wasn't okay. This couldn't be right. Her head was ducked, her hair a curtain around her face, making it impossible to see her friend's expression. Lily looked up, scan-

ning the area, praying that Ely would come back. That he'd be able
to do something. But he didn't.

She was all alone, standing in the aisle of a looted Wal-Mart
with a girl who was clearly, painfully in labor, and she was helpless.

Then, slowly, McKenna's fingers loosened their grip on her arm.
Her shoulders rose and fell as she sucked in a breath. Then another. Her legs must have felt weak, because she wobbled before
straightening.

"I'm okay," she gasped.

"No," Lily argued. "You're not okay. You're in labor."

She shook her head, despite being pale. Despite being weak and
shaken. "I'm fine. It's just those fake contractions. This is normal."

"McKenna—"

"I'm fine!" Whatever strength her body lacked, she more than
made up for with her conviction. "Even if I wasn't, there's nothing
you can do now. We'll be at the border soon. We can't stop until
we get there anyway. And I'm fine."

Lily studied her friend's expression. Her skin was still blood-
less. The circles under her eyes as dark as bruises. She wasn't fine,
but she was right.

There was nothing they could do here.

"We could go back to Base Camp," Lily said.

McKenna shook her head. "Base Camp is farther away. And
there's not even hope of a doctor there. We should stick with the
plan."

Lily bit her lip, thinking. Despite what McKenna had said, this
clearly wasn't one of those Hicks things, whatever they were. This
was real labor.

"Okay, we'll head for Mexico and we'll drive fast. Ely will get us
there."

McKenna nodded and they started walking for the door. They ran into Ely outside by the SUV. He shot them an odd look, but Lily just shook her head so he'd know not to say anything in front of McKenna.

She got McKenna situated in the front seat of the car and headed over to the driver's side to talk to Ely.

"What's up?" he asked, the question obvious in his eyes.

"I think McKenna's in labor."

"You *think?*"

"She says it's just a Barton Hicks thing but—"

"Braxton Hicks?"

"What?"

"Braxton Hicks. They're early contractions. False labor."

"Yeah. That must be what she meant. She said she thought that's what it was, but it seemed really intense."

Ely clenched and unclenched his jaw. "How far apart are they?"

"I don't know." Then she thought it through. "No, wait. When we went to the bathroom, she was in there a really long time. She could have had one then. Which means . . ." They'd come out of the bathroom, gathered up their stuff. Walked through most of the store. And McKenna had been walking slowly. "Maybe fifteen minutes?"

Ely nodded. "Okay. We won't panic until they're five minutes apart. Until then, we pack fast and we get the hell out of here."

"How do you know so much about this stuff?"

He gave a humorless chuckle. "Hey, it's a cliché, but I'm Latino. I'm the oldest of three and I've got a shitload of cousins." His expression darkened. "*Had* a shitload of cousins. Guess I've just been around more pregnant women than you."

He turned and walked away before she could say anything else.

She watched him for only a second before heading back to the storeroom for the last of their stuff.

Ely seemed like such a loner. He could have stayed at Base Camp, or even infiltrated the Farms with the other retrieval teams. Instead, he spent all his time on his own, just searching.

He'd gotten a lot of people out of Farms. Carter had said his retrieval rate was higher than almost any other Elite's. All those people he'd gotten out and none of them had been the family he'd been so desperate to save. How must that have fucked with his head? She'd been so desperate to save just Mel. She'd failed and it had nearly killed her. Wouldn't it be worse, so much worse, if it wasn't just Mel, but a whole shitload—to use his word—of family members?

She grabbed the last few things from the walk-in and made her way out of the store toward the waiting car. Only when she looked up at the ceiling, at the signs hanging from the rafters, did this look like a Wal-Mart rather than a battlefield. Somehow, the signs were intact. Big, cheerfully colored signs with pictures of smiling kids and busy moms. Over what must have been the child-care section hung a five-foot-by-five-foot close-up of a gurgling infant.

She nearly stopped cold. That baby. That was what McKenna had in her belly right now. Not that exact baby, obviously, but a real, living person. She'd avoided thinking about her bump that way until now.

It seemed stupid not to look. Just in case. She crept through the store toward the child-care section. It wasn't a part of the store that she'd ever paid much attention to in the past. In the Before, she'd had zero contact with babies. She stared at the rows and rows of looted products. Most everything had been picked clean. The empty shelves alone were enough to scare the crap out of her. How was it possible that babies needed this much stuff? How on earth was McKenna going to do this? How would she even keep this baby alive once it was born?

Just thinking about it made her heart pound.

So she stopped thinking and just dug through the piles on the floor. There was more stuff in the debris than it looked like at first. No food or formula. Those kinds of thing would have been the first to go, but she did find some clothes, a few blankets. A couple of packages of diapers that looked way too big—but hey, she wasn't going to be picky—and a pacifier.

It wasn't enough. Lily couldn't help feeling like nothing she did would be enough. But it was better than nothing.

CHAPTER TWENTY-SIX

CARTER

There's a lot of shit I've had to get used to since the Tick-pocalypse. The burn of gasoline in my mouth and sinuses when I suck too hard when siphoning gas. The constant, low-grade hunger and the way it makes you think about food all the time. The relentless cold of living in a cave that's sixty-five degrees year-round. The muddy taste of boiled, bleached water. The nostalgia for fresh fruits and vegetables. I've learned to live with all kinds of crap.

But there's one thing I don't think I'll ever get used to: the sight of a rotting body staked up by a chain outside the fence of a Farm.

Every Farm had them. The Dean of Lily's Farm had made it sound like some kind of precautionary measure. He'd claimed the decomposing bodies kept the Ticks away as strongly as the scent of fresh blood lured them closer. I didn't know if the sight and smell repelled the Ticks, all I knew was that they sure as hell repulsed me.

I would never get used to it. I didn't want to.

It had taken us just about twenty-four hours to get from Utah to San Angelo. I only hoped we'd gotten here soon enough.

As stupid as it seemed to be hanging out a hundred yards from a Farm during the day, I knew from experience that the middle of the afternoon was the best time to sneak up on a Farm. The shadows were starting to lengthen, but it wasn't dark yet. At dusk, the

Collabs started to scramble. By full night, they were alert and trigger happy. This time of day, most of them were still asleep.

I stood, back pressed against a brick wall about fifty yards from the fence—about forty-five yards from the dead bodies. Zeke was a few feet in front of me, crouched behind a shrub as he set up the sat phone antenna. I suppose this must have been the main drag, back when the Farm was still a college. It was a solid block of fast food restaurants, bookstores, and shops. I was in the alley beside a Subway, serving as lookout while Zeke set up the antenna that would allow us to use the sat phone from anywhere within a one-mile radius.

He'd been fumbling with the thing for several minutes. Sure, it would have taken me a lot less than that, but I never liked to be on a mission where I was the only one who knew how stuff worked. That was just asking for trouble. If shit went bad—and it almost always did—you needed as many people as possible who could get you out of it.

Across the street was an expansive student parking lot and then, right up next to the buildings, the double row of electrified, razor wire–topped fences. And outside those fences were the remains of Greens, which Collabs had left chained there to die. I didn't ask myself if Zeke had been the one to chain any of them up. But I did make myself look at them. I relished the surge of anger, the raw scrape of it against my nerves. I needed it. I'd need it for when Zeke and I broke into the Farm. I'd need it for what I had to do later. Because later, there was a damn good chance humans were going to get hurt. And that I'd be the one doing the hurting.

This wouldn't be the first time I'd kicked a Collab's ass. But in a world where humans were an endangered species, I had to psych myself up for it. I had to remind myself that whatever I dished out, they deserved. I wasn't planning on killing anyone, but in a fight with someone who'd betrayed the human race, I couldn't be the one to hesitate.

So while Zeke worked on setting up the antenna for the sat phone, I studied the bodies outside the fence. In the mid-afternoon light I couldn't tell exactly how many there were. At least a couple that were fairly fresh if the stench in the air was any indication, but there were other, older bodies around, too, their white bones stark against the black asphalt. Turkey buzzards roost in the nearby trees, their bodies fat enough to bend branches.

We'd driven down from Utah in five cars of five. The plan was simple. Sort of. There were two cars along with Tech Taylor, and that group was going to find whatever power source was feeding the Farm and try to secure it. Most of the Farms had more than one source powering the fences, a solar grid, and wind turbines, as well as a generator. The other cars were out working on the backup plan. If we couldn't keep the electricity online, we'd need some way to keep the Ticks away.

The car Zeke and I had driven down in had dropped the two of us right at the fence line. Our goal was simple: get the antenna set up and then walk in through the front gates. Hopefully, by morning, we'd either have subdued the other Collabs or won them over to our side. If Zeke was right, the Dean was long gone.

If Zeke wasn't right . . . well, then I had bigger problems to worry about. I didn't want anyone else inside the fence until we'd secured the Farm.

Beside me, Zeke straightened and asked, "That good?"

I looked down at the antenna. "Yeah, basically. Just make sure it has a clean shot at the sky and we should be set." I handed him the sat phone. "You'll want to do a test call to make sure it's working."

He called the second car, whose antenna was installed on the car itself. A minute later he ended the call. Instead of handing the phone back, he slid it into the pocket of his jacket.

I felt a weird little trickle of apprehension work down my spine. I held out my hand. "My phone?"

He gave a nonchalant shrug. "I've got it."

"No offense, but if I'm going to waltz into a Farm, I'd be a lot more comfortable with my phone where I can reach it."

Zeke narrowed his gaze at me. "Yeah, about that." Before I could reach for my own weapon, Zeke whipped out his gun and had it aimed at my throat. "I've got a better plan."

My hand dropped to the Glock at the back of my jeans.

"I took the clip out already," Zeke said quickly. "But you're welcome to check it to verify if you want."

I pulled the Glock out and instantly realized he was right. My previous full clip had been replaced by an empty one. I hadn't even noticed the difference in weight. Jesus. How effing stupid did I feel?

"Down on your belly." Zeke gestured with the point of his gun. "Hands behind your back. Nice and slow."

Yeah, I could have charged him. It's true what they say, that most people, even trained marksmen, can't shoot a moving target, but it's usually true of targets moving away from the shooter, not right at it. I didn't want to risk it.

"You're making a mistake," I said as I laid down, trying to smother my panic so I could think. Okay, Zeke was clearly still working for the Dean. He'd betrayed us all. Had Ely known what Zeke was when he'd brought him in?

No. I couldn't believe it of Ely. He wouldn't betray me. Besides, it didn't make sense. If his goal had been to lure me down here and turn me in to the Dean, then he wouldn't have volunteered to take Lily to Canada. He would have stayed with Zeke to make sure the job got done.

"Trust me, Carter, this is much better." As soon as I was down on the ground, he planted his booted foot in the center of my back and reached for my hands. "They were never going to believe—"

As he leaned over, I reared back and reached up with my hands, grabbing whatever I could. I caught a handful of arm in one hand and scratched the underside of his chin with the other. My upward momentum knocked him off balance. I rolled with the motion and scrambled up, but he was faster. He plowed into my chest, knocking me back a few steps, right into the tangle of the prickly brush. I tripped on the antenna and went over backward. He came toward me again. I scrambled away, but not fast enough.

I couldn't find purchase under my feet and the branches of the bush clawed at my skin. I transferred my momentum into a sideways roll to free myself from the bush but when I came up, I was no longer facing just Zeke and his weapon. Suddenly, there were ten guns—ten tranq rifles.

Zeke was back a little ways, panting. "Hold your fire! Hold your fire!" he called out a couple of times. "He's unarmed."

One of the Collabs—the guy with both a rifle and a tranq gun—said, "Where the hell have you been, Zeke?"

Zeke straightened. "I've been to Utah and back." He put up his hands so they could see the gun he held before he slowly tucked it away in the holster at his side. "I brought us a nice little bargaining chip. Just don't tranq him. He's not alone and I want him awake until we know for sure where the rest of them are."

From my spot on the ground, I could see a few of the Collabs starting to lower their weapons. But the one in the middle, a big guy with dark hair and a scowl that made him look like a pit bull, didn't relax at all.

Zeke nodded toward that guy. "Is the Dean here?"

"No," the pit bull answered. "Haven't seen him since right before you disappeared."

"Well, good. Then we can use his office to question the prisoner." Zeke nudged me in the ribs with the toe of his shoe. "Hands behind your head. No tricks this time." He gave me a kick.

The blow stung my pride more than my ribs. Somehow that only pissed me off more. If he was going to beat me up, he could at least put a little effort into it.

"I'll fucking kill you, you bastard," I growled just low enough for Zeke to hear. But with ten tranq rifles pinned on me, what could I do except put my hands behind my head like a good little POW?

I felt cold metal snap around my wrists, and smiled.

Handcuffs. The idiot had bound me with handcuffs? Zip ties are not impossible to get out of, but you need a knife or something to cut with. And you need the right leverage. Cuffs are so easy to pick, it's a wonder he even bothered. Not that that made me any less pissed at him.

As Zeke hauled me to my feet, he muttered, "See? Told you this was better than the other plan."

The arrogant grin on his face churned the anger in my gut.

So this was who he really was: a Collab through and through. A liar. A self-serving bastard.

I'd trusted the wrong guy and it had come back to bite me in the ass. And now I was caught. Half the Elites were down here with me, as well as Dawn and Darren. Sometime in the next twenty-four hours, they would be done scouring the area for cars and gas and they'd come back here, expecting Zeke and I to let them in. And I'd failed.

My hands had been behind my neck when Zeke had cuffed me. I raised them over my head and pulled them down in front of me as Zeke dragged me forward by the arm.

There was a path big enough for a delivery truck cleared right up to the gate. The trash there was sparser, but there was enough of it in the road to make me think the Farm hadn't had a delivery of any kind in at least a few days.

The pit bull sent half the guys out to patrol the perimeter, looking for the rest of my crew. If my guys were where they were supposed to be, they wouldn't be anywhere near here—at least not for a couple of hours. But it wouldn't be long before they started to check in. And then, one by one, they would be caught.

Lily had been right: the entire human rebellion was a house of cards. This one betrayal had brought it all down.

CHAPTER TWENTY-SEVEN

LILY

Once they got in the car, time seemed weirdly disjointed. Lily didn't pay any attention to Ely's driving but focused solely on McKenna, who had abandoned the passenger seat and was stretched out in the back. Lily could tell every time a contraction hit. She could see it clearly in the rippling muscles of McKenna's stomach.

Sure, she had learned about involuntary muscles in biology, but this was just freaky. This baby inside, this thing, it wanted out.

Soon.

They were long past Albuquerque when Lily leaned across the console and whispered to Ely, "We gotta get her out of here."

He glanced at her and then over his shoulder at McKenna. "Great idea. I'll just pull a hospital out of my ass."

"Well, regardless of what you have up your ass, she's having this baby. Soon. We've got to find somewhere that's not a car to do it."

Ely seemed to be gritting his teeth, but thankfully he swallowed whatever comment he wanted to make. He kept his gaze straight ahead. She pretended he wasn't looking at the clock, but he probably was. They were four, maybe five hours from sunset.

"Pulling over now isn't a great idea."

"It doesn't matter. As nice as this Cayenne is, there's not enough room in the back to deliver a baby. Besides, we can't drive through the night. Even with what we got from the airport, we don't have the gas for it. Not to drive straight through the night."

Because as panic-inducing as looking at the clock was, looking at the gas gauge was that much worse.

"Fine. Where do you want to pull over?"

She scanned the horizon, looking for anything that might be suitable. The next mile marker said the town of Emmet was three miles off. "There," she pointed to the sign. "They'll have a Wal-Mart. A grocery store. Something."

Except Emmet was a one-stop town, without even a stoplight. They passed the cotton gin and the Tractor Supply, but no Wal-Mart.

"You got any other bright ideas?" he asked.

Three minutes after turning on to Main Street, they left town. Lily counted the passing time by McKenna's contractions.

"I got nothing," she muttered. Ely was about to turn the car around when she spotted a white shape looming on the horizon. "Wait. What's that?"

Ely squinted in the direction she was pointing. "The set of a horror movie?" he asked dryly.

"No, it's a house."

At my direction Ely slowed the car and turned off into the driveway. A minute later, we stopped, maybe a hundred yards from the house. Okay, so it did have a sort of gothic-creepy vibe. It was a classic American farmhouse. Two stories, wide, wrap-around porches. Waist-high weeds in the yard. No vehicles except for a beat-up old truck, which looked like it hadn't run even in the Before.

Ely looked at her. "Seriously, you want to stop here? 'Cause there was a Gas-n-Sip back in town. There's at least a beer cooler."

"And that would be better?"

"Wouldn't be worse."

"Look, it's two stories. There's nothing else around it. That means anything comes at us, we'll see it first."

"Oh, yay. Because that's what makes the Ticks so damn hard to kill: my bad vision."

"Come on, in this case the isolation is a tactical advantage. Plus, there's a fireplace."

"What? Did you want to roast marshmallows?"

She gritted her teeth at his comment. "Actually, I was thinking we could at least start a fire and boil water."

"Boil water?" Ely inched the car farther up the weed-strewn gravel drive.

"That's what people always do in the movies, right? Maybe they do it to . . . I don't know, sterilize stuff."

"Well, this isn't a movie." But despite his tone, he pulled to a stop behind the abandoned truck.

The house looked less creepy up close. Clearly, no one had lived here since the Before, but it had been cared for and it had fared pretty well since then. The windows were intact. The door was still on the hinges.

Ely stopped close to the steps and drummed his thumbs on the steering wheel for a few seconds before blowing out a loud breath. "Damn, I wish I still had my dog."

Lily nodded, unsure what else to say. Because, yeah, in circumstances like this, she could see how a dog could make the difference between life and death.

Finally, Ely reached for the door handle. "Okay, I'll go check it out."

"Just don't red shirt yourself, okay?"

He slanted her a grin. "Don't worry. I'm still in the game."

"No, it's a—" Then she broke off. It probably wasn't the time to explain the allusion to *Star Trek*. "Just be safe."

There weren't enough humans left that anyone was expendable.

"Try to get in without breaking a window. Might as well make it hard for them to smell us in case we need to stay the night."

He nodded, but said, "Let's not count on staying the night."

McKenna's eyes flickered open. "Where's he going?"

"He'll be right back. We found a place for you to have the baby."

"We're in Mexico already?" She looked out the window, her brow furrowing even though her gaze was unfocused.

"No, we found a house. Someplace safe." Lily's heart fluttered anxiously at the lie, but McKenna didn't need anything else to worry about.

Lily kept talking, murmuring more lies, making more promises she couldn't keep. Until Ely rapped the glass with his knuckle to get her attention. She thrust the door open and clambered out. "Did you find a way in?"

He smirked. "Yeah. No broken windows, either. Help McKenna in. All the way up to the second floor, if she can make it. I'm going out to the barn to see if I can find something to barricade the windows."

Ely had left the front door ajar. The foyer opened to living areas on either side and a massive staircase straight ahead. The house smelled musty from being closed up so long. The furniture was worn and aging, though well preserved. They took it slow, pausing every four or five steps when McKenna was hit with a contraction. By the time they made it all the way up, Lily was as out of breath and as sweaty as McKenna. Lily's shoulder—which had been feeling pretty good—was aching from supporting her friend's weight.

Lily guided her into the first bedroom they found. It was pink

and frilly with a four-poster bed. She tried not to think about whoever had lived here in the Before, but she sent up a silent hope that
wherever they were, they would understand that McKenna needed
this bed more than they did. Lily could only guess that this was
going to get messy.

CHAPTER TWENTY-EIGHT

LILY

Things didn't just get messy, they went to hell and back. McKenna didn't want to stay in the bedroom just yet, she wanted to move. They paced up and down the length of the hall. Her water broke, drenching the carpet with pinkish liquid that made Lily's stomach flip over. At that point, Lily found McKenna an old nightgown from one of the closets and changed her into it. She seemed so weak, Lily didn't know how she kept moving, but she did.

Ely avoided the entire upstairs as much as he could. He found food in the pantry. He brought them a box of old Saltines and a half-eaten jar of peanut butter. Even better, he brought candles, which they could light as night fell.

He must have gotten the fireplace working, because the scent of burning wood filled the house, and then maybe a half hour after that, he brought up a bundle of items wrapped in a kitchen towel. Lily propped McKenna against the bedpost and unrolled the bundle. The items were still hot from being boiled. He'd included a pair of sharp-looking scissors, a butcher knife, a pair of kitchen tongs, and a binder clip.

Lily frowned and nudged the air above the clip, being careful not to touch it, just in case. "What's that for?"

"You said you needed to clamp the cord."

"With a binder clip?"

"You got any other ideas?"

"Nope."

She was fresh out. Of ideas. Of reserves. Of strength. She was just out. So she wrapped up the stuff and placed it on top of the dresser. Then, she went back to helping McKenna pace.

Ely must have found plywood, because the hammering shook the whole house. Dusk was starting to fall and the sick feeling in Lily's stomach cranked up with every passing contraction. Every time McKenna's groans ceased, Lily listened for the sounds of Ticks outside the house. They never came. Not yet anyway.

She didn't know how much time passed. It felt like days. Finally, McKenna sat weakly on the edge of bed and gasped out, "I think it's time to push."

The words were barely out of her mouth when ripple after ripple coursed over her belly and a moan tore through her chest.

"How do you know?" In the movies, the doctor always told the mother when it was time. But there was no doctor here and Lily was suddenly, painfully aware of her own ineptitude. She couldn't do this. There was no way she could do this. But it didn't matter, because McKenna was pushing. Without Lily's encouragement or her help.

Lily lunged for her, grabbing her arms as she started to slide off the bed. She trembled under McKenna's weight as pain rocketed through her shoulder. She called out for Ely, her cries mingling with McKenna's. A second later, she stopped pushing, her weight sagging.

"Ely! Get in here!" She could hear him moving on the other side of the door as seconds ticked past. "Now!"

"What?" he asked, hovering by the door.

"Help me!"

She was barely standing, keeping McKenna wedged between the bed and her body. She didn't have the strength to hold her up and she could feel her legs slipping out from under her on the soggy carpet.

"Jesus, Lily. Get her up on the bed."

"What do you think I'm trying to do?"

"No. Want to—" McKenna gasped. "Stand."

"Help me get her up!" Lily ordered.

He held up his hands, palm out. "Hey, never argue with a pregnant woman."

"Then hold her!"

He swallowed visibly. Then took a step closer. He didn't seem to know where to put his hands; finally, with trembling muscles, Lily just thrust McKenna at him. McKenna sagged into Ely as she started pushing again.

He wedged himself behind her, braced against the bed, supporting her weight. Thank God Ely was stronger than Lily was. For once, that smart-ass smirk was wiped off his face. Then his gaze darted up to Lily's. "Hey, if I'm holding her, you've got to get down there to catch the baby."

"What?"

"She's pushing, man. That means the baby is going to come out. You need to be there to catch it."

Ah, shit.

"Can't you get her up on the bed?" Lily asked. That was how it was always done in the movies. On a bed. In a hospital. Where things made sense.

"No, man. I wasn't joking. You never argue with a pregnant lady. That's what my *abuela* always said anyway. And she was a nurse. She said you let a woman do whatever she wants because it's her body and she knows."

"Oh, great. If your *abuela* has such great advice, why didn't you trot it out until now?"

Ely didn't answer because McKenna was pushing again. Anyway, she knew the answer. He hadn't trotted out the advice because he didn't want to be here. Not any more than Lily wanted to be here. None of them wanted this.

She stepped back, pushing her hair out of her face while she considered her options. She dug a ponytail holder out of her pocket and yanked her hair back into it. He was right. This was so not what she'd signed up for, but this wasn't McKenna's choice, either. None of this was, and Lily didn't have time to be squeamish anymore.

McKenna's feet were bare and widespread. Ely's feet bracketed hers, keeping them from sliding farther apart. Lily knelt by her feet and tried not to freak out. How had anyone else ever done this?

How was this the beginning of life? This act, which seemed so violent. So primal. How was this how it all began, for everyone? And for most of human history, it had happened just like this. In homes and bedrooms, without electricity. Without doctors. Without medicine or help if something went wrong.

She was not the first scared, eighteen-year-old girl to kneel helpless nearby while her friend labored to bring a life into the world. Logic dictated she wouldn't be the last. And something beyond logic, too.

As wrong and as horrific and as horrible as this all seemed, it also somehow felt right. Like this was how it was supposed to be. Women helping other women to do the impossible. To do this difficult and dangerous thing.

Then, suddenly, McKenna gave one more big push and the baby's head slipped through. And a moment after that, the rest of the baby's body wiggled free. Lily caught her in a towel. Her head was huge compared to the rest of her. She was covered in slime and looked unnaturally pale and wrinkled, but she let out a cry almost immediately, stretching and kicking her legs.

Ely's strength must have given out, because he sank to the ground, bringing McKenna with him. Holding the baby, Lily scrambled back out of the way of sprawling arms and legs. McKenna barely had the strength to keep her eyes open. Her head lolled back against Ely's shoulder. She was shaking and pale. Ely just stared at the baby in Lily's hands. His expression a mixture of horror and awe.

She felt all that, too. Plus a great helping of relief. Whatever else happened from here, the baby was alive. Lily might not know jack about birthing babies, but at least she recognized alive when she saw it. Somehow, in this crazy, messed-up world, in this world where nothing made sense anymore and where no one was safe, somehow, McKenna's baby had made it. She was alive. She was healthy. For now, in this moment, she was safe.

With as much wrong as there was in the world, good things could still happen.

She could regret almost everything that had happened since the Before. But she couldn't regret this.

CHAPTER TWENTY-NINE

CARTER

After the apocalypse, after you've lost your home and your family, after you've buried friends, you might think it'd be hard to know where rock bottom is. You might think it's hard to know exactly when you're beaten.

It's not.

Defeat isn't just being caught. It's knowing there's no one else to blame and no one left to fight for. I mean, who was I kidding? Sure, my goals seemed noble—save humanity, right?

But really, I'd only been in it for the girl. All this time that I fought, that I searched Farm after Farm, liberating people, organizing people. I'd done it for Lily. To find her. To keep her safe.

But what was the point? I couldn't keep her safe. I didn't get to be with her. And obviously, I was a miserable leader.

Right now, the best thing that could happen for the entire rebellion was for me to get caught. If I was extremely lucky, the Elites would figure out what had happened when they couldn't contact me, and they'd get the hell back to Utah. If the best that I could hope for was that I was the only one to pay for my mistakes, then I could live with that.

I guess in the end, I was just so effing tired. I was tired of the constant responsibility, of the fear that I might make the wrong decision. That I might have ruined everything. That I might get everyone killed.

If I could have had Lily, maybe I could have made peace with all of that. But without her, what was the point?

It was all so goddamn hard and for once—just for once—I wanted to take the easy way out. I wanted to just lie down and let the bad guys win, because honestly, I wasn't winning either way. So I might as well just roll over, right?

I walked through the gates of the Farm in handcuffs, my head hung low. It wasn't the first time I'd come in to a Farm this way, but it was the first time I didn't have an exit strategy.

Pit Bull led me through the Farm himself, his tranq rifle poking me in the back every time my steps slowed.

Zeke was up ahead, talking to the other two Collabs, guys Zeke greeted as Victor and James.

"If I'd known that's why he was sneaking off, I never would have let him go," Pit Bull said, giving me another surly poke.

I slanted a look back at Pit Bull. "You didn't know?"

Was Zeke's side trip to Utah something he'd come up with on his own?

"Nah, he just disappeared. If I'd known he had a lead on you, I would have gone with him."

"On me?"

"Yeah. Who would have thought Zeke could have brought in the great Carter Olson. I never would have thought he had the balls to pull off something like this."

This little speech tripped me up. "You know who I am?"

"Shit, yeah. You're one of the most wanted terrorists in the New Republic."

Again, I stumbled. "Terrorist?"

"The New Republic released the news about a month ago. Thirty-four counts of conspiring to commit treason. Twenty-seven counts of aggravated assault. And fifty-four counts of kidnapping a minor." Pit Bull reached out and shoved me in the middle of my back. "You would not believe the pain in the ass the Greens have been since then. Like you're some kind of friggin' hero. You'd think you were Iron Man."

Despite myself, despite being at rock bottom, despite my exhaustion, I laughed at that. Iron Man? Seriously? Because they had no idea how wrong they were.

Pit Bull jerked me to a halt and whirled me around to face him. "You think that's funny? You think that's friggin' hysterical? The fact that you're making my life a pain in the ass? That our Dean has left because of you? That our friggin' food shipments have stopped because of you? You think that's funny?"

"Your Dean has left? Your shipments have stopped?"

Was that possible? Was Zeke right? Because to hear Pit Bull describe it, this Farm was in serious trouble. Just like Zeke had described. So why had Zeke betrayed me?

I was still trying to wrap my brain around it when we reached the Dean's office. It's almost always at the top of some admin building. In the biggest, plushest office on campus. This Dean was no different.

Pit Bull had swiped his security card and opened the door. Victor, James, and I followed Zeke in. A moment later we were piling out of an elevator on the top floor.

The elevator opened up into some kind of reception area. A couple of Collabs sat in front of a flat-screen TV watching one of those Kate Beckinsale vampire movies. Assholes.

Pit Bull marched across the room and hit one of them upside his head. "Turn that shit off." The other guy scrambled for the remote and a second later Kate vanished. "You two go patrol the perimeter. Make sure every Collab here is suited up and on patrol."

"Why? The Dean's not—"

"Unless you want to be chained up outside like a freakin' Green, you'll follow orders."

The two Kate Beckinsale fans didn't even wait for the elevator. They dashed straight for the fire stairs and vanished.

Zeke whirled me around and pushed me through the door into the Dean's office. It was a pretty typical set up. Oversized desk. Lots of book shelves. A couple of chairs against the wall on either side of the door. As soon as the door closed, the Pit Bull started giving Zeke a hard time. I let Zeke push me into one of the chairs, and ducked my head, trying to look whipped, but inside, my mind was whirling. This Farm really was in trouble. And to hear Pit Bull talk about it, I was partly to blame. And right now, I was the only person who could save them all.

And no matter how much I wanted to just give up, I couldn't. Because if I just rolled over now and let these Collabs win, then I would be no better than they were. If I had the chance to save people and let it slip by because it was too hard, than wasn't that worse than what the Collabs did?

And maybe I didn't have Lily anymore, but I still knew exactly what she'd say about that. She wouldn't give up. Ever. She would fight this until there was nothing left in her to fight. And so would I.

All I needed was something to pick the lock with. All I needed was a moment alone to find a friggin' paper clip. Then I could almost do this in my sleep. It was the kind of thing I used to practice, just for the hell of it, back in my room at the academy. Looking back, there were so many things about my time there that made sense only in retrospect.

We had all the normal military school stuff: discipline, exercise, and duties, plus the normal school stuff. But then, we had stuff you'd never want to teach a bunch of troubled teens: combat simulations, military strategy. Real-world covert skills. How to hack a computer system and cut the electricity to a building. How to pick a lock and scale a fence. Real guerilla warfare stuff. Who teaches that to kids?

A vampire building an army, that's who.

But who was I to complain since those skills were going to get my ass out of here. If I could ever get a moment alone to search the desk.

Just then, there was a knock on the door. Pit Bull broke off whatever he'd been saying and glared at me as he walked past. I glanced over at Zeke while Pit Bull opened the door. I expected gloating, maybe a flash of guilt. Instead he frowned at me, shifting his shoulders in a what's up? gesture. What the hell?

He glanced over at Pit Bull to make sure he was still distracted. Then he held his wrists together, like they were cuffed in front of him and then jerked them apart in a sharp little gesture.

By the time Pit Bull turned around a second later, Zeke was playing with the paperweight again. He smirked at me. Yeah, there was that gloating I'd been expecting. But what had that other gesture meant? He seemed to be telling me to break free of the handcuffs.

I ducked my head again and let the sleeves of my jacket cover my hands. Then, slowly, carefully, I eased my wrists apart . . . and felt the handcuffs give. The pressure slipped one of the teeth free, then another.

All this time, I hadn't really been captured. And Zeke apparently, hadn't really betrayed me.

But that didn't mean I was home free. Far from it. Even if Zeke was on my side, we still had to subdue Pit Bull—one of the bigger, nastier Collabs I'd ever run across. Even though Pit Bull was still giving Zeke hell about running off and not paying any attention to me, I was excruciatingly aware of each click the handcuffs made as I eased my hands out of them.

I watched his every move, letting the handcuffs click when he strode to the other side of the room. Letting them click again when his voice rose as he yelled at Zeke about how Zeke should have let him in on his plan. Yeah, I agreed with him there. Zeke and I were going to have a talk about that, too.

Zeke seemed to have realized that I was timing wiggling free of the cuffs to the loud noises in the room, because suddenly he hopped up, his feet slamming heavily to the floor and he dropped the paperweight on the desk.

I got two clicks out of that and was finally able to ease my right hand out of the cuffs.

Pit Bull turned to follow Zeke's progression across the room. He was only a few steps away. His back was toward me. I went for it. I jumped to my feet and wrapped the chain of the handcuffs around Pit Bull's neck, yanking hard before he could get his fingers under the links. He flailed around, but I managed to stay behind him. I had the fingers of my right hand wrapped around the one cuff and my wrist through the other. The metal bit into the skin at my wrist and on my fingers.

He couldn't shake me free, so he stretched both hands up over his head and grabbed fistfuls of my hair. I've been shot. I've had my shoulders sliced open with razor blades over and over again to insert and remove chips. I've been in serious pain. You wouldn't think having your hair pulled hurts in comparison. Trust me. It does.

And he was damn strong. When I still didn't let go, he swung his whole body around and I almost went flying off. Then I heard a sharp little pop and a moment later, Pit Bull's fingers slipped through my hair and he let me go. He sank to his knees and just toppled forward. I let go of the cuffs just in time to prevent myself from being pulled forward, too.

I felt a moment of . . . something. Remorse, maybe? I'd killed Ticks before, but I'd never killed a human. At least not that I knew of. And, yes, it had been him or me. But not even just that. It had been him or me and all of my crew and all of Base Camp. Even knowing he would have killed me in a second in order to save himself, I still felt nauseated. Like someone had ripped out my stomach.

The weight of all those deaths at Base Camp. Yeah, I was prepared to shoulder that. But I hadn't been prepared for this.

Then I looked up and saw the tranq rifle in Zeke's hands.

I hadn't killed Pit Bull. Zeke had just shot him with the tranq rifle.

I sucked in a deep breath and made a conscious effort to slow my heart rate.

When I trusted myself to speak, I said, "Thanks. Good move."

Zeke stood there, the rifle dangling from his hand. His skin looked a little pale.

"Holy crap," he said. His gaze moved up to mine. "Ely said you were hard core, but I had no idea. You freakin' tried to strangle him with your handcuffs."

"What'd you expect me to do?"

"You were four feet away from the tranq rifle!"

I yanked the other side of the handcuffs off my wrist and dropped them on the chair.

"Yeah, well, my handcuffs were only four inches away from his neck. I couldn't risk it." I looked around the room. "You have any real handcuffs? Or better yet, a zip tie?"

Zeke nodded, his expression still dazed. "There's a supply cabinet just down the hall on the left. Check in there."

I crossed over to Zeke and eased the tranq rifle out of his hands. "He'll be out for at least thirty minutes. I'll stay here with him, you go get the zip ties. Act natural. Don't talk to anyone. If you can get your hands on another tranq rifle and more darts, do it."

Zeke nodded mutely. He was almost to the door when he turned back around and said, "I'm um . . . sorry about the . . . you know." He mimed punching me. "I saw the Collabs sneaking up and knew I had to do something."

Funny, thirty minutes ago, he seemed like such an arrogant jerk and I'd been ready to kick his ass as soon as I got out of those cuffs. Now that I knew he'd just been play-acting, I was glad he was on my side. Now that he knew what I was actually capable of, he was rattled. And maybe more than a little scared of me.

Hell, maybe I was scared of myself, too.

It was easy to forget that we—none of us—were as badass as we wanted to be. A year ago, we'd just been kids. I hadn't thought so then. I never would have admitted it. Then.

Now, looking back, I didn't even know that kid I used to be anymore. Sometimes I felt like I barely knew *this* guy.

This guy, the one who had stood outside the Farm, desensitizing himself to death and violence so that he'd have the will to kill another human? When had I become this guy?

Since Zeke was still looking at me with that wary, nervous edge to his eyes, I forced myself to smile at him. "Hey, you could have just told me you wanted to pretend to bring me in like a prisoner."

He gave a nervous laugh. "Yeah, wish I'd thought of that now. But I had to think fast when I saw the Collab out there on the street." He shrugged. "Besides, you needed to seem really pissed off or they wouldn't have bought it. I mean, shit. You're *Carter Olson*. No one would have believed I'd brought you down if they hadn't seen it themselves."

He was gone before I could ask him exactly what he meant by that. He'd said my name in tones of mixed awe and horror. Like I was two parts bogeyman and three parts Keyser Söze. Like I was a big friggin' deal.

Maybe to him, I was. The thought made me uncomfortable. I didn't need any more power or influence than I already had. So I shoved the thought aside and got to work.

Alone with Pit Bull, I turned his head to the side and checked his pulse, which was still strong. I left him where he was for now. It was rare, but every once in a while, people asphyxiated while they were out. I didn't want to have not killed him on purpose only to accidentally kill him later.

Since he was out cold, I searched the room for anything else that might come in handy. In one of the drawers, I found a box of matches, a pocketknife, and a box of Clif bars. In another drawer, under a false bottom, I found a pistol and full clip. I loaded the clip and swapped it out for my handgun since Zeke had emptied mine. I would get the bullets from Zeke later, but it never hurt to have an extra gun.

I thought about what I'd said to Armadale back in Utah, about how Texas had fallen because we were all so damn eager to kill one another. About how fear and suspicion had made things so much worse for us here. All of that was true. I believed every word. And yet here I was, grabbing every damn gun I could find, standing over the body of the guy I'd nearly killed.

We had to find a better way. This shit had to stop.

But it wasn't going to stop with me. There were a lot of frightened kids outside this building who needed someone to kick some ass. For now, I was the only one they had who could do it.

I was sliding the gun into the holster at the back of my waistband when Zeke came back in with the ties and an extra rifle.

I took one from him and quickly tied up Pit Bull. The office had an attached bathroom, so I had Zeke help me drag his body in there. I did a quick survey of the room but didn't see anything that Pit Bull could use to cut open the ties. If he was determined, he'd get out, but not quickly. Then I headed back to the reception area.

I paused with my hand on the knob. "The other two guards still out there?"

Zeke nodded. "Victor and James? Yeah. Now they're watching that movie. Didn't even notice when I went out for the zip ties."

"Did you know either of them before you deserted?"

"I knew Victor pretty well."

"He a decent guy or a fascist bully like Pit Bull in there?"

Zeke frowned. Maybe because he didn't know the meaning of the word *fascist* or maybe because he didn't know my code name.

So I added, "The first officer. The head Collab. That guy I just nearly killed?"

"Oh. Brad."

"Yeah. Him. Either of them as bad as he is?"

Zeke shook his head, but he was frowning. "I don't think so. Most of us aren't. We just—"

But I didn't have the patience to listen to Zeke's excuses. "Most Collabs never meant to hurt anyone. You just took the easy way out. You protected yourself. I get it." I pinned Zeke with a stare. "But that's not who you are anymore. When you throw in with me, that has to change. If you want to take the easy way out, I can

tranq you right now. You'll wake up in thirty minutes, zip tied next
to your commanding officer. If things go wrong on my end you still
have plausible deniability."

Zeke shook his head. "No. I'm in."

"Are you in? Or are you all in? Because if you're in this just to
save your own ass, I don't need that kind of trouble."

Zeke's gaze narrowed and his shoulders straightened just a little. "If I was in it for my own ass, I wouldn't have told you this
Farm was in trouble, would I?"

Good point. Still, I'd had to ask.

"Okay. Do you know any other Collabs who you can trust? Any
you think we can win over to our side?"

"I know of at least three guys. They know something's wrong,
too. They'll want to help."

"Okay. Good. Do you know where you can find them?"

"This time of day, they'll be in the dorms. We all worked the
night shifts together."

"Once we get out of here, securing the rest of the Collabs and
finding the ones who could be allies will be our top priority. After
that, we're going to need to convince some Greens. Who do you
know who's got influence among the other Greens?"

Zeke thought for a minute and nodded. "I can think of a couple
of people. There's a guy. Named Wilson, I think. Real geeky, but
everyone likes him. He's been talking to people for months now
about how the Greens need to be better organized."

"And he's gotten away with it? On most Farms, a guy like that
would be fed to the Ticks."

"He's Brad's baby brother."

"Oh." And Lily had thought she'd had problems keeping her
sister safe. I almost felt sorry for Brad.

"Yeah." Zeke winced. "And there's this girl. Her name's Trinia. She hangs out with Wilson a lot, but I don't think they're . . . you know . . . together." Zeke paused for a second and I thought he might have been blushing. "Anyway, she seems to take care of a lot of other Greens. The younger ones, you know. She watches out for them. They'll go anywhere she goes."

"Okay. We'll start there."

"And there's this one other guy. He was brought in about a month ago. His name is Joe. Even though he hasn't been here very long, people like him. There are even rumors that he was at another Farm and escaped."

I hesitated for a second, wondering. How crazy would that be if this Joe, this guy who had randomly shown up at this Farm in Texas after all these weeks, was McKenna's Joe?

How crazy lucky would that be? How happy would it make McKenna if I could bring him back alive? How happy would it make Lily?

But then I remembered that Lily and McKenna weren't even at Base Camp anymore. Wherever they were, it was far away from me. They were getting farther and farther away from danger—I hoped. And even if by some miracle it was Joe, how would I find McKenna to tell her? Not that it would be him, even if the name and timing were right. Because that's not the kind of thing that happened in this world.

Once, I'd thought it would be a miracle if I ever found Lily again. Now I knew it was just another form of torture. Having her, but being unable to keep her safe. Finding her, but not being able to keep her at all.

"Good," I said to Zeke. "Once we've secured the Collabs, we'll need to find those three first."

I swung the door open. Just as Zeke had said, James and Victor were watching Kate Beckinsale on the tiny screen. They'd even set their tranq rifles down on the receptionist desk behind them, a good six feet from their chairs. I didn't bother securing the rifles yet, because I didn't want to make any noise. Zeke followed my lead; for a Collab, he was light on his feet. Victor and James didn't even look away from their movie until they felt the nose of the tranq rifles on their shoulder blades.

"Listen carefully, boys." I kept my voice soft in case there was someone else on the floor that I didn't know about. "Zeke and I are taking over. Neither of you is stupid enough to think this Farm is still functioning like it should. The Dean's gone. He's left you to die. Unless we stop it, the fences are going to go down soon, too." I inched back a step to give them room to twist in their chairs. When they were both looking at me, I continued. "We've already taken out Brad. We're going to work our way through the rest of the Collabs. Either you're in or you're out. If you're out, I tranq you and you wait this out locked in a room. If you're in, we could use your help. Which is it?"

James's gaze flickered infinitesimally to the desk where his tranq rifle lay well out of his reach. He was thinking about going for it.

"Wrong answer," I said and fired one of the tranq darts into his chest. He jerked to his feet, but swayed almost immediately. A second later, he staggered backward and passed out in the chair.

I turned my rifle on Victor. "How about you?"

He held his hands up in a gesture of surrender. "I'm in!"

Ten minutes later, we'd secured the top floor, had two more Collabs in custody and one more—a guy Zeke swore by—on our side. Better still, Taylor had reported back in that he'd found the site of the solar array and they'd secured it. Which meant we might—might—be able to at least keep the fences working for a few more days while we devised a game plan for getting these Greens out alive.

Maybe I was wrong. Maybe things didn't *always* go bad.

CHAPTER THIRTY

MEL

I know we're in trouble when Sebastian asks me to drive. A passenger all my life, I've never taken the wheel, except for bumper cars at theme parks, but how can I say no when we were hunting all night and he's been driving all day. He seems exhausted, so I slide into the driver's seat. The car feels like it has a mind of its own, lurching all over the road. I control it just barely, like I control my hunger. I wonder if that's why Sebastian makes me drive, but then I notice that he's looking paler as he directs me through the streets of an abandoned town I don't know. We're in the desert somewhere.

Soon he doesn't have to tell me where to go. There is light ahead and I am drawn to it like a moth . Where there is light, there will be food.

Though it is night, the area around the fence is lit up like a football stadium. The fences are taller even than those I've seen around Farms. Though we are surrounded by desert, a perfectly manicured green lawn stretches for hundreds of acres inside the fence. A cluster of pale, five-story buildings sits in the distance. And there are people walking from building to building. Even a crew of workers fretting over the landscaping.

"What is this place?" I say on a whisper. "Is it some sort of Farm?"

Sebastian taps his fingers against his leg in that world-weary way he has. "No. Not as such." He looks at me. "Can you not guess?"

My mind races. He expects so much of me, but never more than I can give. If he thinks I should guess, the answer must be obvious. "This is Roberto's lair."

His chuckle is strained. "Ah no, dear Kitten. If it was Roberto's lair, he would have yanked me from the car long before now."

Okay, not a Farm. Not Roberto's.

I feel a jolt of excitement. "This is the lair of someone else. Some other vampire I haven't met yet."

"Very good, Melly."

Before I can ask more, someone walks out of the guard station at the gate. I roll down the window. He is human. The first human I have seen since my death. The aroma of him is intoxicating. It's infinitely more appealing than the muck running through the veins of Ticks. This human, however, is no defenseless snack. He holds an assault rifle clutched to his chest.

"Can I help you?"

A human? Asking if he can help two vampires? Unless he wants to open a vein, then no. "I doubt it."

Sebastian leans across the console to look out my window, tipping his sunglasses down his nose. "Tell your mistress I am here and that I formally request sanctuary in compliance with my rights as a signee of the Meso-Americana Accords of 1409."

The guard stares dumbly at Sebastian. "What?"

A crash rocks the car as something heavy lands on the roof. The guard stumbles back. I press myself back against the car seat, my pulse suddenly racing in time with a wild new beat. Sebastian glances up and quirks an eyebrow. "Never mind. She's here now."

Without a word to me, Sebastian climbs from the car. I sit there a moment, heart pounding and unsure what to do. Nothing in my weeks as a vampire had prepared me for this—not for this fortified compound, not for the flagrant use of electricity. Certainly not for the presence of another vampire.

Her music is fierce and fiery. Like skate punk and metal death, which shouldn't be feminine at all, but somehow is, though that makes her no less terrifying.

I scramble from the car and scurry to Sebastian's side. As I round the rear of the car, the other vampire pounces lithely to the ground. She is dressed entirely in black leather, with a sheath of long, black hair that gleams almost blue in the moonlight. She has on so much eye makeup, I can't even tell if she's pretty, only that there is a fierce cruelty in her smile.

"Hello, my dear," she coos to Sebastian. "I was wondering if you would stop by or if I would have to run you to ground."

"I wouldn't dream of insulting you by traveling so close to the heart of your territory without complying with our laws."

She nods, but her lips curl in distaste. "So you have decided to seek sanctuary. You have been on the road a long time. Has Roberto edged you out of your territory?"

Her words are an insult. I sense it in the tensing of Sebastian's muscles, but his answer is easy charm. "Not at all, Sabrina. I have merely been busy."

She throws back her head and laughs. And I can see suddenly that the skin of her neck isn't as supple or youthful as I thought at first. "Busy? Is that the most apt description of your meddling?"

"I think so."

Sabrina turns her gaze to me. "And what is this? This little thing you've brought me?" She arches an eyebrow. "Not a snack, surely." She inhales deeply, and I have the urge to shrink into myself. She cocks her head in a way that reminds me weirdly of myself when I was autistic. "No, she's . . ." And then she laughs, clapping her hands together like a giddy child. "Oh, she's just a baby! And you brought her to me. What fun."

Sabrina clasps my arms and holds me out to examine me like a loving aunt about to pinch my cheeks. There is something both maternal and malevolent in her gaze that makes my skin crawl.

Then she spins back to the guard and snaps her fingers. "Show them in." She winks at Sebastian. "I'd offer to race you, but you, poor boy, must be feeling the effects of trespassing. Join me in the penthouse. I'll have refreshments waiting. That should perk you up."

With that, she zips away into the night, a soundless blur of movement. The guard is still baffled. When he makes a move toward the car, Sebastian cuts him off. "I'll drive it myself, thank you."

I slip into the passenger seat. It is obvious to me now that Sebastian has been dragging for the past several hours because of Sabrina. Being on her territory has cost him. How did he describe it? Like a berserker rage. Like an uncontrollable force. Yet, he has controlled it. Still, I can see how that control has worn him thin, though his pain seems to have lessened now that he's formally requested sanctuary.

As Sebastian drives through the gates, I get a better look at the buildings and realize this must have been a business complex, a multi-building campus for one of the premier technology companies in the Before.

I lean forward to look at the logo on the building. "I had their cell phone."

"You and half the population of the United States," Sebastian mutters. "Even I had one of her phones."

"Her phones? She didn't just take over all of these buildings when things fell?"

"Goodness, no. Sabrina has run this company from behind the scenes since the late nineties. How else do you think it became the most respected company in the world? When the Ticks started spreading west toward here, she merely consolidated her kine onto the property."

"Is it a Farm then?"

"I believe she thinks of it more as a free-roaming ranch."

I can't suppress a sneer. "How generous of her."

He slants me a look. "Be careful, Melanie. I have tolerated more freedom in your speech than others might. For now, you are Sabrina's guest. Her hospitality will last only so long as she believes you are maintaining your responsibilities as a guest."

"My responsibilities?"

"Is it not part of the social contract that the guest be respectful of the rules of her host's home?"

"Okay. Got it. Be polite." I look over at Sebastian. We're following a long, winding drive across the lawn. There are no other cars on the road and even the people seem to have scattered. "Exactly how long are we staying?"

"That depends."

"On what?"

"On whether or not she accepts my gift."

"Your gift?"

"Of course, I brought a gift. It would be rude to request even temporary sanctuary without bringing her something in return."

For some reason I don't understand, a shiver of dread tiptoes down my spine. Maybe I should ask him what he means, but I can't make myself do it. Instead I stare at the buildings and the security Sabrina has set up.

"Did she know about the Ticks beforehand?" I ask, studying the landscape. Even though it's night, I can see wind turbines spinning just beyond the fences. What at first looked like ornamental landscaping, I now realize is agriculture. There is no wasted space. It is the very model of compact efficiency.

"I don't believe anyone fully understood what the Ticks would become or the damage they would do." He stops the car in front of a building with sleek modern architecture. "But no, I don't think she knew ahead of time. Why?"

"It's been less that a year since the initial outbreak. She's built all this in such a short period of time."

"You think this is impressive, you should see the Red Empire in Atlanta," he murmured with a sneer.

"The Red Empire?" I repeat dumbly. "There's an empire of blood in Atlanta?"

"No, it's not blood. Don't be so literal." He gives me a look like I'm being exceptionally naive. "Well, there's a reason the cans are red."

Then his meaning sinks in. "Truly?"

He practically snorts. "You don't sell ten billion ounces of soda a day without a whole network of *abducturae*."

"And the bottled water?" I ask, even though this makes the most sense of all.

"Of course. That bit took a lot of power to pull off. Humans are gullible, but they aren't stupid."

"Is that common?"

"What?"

"Major companies—products we all loved—owned and operated by vampire empires?"

"Of course."

Somehow, this makes me sad. Are we humans so insignificant that every aspect of our lives is controlled by monsters? But there's the flaw in my thinking. I can no longer include myself with the humans.

CHAPTER THIRTY-ONE

LILY

They stayed at the house as long as they could, letting McKenna rest, but it wasn't long before they realized they were in trouble.

Suddenly Ely appeared in the doorway. "It's time to get out of here."

"You think?" As if to make Lily's point, the night air was once again rent by the piercing howl of a Tick.

"There'll be time for sarcasm later. Let's move."

She had already been packing some bags and she had a few ready by the door. Just stuff she'd found around the house that she'd thought might be useful. Now, she went back to the bed, where McKenna lay curled around the fidgeting baby, whom McKenna had named Josie. Lily touched McKenna's shoulder.

"Time to get up. We've got to move." McKenna didn't even twitch. A flicker of fear skittered across her nerves. Lily shook her harder. "Come on, honey, get up."

Slowly McKenna's eyelashes fluttered. She turned her head. "Huh?"

"We gotta go. Ticks are headed our way. We gotta get out now."

"Okay." She tried to wedge her arm under her. "I feel so strange."

"You're supposed to feel strange," Lily reminded her as she picked up the baby. "You just had a baby. You'll get your strength back."

"I'm so cold."

"We'll bring the blankets with us. Come on, Ely. Help me get her up."

Lily sat on the edge of the bed and tried to wedge her spare arm under McKenna. The second she touched McKenna's skin, she knew something was very wrong. Her skin was as cold as chilled lunch meat and just as clammy. On instinct, Lily pulled back the covers.

From the waist down, McKenna was covered in blood. Not a little blood, either. More blood than Lily had ever seen. Her stomach flopped over and bile mixed with peanut butter crawled back up her esophagus.

She called out, "Ely!"

He turned around. He went instantly pale and staggered back a step. He said nothing. No vulgar stream of curse words. No gasp. Just deathly silence.

Then slowly he crossed to the bed, shaking his head. "Oh, God, McKenna." His voice broke. "I'm sorry."

She hadn't looked down yet, and when she did, her head bobbed weakly.

Lily thrust the baby into Ely's arms. "We've got to stop the bleeding."

"No," he said. He grabbed her arm before she could reach for the blanket. "You'll get it all over you."

He yanked her hard, pulling her from the bed. Lily's legs wobbled and she would have gone down to her knees, if he hadn't supported her weight.

"No!" She struggled against his hold, but he was gripping her arm in an iron-tight grasp, walking backward toward the door. "Ely, stop! We've got to stop the bleeding."

"No." His voice was cold now. Dead. "We've got to go. Now."

"No!" Lily screamed again. Her heart was being torn from her chest. "No, we can save her! We can get her to the car. We can drive."

He whipped her around so she was facing him. "They'll smell that blood. They already do. That's why they're coming."

They were talking over each other now. Neither listening. Lily didn't care. All she knew was that she couldn't leave McKenna. She couldn't lose McKenna.

"We're faster than they are. We'll—"

"Anywhere we go, they'll be there."

"I'm not leaving her. I need—"

"Think, Lily! We can't—"

"He's right," McKenna said from the bed.

Her words were soft, barely audible, but somehow they both heard her.

"I'm not going to make it," she said, her eyes wide with terror. "You need to go now. Take Josie and go."

"No," Lily said again.

"I can't even walk."

"This isn't what you want. You want to live. I know you do. You want to live to fight for Josie."

She met Lily's gaze dead on and when she spoke, her voice trembled. "This way she'll have a chance. This *is* me fighting for her."

"No!" Lily said again, nearly senseless now. McKenna was right. Ely was right. But Lily couldn't face it yet. She collapsed on the floor, sobbing at the brutal, unreasonable horror of it all.

Ely grabbed her arm, wrenching her to her feet and shaking her until she met his gaze. "Get it together! We have to get out of here. Now. Either you walk out or I carry you out."

"I'm not leaving her," Lily protested.

"You are." He gave her another shake, somehow managing to shake her and hold Josie at the same time. "I promised Carter I would keep you alive and I will. I didn't make any promises about this baby. If I have to put her down to carry you out, I will do it."

She looked into his eyes, nearly recoiling at the cruel determination she saw there. He would do it. He would drop this precious newborn and leave her here to die. He would carry Lily out and leave Josie.

If Lily didn't get it together, Josie would die, along with her mother.

"Do you believe me?" he growled.

She nodded, unable to speak past her grief and her burning hatred.

"Then stand up and walk out of here." He released her arm. Her legs wobbled but she stood. He thrust the baby into her arms. She felt so tiny and fragile. "I'm going to go check outside. You do what you have to do to say good-bye and be out front in two minutes. Don't get any blood on you."

Lily nodded past her tears, her grief, her rage. He didn't see her nod because he was already gone.

Lily walked over to the bed, careful not to look at anything beyond McKenna's gaunt face and hollow eyes, but her peripheral vision caught the bright-red oval of blood, which seemed to be spreading over more of the bed with every minute that passed. How could a human hold that much blood? How could she still even be alive?

She was so pale lying there in the moonlight that she looked almost blue. Lily clasped her hand, even though her fingers were beyond cold and too weak to squeeze back.

"Thank you," she said, and Lily couldn't believe McKenna was thanking her when Lily was the one who was letting her die.

All she could do in response was shake her head. She couldn't even speak. She couldn't even breathe.

Lily's jaw, her chest, everything was shaking with the urge to sob; it took all she had not to give in to it.

She moved McKenna's arm off her chest and lay baby Josie there, carefully placing her hand back over the blanket, so she could hold her baby one last time, even though she was too weak to do it.

McKenna looked down at her child, tears pouring down her paper-white face. "She looks like Joe. She's beautiful."

Lily nodded. "She has his eyes. And your mouth." She forced the words out, not because she believed them, but because it seemed to be the kind of thing people said about babies. And maybe because she wanted it to be true. She wanted to believe that this tiny baby held a part of her friends.

Then McKenna looked back at her. "You take her now and go. You keep her safe."

Lily nodded, her hands shaking as she picked up the baby.

"It's okay," McKenna said, despite the fear that made her voice quiver. "This is a good way to die."

Lily wanted to scream. It wasn't a good way to die. It was a shitty, horrible way to die. And there was a good chance it would only get worse.

Nothing about this was good. A baby shouldn't lose her mother within hours. Newborn babies shouldn't be orphans. Josie would grow up without knowing her parents. She'd never even see a picture of them. If she grew up at all.

As if to echo her thought, the door flung open again as another howl, much closer this time, went out from a Tick.

Ely stood in the open doorway. "We're out of time. They're here. It'll take them a couple of minutes to find a way in, but they're coming in."

Those words snapped Lily out of her daze. "How many?"

"Three." He scanned the room, then strode over to the bags she had waiting by the foot of the bed. He picked up a backpack, unzipped it, and unceremoniously dumped the contents on the floor. "Put the baby in here. We'll have to wait until they're in the house, then we're going out the window."

"Out the window?" But even as she asked, she was taking the backpack from him. She knew it was the only way out. She grabbed a couple of the towels that had fallen to the ground and shoved them in the bottom with her free hand. Then carefully, past the tears streaming down her face, she placed the baby in the backpack. Tiny as she was, wrapped up tightly in the blanket, she fit right in the bottom. Lily carefully tucked the towel around her head and neck to hold it in place and then zipped it up, leaving a hole in the top. Josie hated it and squealed in anger or maybe fear. Probably fear. Then Lily eased the straps over her shoulders.

"You ready?" Ely asked.

"Almost." Lily turned back to McKenna and sat gingerly on a clean spot near her shoulder. She reached behind her and yanked out the ponytail holder that held her hair back and snapped it onto her wrist. She smoothed out a section of McKenna's hair, talking to her as she braided.

"I'll keep her safe. No matter what."

"I know." McKenna's near-blue lips curled into a wan smile.

"And I'll tell her everything about you and Joe. She'll know how much you loved her. How much you both loved her."

McKenna nodded. Her breathing was shallow now, her gaze losing focus.

"Do you want me to—" Lily couldn't finish the sentence.

"The pity kill?" McKenna asked softly.

Lily nodded. So, McKenna had been awake for that conversation in the freezer.

From near the window, Ely muttered a curse.

By then, she'd reached the end of McKenna's hair. She doubled the braid back on itself and snapped the rubber band on near her scalp, so it caught both ends of the braid. She held out her hand. "Ely, your knife." He slapped it into her palm and she quickly sawed through McKenna's hair. She took the braid and tucked it into her pocket. Someday, she'd pass McKenna's braided hair on to the baby. "She'll always have a part of you."

"You done yet?" Ely asked.

She could barely hear him over the fussing of Josie nestled in the backpack and the roar of blood in her ears. That was all the excuse she needed to ignore him for a moment longer. "You tell Joe I said hey."

McKenna smiled, but her breathing came in panicked bursts now.

Then, from downstairs came the sound of crashing glass and splintering wood. They were sounds she couldn't ignore.

Ely flung open the window. "Get out of here. I'll handle it."

With sorrow choking her, Lily climbed out the open window. An icy blast of wind hit her. She was gasping for breath when the gunfire tore through the silence. Three quick bursts. She flinched at the noise, clutching the window frame.

She looked back through the window as Ely climbed out. With the candlelight still dimly lighting the room, Lily could see McKenna sitting in the bed. Her legs were stretched out in front of her, but the angle was all wrong. Like she'd been trying to move them and couldn't. Like she'd been crushed from the waist down.

She'd turned her torso toward the open bedroom door. The dark holes in her forehead almost weren't visible. She'd faced her death head on. Lily was the only one who wasn't ready.

She never would be.

Feeling like her heart was as broken as her body, she turned her back on McKenna's body and looked out into the darkness of the roof. Ely was already a few steps ahead of her. He was crouched down, skittering sideways toward a tree whose branches reached out toward the house. There was something sinister about his furtive movements. She followed him, knowing she must look the same. This was how you crept away when you left a dead comrade. You skulked through the darkness. There was no nobility in it.

She buried her shame and followed, keeping her steps light but careful. She couldn't trip and fall; that would mean certain death for her and for Josie.

Josie was strangely quiet in the backpack; maybe she was confused. Maybe she liked being jostled.

Lily could hear the Ticks tearing through the house below them, destroying this tiny bit of sanctuary they'd found. They rummaged liked the beasts they were, tearing everything to shreds. It wouldn't be long before they followed the scent of McKenna's blood up to the second story.

At the corner of the house, Lily stared out at the branch and felt her stomach drop. Ely had stopped, too. They both just stared at the tree. From the ground by the front of the house, it had looked like the branch reached the house. The tree was a sprawling live oak. It had looked sturdy. But from here, it was obvious there was at least a four-foot gap between the edge of the roof and the branch.

Ely glanced at her. "Here's what we're going to do. I'm going to jump for the branch and try to shinny down to the ground. Once

I'm down, you lower the backpack to me. It's a couple feet drop. Maybe three or four."

"So basically you want me to throw you the baby." His expression twisted and she held up a hand. "I know. Not helpful."

"You have any better ideas?"

"No." Damn it!

She was supposed to be the smart one, so why didn't she have any better ideas?

She wanted to ask what she should do if he jumped for the branch and fell. If he killed or injured himself trying to get across. Carter would have had some backup plan. That was Carter: the guy with five levels of planning to keep her safe.

But Carter was back at Base Camp and she was out of time. Before she could ask Ely for his thoughts, he was leaping through the air.

Ely was short, squat, and immovable. The kind of guy who looked like he could go head to head with a Mack truck and win.

If she'd had to guess, she would have said he didn't have a graceful bone in his body. Yet somehow when he jumped for the branch, he made it look easy. He landed nimbly on the branch. It swayed beneath his weight, but didn't break. She watched in awe as he moved across it, his arms stretched out like a tightrope walker.

A moment later he was on the ground, beneath her. She slipped the backpack from her shoulders and unbuckled one shoulder strap to give herself more play. Then she lay down on her belly and scooted right up to the edge of the roof before she lowered the bag down. The gutter bit into her armpits as she held her arms over the edge of the roof, dangling the bag from its extended strap. What had seemed like an impossible distance before seemed like nothing now. Ely reached up; she felt his fingertips grazing the bottom of the bag and she released it. Letting go, trusting that he would catch it. He did.

From inside the house, she heard the high-pitched yip of the Ticks followed by what had to be feet thundering up the stairs. They were out of time.

She did some quick calculations. Ely was about her height. With his arms extended, he'd been able to just graze the bottom of the bag. With the strap extended, the bag was maybe three or four feet long. So if she lowered herself over the edge, the drop would only be three or four feet. She could do that, right?

"What are you waiting for?" he growled. "Get down here."

"Give me room!" she called, even as she wiggled her legs over to the edge.

She heard him cursing as he stepped back. She was halfway off the roof when she realized her mistake. She'd forgotten about her shoulder. Pain roared through as the weight of her body tore at the stitches. She felt them ripping open. Her fingers slipped on the edge of the gutter. There was a horrible wrenching noise as the screws pulled loose and the gutter pulled away from the roof.

She let go by instinct, dropping the rest of the way to the ground. She landed badly, her ankle crumbling beneath her. She stumbled back a step before falling hard on her ass.

When she opened her eyes, Ely was standing over her, the backpack cradled against his chest. "Jesus, Lily!"

She couldn't tell if he looked more exasperated or impressed. The fall had knocked the air out of her and she couldn't catch her breath past the twin pains screaming up her shoulder and ankle. Shit.

"Get up. We've got to go. Now!"

With Ely barking orders at her, she had to obey. If that hadn't been bad enough, a howl of excitement came from inside the house. They were probably done with McKenna by now. The thought sent a sick squelch of anguish through her, but she didn't have time to think about it. She had to move.

Despite the pain in her heart and her body, she had to move. Because she couldn't die here in this yard. Not when McKenna had given her life to save her baby's. Because if Lily died, then Josie would, too.

She was the only person on earth who loved this baby like her parents would have loved her. It was her job now to keep her safe.

So she moved. She ran like she'd never run before. Past the pain. Through the fear. Despite the panic. She ran.

Ely was ahead of her. She could see the strap of the backpack in his hand as he ducked around the car. A moment later, she flung open the door of the Cayenne. Her breath caught as a Tick crashed through the upstairs window.

For a second, it perched on the roof. Then, in one crazy motion, it leapt the distance from the window to the tree, landing nimbly on one of the branches.

It swung on the branch with the skill of an Olympic gymnast. She slammed the door of the Cayenne closed as the Tick let go of the branch and soared through the air.

"Ely!" she cried in alarm.

He yanked the door closed on his side of the SUV and thrust the backpack into her arms. "I see it."

But his keys were still in his pocket. He raised his hips up and dug into his pocket, but panic must have made him clumsy. The Tick landed a few feet in front of the car. Despite the darkness, she could see its features clearly: the heavy, too-large head. The distended jaw. The thick brow ridge. The jutting lips that couldn't quite contain the leonine teeth the Ticks used to devour their victims' hearts. The fresh blood rimming its mouth. The Tick cocked its head to the side, staring at them through the glass. Puzzling it through.

She could hardly breathe her heart was pounding so hard.

Josie was squirming in the bag, making a confused, mewing sound that was almost crying.

Ely still hadn't found the keys. He was cursing as he patted his pockets frantically. The Tick just stood there in front of them, a pained expression on his face, like he was trying to remember what this strange metal thing was. Or maybe like he couldn't quite figure out how to break open the crunchy, outer shell of the car to get to the yummy goodness inside.

Either way, Lily wasn't going to wait around for him to figure it out. She ignored Josie's crying and carefully lowered the backpack to the floorboard between her feet. Then, she scrambled in the seat so she could reach around into the backseat of the Cayenne for her bow and arrow.

"What are you doing?" Ely demanded.

"I'm protecting us. Find the keys, damn it. Let's just pray they weren't in the backpack when you dumped it out on the floor."

She blew out a puff of breath and thrust open the door.

She put only one foot out the door—her other foot was useless anyway. Agony seared through her left bicep as she extended the bow. Blood seeped through her shirt where she'd ripped through the stitches. But she pushed past the pain and tried to steady the bow as she notched an arrow and lined up the shot at the Tick. He was still ten, maybe fifteen feet away, but she saw the instant he drew in the scent of her blood. She had one chance to get him through the heart. One chance for the clean kill or she wouldn't have time to notch another arrow. She waited until he roared right before he launched himself at her. She fired, but didn't wait to see if she'd landed the kill shot. The Cayenne's engine rumbled to life as she ducked back in the car. The momentum of the car lurching forward slammed her door closed. The Cayenne rammed right into the Tick and for one horrible moment, he clung to the hood of the car, the arrow piercing his chest, his face contorted into an expression of too-human horror. Then Ely cut the steering wheel hard to the right and the Tick flew off the hood before the Cayenne sped away into the night.

For a long moment, she just sat there, struggling to suck air into her lungs despite the pain wracking her body and the shock wracking her mind. Beside her, Ely was still cursing. His anger or maybe his fear made him mean. As for her, she had nothing left in her except the need to see Josie. To make sure the baby was okay.

Her hands shook as she reached down to the backpack. Josie was still crying, so Lily knew she was alive, but was she hurt? She couldn't tell from the increasingly frantic cries.

She unzipped the backpack and spread it open. It was too dark to even see the baby, so she fumbled for the overhead light and flicked it on.

Lily slipped a hand beneath Josie's head and slowly raised her up out of the bag. The sheet that they'd wrapped her in had unraveled, revealing her tiny, naked body. At some point, they would have to stop and get the diapers out of the back, but for now Lily just looked at her. She was tiny and fragile, her limbs wobbly; even her skin looked thin. Her crinkly red skin and scrunched-up face hardly looked human. Despite that, Lily felt an almost overwhelming need to protect her. To actually curl her own body over the baby's and shelter her from everything.

Looking at Josie, Lily felt a strange sense of peace.

Strange because she should have been overwhelmed. She *was* overwhelmed. And afraid.

She had just lost McKenna. Her best friend had just died. A

horrible and pointless death, which Lily would never be able to make peace with.

And to make things worse—she was wounded. The gunshot wound on her arm had broken open. And she was pretty sure she'd sprained her ankle when she landed from the roof. Worst of all, she was with a guy who thought anyone who wasn't able-bodied was a liability.

Despite that, she felt a renewed sense of resolve.

Strangely, the ease with which Ely had handled McKenna's death brought her comfort. Three shots across the forehead. There would be no coming back from that. He'd been freaked out, but he'd done it. That meant, if the time came, he would do the same for her. But it wouldn't come to that. She would protect McKenna and Joe's baby. No matter what.

CHAPTER THIRTY-TWO

LILY

"What the hell are we going to do with this damn thing?"

She looked up at Ely. The dome light in the car was still on and she could clearly read his expression of pure disgust.

Lily just shrugged. She didn't know what to do with Josie. She'd dug out one of the way-too-big diapers and sort of had it on her, but beyond that, Lily was lost. Josie's tiny body looked so pale that it was nearly blue, even though the light had a decidedly yellow cast to it. "I don't know," she admitted. "I don't know anything about babies."

"Obviously."

"Aren't you supposed to be the expert? All those siblings and cousins. Isn't that what you said?"

He scowled at her, then turned his attention to the road ahead and didn't answer.

"Are you just full of crap or what? Do you know anything about how to take care of babies or not?"

Ely made a grumbling noise, almost like a growl. He glared at her. "Cover her up."

"What?"

He gestured toward Josie. "Can't you tell she's cold? It's friggin' freezing in here for me and I wasn't just born an hour ago."

"Oh." God, Lily felt like an idiot. She quickly wrapped the sheet around Josie like she was a burrito, but didn't know what to do with the ends of the sheet, so she tucked them under and then brought them back around and tied them in a loose knot. "Better?" she asked.

He frowned, but nodded.

She thought back to when she and Mel were on the Farm and she hadn't been sure if she could get them out. Back when she had sole responsibility for keeping herself and Mel alive. Back when things seemed really bad.

That was nothing compared to this.

Mel had known how to take care of herself. She'd had her own thoughts and ideas. Sometimes that made her a pain in the ass, but other times, her ideas were better than Lily's.

But Josie? Josie was really, truly, one hundred percent dependent on her. For everything.

She didn't know how long a baby could go without starving to death, but it couldn't be very long. They needed to find food, and they needed to do it soon.

The sun would be up within the hour. The Ticks would nest down for the day. When that happened, they would have to start scouring stores and homes and anywhere else they could find food and supplies. Slowly, she noticed the sky lightening on Ely's side of the car.

"We're still heading south," Lily said.

"Yeah."

"Do you have any idea where we even are?"

"I figure somewhere in the panhandle."

She laughed then. "We're in Texas?"

"Yeah. You got any better ideas?"

She knew what she wanted to do. She wanted to ask him to turn the car around and take her back to Carter. But she couldn't do that. Her reasons for staying away were the same as her reasons for leaving in the first place.

"No," she said. "It's just that I worked pretty damn hard to get out of Texas. But I can't go back to Base Camp. Not after I lost McKenna."

"You *lost* McKenna?" he asked. "Christ you've got some kind of martyr complex."

She shot an annoyed look at him. "No, I don't."

"You do. It's pathetic. You didn't lose McKenna. She bled out. That happens, and you happened to be there. That doesn't make it your fault."

"I could have—"

"What? What could you have done? A doctor, in a hospital, with tons of support staff and maybe she could have made it."

"But—"

"No. There's no 'but' to that. You can't save everyone. Get over it."

She clamped her mouth closed and didn't say anything else. She wasn't going to argue with him. Ely liked to pick fights and she wasn't in the mood. Maybe he was right. Maybe there was nothing she could have done anyway.

After a moment, he added in a gentler voice, "Look, I didn't mean—" He jammed his hand through his hair. "I didn't mean you shouldn't mourn her. And I'm sorry I made you leave. It was the right call. I did what I had to do."

"She was my friend and she trusted me to keep her safe. Now she's dead. That's not something I'm going to just get over."

He was silent for a minute and when he spoke again, his voice was softer than she'd ever heard it. "No. I don't guess you will. Losing someone like that. You don't get over that. Probably ever. But even though she was your friend, she didn't expect you to take care of her. You didn't let her down. This wasn't your fault any more than it was hers or mine. Things just happen. Just don't blame yourself, okay?"

She nodded, pretending to consider his words. He was probably even right. But the truth was that she was too damn tired to even think beyond her crushing grief. There would be plenty of time for her to wrestle with her guilt later.

Nestled in Lily's lap, Josie's eyes were drifting closed, and her own eyelids felt heavy. The steady rhythm of the wheels on the asphalt lulled her to drowsiness. She hadn't intended to sleep. She'd planned on staying awake to help Ely look for somewhere they could stop to search for baby formula, but before she knew it, her eyes were closing. She would have to trust that Ely would wake her up when there was somewhere to look. Trust had never come easy for her, but sometimes, you just didn't have much choice.

CHAPTER THIRTY-THREE

CARTER

I should have known it wasn't going to be easy. It's never easy.

"Why should we trust you?"

Wilson and Trinia stood shoulder to shoulder glaring at me with equal expressions of animosity, but it was Trinia who had spoken.

I had sent Zeke out to find Trinia and Wilson the night before, but he hadn't found them until the next morning. Thankfully, I'd at least gotten my whole crew in before dusk. That was the only thing that had gone right. Unfortunately, by the time Zeke actually found Trinia and Wilson around noon the next day, he brought them to the Dean's office, where I'd set up command. So to them, it looked as though I was nothing but some random Collab who had taken over in the Dean's absence. Despite Pit Bull's claims that I had the reputation of a superhero, they were clearly suspicious.

"You don't have to trust me," I told them. Except, they did have to trust me; this plan of mine wouldn't work if they didn't. "You're not idiots. You must have noticed things are going to hell here."

Wilson and Trinia exchanged a look. They obviously knew each other well enough that they were able to have a whole mini-conversation with their eyes.

"Look, I'm not a Collab. I came here to help. Here's the situation as I know it: your Dean has pulled out. You've got a Farm here of roughly a thousand Greens and around twenty-five Collabs holding it together. As far as I know, there's a plan in place to bring the fences down and let the Ticks have you, because the powers that be think it'll make the Ticks easier to kill. Either you believe me or not. Either you let us help you or not. Your choice."

They still looked unconvinced. I wasn't even sure I blamed them.

But, frankly, I didn't have time for this.

I marched over to the door and stuck my head out. "Hey, Zeke."

Zeke looked up then hopped to his feet. "Yeah?"

"You said there was another guy. Joe. Where is he?"

"I don't know."

"Find him. I want to—"

"Preacher Joe is—" Trinia started to say, but then she broke off when I whirled around toward her.

"Preacher Joe?"

"Yeah. That's what we call him. He's . . ." She wrinkled her nose, not in distaste, but more in confusion. "He's started up a church, I guess. People meet in one of the lecture halls and listen to him."

"What does he preach about?"

"Hope," Wilson said simply.

Could Preacher Joe be the Joe I'd known? When I'd met him at Lily's Farm, Joe had been known as Stoner Joe. He'd set up a shop of sorts where people came in and traded for things they wanted or needed. Joe had been an easygoing guy who was hard not to like, but he'd also been fiercely devoted to McKenna and their baby. He'd been a good guy. He'd also been one of the few people I'd met since the Before who still held out hope that there might be a God somewhere who gave a damn about humanity.

Had Stoner Joe turned into Preacher Joe? Stranger things had happened.

If this Preacher Joe was the guy I'd known, then I sure as hell needed him here to convince these people I wasn't here to butcher them.

"Find Preacher Joe," I ordered Zeke. "Get him in here."

"You can't just arrest people!" Trinia launched herself toward me, but Wilson grabbed her and held her back. "People won't stand for you arresting Preacher Joe! We'll rebel! You can't—"

I'd had enough, so I grabbed her by the arms. Wilson instantly bristled, but I didn't do more than hold on to her to get her attention.

"Listen to me! I get it. You feel completely overwhelmed with the responsibility of taking care of all these Greens. That's what Zeke said about you, that you take care of all the young kids. All of them. Was he right?"

Trinia's eyes filled with tears. She was still looking at me with undisguised hatred, but with fear, too. Not for herself even, but for all those kids she'd put herself in charge of. Slowly she nodded.

"So you're taking care of all the kids who are thirteen to . . . what? . . . fifteen or so? That's about one-third of the Farm. You've appointed yourself the savior of over three hundred kids."

She swallowed, but nodded again.

Yeah, I knew her type. That's the kind of thing Lily would do. When bad shit like this happened in the world, you had to find some reason to go on. Some reason to keep putting one foot in front of the other. For Lily, it had been Mel. For Trinia, it was those kids. And unless I was mistaken, for Wilson, it was Trinia.

"You feel like if you make the wrong choice, it's not just you who pays, it's all of them. And it terrifies you."

She dropped her gaze and averted her face. I let go of her arms and stepped away. She immediately went to Wilson, and he just held her.

"Hey, I get it. I wouldn't want to trust me, either. To make matters worse, I can't even promise we're going to do any good here. I can't promise we can get the fences back up and even if we do, that's only a temporary fix. If it's been three or more weeks since a food truck has come, then you're all short on energy. We have to get out of here and fast. But I'm not going to lie. I have no way to get all of you up to Utah, where maybe—maybe—it's safe. We're going to have to find cars. We're going to have to caravan it. I'm not going to sugarcoat it. We're in trouble. Serious trouble. I can't promise that we're all going to make it, okay. Hell, I can't even hope that. All I can promise is that there are guys here who know how to kill the Ticks. People who will help you fight them."

Trinia was openly sobbing now, but her fear, her gut-wrenching terror, seemed to have morphed into something else. Determination, maybe. Despite the tears, she seemed stronger than she had when she'd first walked in.

Wilson stroked the back of her head reassuringly, but looked up at me. "Can they really be killed?"

"Yeah, they can. I've killed them myself."

"God, I hope you're right."

Yeah. Me, too.

CHAPTER THIRTY-FOUR

LILY

Lily felt hungover when she woke up. Dry-mouthed, disoriented, head and body aching.

She sat up, shaking her head. It was dark. She was in the front seat of the Cayenne. Her neck hurt from sleeping sitting up. In fact, every muscle ached, especially her left bicep, which throbbed angrily. Blinking, she ran her hand down through the neck of her shirt to the spot on her arm where the bullet had grazed her shoulder last . . . when had that happened? Why couldn't she remember?

She gingerly poked at the skin around her wound. The skin felt hot and too tight. Cringing from the pain, she tried to put the pieces together. She was alone in the Cayenne. The Cayenne wasn't moving. It was dark outside, but where was she?

Ely and McKenna wouldn't just leave her alone unprotected. Her brain stuttered over that thought. There was something she wasn't piecing together. Again there was that foggy feeling. Her mind wasn't working at full speed. What the hell had happened to her?

She patted at the wound through her sleeve and her fingers came away damp with blood. She had torn through the stitches. She'd jumped out of a tree. Or off a roof.

That's when it all came rushing back to her. The farmhouse. McKenna. Josie.

Oh, God. Josie!

Where was she now?

And why the hell had it taken Lily this long to figure out she was missing? What was wrong with her brain?

She pushed the door open and stumbled out of the Cayenne. Her head spun and nausea hit her stomach. Sucking air in through her mouth, she sank back onto the seat and dropped her head between her legs. She knew this feeling. This dizzy nausea and foggy disorientation. She'd felt this before. This wasn't a hangover. This was how she'd felt when she'd been shot by a tranquilizer dart back on the Farm. But who had shot her this time? And why?

Ely.

Shit. Shit, shit, shit!

"Don't blame yourself," Ely's voice called from somewhere nearby.

Ely's words sent a burst of hatred through her. She brought her head up, looking around through the haze of her nausea and anger.

"You're probably already thinking about things you should have done differently."

His voice came from the other side of the car, but not from nearby. Surreptitiously, she looked around, trying to pinpoint his location. On her side of the car, she could see dawn starting to peek over the horizon, a faint patch of gray. When she looked out the driver's-side window, she could see a low, squat building not far from the Cayenne.

She couldn't see him, but as he kept talking she could tell he was somewhere in that direction.

"You're probably wondering how you didn't see this coming."

"Fuck off," she growled.

Only then did she notice a mewling sound somewhere in the distance, coming from where Ely must be.

Terror shuddered through her as she realized what the noise was. Josie.

That's why she wasn't in the car. He was leaving her here. Leaving them here.

Instinct pushed her to her feet. But her right ankle throbbed in time with her arm, and it crumpled beneath her weight.

She ducked her head and scanned the interior of the Cayenne, looking for a weapon and cursing her sluggish brain. She didn't see her bow and quiver, which meant Ely must have moved it. She couldn't let him drive away.

In the backseat, all she saw was the blanket from that first night. She grabbed the blanket and pulled it into the front seat with her, but there was nothing else back there. Which meant Ely had at least the tranq gun with him.

If she made it to the back of the SUV, if she could pop the trunk, if her bow and arrow was back there, then she'd have at least a fighting chance. But that was a lot of ifs.

"All I'm saying is that you shouldn't blame yourself. It's not that you're weak. It's not that you're gullible or too trusting. I would have betrayed anyone. And there wasn't a damn thing you could have done to stop me. So don't beat yourself up over it."

If she had to guess, she would say Ely was still talking for only one reason: he was trying to distract her. Because right now, all her attention was focused on two things: fighting her pain and talking to him. He knew how bad her injuries were.

As long as he kept her standing here talking to him, he could be sneaking up on her through the darkness. And here she was, standing right next to the Cayenne with the dome light on in the car. The only bright spot in the entire wasteland. Jesus, she hated what those tranquilizers did to her brain.

Think, damn it!

Okay, tranq guns are powerful, but unless you were a helluva shot, you weren't going to hit someone with one from a distance. They didn't have the accuracy of a rifle. So he'd have to be within twenty or so feet from her. Which would be perfect if she had time to get her bow out of the back. But she doubted Ely was going to wait for her to arm herself. Tranq guns were also most effective if you took the dart in the neck.

Last time, she'd been shot in the ass and she'd woken up pretty quickly. This time, from the pain, she was guessing he'd got her in the left bicep, not far from her other wound. That was why it hurt so badly. And again, she hadn't been out long. This time, if he got close enough to get her neck, then she'd be out for a while. Josie's screams—and she was definitely screaming now—would attract wildlife, or worse, and they'd both be dead before she even woke up again. Forget whether or not they had the Cayenne.

Ely had all the weapons and his brain wasn't foggy.

Right now, her best shot was to minimize the effect of the tranq dose he was about to shoot her with. She grabbed the blanket off the seat and wrapped it like a cloak around her shoulders, bunching it up around her neck to provide as much protection as she could.

She stepped away from the door before shutting it and plunging the desert into darkness. That would make it a little harder for him to attack her.

She moved down the length of the Cayenne, hopping on one foot and praying she could be quiet. To cover any noise she made, she started talking again.

"Can I assume this heartfelt apology means you're not working for the rebellion anymore? Is Carter in danger?"

"God, you are so predictable, Lily." Ely's voice took on a hard note. "Your inability to live without the people you care about isn't altruism. It's not a virtue. It's your greatest weakness."

He was closer now. She could hear it, but she still couldn't see him and Josie's crying covered the sounds of his approach.

"I'm sorry you think that." She reached the back of the Cayenne, panting. She was tired, groggy, and defenseless and facing an unknown number of opponents. In short, she was screwed five ways to Sunday. Just another day in the Tick-pocalypse.

"That's the thing about people like you and Carter," Ely was saying. His voice held an edge, an intensity that was usually hidden behind his indifferent attitude. "You think you're so noble. But you really aren't. None of this is for the greater good. You're not doing this because you want to protect other people. You're just protecting yourself. You can't live without the people you love."

She looked around the ground for a weapon, even though she was pretty much screwed. Unless she found a bazooka just sitting there.

Her eyes had adjusted to the dim lighting and she could see a rock about the size of a grapefruit lying on the ground maybe fifteen feet away. It was better than nothing.

Unfortunately, nothing was what was between it and her. Nothing to grab hold of. Nothing to hang onto as she hopped across the ground. Crap.

She friggin' hated this. She hated being weak. She hated feeling vulnerable. Worst of all, she hated knowing that Ely was right about her.

All these sacrifices she'd made to protect the people she cared about . . . they hadn't benefited others at all. All those "sacrifices" had been for her. Because she needed the people she loved. Because she couldn't imagine her life without them. Her sacrifices were only selfishness.

Mel was proof of that. Lily hadn't begged Sebastian to turn her because she'd thought Mel would be better off as a vampire, she'd done it because she couldn't live without her. The same was true of McKenna.

But that didn't mean she was going to give up. She still had Josie to think about. She needed to be strong for the baby.

She lowered herself to her hands and knees and began the painful, awkward crawl toward the rock.

"You know I can hear you panting out there in the darkness, don't you, Lily? I can tell how much pain you're in. Why not just give up?"

She ignored his question and his jab. No way was she going to let this guy win.

"So tell me something, Ely. Why exactly did you betray the rebellion? Are you working for Roberto? Did he promise you safety? Money? What?" She was just throwing words out there. She didn't give a damn what his answer was. "No, that's not it at all," she muttered. "You've been looking for your family. Is that it? Did Roberto get to them first and promise he'd keep them safe if you'd find me and kill me?"

She could see the rock just a few feet ahead. Maybe five. Far enough that she couldn't just reach out and grab it, but close enough that she wanted to. She was so close.

"But that's what I don't get. All this time, you kept saying you'd promised Carter you would keep me safe. So what's up with that? You were just lying? Why bother?"

By now, even her good limbs ached. Pain shot through her body with every inch she moved forward. And she was pretty sure her arm was starting to go numb.

"If you weren't keeping me safe because you'd promised Carter you would, then why? Why not just kill me?"

The rock was only a foot or so away now. But she'd been so busy talking and crawling, she hadn't heard anything from Ely in too long.

Damn.

She reached out to grab the rock, but before she could get it, a black boot came down on her hand.

Ely squatted down. It was almost like he was trying to save her the trouble.

He held the tranquilizer rifle in his hand. God, she hated those things.

Again he flashed that annoying smile of his. "You're quite the fighter." The bastard winked at her. "Your daddy would be proud."

If she'd had any fight left in her at all, she would have punched the jerk right there and then, but she was down to zero. She was just out. Between the pain and exhaustion and the grief, she had nothing left. She clenched the blanket tighter around her neck. Even at zero, she still wasn't willing to give up entirely.

Slowly, Ely took his foot off her hand and stood up. "Come on, Lily. Have a little dignity. Just put down the blanket and give me a clear shot at your neck. This will all be a lot easier once you're out."

"Why?" she asked. Why should she make this any easier on anyone? Life wasn't about doing what was easy. It was about fighting, no matter what. "Why not just walk away now and leave us here?"

He shrugged like he didn't really care either way. "I promised I'd keep you alive no matter what."

"If you're betraying Carter anyway, why keep me alive just for him?"

Ely shifted his weight back a step, nudging the nose of the rifle in her direction. "Come on."

"I'm serious," she whined. She knew she was acting like a big baby, but she didn't care.

She was hurt. She was tired. She was beaten. She wanted Ely to see that he'd won. He had her at his feet.

He had every advantage but one.

That would be the knife strapped to the outside of his boot, and he'd obviously forgotten about it.

She looked up at him trying to keep him talking long enough for her to grab the knife. "If you're keeping me alive just because you promised Carter, don't you think he'd rather you put me out of my misery?"

But she didn't give him a chance to answer. She flung the blanket off her back and toward Ely, hitting him in the chest. With her other hand she lunged for the knife. Her hand closed around the handle even as her momentum carried her forward into his legs. They both went down in a tangle. She heard the soft *whoosh* of the tranq rifle being fired, but the shot went wide, landing in the dirt. She tugged the knife free of its sheath and stabbed blindly. She was aiming for his thigh but thought she hit closer to his knee. Either way, he cursed and grabbed at his leg, losing his grip on the tranq gun.

She scrambled for the gun and twisted it around. She wasn't one for pretty speeches. As soon as her finger found the trigger, she just fired the damn thing.

Ely fell back, looking down in shock at the dart sticking out of his chest.

She stumbled to her feet, backing out of his range. Tranq rifles only held three darts. So she turned it around and held it butt out, like a bat, ready to swing it at him if she had to.

Ely ripped the dart from his chest, but his eyes were starting to glaze.

His lips twisted into a sneer. "You stupid bitch."

"You want to know the sad thing? It's not that you betrayed

Carter. It's that if you'd gone to him for help, he would have done anything for you. Whoever it is that Roberto has, Carter would have gotten them out."

"No . . . good . . ." Ely gasped. "Wasn't going to leave you . . . here . . . never could see the big picture." He gasped, wincing as his hand clutched the knife. "Carter's not the only one who wants you alive."

Then, with another gasp, his eyes flickered closed and he was out.

CHAPTER THIRTY-FIVE

LILY

Lily didn't have a lot of time to consider what the hell Ely had meant when he'd said Carter wasn't the only one who wanted her alive. She had to get Josie and get the hell out of there.

She started out by kicking Ely soundly in the ribs a couple of times just to be sure he was really out and not faking it. Then she kicked him once in the groin for good measure. She grabbed the knife, quickly unbuckling the sheath from his boot and taking it as well. Good gear was too hard to find to leave something like that behind.

A quick search of his body uncovered the keys to the Cayenne—thank God—a flashlight, one more knife, a Glock with a full clip, and a little pistol. She emptied all but one of the bullets from the pistol and left the loaded gun a few feet away from him, where he'd be sure to see it when he woke up in an hour or so.

After that, she ran, stumbling, toward the sounds of Josie's crying in the building. It turned out to be an old bunkhouse of some kind. A single room deep, three rooms long. The windows were long gone, the door hung on its hinges. Trash and debris littered the floor. And there, in the center room, on a disgusting old mattress lay Josie, squalling in the shadows.

The building offered her some small level of protection.

She scooped Josie up and held her to her chest as she stumbled back to the Cayenne. Josie gave an exhausted little hiccup. But by the time they were back in the Cayenne, she was crying again, and Lily's brain was starting to clear enough to know they were in serious trouble.

She didn't know how long she'd been out for sure, but it was dawn. Josie had been born more than six hours ago and still hadn't had anything to eat.

She had no idea how long babies could go without eating, but she was guessing it wasn't as long as she could. She needed to find food, and she needed to do it fast. She didn't know where the hell they were, but she knew even if they headed back to Base Camp now they wouldn't get there anytime today. She didn't dare risk driving at night and attracting Ticks on the way. She needed to find food for both of them before dark.

She held Josie close to her chest with one hand as she fumbled with the keys in the other. She scrambled into the Cayenne, slamming the door behind her and jamming down on the lock button on the door's console of controls. In the rearview mirror, she could see the dark shape of Ely's body on the ground maybe twenty feet back.

Heart pounding in her chest, she tried to jam the keys into the ignition one-handed without ever taking her eyes off that dark lump on the ground. Finally the key engaged and the engine roared to life. As she slammed the SUV into gear and drove off, she could have sworn she saw a flicker of movement from the black mass in the mirror. Was Ely waking up or was that just a trick of the wind? Or a trick of her mind?

The road seemed to stretch for endless miles through the featureless west Texas, so flat and so broad, it seemed like she could actually see the curve of the horizon off in the distance. It was emptiness like nothing she'd ever known. She passed abandoned houses too run-down to bother searching, broken pump jacks, and more tumbleweed than she could count—if she was counting, which she wasn't. Josie finally screamed herself to sleep, and still Lily drove, just to put distance between herself and Ely. And also because she simply didn't know what else to do.

Finally, the houses seemed closer together, the road merged with another, and eventually she reached a town that looked as barren as the surrounding desert. Sweetwater was the town's name, if the sign on the car dealership was any indication. Five gas stations and innumerable houses later and she'd found jack. At one of the gas stations she'd come across a map and a handful of beef jerky sticks. Standing in the parking lot, she ate one of the beef jerky sticks, scarfing down the first three bites quickly and then forcing herself to slowly gnaw on the rest while she considered her options. It almost took the edge off her hunger. She thought about offering a second piece to Josie. And, yeah, she knew babies didn't need beef jerky, but the sucking alone might be enough to calm her. Except beef jerky was so damn salty. From what she knew about dehydration, salt would only make it worse so she dribbled a little water in Josie's mouth instead.

Lily changed Josie's diaper the best she could. The fact that the diaper was barely wet didn't comfort her at all. Being snuggled in the backpack seemed to comfort Josie as much as anything, so Lily wrapped Josie back up like a burrito and carefully placed her back in the bottom of the backpack, folding down the top flap so she got plenty of air. Then she put the bag on, over her chest, so Josie rode in front. Sure, it wasn't exactly like those sling things she'd seen parents using in the Before, but it had to be better than letting Josie roll around on the floorboard of the car.

Josie was still crying, but her cries had lost their intensity. She seemed almost to be giving up the fight and that made Lily want to weep, too.

Since it was still light, Lily opened up the back of the Cayenne to survey the last of the supplies. She had two gallons of water left—which was maybe enough for another two to three days, if she stretched it.

Other than that, there were the four remaining beef jerky sticks, the rest of the tub of peanut butter, two cans of tuna, and about a dozen big glass jars of vegetables. Ely must have found those at the farmhouse and loaded them up, because they looked homemade and she hadn't seen them before. There were six jars of tomatoes, four of green beans, and one jar of peaches.

None of it was the case of pre-mixed formula she'd been hoping to miraculously find stashed in the back, but surely peaches were a better option than beef jerky. She would give Josie more water if it came down to that, but the baby needed nutrients, too. She needed milk.

Praying she wasn't going to make things worse, she opened up the jar of peaches, used her knife to slice off a tiny bite, and nibbled on it herself. She hadn't had real fruit since the Before. The sweetness of it hit her tongue in an explosion of flavor that flooded her mouth with saliva and made her taste buds burst. It was all she could do not to fish out the entire slice and gulp it down.

But she wasn't eating it for herself. This was for Josie, and the only reason she'd even tasted it was to make sure it was okay. She let the flavors linger on her tongue, waiting for that metallic zing that would mean it had gone bad. Since it tasted fine, she fished out another slice and dropped it in the sippy cup from Wal-Mart. Then she dribbled a little juice in, too, and mashed the peach up with her knife as finely as she could before fitting the lid on. She climbed into the backseat of the Cayenne, locked her doors, and lifted Josie out of the bag. Then she stretched the baby out on her legs and tried to coax Josie into eating. Josie turned her face away from the bits of peach, pushing them out of her mouth with her tongue. But the peach juice slowly dribbled in and she drank it— thank God.

Lily had no idea how long Josie could live on canned peach juice. She was guessing not very long, but it was better than dehydration, right?

Lily sat there, coaxing Josie into eating, nearly starving herself and wondering what the hell she was going to do.

None of this—nothing—had turned out the way she'd planned. Even if these peaches kept Josie alive, how long would they last without refrigeration? A day? She had to find real food. Formula. Milk. Anything. She couldn't keep wandering around Texas. She needed a plan. Fast. She didn't have enough gas to drive back to Base Camp. She was exhausted from being up all night and doubted she could make it in one trip even if she did. She obviously wasn't thinking clearly because only one solution came to mind. She could think of only one way to save baby Josie.

She had to bring her to a Farm.

The Farms had tons of pregnant Breeders. They had to have some plan for dealing with the babies. They'd have supplies. Diapers. Formula. Medicine, if Josie needed it. All the things it took to keep babies alive.

The cynical, bitter, darkest part of her brain asked the unthinkable: What if the Farms had never intended to keep the babies alive? What if they were just more food for the Ticks?

But that didn't make sense. Not really. Yes, they'd be food for the Ticks in the sense that, at some point, they would be giving blood donations. But Farms needed Greens to replace the Greens who were aging out of the program.

She had to believe that if she brought Josie to a Farm, the Farm would be able to care for her.

It would mean turning herself in. It would mean going back to a Farm herself. But she could live with that, because she had no one else to protect except Josie—she had no one else to love.

But before she did that, she had one more thing to do. She had to tell Carter what Ely had done. Ely had betrayed her. He'd tranqed her and kidnapped her. Why? What was it he'd said? That Carter wasn't the only one who needed her alive.

What exactly did that mean? Ely hadn't confirmed he was working for Roberto but who else could possibly need her alive? Why her?

Obviously someone still thought she was an *abductura*. That was her only value, right? But who?

The Dean from her Farm had obviously believed she had powers, but he was dead. Had he told someone else she was an *abductura* before he'd gone chasing after her and Mel? He must have, but who had he told? Another Dean? Unlikely, but not impossible. The more likely answer was Roberto.

She knew nothing about Roberto other than what she'd learned from Carter and Sebastian. They believed that he had at least one, but possibly more, powerful *abducturae* working for him. That he had bred the Ticks on purpose so that he could take control of some vast swath of territory in the former United States. And that he'd used the one-two punch of the Ticks and the *abducturae* to convince humans that the Ticks were unbeatable and unstoppable. They could only guess what his endgame was.

But whatever his motives were, it was a safe bet he'd do anything to get an *abductura* working for him rather than for Sebastian.

So if Ely was working for someone else, it was most likely Roberto. Just because she'd escaped Ely, that didn't mean she'd escape whoever Roberto sent after her next.

She didn't dare go back to Base Camp, even if she could make it. The only solution that didn't endanger Carter and the rebellion was to hand herself over to Roberto. And finding him wouldn't even be a problem. All she had to do was find the nearest Farm and present herself to the Dean.

She could live with turning herself over to Roberto. After all, she had no powers, so she would endanger no one but herself. But first she had to find a way to contact Carter.

By now, Josie had drifted off to sleep. A fitful, hungry sleep, but sleep nonetheless. So Lily moved the baby off her lap and onto the seat. Then she started searching the Cayenne. Ely had a lot of crap in the back of the Cayenne. He'd been living out of it for months. He had the same training as Carter. Carter never went anywhere without his satellite phone. She was betting Ely would have one. If she could just find it.

Searching the backseat turned up a dozen Clif bars, a flashlight, and a well-stocked first aid kit. Since she was starting to feel punchy from the lack of sleep and her arm was still aching, she ate one of the bars and took an Advil for the pain then went back to the search. Finally, she found what she was looking for, wedged into the Cayenne's spare-tire compartment. It took her a few minutes to figure out how to set up the antenna, but she'd seen Carter do it and it wasn't that hard. A few minutes after finding the phone, she was still working up her courage to call Carter. She was worried that just the sound of his voice might weaken her resolve. She couldn't risk him talking her out of it.

While she thought about what she was going to say, she watched Josie as she slept in the backpack. She had strapped the seatbelt through the straps on the backpack. Yeah, it screamed "bad idea" as a car seat, but it was the best she could do.

That pretty much summed up the entire situation. It all screamed bad idea, but she was doing the best she could.

CHAPTER THIRTY-SIX

CARTER

I didn't know if I'd actually convinced Wilson and Trinia, but at the very least Trinia was no longer yelling at me and trying to gouge my eyes out. That was an improvement, right?

The not-having-my-eyes-gouged-out wasn't much comfort when I got the news from Taylor: The generator couldn't be expected to hold for more than another night, even if we turned off everything but the fences. Which meant we had less than twenty-four hours to devise an exit strategy. Without sounding like I had a Messiah complex, I couldn't help wondering if Moses had had these kinds of problems when leaving Egypt.

I had teams outside the Farm now, looking for vans and trucks we could use to transport the Greens to Utah, and to siphon what gas they could find. I was talking with Victor about organizing teams of Greens to look for food and weapons when my satellite phone rang. If anyone was calling me, it should have been one of the other Elites, hopefully with good news about . . . oh, I don't know, finding an RV park or something. Instead, it took me a minute to recognize the number.

I gestured Victor out the door of the Dean's office as I picked up. "I hope to hell you have good news, Ely, because I could sure use it."

There was a moment of silence so long, I wondered if maybe

the connection had gone dead. Maybe the phone's antenna had broken.

Then a quiet voice said, "This isn't Ely."

"Lily?" My heart rate jumped.

"Yeah. Hi, Carter."

A thousand questions raced through my head. Where was she? Was she safe? Had they made it to Canada? Instead, I asked the stupid question. "Where's Ely?"

"He's, um . . ."

I would have heard the hesitation in her voice even if she hadn't been stuttering. Then it hit me. That wasn't just hesitation. She was crying.

"Lily, what's wrong?"

In the moments of her silence, my mind raced. Lily wasn't a crier. I'd seen her go through some crazy shit. Crap that would have had grown men sobbing, and she hadn't broken down. If she was crying now . . .

"Are you hurt? Where are you? If you—"

"I'm okay," she broke in, her voice trembling. "I'm not . . . Jesus, I'm sorry. I thought I could do this without crying."

"Do what?" Shit. If she didn't tell me what was wrong soon, I'd frickin' leap through the phone and—

"It's Ely."

"Is he hurt? Is he—"

"No. He's fine. I mean, sort of." I heard her take a shuddering breath. "Carter, he can't be trusted."

"What?" I heard her words, but they didn't register.

"I know he's your friend and you've known him forever, but he's not on our side and I need you to believe me and—"

"Lily, of course I believe you." My mind was still reeling. What-ever had happened, it had obviously messed with her head. Because this was Lily. She was always coherent. She could always make a cogent argument. Always. I'd never heard her fumble for words or ramble like this. Ever. That just wasn't her style.

"Of course I believe you." But Ely had betrayed her? He couldn't be trusted? It made no sense. "Back up. Tell me exactly what happened."

"Okay." Another rasping, quivering breath. "Things went bad." There was another pause and I could tell she was trying to figure out what parts of the story she should say aloud. What was important enough to push through and what could be left out. "He tranqed me. He was taking me somewhere. To someone, but he didn't say who. Only that they wanted me alive."

I felt a white-hot rush of anger blast over me. Anger hotter than a windstorm in the Texas summer. So strong it burned my skin and blurred my vision.

I had trusted Ely. With my life. With all of Base Camp. With Lily.

He had promised to keep her safe. He'd said he would guard her with his life.

And then he had tranqed my girl—*my girl*—so that he could deliver her to God only knew who.

"Where are you now? Are you safe? Did you get away from him?"

"I'm . . . yeah, sure. I'm safe."

"I'm going to kill him." I hadn't even meant to say it aloud because I knew Lily would argue. Screw it. "I'm gonna fucking kill him."

She made a sound that—over the sketchy connection of the satellite phone—almost sounded like a strangled laugh. "That might not be necessary."

"Why?"

"Because I kind of kicked his ass and left him out in the middle of nowhere without a car."

And that, that right there, was just one more reason I loved this girl.

Ely was as tough as they came. But my Lily, she was tougher. She never gave up. No matter how hopeless things seemed, no matter how helpless she might appear, she never just laid down and accepted that. She fought.

Despite everything, I found myself chuckling. "Yeah, you did."

It sounded like maybe she was chuckling, too. The kind of desperate, frenetic laugh of someone very close to the edge.

"Carter, the thing is, I don't know who he's working for. I don't know if it's one of the Deans. Or Bob. Or who. I have no idea. But we have to assume the worst."

"You think he gave away the location of Base Camp?"

"I don't know. But if he did, then everyone is in danger. You have to get those kids out of there. You have to be ready. You could—"

"Let me worry about Base Camp," I said. Then it occurred to me that her "Yeah, sure. I'm safe," hadn't been particularly reassuring. "Let's get you home first. I mean, unless you guys are in Canada already. You should be there by now, right?"

"That's the other thing." Her voice caught. I could hear the tears in her throat, choking her. "McKenna didn't—"

I cursed again. "Did Ely—"

"No." Another long pause. "She went into labor. She bled out. There was nothing—"

I sagged against the side of the desk. It felt like my heart actually stop beating. Like it was being squeezed by all the grief and sorrow. McKenna. Gone.

Since losing Joe, McKenna had seemed fragile and worn, not quite of this world. But everyone had loved her. She was hope. The crazy, insane hope that somehow we were all going to make it.

"The baby?"

"Is fine. She's here. She's beautiful. But Carter, I can't feed her. I can't take care of her. I can't—"

"Where are you? Wherever you are, I'm going to come and get you. You hunker down. You stay safe. I'm coming."

"No. Carter, it's okay. I have a plan."

"What? What's your plan?" And it had better involve staying safe and waiting for me to get there.

"Shh," she murmured reassuringly. "It's okay. I know what I'm doing. I'm going to find the nearest Farm and turn myself in. They take care of—"

"No! You stay where you are. I will come for you. I can leave here in five minutes. I can be there in—" Shit. She was most likely in Montana. Even if I took the fastest car, even if I drove through the night, it could be days before I got there. "You just stay low. Stay safe and keep her alive. I will come for you. I'm leaving right now. You just tell me where you are and I'm coming for you."

"No, Carter. It's—"

"Just tell me where you are." I'd be walking out the door already but I was terrified of losing the phone signal.

"This is a good plan."

"You cannot be serious!"

"I am. Listen, at a Farm, they'll be able to feed Josie. They can keep her alive. They've got to be set up for this kind of thing, because some of the Breeders should be ready to give birth soon, right? So they have to be able to care for a baby. And as long as you know where she is, you could come get her. You could rescue her when she's older."

"And what about you? You're eighteen. And you risked your life to get off of a Farm. You can't—"

"No, I've thought about that. If I turn myself in to a new Farm, they won't know how old I am. I can lie. And you . . ." I heard her swallowing. "You can come and get me. You saved me once. You can save me again."

There was something in her voice that I didn't trust. It took a second, but I figured it out. She suspected that Ely had planned on turning her over to Roberto. Roberto wouldn't stop looking for her. Which meant she was planning on trading Josie's safety for her own life. "Just tell me where you are."

"Carter, I—"

"Where are you? Montana? Idaho? Somewhere in Canada? Where?"

"Canada?" She sounded baffled for a second. "No. I'm not in Canada. We changed our game plan. We headed for Mexico instead of Canada. I'm in Texas."

And then, it hit me. Like a speeding train. Right in the chest. "You're where?"

"In Texas. Some tiny town. Sweetwater, I think."

"You're in Texas?"

"Yeah." Her words slowed to a trickle. "It seemed like a good idea. Because of the guns. And the cartels . . . and . . ."

My string of curses cut her off.

"I'm there, too."

"You're in Texas?"

"Yes."

A long moment of silence, and then, "Oh."

We were both in Texas. And frankly, there was no way in hell that we'd both ended up here by accident. "Tell me exactly why you're in Texas because of the guns and the cartels?"

"Ely said—"

I cursed again.

She ignored me and kept talking. "That Canada had probably fallen. Their army wasn't as well armed as ours, so they wouldn't have been able to fight off the Ticks. He said he'd been all the way down to the wall and he thought the drug cartels had kept the Ticks from going farther south than that."

I cursed some more. Even though I could see how perfectly logical that argument was.

"Why are *you* in Texas?" she asked.

"Because of Ely." It seemed so obvious now, looking back, that he'd been driving us both here. . . . No, wait. Not both of us. Just her.

He'd said it during that first conversation he and I had had about the Farm in San Angelo. "Bring Lily down there. She can convince them to fight." He hadn't actually given a damn whether or not I came to Texas. He'd been angling for her all along.

In fact, after she'd agreed to leave Base Camp with him, he'd lost interest in our plan to go to San Angelo.

Why did he want her here?

Not that it mattered.

Because here's what it came down to: Lily was scared and alone with a baby she couldn't care for, being pursued by people whose motives we could only guess at. I didn't need to know any more than that.

"Okay," I said again. "I'm coming for you. Don't turn yourself in. Do you promise me?"

"Carter, I—"

"Just give me until sunrise. If I can't find you by sunrise, then . . ." Well, then I still wasn't going to be frickin' okay with her turning herself in, that was for damn sure. "Well we'll worry about that after."

"After what?"

"Your goal is just to stay alive and keep that baby alive. Got it?"

"Okay," she said finally. "Where are you in Texas?"

"San Angelo. And Dawn is here. You remember Dawn, right?"

"Dawn Armadale?"

"Yeah. She talked her way into the car. She's a nurse, right? So she'll know what to do for Josie. And surely you trust her more than whatever nurse a Farm would have."

I could practically hear her mulling it over on the other end of the phone. "Yeah. I guess."

"I'll be there around midnight. Just stay safe. Stay alive. And keep your phone on."

"Okay." Her voice sounded steadier than it had even just a few moments ago. She was pulling it together. I'd never had any doubt she would.

I got off the phone with her quickly after that, which was one of the hardest things I'd ever done, because I wanted to keep her on the line. I wanted that reassurance that she was following my orders and that she was staying safe. Because it felt like the only way to actually keep her alive was to maintain that connection to her. But I hung up anyway because a fully charged phone was too precious to waste.

As soon as I hung up, my mind started racing through the list of things I'd need to get out of here fast. I grabbed my bag of gear and headed for the Dean's personal stash of food. Zeke walked in as I was zipping up the bag.

He stood in the doorway, blocking my way out. "What's up?" he asked, frowning. "You look like you're packing."

"I am. I'm heading out."

"You're bailing?"

"No, I'm just—"

"Jesus! After all your big talk about how we need to save these people, you're bailing."

"I'm not bailing." Except I kind of was. "Look, Lily is in trouble. I'm going to get her."

"Lily, your girlfriend?" His sneer said it all.

"Yeah. She's in trouble. Serious trouble." I stepped closer to him, waiting for him to get out of the way.

Instead, he gave my shoulder a shove. "There are a thousand kids here at this Farm who are in serious trouble. You're going to throw them to the Ticks to save your girlfriend?"

I didn't even have to think about it.

Yes. Yes, I was.

I knew it made me a bastard and a total ass. Hell, maybe it made me a sociopath.

I knew—*I knew*—that the needs of the many should outweigh the needs of the few. And ninety-nine percent of the time they would. But not today. Not now. Not when Lily was in trouble. Because she meant more to me than all those other kids combined. She was all that mattered.

"Yes," I said slowly, "I am. And unless you want to throw down right now, you can't stop me."

The anger in Zeke's gaze wavered and bled into fear. "You can't leave us."

I gripped the back of his neck and gave it an encouraging squeeze. "The fences will hold at least through tonight. Tomorrow, you take whatever blood donations are fresh and you have someone dump them far away. It'll keep the Ticks away for at least tomorrow night. It won't matter if the fences aren't on if the Ticks aren't nearby to test them. There are twenty-five guys here who know as much about fighting Ticks as I do. Dawn is level-headed. Besides, I'll be back in two days. You'll be fine."

By the time I was done talking, Zeke even looked like he believed me.

He nodded and blew out a breath of resolve. "We'll be okay."

Before I could give him any more instructions or reassurances, someone knocked on the door frame behind him. He stepped aside. Victor was out in the hall.

"Hey, boss," he said. "We found Preacher Joe. Someone's bringing him up right now."

Standing in the doorway, I had a clear shot of the elevator. My heart started pounding as the doors slid open. There was Joe. Preacher Joe really was Stoner Joe. When he saw me, a big-ass grin split his face.

If what I'd heard was right, then Joe was the kind of guy who prayed. And he'd probably been praying for something exactly like this. Praying that someone would come who could help the Greens here at this Farm. Praying that he'd find some connection to the world outside this place, some connection to the girl he loved.

Right now, I was the answer to his prayers.

And I had to tell him that McKenna was dead.

CHAPTER THIRTY-SEVEN

LILY

Sweetwater, Texas, didn't have a Wal-Mart.

Lily had driven down the town's two main roads looking for one. She'd even broken into a house to check the phone book, just to be sure. The phone book had turned up no superstores of any kind, but the house was a treasure trove. There were two cars in the garage with gas in both tanks. The pantry had a bag of beans and rice. Five cans of veggies and four of tuna. A bottle of vitamin C and the real brass ring: three cans of evaporated milk.

It still took a while to get Josie to drink from the cup, but by now, the baby was starving and eager. Once she got going, she drank and drank. It wasn't perfect, but it would keep her alive.

Lily gave the house one last pass, finding a stash of soda in the garage and bag of Halloween candy in one of the drawers in the master bedroom. As she drove down the road toward the town's only grocery store, a Town and Country, she ate a fun-size Twix bar. There was a mini-roll of Rolos, too, but she set those aside for later.

Carter was coming for her. She'd share the Rolos with him when he got there.

Josie was asleep by the time she pulled into the parking lot of the Town and Country. By the standards of a Wal-Mart, the place was tiny.

She left Josie asleep in the car when she went in to secure the freezer. Something—something other than Ticks, if Lily had to guess—had knocked holes in the roof in a couple of places. Maybe a tornado had come through here in the past few weeks. This was prime tornado alley.

A little moonlight filtered through the gaps in the roof, making it possible for her to forage as she searched for the freezer section. Along the way she found a few cans of food and some bottles of Gatorade. They even had some cleaning supplies. More bleach, which was always useful, and five mops. She brought Josie inside before carrying in load after load of plants and the other supplies she'd found. She set up the antenna for the sat phone just outside the car. Once she had locked herself and Josie in the freezer, she spent a few hours whittling the mop handles into stakes. There were some things you could never have enough of. Food was one. Stakes were the other.

Logic said she should sleep when Josie did, but her mind wouldn't quiet. Had she done the right thing? Maybe she should have argued harder against Carter coming to find her. Maybe she shouldn't have told him where she was at all.

Not calling him hadn't been an option. He needed to know about Ely. And as much as she wanted to pretend that she was strong enough and independent enough to handle anything, she wasn't. Everyone needed help sometimes. That was just part of life. When she and Mel had been planning their escape from the Farm, she'd tried her damnedest to do it all on her own. To rely on no one. But that hadn't worked. Her stubborn self-reliance had caused more problems than it had solved. She wasn't going to make the same mistakes twice.

By midnight, roughly the time that Carter had said he'd be rolling into town, she was even more keyed up. By one A.M., she was downright jittery.

She'd told him where she'd be, but maybe he hadn't understood. She tried calling him again, but her phone must have been too far away from the antenna she'd left at the Cayenne. Which meant if he was trying to get in touch with her, he wouldn't be able to.

By two A.M., when he still hadn't shown up, panic was eating away at her. Josie had woken up, eaten, and gone back to sleep. Too jittery to even sit still, Lily cracked open the freezer door and stuck her head outside, listening for the sound of . . . anything.

She thought about what Ely had said. If the Ticks couldn't hear you or smell you, you weren't there. But that assumed there were Ticks in the area. She hadn't seen any sign of them all day long. Signs of human looting and destruction, yes. Signs of Ticks, no. Maybe there just weren't any here.

She was hours away from a Farm. They tended to congregate near their food source. So it was feasible that this entire town was as Tick free as an indoor dog.

She waffled for a few more minutes. Leaving the freezer to get within range of the antenna maybe wasn't the smartest thing to do, but wasn't being out of range of the antenna just as dangerous? It was a tradeoff.

Grasping the phone in one hand, she snuck out the freezer door and crept to the front of the store, opened the door, and stepped right outside. About a minute after the signal icon on her phone lit up, a beep sounded letting her know that someone had tried to call her. The number was Carter's. From a half hour earlier.

She listened to the message with a pounding heart.

"It took longer than I thought to get out. We're almost there now. Thirty minutes. Tops."

Okay. Thirty minutes. So he should be walking through the door any second now.

She'd already made it back to the freezer compartment when

she heard a noise from beyond the freezer. Not the quiet shuffle of human footsteps, but a loud noise. Something crashing—a noise that, under the circumstances, Carter would never make.

She waited, heart pounding, for the howl of a Tick. It never came, but the store echoed with more crashing. Shattering glass. Shelves being knocked over. It didn't sound like Ticks. Ticks traveled in packs. They moved fast. They yowled and yipped to communicate over long distances. They didn't forage in stores.

So who or what was this?

What kinds of creatures prowled around this part of Texas at night? There were all the benign small things: rats, possums, raccoons, and nutria. Then there were the bigger things. Coyotes. Bobcats. Mountain lions. None of those were animals you wanted to meet in a dark alley. Or an abandoned grocery store.

Had she attracted the attention of some creature when she'd stepped outside to listen to the phone message? She must have. Crap. That was a newbie mistake. And Carter would pay the price. Because he was about to walk into the store and come face-to-face with whatever beast had followed her scent.

He was about to walk in unprepared. Because of her stupid mistake.

And she couldn't warn him. She couldn't call him. She had no way to let him know. Unless she walked out of the freezer and faced down this creature herself. Except, if she was wrong, if this thing was a Tick, then going out there was the last thing she should do.

Christ, she hated feeling useless. Hated knowing that her genetic makeup made her a risk to everyone around her. It was like her very blood had turned against her.

For a few heart-wrenching moments, she paced back and forth, listening to the sounds of the beast out in the store and watching baby Josie sleep. She clipped the holster she'd gotten off Ely to the waistband of her jeans. She checked the clip before sliding the gun into the holster. Seven bullets wouldn't kill a Tick, but it would sure as hell get the beast's attention. She picked up one of the mop handles and tested the jagged point against her thumb before sliding it through the belt loop of her jeans. She picked up her bow and quiver only to put it down again. Was she really doing this? Was she being smart or foolhardy?

Then, finally, she snatched it up and headed for the door. She didn't have to go all the way out into the store. There was a refrigerator section right beside the deep freeze in back. She could sneak in there and look out into the store though the glass doors. If the doors were well-sealed, whatever was out there wouldn't be able to smell her. It might see her, but it might not. She wouldn't bring a flashlight. Her night vision was good enough that she should at least be able to tell the difference between a Tick and a mountain lion.

She waited for another burst of racket from the main part of the grocery store, then opened the freezer door, snuck out, and shut it tight behind her, all the while praying that Josie wouldn't wake up and start crying.

A few steps later through the darkened backroom, she found the latch to the dairy case and slipped inside.

The stench of rotting food made her nostrils curl. No wonder Ely had thought these freezer sections would hide them. If the Tick's sense of smell was strong like an animal's, then this had to be horribly offensive to them.

Breathing shallowly through her mouth, she wended her way through discarded boxes and other trash to the shelves that made up the dairy case. Most of the food was long gone. She quietly removed the few plastic tubs and bottles that remained at eye level, and stared out.

At first she saw nothing. She could still hear something rummaging, she just couldn't see it. It didn't sound like a raccoon. Something bigger then. Would a mountain lion be better or worse than a Tick? Surely both would be equally dangerous, if they were hungry and hunting.

Then she saw a flicker of movement maybe twenty feet away. Then that movement morphed into a recognizable shape. Not the low, svelte swagger of a panther or mountain lion, but a hulking, upright form. A Tick.

Her heart seemed to thud to a stop. She didn't even dare breathe. Suddenly, the dairy case seemed like a bad idea. A very bad idea.

Theoretically, it was securely closed, but that didn't make her feel much better. The freezer section had only one door. This thing had a dozen and they were all glass.

She had to get out of here. She took one, extremely slow, step backward. And then another.

Unfortunately, he was also moving. Toward her hiding place.

Why was he alone? Ticks were pack animals. They hunted in groups. Except Ely said their behavior was changing. That the Farms had poisoned the blood at the feeding stations and killed off all but the smartest of the Ticks. Was that why this one hunted alone? Was he all that was left of his pack? The smartest of the bunch?

He was too far away for her to tell for sure, but he didn't seem to be looking at her. He kept sniffing the air. Like he was following her trail. Okay, then. Unless something else distracted him first, he would find her. He would follow the trail right to the door of the dairy section. Or would the stench of the rotted dairy confuse him? Was the human scent of blood stronger going to the freezer section? Would he go there first? Would he be able to open the door or would he get discouraged and wander off? If he did follow her to the dairy case, the door handle's mechanism was less complicated. He might be able to open it.

And all of this would be a moot point if Carter wandered in here in a few minutes. The Tick would catch the scent of his blood, nearby and unmuddied by rotting dairy. The Tick would bound across the store in maybe five or six leaps. Carter might have a chance to raise a weapon, if he had one handy.

No. Carter *would* have a weapon. He always did. He was cautious. He always had a plan.

The Tick moved closer to the glass door; he was the biggest she'd ever seen. When they ran or attacked, they moved with grace and speed that was as unnatural as it was terrifying. But Ticks were at a disadvantage when they walked. Slow and awkward on his feet, this guy shuffled forward upright for a few steps, dropped to his knuckles and scuttled another ten feet closer in a few easy movements. This guy was huge. In life—in human life, that was—he must have been more than six feet tall. He paused, raised up on his knuckles, head tilted to sniff the air. He resembled a gorilla way more than the human he'd once been. His body was covered in patchy hair that didn't quite hide his bulging muscles.

Lily had no doubt, none at all, that he could crush her chest with one hand. That he could close his fist around her heart. He took another shuffling step forward, into one of the beams of moonlight. And he stood. Except for his pelt, he was naked—of course, Ticks didn't wear clothes. She'd just never been close enough to a male Tick before to think about it. A shudder of pure disgust went through her, and she was hit with a punch of nausea that had nothing to do with the scent of rotting dairy. Bile pooled in her mouth, but she fought the urge to spit it out. She didn't dare move.

He was close enough that she could see his eyes flash to black as his pupils contracted. If she so much as twitched, he'd see her. Hell, he could probably see her now. She was just counting on his diminished brain capacity to overlook her if she didn't move.

Even then, her heart was pounding so strongly, she was sure he could see her pulse. Afraid to even breathe, she held her breath so long her head swam.

Then he dropped back down to his knuckles and twisted away to sniff at the air in the direction of the freezer.

She sucked in a deep shuddering breath that did little to calm her racing pulse. Okay. It was go time. She couldn't dawdle anymore. If he was heading for the freezer, she had to act. She crept toward the door out of the refrigerator. If she timed it right, she'd fling open the door right as he reached the freezer door. She'd be close to him, but she could still get off a shot with her arrow. And she still had the stake. And the gun. Of course, she had no way of actually timing it. It'd be guesswork at best. But given the choice, she'd rather take a chance than wait for him to find her—or worse, find Josie.

At the door, she pulled an arrow from her quiver and notched it. She would nudge the latch with her elbow and step out of the door ready to fire. It was the best she could do.

Except before she got the door open, she heard something behind her. Nails on glass.

She whirled around to see the Tick back at the glass-fronted door to the dairy case. He hadn't gone around to the freezer at all. Either he'd seen her move, or he'd tricked her into revealing her location. Could a Tick be that smart?

She spun to face him, keeping the arrow up and notched.

He lifted one massive paw and slashed at the door again. The grating sound of claws on glass rent the air. He pawed at the door with one hand and then the other, his massive brow furrowed into a frown. He clearly saw her but couldn't figure out how to get to her. He tipped his head back and howled with rage. The sound sent her pulse racing, and pumped adrenaline through her body, making her hands shake. Adrenaline and standing still: not a great combo, but at least the adrenaline deadened some of the pain in her shoulder.

He clawed at the door again, yipping his frustration. And one of his nails caught on the edge of the door, pulling it open for a second. He stopped instantly and tilted his head to the side staring at the door for an interminable moment. Then he brought his hand forward, that same finger extended and caught his nail on the edge of the door a second time. Deliberately. It pulled open, then slipped from his nail and slammed closed. He stared at it, fascinated.

And she stood there, simply watching, unable to do anything. She couldn't shoot an arrow through the glass. She could fire her gun, but that would do almost nothing. Unless he got the glass door all the way open, she was screwed. And if he got the door open, then she'd have exactly one chance to put an arrow through his heart.

"Come on," she murmured softly, "Use that ugly brain of yours."

He ignored the handle, but he obviously understood the concept of a door. He repeated the action several more times, catching the door, opening it, letting it slam closed before he thought to wedge his hand between the door and the frame. Then he opened the door all the way. And he looked at her, his features twisting into a horrible mockery of a smile.

The metal shelves of the dairy case blocked him, but he lunged forward, his arms reaching between the shelves. She pulled back the string a fraction of an inch and let the arrow fly. But her hands were shaking too much and the shot went wide, bouncing of the shelf with a clatter.

The Tick frowned, obviously baffled by the sound.

Her breath caught. He threw himself at the shelves again. This time the entire unit scooted forward a few inches. Okay, maybe she had another shot. Looked like today was her lucky day. She whipped out another arrow, forcing herself to walk closer to him. If she wanted to hit him, she'd have to get the arrow straight through that gap. It'd be like threading a needle.

Heart pounding, she stopped three or four feet away. She sucked in a deep breath and held it before letting the arrow fly. She notched another and let it loose before she even knew if she'd made the shot. The Tick staggered back, howling in pain, the arrow protruding from his chest. Right in his heart. She hoped. The door to the dairy case slammed closed.

Moving quickly, she slung the bow over her shoulder and booked it for the door. She plucked the flashlight off the floor and palmed a stake before throwing open the door and panning the light across the store. Not that she needed the light to know right where the Tick was. His angry thrashing gave away his position.

She followed the sounds of crashing metal and breaking glass. Back in the freezer, Josie must have woken up, because underneath the sounds of the dying Tick, she could hear the piercing scream of the baby. Combined, they were making enough noise to attract the attention of every creature in the county.

On the upside, Carter wouldn't be able to miss them when he finally got there.

She took one small step toward the Tick's thrashing body just to be sure he wouldn't be getting up. His hands grabbed at the arrows, smashing their shafts so only stubby ends protruded from his chest. He wasn't dead yet, but he would be soon.

From what she understood, the Tick's blood had super healing properties. A Tick could survive from almost any wound as long as its head was still on and its heart was pumping. The stake through the heart—or in this case the arrow through the heart—kept the heart from pumping. He wouldn't really be dead until she cut off his head, but until he'd stopped twitching, she didn't want to get close enough to do it.

So she stood there for several long minutes watching him die, her heart pounding with terror, her throat clenching up. This whole thing . . . it was just too much. Too much fear. Too much death.

She still couldn't help wondering about the man he'd been before he turned. And what kind of Tick she would be, if she ever turned herself.

Even though she'd never been particularly religious in the Before, now, she closed her eyes and said a quick prayer, for his soul, if he still had it. And for her soul as well.

Not because she really believed it would make a difference, but because she knew all too well that someday there might be someone standing over her mutated, monstrous body. And she hoped the person who stopped her heart with a stake would do the same for her.

CHAPTER THIRTY-EIGHT

MEL

Sabrina makes us wait. Which, I suppose is the right of the host when guests stop by uninvited. But we are shown into a lobby and taken up to a sprawling office on the top floor. There is little view from the windows, just the twinkly lights from the campus below, bleeding into the darkness. There must be an empty town outside these fences, but it's unlit and easy to ignore in the pitch-black night.

There is sleek furniture in the penthouse, and fresh-cut flowers and guards at the ready, but nothing refreshing. Nothing in this place soothes me. I can sense the strain of Sebastian's fake calm. His jangling nerves make me jittery. He hates being here more than I do. It's his spidey sense. Even though mine isn't developed yet, I can sense it in him. Or perhaps it's just that I know him well by now.

I prowl the length of the windows while we wait. Back and forth, back and forth. I have to keep moving, because hunger is crawling along my skin, twitching my nerves. Smothering me. I haven't been near this many humans since I turned. It's harder than I thought.

Finally, the door to the back slides open and Sabrina enters, surveying the room. She frowns when she sees the guard standing by the door then turns to Sebastian. "You weren't hungry?"

"You know I don't drink directly from humans. I won't risk infecting another."

"I thought perhaps your tastes had changed," she says with a look in my direction.

My heart stutters as I realize the implications of their conversation. First, unlike Sebastian, Sabrina clearly drinks from humans with no concern for turning them. And secondly, the "guard" isn't a guard at all. *He* was the refreshment she'd offered us.

She smiles smoothly. She strokes the fingers of one hand across the tips of the other. On another woman, the gesture might look diffident, but on Sabrina, it's menacing. Her nails are as long and pointy as a lion's claws. "But surely you'll at least share a drink with me. We have glasses aplenty on the sidebar."

She is not merely playing with her hands; she is testing the edge of her weapon, preparing to slice open a vein on the man standing stupidly in the corner.

I'm backing away, panicked. I can't drink human blood. I *can't*. But I muffle my screams, because Sebastian's warnings are too loud in my ears. I edge back away from her, but Sebastian grips my arm, keeping me in place.

"No, thank you," he says. "I remember the ancient laws as well as you. I will not partake of your kine."

She nods graciously. "If you do indeed remember the ancient laws, then you know as well as I that I had to offer."

"You did not have to make the offer so enticing."

She throws back her head and releases a husky chuckle. "So enticing? Your straits must be dire indeed if a single pint of human blood is enough to entice you."

Sebastian makes a sound low in his throat that is almost a growl, but I'm unsure if she even hears it.

She is still laughing as she waves the guard from the room. She slinks across to the sofa in front of the windows and curls into a seat. "Now, down to business. I assume since you refused to drink, you are not ready to pledge your loyalty to me and become my vassal."

Sebastian snorts in derision. "You know I am not." His hand is at my back, guiding me to a seat opposite Sabrina. I want to fly against the glass like a hummingbird caught in the skylight, but Sebastian nudges me forward now and so I sit. "But I noticed Jackson has fallen."

I have no idea what Jackson is. A city, maybe?

But Sabrina knows instantly what he means, because her smile freezes. "Your intel is extensive."

Sebastian smirks. "Please. We crossed through his territory on the way here. You think I would not notice this weakness along your border."

"Notice? Or prey on?"

Sebastian's chuckle sounds genuinely amused, as if he's enjoying this game of wits, despite the strain of being with her. "If I was going to prey on your weakness, I would never have come close enough for you to even know I was here."

Sabrina's smile widens. "And yet you *have* sought sanctuary," Sabrina purrs, and her eyes light up as she sweeps her hand toward me. "And you brought me gifts. To help with my little problem?"

It takes me a moment to figure out what she means, but I still answer before Sebastian does.

"Gifts?" I ask, speaking for the first time. I bob to my feet. "I am *not* a gift."

"I couldn't agree more," Sebastian mutters.

Sabrina grins, clearly delighted by my outburst. "You didn't tell her? Oh, Sebastian, you are so deliciously naughty I could just eat you up. And if you were human, I suspect I would."

I turn on Sebastian. "Did you bring me here to get rid of me?

So she could, what?" My mind races, but I have no answers. I am out of my depth and drowning. "Why?"

Sabrina comes to her feet and pulls me into her arms. "Now, dear one, you needn't fret."

Needn't fret? I jerk away. "I have less than six months before my own territorial instincts kick in and Sebastian is trying to hand me over to you like a . . . like a . . ." But I don't even know what. I know so little about being a vampire. Sebastian has been my lode stone for the past six weeks. If he abandons me now, I don't know how I will function.

She strokes a hand down my arm. "My dear, you are being a tad overdramatic. Perhaps if you could . . . what is that phrase? Reign it in?"

I nod without really agreeing.

"If you become my vassal, I promise I will take very good care of you until it is time for you to leave."

Her words are tender, but they still chill my heart. I look to Sebastian, but his expression is unreadable.

Why? I want to scream at him. *Why are you doing this?*

But instead I ask that other great question: "How?"

Sabrina slithers closer. "Sebastian is very . . ." She savors choosing the word. "Pragmatic, shall we say. Not all vampires are isolationists like he is."

"So then you *can* be around other vampires?" I ask, something strangely like hope filling my heart.

"No. Not in that sense. Not long-term. Once you were fully grown I would boot you out, so to speak. But we would have so much fun in the meantime."

"Oh," I say. I shudder at her words, unwilling to imagine what her idea of fun might be. I can't help but look at Sebastian, who is lounging disinterestedly on the sofa. "It's only a few more months. Why not just let me be? Is it so awful, being my mentor that you can't just let me stay?"

He returns my gaze, looking more bored than concerned, then he turns to Sabrina. "Perhaps you could give us a moment?"

She has been watching the exchange, her gaze bright with interest. Her face falls as she realizes she's being asked to leave. Her lip juts out in a pout. "Very well."

A moment later we are alone.

My emotions roil inside of me. I never used to be like this: awash in feelings. In my Before, everything was so much simpler. I lived within myself, under a bell jar made of music. The jar protected me, from the world and from the darker parts of myself— the parts that feed on my control and weaken it. The parts that want to rise up and howl, Tick-like.

Alone with Sebastian, I pace, trying to outrun my anger and fear.

"Come now, Kitten. Surely it's not as bad as all that."

I whirl on him. "You tried to barter me to that woman in exchange for sanctuary!"

"Did I?"

"Yes! She thought I was some sort of hostess gift."

"I am not responsible for what she thought, only for what I intended."

"What you intended was to get rid of me."

"Was it?"

I'm tired of his oblique questions. "Yes! You brought me here to ditch me so that you wouldn't be responsible for training me. You never wanted to turn me. You turned me only because Carter made you do it."

Sebastian raises his eyebrows at this and for a moment, he looks disconcerted. "Carter made me? You believe there was *anything* that boy could have done to make me turn you?"

"What other explanation is there? You hate turning vampires. You'd rather go hungry than risk it. And yet now you're stuck with me and so you're trying to ditch me."

"My dear, if I was that desperate to be rid of you, I would have merely waited until Carter and Lily had left and I would have beheaded you. If I wanted you gone, you'd be gone. I brought you to Sabrina's not for my benefit or for hers, but for yours."

"Mine?"

"Of course. Sabrina has fared quite well since America fell. Much of her financial and personal empire is intact. Most of her enemies have fallen. She is in need of powerful allies on her border, and would likely do much to help you establish your own empire. You could do far worse than to become a vassal to a vampire of her strengths."

Everything inside of me stutters to a halt. Is that possible? That Sebastian has not brought me here to drop me off like a bag of kittens to drown but for some other reason? I don't even know what to think of that, so I admit, "I don't know what a vassal is."

He pushes himself up from his seat and comes to stand close to me. "She would be your mentor until you are fully vampire. Then she would secede you a territory adjoining hers."

"And if I was her vassal then I could be around her? Even after I'm fully vampire?"

"No. Not all vampires are as unsociable as I am, but when the time comes, you will not want to be in her company, I promise you that."

"You are in her company," I point out.

"Only because I've requested sanctuary. And it is not easy. Not for either of us."

I want to argue the point, but even I can see the strain around his eyes.

"Being her vassal would provide you some small protection. You would be allies of sorts. You would owe her an annual tithe, but in exchange, she would send resources to protect your lands if you were ever in dire distress."

It all sounds very feudal and not at all comforting, but I'm putting the pieces together. "Jackson was once her vassal."

"Yes."

"But his territory fell?"

"He did. But that doesn't mean that you would. This would be a smart move for you. Unless you have a different plan. What is it that you want out of all this?"

"I don't want to be her vassal. I don't want an empire. I just want—" I break off as my tears nearly choke me.

I have been asked this question so rarely, I have no answer. Even in the Before, even with my mother, who tried so hard and my sister, who loved me so dearly. Even they did not often ask what I wanted.

I have no ready answer to the question. Heart searching is harder than it should be. What do I want?

I want my life back. My easy, autistic life with its simple rules and solid structure. I want my mother. My sister. Even my willy-nilly father, who never writes or calls. I want all of those things. And I want a choice. An opinion.

This is what Sebastian is giving me, which no one else ever has.

Oh, Lily and my mother tried, but my safety always trumped my voice.

"I want . . . I want to make a difference." I want the chance that

Lily took from me when she begged Sebastian to turn me. It's not that I didn't want to be a vampire—though who would choose this?—it's that I wanted my choice, my actions to matter. Lily took that from me, but Sebastian is giving it back. "I want to fight. I want to help people."

Sebastian tips his head to the side, as if mulling over my words. "You could help people without fighting. Sabrina protects many subjects from the Ticks. She provides for them. She—"

"She feeds from them and calls them kine," I sneer.

"You didn't see her guards arguing, did you?"

"Because she no doubt has a powerful *abductura* who convinces them to stay with her."

Sebastian sweeps a hand toward the windows and the world beyond Sabrina's kingdom. "Did you not see her defenses? Do you think the people here would want to leave? The world outside is gone. Where would they go?"

"She feeds from them."

"And they gladly let her, because she protects their families."

"She lays them out as appetizers before her guests. What would she have done if I had eaten that man? I could have killed him."

"If you had dined in her territory, you would have been her vassal, like it or not. Those are the ancient laws of hospitality."

I reel back from this news. As indignant as I had been on behalf of that nameless stranger, I am repulsed on my own behalf. And betrayed. Sebastian's endless mind games have laid me bare. "So you set me up?"

"I merely tested your resolve. I did warn you to be polite."

"In some cultures, it's considered rude to refuse food!"

"And in many ancient cultures, sharing food forms a binding contract." He waves a dismissive hand. "I'll not quarrel with you over what might have been. If you didn't have the strength to resist eating the man, you would have been of no use to me. But—"

"Of no use to you? What of me and my choices?"

"Strength earns you choices. This has always been true. It's as simple as that. You want the right to determine your own destiny, you fight for it." He smiles. "And you maintain your self-control."

I'm still pissed, but I don't argue. Maybe because I know he's right. Maybe because it doesn't matter. I was strong enough and that's earned me the chance to make a difference. If I can convince him to let me.

"If I don't want to stay with her, can I leave?" He arches an eyebrow in question, so I continue. "You were exchanging me for sanctuary."

"Was I?"

"Yes! You said I was a hostess gift."

"Ah, poor, Melly. You jump to conclusions so quickly."

"Because you aren't being straightforward!"

"Have I ever been?" Then his expression softens and he trails a soothing hand up my arm. "I didn't bring you to her in exchange for sanctuary. I sought sanctuary so that you would have an option of becoming her vassal. If you want to leave with me, you may."

I'm confused not just about these complicated rules that govern vampire behavior, but also by Sebastian's distracting touch. "But what about the ancient laws of hospitality? Don't you owe her something?"

"And you just naturally assume that you are the only asset I have?" He chucks my chin playfully. "Have a little faith, my dear. I have many resources. I will strike a bargain with Sabrina, if it is what you choose."

"I do not want to be her vassal."

"Are you certain? You can't change your mind."

"When you leave here, you're going to continue to fight against Roberto?" I ask.

"Of course."

"Then I—"

"Do not make this choice lightly, but consider what you're giving up. You could do what Sabrina has done: establish a territory here in Arizona. She would expect you to cultivate your own kine."

I shudder at the word. I cannot bring myself to think of humans as my food.

Sebastian sees my reaction and grabs my chin. There is nothing gentle in his touch. "No. Do not flinch from this. They are your food. You were made to consume human blood. We are the check that balances the human population. I will not always be here to remind you of this. For now, you feed on Ticks, but what will you do if the Ticks are ever wiped out? That is the point of Carter's rebellion, is it not? To destroy the Ticks? What if he succeeds? What will you eat then? And do not entertain any fantasies about dining on deer and dogs. If the Ticks are gone, you will eat humans. Accept that."

Hysteria bubbles up inside of me. I cannot accept that. I will not. There must be another way.

I shake my head, but he keeps talking.

"If you really want to help the rebellion, then you should do this. Establish a territory here. All of those people at Base Camp, make them your kine. You want to fight against Roberto, then fight that way."

"Why are you so desperate to get rid of me?"

He lets go of me and turns away now. I still can't read his moods. Is he annoyed with me or merely tired? Is the strain of being near Sabrina wearing on him, or is it the strain of being my mentor?

When he turns back to me, I think it must be both.

"I will do anything to bring down Roberto. If you stay with me, the path ahead will be difficult. I don't want to be rid of you, but I would not force this on you."

"Why?" I ask. "Why is destroying him so important? Why do you hate him so much?"

Sebastian arches an eyebrow. "Kitten, in two thousand years, when everyone you've ever loved has died, when you've been alone so long you cannot remember how to be with any living creature, when you've watched the world crumble at the whim of one man, then, perhaps, you'll hate me as much as I hate him."

As always, Sebastian hasn't really given me an answer. No real specifics anyway, but I understand him now. I don't even have to think of my reply. "If I get to choose, then I choose to stay with you. I want to fight Roberto, too."

But even as I say it, I am questioning motives—not his, but my own. Have I picked this because of my strength or my weakness? Do I want to bring down Roberto because he is a monster? Or is it because it's easier to destroy another monster than to admit I have become one myself?

CHAPTER THIRTY-NINE

CARTER

In a perfect world, I would have found Lily hunkered down for the night, somewhere safe and secure. Like an army compound surrounded by armed soldiers. And watched over by Iron Man and Thor.

But the last time I'd seen armed soldiers (via news footage, but still), they'd been running away from Ticks. And that guy who played Iron Man was worth like a gazillion dollars. I was pretty sure all the people rich enough to afford it had bailed on the United States and were off on some tropical island somewhere. Hell, it's what I would have done if I'd had my own jet.

But this was Lily. She never played it safe. So instead of finding her locked in the freezer section like she promised me, I found her standing over the body of a dying Tick, contemplating how to cut off his head.

She turned when she heard me. Her face was pale and drawn. Her hands were shaking so badly the flashlight she held cast a trembling circle on the floor.

She dropped the stake from her other hand and launched herself into my arms. "God, it took you long enough to get here!"

I held her for a long moment. I wanted to kiss her so badly I was nearly shaking, but instead I pulled away enough to look down at her. "I thought we'd talked about you not risking your life. Especially not when there are Ticks out there."

She looked at the dead Tick and gave a little shrug, looking diffident for a moment. Then she shrugged it off. "I couldn't do it. I'm not even going to apologize. I wasn't a hundred percent sure he couldn't reach the baby. I had to protect her. Besides, I knew you were on your way and I wasn't about to let you walk in with him wandering around."

"Lily, we've been over this. You can't—"

"I know I'm vulnerable, but a Tick can kill you just as easily as it can me."

Even knowing she was right, I didn't want to hear it. I blew out a breath but before I could talk, she continued.

"Besides, I had a choice. I could have waited for him to find me, or I could stand my ground. You're the one who taught me to always stand your ground."

She was right. I was the one who told her that. And I hated to have my own words thrown back at me, so I changed the subject.

"Leave me here to take care of this guy. Get the baby and get out to the car. We've got plenty of gas, we're going to drive through the night."

She nodded tearfully, and pulled away from me to head for the freezer at the back of the store. I could hear the baby's plaintive cries even from here.

I was almost out the door when she called out, "You should check the back of the Cayenne. I think I saw an ax back there. You know, for . . ."

She let the words trail off with a curl of distaste to her lips. She had paused and turned back to face me.

Her distaste was mingled with amusement, like she was laughing at herself for not being tougher. I smiled, too, because that was so like her. And because just yesterday, I thought I might never see that smile again. Seeing it now made something in my chest ache. Maybe this was enough. Just this moment. Regardless of whether I could keep her safe forever. Maybe it was enough to keep her safe for now. For each day we had together.

Before the thought could even crystallize in my mind, shit went bad. I saw it in her expression before I heard the scraping of the Tick's movements. I saw the flash of fear in her eyes. The mute terror as she fumbled for words that she couldn't get out fast enough.

I whirled to see the Tick stumbling to his feet. He clutched a bloody arrow in either hand. Arrows he'd ripped from his own chest. The wounds gaped, pumping blood out onto the floor.

Lily screamed, the sound piercing the air even as I pulled the shotgun from the scabbard slung across my back. I fired at the guy, one round of buckshot and then another. It hardly seemed to faze him. He shambled forward a step and then another. My shotgun was nothing fancy. Its greatest virtue was simplicity, not speed, and it took me precious seconds to reload. If the Tick hadn't been wounded, I'd be dead already. But the holes in his chest were pumping a lot of blood. Too bad he wouldn't bleed out and just die peacefully. Instead, his extraordinary wounds just made him that much hungrier.

I needed a stake. Something thick and strong. Something he couldn't pull out. Too bad I was fresh out.

"Carter!" Lily yelled.

I turned toward her and saw a stake—a whittled-down broomstick—in her hand. She tossed it underhanded toward me but she must have been nervous because the toss fell short by several feet. The Tick was on me by then. I grabbed the barrel of the shotgun in both hands and slammed the butt into his face. The heat of the metal seared my palms. I rammed it at him again, hearing a sickening crunch that didn't even phase him. He automatically dropped the broken arrows and grabbed the shotgun, too, trying to pull it out of his way. He literally lifted me off my feet and flung me aside like a ragdoll. I was out of weapons and ideas.

Then, suddenly, the Tick froze. The shotgun clattered to the floor as he looked down. I followed his gaze and saw the pointy end of a stake sticking out of his chest.

He flailed mutely for a moment, then reached for the stake Lily had thrust through his heart from behind. He howled with rage, but his hands were too slippery from the blood to gain purchase on the shaft. Then he stumbled and whirled around. He fell to his knees and reared up one more time. At first I thought he was trying to get back up. Then I saw the arrow in his hand again. I was too far away to do anything about it. In one quick and deadly movement, he stabbed the bloodied arrow through Lily's shoe.

CHAPTER FORTY

LILY

Lily didn't even see it happen, just felt the sharp and sudden pain flare through her foot. When she looked down, it took several long heartbeats to process what she was seeing at all. What was that in her shoe? How had it gotten there? What the hell?

By the time she put the pieces together and figured out it was an arrow, Carter had already picked her up and was running through the store. Away from the Tick, but also away from Josie.

She bucked in Carter's arms, twisting and yelling for him to stop, but his crushing grasp was too tight. "The baby!" she cried. "You can't leave the baby!"

He ignored her. A moment later, he burst out of the store and into the night. The Cayenne and a smaller Mazda were parked right out front. He deposited her on the passenger seat of the Mazda.

The trunk of the Mazda was open. And beside the car stood Stoner Joe. Who she'd thought was dead. The shock of seeing him warred for attention in her already scrambled brain. She dismissed it. She'd process that later. After.

Joe, who had been siphoning gas from the Cayenne into the Mazda while moving supplies from one vehicle to the other, stopped what he was doing.

Unnaturally pale he asked, "Where's the baby? What happened?"

Carter was already rummaging for the ax she'd told him about. He seemed not to even hear Joe's questions.

The arrow . . . the Tick . . . But Lily couldn't think of that yet. They were still in danger, and Josie wasn't out yet. The longer they all stood here talking, the more likely it was that another Tick would show up.

So she pushed aside her shock and answered. "There was a Tick. We've killed it. I think. He's going to make sure." By the time she finished the sentence, Carter had found the ax and disappeared back into the building. "You should wait a minute then go in after Josie. She's upset, but fine. The freezer in the back. There's food there, too. In a backpack. Don't leave that. We'll need it later. And there's a sippy cup with some milk in it. Don't forget that. And—"

Her words trailed off as her head suddenly spun. She'd forgotten to breathe there for a minute. "Just go," she ordered. She just needed a moment. To be alone. To think. To plan.

Joe bolted for the door.

She was immediately sorry she'd sent him away. Not because sending him into the building was dangerous. Carter was finishing off the Tick right now. Not because she didn't think Josie needed rescuing, because of course she did.

But because now that he was gone, it seemed impossible that he'd really been there.

Joe was dead. She was so sure of that. If he hadn't been dead these past two months, then where the hell had he been?

She couldn't believe that McKenna had died, only to have Joe show up alive, hundreds of miles from where he was supposed to be. Here. Now. When Josie needed him so badly.

It was unimaginable.

So had she imagined it?

Was this how it started? With hallucinations?

Because—holy crap—she'd thought she'd have more time. Three days, right? That's what the news shows had said. Three days of extreme flulike symptoms before the transformation happened.

But maybe the news had been wrong. Maybe it was three days normally, but not if a friggin' Tick stabbed you with an arrow covered in friggin' infected Tick blood. Maybe when that happened it was three minutes instead.

Jesus.

Fear and panic wrestled inside of her, fighting for dominance, but she couldn't let them win. Because in just a few minutes, maybe less, Carter was going to walk out the door, and she needed to have a plan by then. Carter wouldn't be thinking clearly. So she'd have to think clearly enough for all of them.

But all she could think was that she didn't want to go like this. All the times she'd thought about it and planned for her own death, she hadn't really believed it would go down like this. She'd been arrogant enough to think she was too smart to be infected. Too prepared. Too strong.

Christ, she was an idiot.

She forced herself to look down at her injury. Just seeing the arrow sticking out of her shoe made the pain pulse up her leg. Okay, first things first, get the arrow out. It would hurt like hell but it gave her something to focus on. Something to do. Some way to clear her mind of the racing clutter.

She reached into her back pocket and pulled out the pocket-knife. Her hands were shaking so badly she had to use her teeth to open it. The arrow went straight through the tongue of her sneaker.

She pulled the lace out of the shoe and flared open the sides. She moved quickly, ignoring the pain. The pain didn't matter. What mattered, what really mattered, was that she see it with her own eyes. That she see the bloody arrow, penetrating her foot. Otherwise, how could she do what needed to be done next? Unless she saw it, she wouldn't be strong enough.

She slid the flat of the blade between the tongue of the shoe and her foot and sawed the knife back and forth, cutting the tongue off. Every slice of the knife jostled the arrow and she had to clench her teeth to keep from crying out. Then she pulled the shoe off her foot, leaving the arrow. Just as she'd thought, the arrowhead was embedded entirely in her foot, the point protruding from the bottom. Pulling it out would do more tissue damage than pushing it cleanly through. She sucked in five sharp inhalations, then held her breath as she drove the shaft of the arrow the rest of the way through her foot and pulled it out.

Choking back a sob, she let the arrow drop to the ground and she collapsed in the seat, her head rolling to the side.

Her mind raced with treatment options, even though she knew none would work. She'd been to Girl Scout camp every summer since she was six. She'd taken dozens of first aid classes. Yeah, she wasn't a doctor or a nurse, but she didn't need any formal training to know she was screwed.

"Joe, get me the first aid kit, a bottle of water, and the soap out of the back."

She opened her eyes to see Joe standing maybe ten feet away, cradling baby Josie in his arms. Carter was a bit farther away, stripping down to his underwear. Again she blinked, trying to force her spinning head to reason. Was she hallucinating?

She looked to Joe. "You're alive? And here?"

He nodded as he pulled out a gallon jug of water and tossed a bar of soap to Carter. "Yeah. I've been at a Farm. I got picked up on the way to Utah. It's a long story." His gaze dropped to her foot. "Lily, man . . . I'm sorry."

Carter chucked the last of his bloody clothes into a pile and started washing his hands. He responded to Joe's comment before Lily could. "It's okay. She's going to be fine."

"Carter, I'm not—"

"You're gonna be fine. We'll clean the wound. Flush it with water."

He rinsed his hands and gave them a shake, looking over his own body for more blood. When he didn't see any, he disappeared behind the back of the Mazda and she could hear him rummaging around for clean clothes. He came out a moment later, dressed in jeans and gray hoodie like the one he'd been wearing when he rescued her from the Farm.

The sight of it made her heart ache even more. He'd done so much for her. This was going to be hardest on him. So much harder on him than on anyone else.

"Listen to me, Carter." Her voice shook with fear, but she pushed it aside. "A wound like this can't just be cleaned. I'm infected."

"No. You're not."

"The Tick's blood—"

"It's just like snake's venom. I'll suck it out. It's only been, what, five minutes? That's soon enough."

"No. It's not. Trust me. Twelve years of summer camp first aid classes. If you're bitten by a venomous snake, the venom reaches your heart within sixty seconds. There's no way to suck it out. The human heart beats too fast."

All this time she'd thought that the human heart would save

them all—that love would rescue them. And now her own heart had killed her. Just as surely as the Tick had.

Carter came over to her, crouching to look at the wound. After his careful scrub-down, he didn't touch her foot. A sign that some part of him knew she was right. He wouldn't say it aloud. She didn't blame him. She didn't want to say it either, but it had to be said.

She scooted to the edge of her seat and took his face in her hands. That beautiful face she loved so much. She made him look at her. "Here's what's going to happen. You're going to get in the Cayenne with Josie and drive away."

"No!"

"Just a mile down the road. There's a"—she frantically tried to remember what else was in this Godforsaken town—"a Dairy Queen. It's just down Main Street. You're going to wait there. Joe will meet you there in five minutes. Ten, max."

"No," Joe said quietly, shaking his head and holding Josie even closer.

Carter said nothing, but his gaze dropped and he couldn't look at her.

She looked up at Joe, who stood there holding his beautiful baby girl in his arms. She'd sworn she would do everything in her power to keep Josie safe. Letting go now, knowing that she couldn't do that in person, was like ripping her heart out. She didn't want to die.

And yet, she was doing everything she could to protect Josie. She understood now what McKenna had meant about that. This was her fighting for Josie. Making them do the right thing. Choosing death when life was no longer an option. That was fighting, not giving up.

"You can do this for me, right Joe?" He was shaking his head.

"Yes. You can. I know you don't want to. But it's the right thing. It's easier to do it now. We have no idea how long I'll have. I'd rather go now than risk putting anyone else in danger."

But Joe was still shaking his head. "No, Lil. I don't think I can."

What was she going to do if she couldn't convince either one of them?

She still had her handgun, but there were no guarantees that a gunshot would kill her. She was still mostly human, but who knew how long the virus took to kick in. For all she knew, her epigenetics were already switching around to change her body. When Sebastian had turned Mel, it had started so damn fast.

No. She needed one of them. Even if she shot herself, she needed someone to dispose of the body and make sure she didn't regenerate.

"Joe, listen to me. You can do this."

"No, Lily. I can't."

She saw the resolution in his gaze. Saw what it would cost him. Dear, sweet Joe. Joe was a pacifist. And he'd just found out about McKenna. Carter must have told him on the drive down, because his eyes were red-rimmed. Besides, he hadn't asked about her, which he surely would have done if he didn't already know she was dead.

The guy had just lost the love his life and now she was asking him to do this horrible thing. To someone he liked. Shit.

Still, it needed to be done and Carter wasn't going to do it. So she dug deep, wracking her brain for something that would make this easier for Joe. "I was there when McKenna died. There were Ticks coming. She was bleeding out. And I left her there so Josie and I could escape. I let her die."

But he just shook his head, like he didn't believe her. "Nah, Lily. You wouldn't have done that. And I can't do this."

"Damn it!" she cursed. "Don't you two get it? I'm turning into a monster. Already! You have to do it now while you can!"

Carter shoved himself to his feet and stormed around to the other side of the car and started digging through a bag on the driver's seat.

"No. It's not going down like this."

She turned in her seat to watch him. What did he mean, it wasn't going down like this? It had already gone down. There was nothing any of them could do.

Yeah, she got it. The situation sucked. They hated having this choice thrust on them. They hated feeling helpless. She got that. That was how she'd felt when Mel . . .

And that's when it hit her.

"Carter, no!"

But the phone was already in his hands. He'd already dialed Sebastian.

CHAPTER FORTY-ONE

CARTER

I couldn't even look at Lily when I made the call. I even blocked out the sound of her protests until she'd hopped around the car to pound on my chest with her fists.

"I will not let you do this!" she yelled.

"It's not your choice," I said simply. I made it sound simple anyway, to hide how complicated this really was. I'd lied of course, because it should have been her choice. This should never have been my decision at all. But I couldn't kill Lily. I couldn't let Joe kill Lily. There was nothing I wouldn't do to save her.

I pretended not to hear her yelling. Instead, I climbed into the car and shut the door behind me then reached across and pulled the passenger-side door closed as well. A quick jab of the door-lock key and I was locked away from all the things I didn't want to hear. I couldn't bear to hear.

Sebastian was slow to pick up. Really slow.

Of course, it was the middle of the night. He'd be out hunting. With Mel.

"Ah, if it isn't my young padawan," he drawled when he answered the phone.

"I need your help."

"Of course you do," he said with the typical sneer in his voice.

"Lily—" My anger closed around my throat and I had to swallow before continuing. Shit. I had to get through this. "She got hurt. She's been exposed."

"Exposed to what?" he asked politely. Like he was inquiring about the friggin' whether. "Is she coming down with a cold?"

"Stop being so damn coy. You know what I mean. She was exposed to the Tick virus. You have to come help us."

"Help you how, exactly?"

I gritted my teeth, unable to believe I was about to say this aloud. "You have to come bite her. Turn her before she can turn into a Tick."

"No," he said calmly.

"What? You can't just—"

"No!" This time there was real anger in his voice, hidden beneath the crisp overpronunciation he fell back on when his emotions ran high. "No. It is you who 'can't just.' You can't just order me around. Do not forget which of us is the more powerful one in this particular venture."

I blew out a breath, trying to calm myself down. "Please, Sebastian." Even as I said it, I knew the word *please* wouldn't cut it. "She had direct, blood-to-blood contact. She's definitely infected."

"Well, then, I suggest you act quickly."

"Come on, you know I can't—" I couldn't even bring myself to say it. How the hell was I going to do it? "Please, just come down to Texas. Just do it." I was begging now. Not ordering. Not even hoping. Just outright begging. "Hell, you don't even have to train her. Just turn her and walk away. By now, Mel could . . ."

But I didn't even have an end to that sentence. I had no idea how Mel was doing. She hadn't had any contact with any of us. For all I knew, she was miserable. She may hate us all for what we did to her. Was that the fate I wanted for Lily? Was I just being selfish?

Yes. And yes.

No doubt I was being selfish, but if I had to choose between killing her and letting her live, as a vampire, it was a choice I would make again and again.

"Just get your ass down here and do something. Please."

"No," he repeated calmly. "That particular ticket could only be redeemed once. No matter how you curse and beg and plead, I will not come solve your problem for you." He paused. For a moment I thought he was done. End of conversation. End of hope. Then he added, "I might, however, have a suggestion that will help you."

"Okay. Anything."

"You mentioned you were in Texas?"

"Yeah. A little town called Sweetwater. Not far from Abilene."

"Excellent. Then you're practically in the den of the lion, as it were."

"The den of the . . . What the hell are you talking about?"

"About Roberto, of course. You don't really think he created the Tick virus without also creating an antidote, do you?"

"I . . . I hadn't thought about it." Was that even possible? A cure for the virus? "There's a cure?"

"Yes. I do believe there is."

"A cure?" I said again stupidly.

"Is our connection bad?" Sebastian asked smoothly.

"If there's a cure, why the hell haven't you mentioned it before now?"

"Well, for starters, I don't know if it'll work. And I'm almost certain it won't work on Ticks who are fully developed. Yet. And besides, I did mention that it's in the hands of Roberto, did I not?"

"Oh, jeez, you make it sound so easy."

"I'm sorry. If saving your girlfriend's life is too difficult for you, then by all means, skip it and play some video games instead."

"Screw you." I was so pissed off at Sebastian, it was all I could do not to just hang up on him right then. "So you're saying, what? That I should break into Roberto's secret lair and steal the cure?"

"Oh, I don't think that will be necessary. You shouldn't have to break in."

"I just walk up with Lily and ask for it?"

"You'd be surprised how much a polite request will get you. That's something your generation never—"

"Focus!" I barked.

"Very well. Yes, just walk up to the front gates. I've been working on a little theory about the Price sisters and—"

"What, now you think Lily is an *abductura* after all?" I asked.

"Sarcasm will get you nowhere."

"Fine. Tell me about this theory."

"Never mind." Sebastian's voice oozed with disdain. "I'll let you find out for yourselves. If you still have that tranquilizer gun of yours, you should use a dart on Lily. An artificially repressed heart rate should slow the progression of the virus. Go to Roberto. He will help you."

Chances were much better that Roberto would kill us where we stood. But I guess I could live with that. Being murdered by Roberto was better than having to murder Lily myself. I'd said I would do anything to protect her. And I guess this was it. My deal with the devil. My unthinkable bargain. I would go to Roberto and ask for help from the man who had destroyed humanity.

"Fine. Tell me where to go."

"Roberto owns the largest contiguous ranch in Texas. In the entire United States, for that matter."

My mind flashed back to my Texas history class. "King Ranch?" I asked.

Sebastian laughed. "No. Vampires haven't maintained their anonymity for three thousand years by cutting endorsement deals with Ford."

"King Ranch is the largest ranch in Texas," I said through gritted teeth.

Lily was dying. Every second we wasted she was a second closer to turning into a monster I would have to kill. And this asshole was here making jokes.

"No. King Ranch is reputed to be the largest ranch in Texas. Roberto's ranch, El Corazon, is the one Richard King tried to build when he started buying up property back in the eighteen fifties. Roberto's ranch isn't nearly as publicized. In fact, I doubt there's anyone other than Roberto himself who knows exactly how big his property is. It is not marked on any map. It's not listed on any county records."

"Well, great then. I'll just drive south until I reach Area 51."

Sebastian chuckled again. "Good plan. Head for Calhoun County, take Ranch Road 3214 until someone either kills you or invites you in."

CHAPTER FORTY-TWO

CARTER

After I hung up with Sebastian, I sat in the car for a minute, mulling, planning, and bracing myself for the shitstorm that was to come after I told Lily what I'd learned.

I thought of Sebastian's suggestion. Actually just tranqing Lily when I got out would probably be the easiest way to go. Not that I was going to do that. I'd done it once, as an absolute last resort. Back when she didn't trust me. I wasn't going to do it again. Even if it would make things much easier. I'd just have to convince her that this was for the best.

Yeah. Because she was going to be so excited to throw in with the man who'd brought down all of humanity.

I climbed out of the Mazda to find her standing with her arms crossed. I held up my hands in a gesture of surrender as I shut the door behind me. Joe stood a little ways away. Out of the blast zone, I guess.

"I am not letting him bite me," she growled.

"Don't worry. He said he wouldn't."

Her brow creased in a frown. "Oh."

"He had another plan." Her frown deepened. "You aren't going to like it any better."

She didn't protest as much as I thought she would. Instead, she listened, quietly. Thoughtfully. Head tilted to the side like she did when she was thinking through a problem.

Then she looked up at me. "He has the cure?"

"That's what Sebastian said."

"And Sebastian really thinks we'll be able to just walk through the front door. That Bob will just let us in?"

"Yeah. He does. And maybe he's right. The Dean obviously thought you were an *abductura*. Maybe he told Roberto. Maybe that's where Ely was going to take you."

Her eyes flashed. "Then he will have to cure me. I'll be useless to him as a Tick. If there are no vampire *abducturae*, then I'm pretty damn sure there won't be any Tick *abducturae*, either."

Joe had stepped closer. He was rocking slightly back and forth the way people always do when they hold newborns. Somehow he made it look tough. And right.

Stoner Joe. Trader Joe. Preacher Joe. None of those names had ever really seemed right to me. But "father" did.

"But Lily, you're not an *abductura*," Joe said.

"No. But Roberto doesn't know that, right?" She smiled as her mouth trembled. She seemed terrified still, but determined. "And we can get in there, to wherever he keeps the cure. We can steal it. Then we kill him."

CHAPTER FORTY-THREE

MEL

I do not know what bargain Sebastian struck with Sabrina, only that they spoke for a long time in privacy. Sebastian and I left a few hours after we had arrived. Sabrina herself escorted us to the gates of her compound. She gave me a motherly hug that almost felt benign, but she smiled cruelly as she pulled back. "I suppose it's just as well, my dear. Enemies are so much more amusing than friends, non?"

Before I could respond, she darted back into the night and Sebastian ushered me into the driver's seat. Again, I drove, since he was still worn thin from being on Sabrina's territory. He merely told me to head east, so I drove toward the rising sun, unsure what my future would hold.

Sebastian slept for hours while I drove in silence, thinking of all I didn't know about this new world. He wakes near dusk, hungry and strained.

"We just passed a town," I tell him. "Amarillo, I think. I'm sure there will be Ticks there. Do you want me to go back, so you can hunt?"

"No," he answers without even considering. "Let's do something different this time."

Dread tiptoes across my skin. I've had too much different. I would prefer routine.

"Circle back, but head just south of town. There's a Farm in Canyon."

"A Farm?" I ask stupidly. We have not yet hunted near a Farm.

"That makes you nervous?"

I shrug. Trying not to sound nervous, I say, "There will be many humans around."

"You were much closer to far more humans last night. Your control can be trusted."

"But is it smart?" I ask. Is it necessary?

But I don't ask that aloud because I don't want Sebastian to know that I'm afraid of being too near a Farm. Too near humans.

Yes, I was near humans last night at Sabrina's but that was twelve hours of hunger ago. Besides, I'd been afraid of Sabrina and the rifles her guards held. Fear had restrained me. Since I don't want to say any of this aloud, I ask Sebastian, "Why should we hunt near a Farm now, when we haven't in the past?"

He gives a disinterested shrug. "Because I am hungry and tired. The Ticks who live near Farms are lazy. They'll be easier to kill."

I don't question him, because his logic makes sense. Besides, he hasn't once led me astray. He has berated me and pushed me. He has tested me and hurt me. But every trial has made me stronger. Every test has given me new focus. If I can't trust his judgment, then what can I trust?

If he believes I'm ready to be near humans without losing control, then I believe him. If he is gearing up for a battle against Roberto and he believes I can help, then I will. I can be a force for good. I can turn the tide in this battle.

We park a few miles from the Farm and leave the car in the parking lot of a strip mall. Sebastian brings his Arkansas Toothpick, a wickedly sharp fourteen-inch dagger. He uses it to kill Ticks, neatly slicing off their heads before draining their blood.

Before we leave the car, he pulls out another blade. It's longer than his—about two feet long with a gently curving blade. Holding the blade on the flat of his palm, he extends the handle toward me.

"For me?"

"It's a katana. Sabrina thought you might like it."

"That's … generous," I say, automatically suspicious.

"Even doing as well as she is, she can see the benefit of thinning out the Ticks. Besides, I think she liked you."

I shiver and I'm not sure if it's trepidation at the thought of Sabrina's fondness or if it's excitement. The katana speaks to me. Murmuring my name. Almost singing to me in a way that no thing has done since I was turned. Everything sang to me when I was human. Now it's only other vampires and Ticks. And this sword. In my palm it feels as if it was made for me. It is light and nimble and makes me feel like Uma Thurman in *Kill Bill*, which my mother never let me watch. And now I'm the sleek assassin. For once, I feel powerful. And strong.

We run the Ticks to ground outside the Farm. The fences are silent and dark. I know there are people inside, because I can smell them, distantly. Behind the layer of ozone of the high-voltage fences. The fences smell like death and steel, but still I know why the Ticks can't stay away. Also, there is the faint buzzing, which at first I think must be the thrum of electricity through the wires, but when I ask Sebastian he shakes his head.

"It's the tracking chips."

Each of the Greens inside the Farm has a chip implanted in his or her neck, which tracks their diet, their health, and their location. When we had first escaped from the Farm—back when I was human—Sebastian had said he thought the chips attracted the attention of the Ticks. I can see why he thought so. It's a constant *thrum, thrum, thrum* in my ears. I can see why it would drive someone mad. The Ticks howl with rage when we corner them.

I kill them quickly, taking off their heads. I will drain them and feed later, just like Sebastian has taught me. Their muddied blood is an easy temptation to resist. Like eating catfish. It's not bad if you don't think about the mud and the muck the fish lived in all their lives. About the excrement they ate to survive.

I'm still waiting to feed when Sebastian calls my name. The wind shifts and I smell it at the same time. We are not alone out here.

Before I can stop myself, I bound over the bodies of the Ticks and run. My mind is screaming. *No! The other way! You know what's there! Why are you going there?*

I round the corner of the fence and stop cold. Despite my hunger. My hunger that is not a hunger but a bone-deep, craven need. A compulsion. Despite that, I stop when I see them.

Greens. And they are almost green in the moonlight, unnaturally pale and gaunt. There are three of them. Sebastian uses the tip of his Toothpick to break open the locks that keep them chained beside the fence. The two boys are free first and they bolt like frightened deer but with none of the grace. The girl, he grabs by the scruf of the neck.

"Come here," he orders.

My mind and body war. I am less than ten feet away before my mind wins.

Sebastian has a hard grip on her shoulder, holding her in place. She cringes under the weight of his hands, too terrified to fight him.

"Please," she begs, so softly the register of her voice is almost inaudible over the delicious beat of her heart.

He uses the tip of his Toothpick to flick her hair off her shoulder. To me, he says, "You've hunted vermin long enough. You deserve a real meal."

My mind stumbles as clumsy as those Greens thrashing away in the darkness. He has told me over and over again that I can't eat from a Tick. I can't eat from a human. And yet he is offering one to me. I have learned to obey his every order, but which command do I follow—the one to abstain or the one to indulge?

I take another step closer. Then I hesitate. My mind catches and falls over itself.

I knew I was a monster, but until now I didn't know how monstrous I was. I question his orders *before* I question whether or not I should eat. I think of him before I think of my own morals. He has become my compass. Have I lost true north forever?

I take a step back. I cannot let him control me. Not if I want to be me. To be Mel.

I am shaking my head, backing away. Not just one step, but several.

"No!" he barks. "You can't deny your true nature. You want to drink her blood. You will drink her blood."

His words finally pierce her shock. Her gaze darts to mine as terror grips her. She claws at his hand, trying to wrench herself free, but he simply lifts her up into the air so her feet kick uselessly. He is both right and wrong. I will not give in. I cannot lose so much of myself. Despite what he said back at Sabrina's compound, I am determined to resist. Even if the rebellion succeeds, even if there are someday no more Ticks, I still won't feed on humans. I cannot.

"No," I say again, barely daring to say it aloud. I am sure he will retaliate. I am sure he will pounce on me and make me submit to his will again, with teeth and force.

Instead, he stalks toward me, dragging the Green behind him.

He holds her in one hand and sheathes his dagger in order to grab me with the other. He gives me a shake.

"Look at her," he orders. "What do you see?"

I make myself look. Not only because he orders it but because it's impossible not to look. At first all I see is the lovely webbing of blue and red veins, brilliant against her fragile skin. Calling to me.

But then I force myself to look beyond her blood. She is young. Tender. Long, dark hair. High cheekbones. Eyes so frightened, she must be in shock. Her heart is beating so hard against her skin, I'm amazed it doesn't burst right from her chest.

Suddenly, she isn't food. She is fear. She is me. The me I was just a few weeks ago. The me I was my whole life.

My stomach turns. I am no longer hungry.

I look at Sebastian. Was this what he wanted me to realize? Was this what he wanted me to see? I am as shocked by his behavior as I am by my own. By his own unexpected display of humanity. He seems so cold and heartless, but he isn't.

All the anger and resentment I've felt melts away. He is not my enemy. He is my mentor. My friend.

But when I meet his gaze, I don't see that spark of humanity. I see brutal cruelty.

"No," he says softly. "Look again. You made yourself see her as a girl. A living human. But look again."

I do. This time I see both the blood and the girl. I see the fear and the food.

"She is not you," he murmurs, his words as seductive as they are chilling. "She is not your sister. Not your friend. She is your food. The sooner you acknowledge that, the better." He jerks her forward until she is right under my nose. I breathe through my mouth to make her less appealing, but I can feel her scent on the roof of my mouth. "She is veal. She is meat. She is the best steak you've ever eaten. She is a Kobe burger from the best restaurant. She is the hot dog from that childhood backyard barbecue. Your favorite ice cream melting on your tongue, an icy Popsicle on a scorching day. That last perfect day of summer. The last time your family was all together. She is the last meal you will ever eat. Once you taste her, all of those other flavors will pale in comparison. You will never want anything else again."

I try to resist. I rub my tongue against the roof of my mouth, trying to scrub away the scent of her blood. I make myself look at her eyes. To see her pain. Her fear. Her anguish. I even remind myself of what Sebastian once said, back when I was still human. That those particular human emotions make the blood bitter. That she will not be as delicious as he has made her sound. She will be bitter with terror.

Despite that, when I look in her eyes, all I see are the tiny blood veins clutching her irises in their grasp. All I see is that ephemeral pulse against the white.

I make myself close my eyes. I blot out the reality of this girl and imagine she is Lily. She is my sister. My mirror image.

Slowly, torturously, I move away. I pull myself from his grasp. He holds tight, but he is holding her and me. I slam my arms down on his hand and he lets go.

"No!" he barks again and I find myself frozen by his words. "You *will* drain her. You will kill her. If not her, then someone else like her. You are trying too hard to think like a human. You are still denying who you are, but someday you will snap and you will kill."

"I didn't at Sabrina's. I was strong enough to resist then. You don't know that I won't always be this strong. Just because you weakened and gave in to your baser instincts. That doesn't mean I will."

He doesn't even flinch at the insult. "Back at Sabrina's you'd fed recently. You weren't hungry. Besides, you were too frightened of Sabrina. You have to train yourself. You have to learn to keep your instincts in check. You do that by giving in now."

"I will not do this."

"You will. The question is, who do you want your first kill to be? This girl? Or some other girl? Lily, maybe? Or even Carter. Which would be worse for her? Dying or losing that whelp of a boy she adores? Which would be worse for you?"

I look at the girl again, trying to make myself see the girl and not the blood.

"Please," she whimpers, her thrasing still now. "Let me go."

I back away a step. "No," I say, shaking my head.

"You will drain her," Sebastian repeats.

I am sure he is wrong. I am sure I can resist. As delicious as she smells, I am sure I will not devour her. Just as I am sure I would never devour my sister.

But he does the unthinkable. He draws his dagger and slices open her arm from shoulder to elbow. A long, curvy slice down her bicep. Her blood leaps through her skin and she screams in pain.

I lunge for her, managing—just barely—to dart out of the way at the last instant. I follow my body's momentum. I run. I flee from Sebastian and the girl and all that delicious blood seeping onto the ground. The air is thick with it. I taste her on every breath. I feel her death creeping into my nostrils. Through the pores of my skin.

Even as I run, I fear it will not be far enough or fast enough. It will never be enough. Because I can't run from my own gut. I will never outrun my hunger. I am not fast enough to outrun him.

And I am right.

He is on me before I even reach the woods. He knocks me to the ground only to pick me up again. He throws me over his shoulder and carries me back to her. She is scrambling away, clutching at her arm. Her movements are slow and jerky, like stop-motion animation.

He thrusts me at her and we both tumble to the ground. I try to use the movement to roll right off her, but her blood covers her body. It's on my hands. And before I can stop myself, it's in my mouth. Just a drop. Then a gulp. A pint. A gallon. I can't stop. I don't want to. My whole body sings with the delight. Feeding on her is rapturous. Intoxicating.

I drink her fear and it is heady on my tongue. It is bitter, but not unpalatable. Like Granny's mustard greens and vinegar. Like Swiss cheese drizzled on broccoli. Her blood is soul food.

It nourishes me. Feeding from her with Sebastian, I am more powerful than I have ever been. I am more powerful than a mountain lion. Deadlier than an orca. A predator like no other on earth. And my whole body sings with the joy of it. More than that, my world sings. The music, which I missed so sorely, so achingly, vibrates in the air around me.

Sebastian and I are one in our hunger. It is a frenzy of feeding by immersion, to satiation and completion. To a state of total insentience.

When I am myself again, when the euphoria fades and the endorphins peter out, when the reality returns, I am full as I have never been before, but my soul is empty. What is left of my clothes is bloodied and tattered. I am unclean and impure. The girl is not the only human who died here, for I am gone as surely as she is.

I back away from her corpse. She lays on the ground, her body all awkward angles. Her dead eyes stare at the heavens, unseeing. But I see. I see her body sprinkled with bloody wounds. I am terrified by myself. But the blood that has been spilled tonight is everywhere. Yet, it is not until I see Sebastian unsheathing my own katana and handing it over to me, that I understand the last violation I must commit. I have killed this girl. Now I must guarantee she remains dead.

It is done with one clean slice. Then I clean the blade on the grass and return to the bodies of the Ticks and do the same to them, making sure her blood does not mingle with theirs. I don't know if this is respect for the dead or protection of the living. My venom is in her blood. Perhaps they could regenerate as vampires. Perhaps I am merely being superstitious.

It is nearly dawn and when I see Sebastian watching me, I take off, bolting for the tree line and running through the woods. I don't care if he follows me. I don't even care if he catches me. I don't know what I'm looking for until I find a stream with icy water. Even that doesn't wash away all the blood. I scrub with sand and dirt until the last traces of it are gone. And still I am not clean.

Sebastian finds me. He stands on the bank of the stream and watches. If I didn't know better, I might imagine there is regret on his face. But it is the distance and the play of light that make it seem so. Vampires regret nothing.

Only my ire exceeds my disgust.

"Why?" I scream.

He watches for a moment, stoic and silent. "Why what?"

"Why did you make me do that? Why?"

"I didn't *make* you do that. You were made to do it."

But I am in no mood for his irritating sophistries. "Were you trying to prove how weak I am?"

He cocks his head, looking baffled for a moment. "How weak you are? If I thought you were weak, I would have left you with Sabrina. I would not have given you the choice to come with me at all. No, my dear, of course not. I didn't prove you are weak." He stalks down the bank until he is standing before me. I shiver in the cold, but have no clothes to hide beneath. "She *was* weak. She was vulnerable and defenseless. Yet you resisted. She was bleeding and you resisted. It was not until her blood was in your mouth that you broke. I didn't do this to show you how weak you are. I did it to show you how strong you are. You know that you can be around a human without feeding and killing. Even one who is defenseless. Now you know where your breaking point is. Some vampires are hundreds of years old before they know that. Now you know yourself. Knowledge is strength. And you will need every ounce of your strength."

"So you keep saying. But what exactly am I supposed to use this strength for? To hunt Ticks? To kill other monsters? Because I was doing that before now."

"The Ticks are not the monsters I've been priming you to kill. You're going to kill Bob."

"You're crazy." I bark with laughter. Or is it hysteria? Or Post-traumatic Eating Disorder?

"No," he says softly. His normal sneer is completely gone. There is no bitter derision. No barely contained amusement. "I am not joking. I am not crazy. He has to be stopped, and you are the only one who can do it. No one but a vampire is strong enough. You are the only vampire young enough to walk onto his compound un-noticed. It must be you."

My legs wobble beneath me. My mind races back through the past weeks and I know he is right. I have known all along that he wanted revenge against Roberto. I have even agreed to help him bring down Roberto. And he was cunning enough to let me think that was my own decision.

I know this is the real reason he made me. Not because Carter and Lily asked him to do it, but because it would help him kill Roberto. I was always part of his plan to kill Roberto.

"I will not be your puppet."

"You will. Because your sister has been infected with the Tick virus."

Shock roars through me and my knees go out from under me. No! Not Lily!

"You know what this means," Sebastian says softly. "She is your twin. She, too, has the regenerative gene. She will not merely die from this infection. She will become a Tick."

Instantly I think of the Ticks I've killed. Of their dumb eyes and their flaccid, drooling mouths. Of their rough hands. Hands that break ribs and grab hearts.

This is what Lily will become. Lily, who has always been quick-witted and strong-willed. Lily, who was always my lode stone—before Sebastian, that is. How can this be? How can I let this be? My own death would be preferable. If my own death were even possible.

Sebastian grabs me and pulls me back to my feet. His touch is gentle but firm. "Listen to me. Wailing in grief will not save your sister."

I blink in surprise, because I realize I have been wailing, making that low keening noise I've always made when I'm distressed.

"Roberto has the cure. She and Carter are on their way to his compound right now. Once they are there, I am sure he will not let them leave. As long as Roberto is alive, his *abductura* will guarantee they don't even want to leave. Which means if you ever want to see your sister again, you have to go there and kill him."

Hope bursts through me—there is a cure! Lily may yet be saved. And then hot on its heels is another realization. Sebastian is right. Of course I will go to Roberto's compound. I will do it to save my sister. If I need to, I will kill Roberto. I will probably even enjoy doing it. The bastard who has destroyed civilization as we know it deserves to die. If I'm the only one who can do it, then I will do it.

But the personal cost will be huge.

This is why Sebastian made me feed from this girl. So that I will never forget what I'm capable of. I have taken a life, but it was the by-product of my hunger. It wasn't deliberate or planned out. It was not something I intended.

Killing Roberto is different. It will be premeditated. Calculated. Roberto will have surrounded himself with his human kine as well. And some of them may die when I go to rescue my sister. To pull this off, I must be smart and strong. I must be as manipulative and cunning as Sebastian has always been. I return to the girl's body and perform one last violation. This time when I bring the katana to her neck, I don't even flinch.

Sebastian turned me into a vampire eight weeks ago, but tonight he turned me into a monster.

CHAPTER FORTY-FOUR

CARTER

Joe left at dawn. He took Josie and the bulk of our supplies and headed back to the Farm at San Angelo. He'd probably be there by noon. I had told him that no one would blame him if he wanted to bail on the Farm and head straight for whatever safety could be found at Base Camp. He had Josie to think of now.

He disagreed. Yes, he had Josie. But there were also nearly a thousand other Greens in San Angelo and they needed help, too. As he pointed out, his return would go a long way to convincing the Greens that there was hope they could actually fight the Ticks and survive. The very fact that he believed it enough to bring a baby into that fight might be the edge they needed. And I let him go, because I understood that he needed to be somewhere he was familiar with and that it would be too painful for him to be where McKenna had been.

I called ahead and talked to Dawn. I wanted her to know Josie was coming so she'd be able to get whatever supplies she needed to keep Josie alive. She sounded exhausted because she'd been up most of the night treating Greens for various injuries that had been ignored too long. Listening to her talk, I sent up a silent thanks that she'd convinced me to bring her and Darren. Competent medical care had gone a long way toward convincing the Greens to trust us. Far more than my reputation had, that was for sure.

Watching Joe drift off, I run through the situation in my head.

I'd been doing the math, thinking about the statistics until my head spun. My father had always been great with manipulating numbers so things benefitted him. When you were the CFO of a multinational corporation, that was just part of the job description.

There is no good and evil, he used to say. There are only facts and numbers. It's all about making the math work for you.

I'd thought a lot about that as Joe was packing up. A thousand kids were waiting to be rescued in San Angelo. Another hundred or so up at Base Camp. Plus the people who lived in Elderton. If I rounded up, that was close to three thousand humans. There was no way—no way—those three thousand lives were worth trading for one life. Lily's life.

Despite that, I would never be able to stand by and watch her suffer, because even though she was just one person, she was the one person I loved.

After Joe was gone, I handed Lily the tranq rifle. "I know you hate these things. Since it has to be done, you should do it yourself."

She held it clumsily, like she didn't quite trust it to do what it was supposed to do. "Based on the map I found in the gas station, Roberto's ranch should be a couple of hours away, somewhere between San Angelo and San Saba. Even if I go for the neck shot, which would be the most potent, it'll wear off before that. You may have to shoot me a second time."

I nodded. I kept my gaze on hers as she did it. No matter how many times I told myself this crazy plan would work, part of me knew this might be the last time I really saw Lily when I looked in her eyes. I didn't want to miss a second of that.

As I drove, I pretended that Lily was asleep in the car next to me. That she hadn't been tranqed. That there was nothing dangerous beneath the bandages I'd applied to her foot right before she knocked herself out.

Could this have been our life, if the Tick-pocalypse had never happened? Maybe if I'd never been sent off to Elite Military Academy.

I had told her once that I'd stolen my father's car that day because of her. Because I'd been scared of what she made me feel and because I knew stealing his car was the one thing he couldn't ignore.

I'd been telling the truth, but not the whole truth. At the time, when I was that dumbass fifteen-year-old, I'd been scared of her and of how much I wanted her. But that wasn't all I was scared of.

Those nine months were the longest I'd lived at home since Giselle—my mother—had gotten tired of having a kid and shipped me off to boarding school when I was ten. At ten, I'd worshipped my father and loved my mother, even though they were indifferent to me. By eleven, I'd learned that rotten behavior got visits from home more reliably than straight As. By fourteen, I hadn't cared about visits nearly as much as my freedom. When they'd enrolled me at Richardson High School, it had been my ticket to unmonitored free time, fast cars, and more spending money than even I knew what to do with. But the price had been watching my parents up close and personal. Seeing them interact on a daily basis. Learning firsthand what total assholes they were. My mother's vain indifference hardly mattered. It was my father who scared me. The casual cruelty with which he controlled everyone around him. Everything he wanted, he got. People adored him, and he treated them like crap.

My father was an ass. I could live with that. What I couldn't live with was the pieces of him I saw in me.

It only got worse when I met Lily. I couldn't stand the open yearning with which she watched me. Couldn't stand how much I wanted her. How badly I treated her despite that. I hated her for how vulnerable she made me feel. For how much I wanted her. I was a monster. Just like my father.

So I'd bolted.

But what if I hadn't? What if I'd stayed around?

I had this fantasy sometimes that I had stayed. That I'd let my ego take the hit. That I'd asked out the geeky girl from my biology class and that we'd spent the past three years dating like normal kids did. Then, maybe, we wouldn't be driving across a barren wasted landscape right now. Maybe we'd be taking a spring break road trip. Maybe we'd be going on college visits our senior year. And she wouldn't be tranqed beside me in the car. She'd just be asleep. Driving to El Corazon Ranch, that's what I let myself imagine, because thinking about the reality of the situation, that just . . . that just didn't work for me.

I figured we were getting closer when I saw the windmills on the horizon. The dusty plain lay spread out before us, flat and interminable. Then, we crested a rise in the road and there it was: a vast plateau looming over the land. The windmills dotted the jagged edge of the plateau. I had known that this part of the country was a leader in wind power. Now it kind of made sense. Of course Roberto would be in favor of that. He'd need a reliable and endless source of power to secure his holdings. Those windmills would provide more than enough energy to operate his ranch. I guess energy independence is a top priority when you're staring down the barrel of the apocalypse.

As we approached the plateau, something seemed to shift in the air. A subtle change, but I could feel the tension dancing along my nerves. Or maybe I imagined it. Maybe it was just the weather.

The wind, pressing hard against the sheer face of the cliff, buffeted the car. The steering wheel lurched in my hands. I gripped it tighter. I wouldn't lose it now. Not when I was this close.

We zigzagged closer to the ranch. One county road, leading us to another, smaller, Ranch Road, which in turn led us to number 3214. It was a tiny, piece-of-crap dirt road marred with enough potholes to break the axle of a Hummer. Navigating the Mazda around them was like driving through a friggin' maze. I couldn't avoid all of them. The bigger potholes jarred Lily's head from side to side, and I slowed down to twenty and held her head cupped in my right hand to soften the blows.

She murmured sleepily, turning her cheek into my palm, and something tightened in my chest. She looked so damn vulnerable like this. Her lashes dark against her cheeks, her lips parted slightly. A lock of inky-dark hair brushing against my hand. I couldn't lie to myself anymore. She was sick. It was only going to get worse. And it was my fault. I had to make this right. Failure wasn't an option. I would convince Roberto to give us the cure, or I would die trying.

She groaned and squirmed in her seat as she started to wake up. She pulled away from my hand. I trailed my thumb across her cheek one last time before letting my hand drop back onto the steering wheel.

She blinked her eyes and stretched. Her gaze was soft and dazed. She smiled sleepily at me and I could tell she hadn't remembered yet. Slowly a frown settled over her face as the memories came back.

"How's your stomach doing? You need me to stop the car?" The tranquilizer always made her queasy.

"No," she answered softly. She straightened, pulling in to herself. "Are we almost there or should you give me another dose?"

"We're close. I think you're okay."

Not a great choice of words, since she wasn't *okay*. Not at all. If she didn't get that cure, she would never be *okay* again. She'd be a bloodsucking monster. Not that I was going to let that happen. One way or another, I was here to prevent that.

She nodded, wrapping her arms around her chest.

"Are you cold?"

"Aren't you?" she asked.

It was one of those beautiful, perfect days that we sometimes got in the early spring in Texas. The kind of day when the air was crisp and clear outside and the sun was shining so brightly that the inside of a car could get up to the mid-eighties. And she was cold. I could see the goose bumps rising on her skin and a shiver making her arms twitch. This wasn't good.

But making her panic wouldn't help, especially if Sebastian was right and a low heart rate would slow the progression of the disease. Hell, even aside from that, I just didn't want her upset.

So I smiled at her and shrugged. "No worries. I'm sitting on the sunny side of the car. Here, let's turn on the heat."

She nodded, the frown not quite leaving her face.

When she wasn't paying attention, I sped up the Mazda. Yeah, west Texas seemed to go on forever, but this was frickin' ridiculous.

I had to slow down again when the potholes got worse. Eventually, it felt like we were crawling there. I drove with the Mazda half off the road, dodging tumbleweeds taller than the car. Letting Joe take the Cayenne seemed like a great idea when we were packing it full of supplies, but now I was really missing the clearance of the SUV.

Then we drove across a cattle guard and onto a paved road. Not the crappy asphalt of a county road, but a concrete road, like you saw in high-end neighborhoods. I sped up to fifty, and a couple of minutes later, I saw the guardhouse ahead.

Towering fences stretched out on either side of the guardhouse, one dead-ended straight into the cliff, the other shot out for maybe another hundred yards before turning and running parallel to the road. The guardhouse itself looked like something out of a maximum-security prison. A series of three gates, one right after another, a dozen guards outfitted in full combat gear, and no fewer than eight pit bulls, two of them between each of the gates and another four on leashes on the other side. And beyond that, there were three tanks.

The Farms weren't half this well-guarded. No surprise there, I guess.

This place would be impossible for a team of trained special forces guys to break into. Forget a mindless Tick. Or a desperate guy.

Suddenly, driving up to this thing in a beat-up Mazda seemed like an incredibly stupid idea. Did I mention the pit bulls? And the tanks?

Beside me, Lily blew out a breath. "Did we remember to pack the Milk Bones?"

I smiled. "I think I have a stick of beef jerky," I joked back. "That'll work, right?"

I slowed the Mazda to a stop about twenty feet from the gate. The guards on the other side were already scrambling. A dozen rifles were aimed on us. The dogs were on point, their muscular bodies coiled with energy. And—I'm not even kidding—the cannon on one of the tanks swiveled toward the car.

"Wow," I muttered. "I wonder if Bob feels inadequate much."

I glanced at Lily, hoping to see a smile. Instead, she'd twisted to face me. "Here's what we're going to do. I get out of the car and walk up on my own. You take off in the other direction. They'll deal with me first. You'll have plenty of time to get away."

I just shook my head. "Stop."

"What?"

"Just stop, okay? When are you going to get it? I'm not leaving you. Ever. I am in this for as long as you are you. Longer. I'm not ever going to turn my back on you."

"But—"

"Ever."

"But when I—"

"That's not going to happen. We'll find the cure."

"If we don't—"

"Then I'm still in. I'm here. To do whatever you need me to do."

She turned and looked out the window. And I knew that she was blinking back tears, even though I couldn't see them. And that was okay. I could live with that. I totally got that thing she had about not wanting other people to see her as vulnerable.

"Okay," she finally said, her voice quiet. "So how do we want to play this?"

I felt my heart sink. I usually didn't walk in to any situation without plans A, B, *and* C ready to go. I had backups to my backup plans.

But I had no plan for this. I had no backup. No strategy for surviving Lily turning into a Tick.

Before I could think of a response to her question, there was a sharp rap on the driver's-side window.

I about jumped out of my seat. When I turned around, one of the soldiers was leaning over to peer in the window. That was fast.

My mind raced as I rolled down the window. What the hell was I supposed to say to this guy? How could I get us out of this? I could take him. Even armed as he was, I could probably take him out. But there were a dozen more guys—all just as armed—waiting behind him. Besides, that would defeat the purpose. We hadn't come here to storm the gates. We'd come here to beg.

The guy looked at me from behind mirrored glasses so I couldn't see his eyes. He nodded in Lily's direction and then mine. "Ms. Price. Mr. Olson. We've been waiting for you."

CHAPTER FORTY-FIVE

MEL

Sebastian drives through the night; I'm huddled in the back, feeling sleepy and lethargic. There's fear. Confusion. Anger. But somehow it's all buried beneath heavy doses of sated contentment. That too-full sleepiness that hits sometime between the pumpkin pie and the final touchdown of the Cotton Bowl. This is how those snakes in the Amazon must feel after eating an entire wild boar.

I'm starting to perk up by the time he pulls the car over on the outskirts of San Angelo. We're parked in a neighborhood as quiet and desolate as my mind. He's gone maybe twenty minutes then comes back with a bucket of warm water, a bar of soap, and fresh clothes. Only then do I realize that the shreds of clothes I have on are still covered in blood. And my skin is still sticky with it. All my icy scrubbing accomplished nothing. I am sure I will never feel clean again, but the warm water and soap go a long way. In the new clothes I feel almost human again. Then I inhale and the scent of whoever last wore the clothes hits me. It's faint but delicious. Maybe I will never feel human again after all.

Maybe that's what Sebastian was trying to teach me.

He returns again, this time with a new car and map with the route all marked out. He hands me the keys.

I don't bother to ask if he's coming, too. We both know he can't. I can see the tension already. We must be in Roberto's territory.

Sebastian is twitchy with the need to move on. Somewhere out there, is Roberto twitchy, too? Does he know how close his enemy is? Does he sense that death is stalking him?

"I've never driven alone before," I admit as I take the keys.

"You're a smart girl, Kit. You'll figure it out." He unfolds the map and spreads it out on the hood of the car. Only then do I notice that he's hand drawn a few more roads as well as several buildings. Just rough squares where buildings must be on Roberto's compound. He traces a road on the map with his finger. "You'll come in from the northwest. The guard station is here."

Of course Roberto would have a guard station. And fences. Lots of them, just like on the Farms. But instead of untrained Collabs armed with tranq rifles, Roberto's compound would be guarded by elite ex–special forces—the best of the best.

It had taken every scrap of will and planning and bravery I had to plan our escape from the Farm and its security was a joke compared to this. "How am I supposed to break in?"

"You don't." Sebastian taps his finger on the box he's drawn for the guardhouse. "You drive up to the front gate. You knock."

"And then just drive on in?"

Sebastian pauses and I sense that he's trying to decide what to say. "Look, Kitten, you know what you have to do once you get there, right?"

"Right." Save Lily. Kill Bob. It was simple.

"Don't forget: a mere stake to the heart won't do it. It will slow him down, maybe even long enough for you to finish him, but to guarantee he's dead you need to chop off his head."

"I know," I growl. "I've been killing Ticks too, you know."

"If killing Ticks alone was enough to prepare you for this, then anyone could do this." He gives my chin a simple nudge. "No, Kit, only you can do this. Only you are fast enough and strong enough to bring down the most powerful vampire in the world."

I feel a strange burst of pride that he's trusting me with this task. But doubt as well. "What if I choke?"

"You won't. You have the killer instinct."

And somehow it seemed even simpler, more cut-and-dry, maybe, now that my head had cleared. Now that I'd fed and the ragged edge of my hunger was worn down. Was that why Sebastian had made me eat? Was that why he forced me to face the most awful parts of myself? Because once I'd killed a helpless human girl, then I'd have the strength to kill a monster? Or was it something else? Maybe he thought that once I'd experienced firsthand how monstrous we vampires were, I wouldn't hesitate to kill one.

Whatever his motives had been, the result was the same. I will kill Roberto. I will not hesitate to destroy him. Destroying him means saving my sister. It's what she would do for me.

I looked up at Sebastian. "I'll kill Roberto."

"Right."

"Will no one stop me?"

Sebastian chuckled. "Melly my dear, everyone will try. He has at least two hundred head of kine in his herd, plus at least fifty soldiers in his employ. You'll have to be careful because once you're in, you'll need to assume every move you make is being watched and listened to. If they know what you're up to, they'll kill you. And Lily and Carter as well. The only advantage you have is that I can help get you in. I know some people in Roberto's herd. I'm going to call and tell them you're on your way. Carter and Lily will probably get there first. I can almost guarantee they'll let all of you right in."

"Why?"

"Because they've been looking for you for months."

Of course they had. The Dean of our Farm hadn't wanted to let us go when we'd escaped. He'd figured out that one of us was an *abductura* and he'd hunted us down, chasing us over half the country. I guess it made sense that he'd told someone else about us before he'd died. "Because he thinks I'm an *abductura*?"

"Because you are extremely valuable and always have been."

CHAPTER FORTY-SIX

LILY

"I'm fine." Lily tried to keep the tremor from her voice, but the shiver wracking her body made it almost impossible. She had meant to reassure him. In the future, it would probably be better to keep her mouth shut and just shiver in silence. Not that she had much of a future.

Carter stalked over to the door.

"Come on, somebody open up right now!" Carter pounded on the door. When nobody answered, he gave the knob a violent rattle—for about the hundredth time in the past hour. When it didn't budge, he slammed his foot against the door.

She understood his frustration. This was not how either of them had pictured this going. They had come here to confront Roberto. To get the cure. And maybe to turn the tide in the battle. Instead, they'd been locked in this empty room for over an hour.

After they'd talked to the guard at the gate, they had been escorted through the compound in a pair of Hummers. The guard had refused to answer any of their questions. So what the hell had he meant when he'd said they'd been waiting for them? They'd driven through acres and acres of open ranch land before finally reaching a cluster of buildings that could only be described as a village. There were a few dozen houses, a general store, a school, and even a medical clinic. It all looked very peaceful if you ignored the military barracks.

They had been shown into a room in the clinic. A medic had come in dressed in full hazmat gear. He had checked her over, given her a shot, all without saying a word. He'd given another shot to Carter. Carter had obviously been tempted to hassle the guy, but the armed guard watching over them with an AR-15 kept him in check. Then, both the guard and the medic left and locked them in. The room was completely empty: bare walls, no chairs, no storage. Since they'd been patted down on their way in, they didn't have much to work with. Carter would have been able to open a normal door with the bobby pin he'd kept hidden in his shoe, but the lock on this door was operated with an electronic passkey and foiled all his attempts.

In the hour or so that they'd been in the room, Carter had become more and more frustrated. Lily, on the other hand, was feeling worse by the minute. The chills wracking her body made it hard to do more than curl up on the floor. Carter had given her his hoodie and his shirt, but she refused to let him hold her in his lap to share warmth.

In the last days of the Before, the newly formed National Pandemic Disease Control Organization had said that the virus was spread by direct contact and that it was not airborne yet, but she wasn't ready to trust that. For all she knew, she'd already exposed Carter merely by riding in the car with him for those few hours on the way here. She had tried to keep her mouth covered, but clearly the disease was very communicable.

"You're freezing," Carter said.

She looked up to see him standing by the door. She'd made him promise to stay on the other side of the room as much as possible.

"I'm okay," she said, burrowing deeper into his hoodie. She

had her legs pulled up under the hoodie and her arms wrapped around her body.

Carter let out a string of curses, which nearly made her smile. He didn't handle this kind of thing well. She didn't blame him. The situation sucked, even more for him than for her. She had the aches and pains to distract her from the threat of imminent demise.

"Do you think this is their plan?" she asked.

"What?"

"Just lock us in here and wait for me to turn? Takes care of both problems, right?"

"Lily . . ."

"No. I shouldn't have let you come. We needed the cure, fine, but I could have driven myself."

"You really think I was going to let you do that?"

"I could have taken the car and just driven off."

"I would have followed."

"I could have—"

"No matter what, I would have followed." He blew out a breath and turned away, running his hand through his hair. "If this is their plan, then fine. If we go down together, there are worse things. If—"

Before he could finish his thought, the lock on the door gave a little series of beeps.

Carter whirled toward it, automatically widening his stance to face whatever was coming through the door. Except it was the last person she expected.

Mel walked into the room.

If Lily hadn't already been sitting, the shock would have knocked her to the ground. The phrase *shaken to the core* might have been appropriate, but she was already shivering so much that her whole body trembled.

Mel stopped just a step inside as the door closed behind. Tension radiated from her body. She stood as if poised for flight, though where she would go in that tiny room, Lily couldn't guess.

Lily wanted to throw herself at her sister. To wrap her arms around her. To hold her for hours, sobbing.

But Mel hadn't liked that kind of display of affection even before she'd been turned into a vampire. Besides, Lily couldn't stand, much less walk.

So instead, she simply looked at her sister. They'd been apart for nearly two months—longer than they'd ever been separated in their lives—and Mel had changed so much in that time. Which was all the more disconcerting because Mel had never really seemed to change much as they grew up. Her social skills had developed as slowly as her language. She'd never gone through the stages of adolescence that girls went through. Grooming and physical appearance had never interested her. So she hadn't seemed to mature like other girls. She had only seemed to grow, so that as she aged, she'd looked like a bigger and bigger version of the little girl she'd been.

At least, that was how she had seemed to Lily.

Except suddenly, she looked not like a girl at all. And not like a teenager either, but like a woman—an extremely fit and beautiful woman. Despite the cold, she wore only skinny jeans and a capsleeved T-shirt—or maybe it wasn't cold at all. Maybe it was only Lily who felt cold.

Carter clearly wasn't ready to trust Mel not to lunge for their jugulars, because he immediately stepped forward and put himself between her and Lily. "Okay," he said slowly. "This is interesting."

Mel looked from Lily to Carter. The old Mel had never seemed to focus on people much. Lily had always felt like she knew where everyone in the room was, but she never cared much what they were doing or why. With this Mel, it was the opposite. She seemed hyperaware of them. Like her attention was completely focused on them. One hundred percent.

Mel looked back at Lily. "How are you?"

"Great," Lily muttered, "except for the likely possibility that I'm turning into a monster."

"Sebastian told me," Mel said, taking a step toward Lily.

Lily nodded. "Yeah, I figured."

Carter didn't budge, still standing between them. "More important, are you good? Can you control yourself?"

Mel flinched and dropped her eyes. "Sebastian always could, couldn't he?"

"He's had more experience with it than you."

"Sometimes old dogs have new tricks for new dogs." Mel's words were almost like the kind of singsongy thing she'd have said when she was human. Almost.

The words were right, but her tone was all wrong. Thoughtful and self-aware in a way she had never been when she was human.

Plus there was that eye-contact thing. When she was human— and autistic—Mel hadn't liked to look people in the eyes, at least not dead on. Instead, she'd turn her head to the side, bird like, and look at you sideways.

Now, she maintained normal eye contact. No twitches, no hiding. No hair pulling.

So why was she still relying on her rhymes?

Then she stepped closer to Carter and made as if to hug him. Lily felt only a stab of confusion until she saw a flash of something dark and plastic in Mel's hand. Then Mel came to her and knelt down. This hug was even more awkward, but she knew why Mel had done it. In the instant her arms closed around Lily, her hand slipped up under the edge of Carter's hoodie and pressed something into her hand. It was plastic and heavy. A little bigger than a cell phone. Too small to be a sat phone, but with a rounded nub on one end. An antenna? So it was a radio of some kind.

The guards had patted both her and Carter down thoroughly. They'd found and removed her spare gun and both her knives. Mel couldn't have snuck in three radios; she must have stolen them from the guards. Which meant they were probably tuned to the guards' frequency, and they would have to be changed before being used. How would she know what frequency to use?

Mel pulled back to look at Lily. "One a penny, two a penny. Hot cross buns."

The nursery rhyme made Lily's head spin. How? How was she supposed to figure out what that meant? "Jesus, Mel," she muttered.

But before she could complain about the rhyming, Mel blurted out, "Three blind mice. Hear no evil, see no evil, speak no evil. See how they run?"

Another, deeper shudder went through Lily's body.

Did she see how they ran? No, she didn't. Not at all.

And she didn't even understand why Mel was talking in rhymes. Sebastian had said she wouldn't be autistic anymore. Had he been wrong? Or was this a trick? Was Mel trying to tell them something? Why not just say it out loud?

Lily looked over at Carter. She couldn't tell if he was just as confused as she was. "I don't understand. Mel, I'm sorry. I just don't get it."

"The itsy-bitsy spider went up the water spout. Down came the rain"—Mel seemed to pause on the word *rain* and she tapped her chest. Just once and Lily wasn't sure she hadn't imagined it—"and washed the spider out."

"You're the rain?" Lily asked.

"Three blind mice," she said slowly. "Three blind mice. See how they run?"

Instead of answering, Lily just pulled her knees closer to her and rested her swirling head.

When they'd been on the Farm, it had taken her months to figure out what Mel had meant when she'd said "Red rover, red rover," over and over again. How on earth was she supposed to figure out "three blind mice" in a matter of hours? There were three of them. Maybe they were the three blind mice. Or maybe three was one of the numbers in the radio frequency. "One a penny, two a penny" had numbers in it, too.

Suddenly, it all seemed like too much to bear. She'd fought so hard. Done so much. Maybe it wouldn't be awful to go like this. Just so long as she didn't take anyone with her. That was all she wanted now.

That and to know that Mel had forgiven her. She'd made so many mistakes when it came to Mel. Maybe the biggest one was asking Sebastian to turn her into a vampire. Had she made the right decision? She couldn't tell. She had no way of reading Mel now. No way of knowing if Mel was okay or would have been better off dead. She could only hope that someday Mel would understand what she'd done. Maybe that was the most anyone could hope for: understanding from the people they loved. Or maybe even that was asking for too much. Maybe she should just be thankful that she'd had the chance to see Mel one last time. No matter what else happened, she was luckier than so many other kids. She'd had a chance to live outside the Farm. She'd made a difference. And she'd had Carter.

Then the door emitted another series of beeps and started to swing open. Somehow, Lily knew. This would be it. This would be the guard who would take her away and execute her. The door opened and a guard walked in. But instead of crossing to her, he stepped aside and left the door open for another man to enter.

For a moment, Lily just blinked at him in confusion.

Carter took a step toward the door. "Who the hell are you?"

Mel turned around, but—despite her newfound verbosity—couldn't find the words.

So it was Lily who answered. "He's our father."

CHAPTER FORTY-SEVEN

CARTER

"What?" I demanded, studying the stranger in front of me.

It's the other guy I was worried about.

He was a tall, fit man, with dark hair, graying at the temples. He was dressed like the classic rich good ol' boy—boots, dark wranglers, and shirt so well pressed it was stiff. Just the sight of him gave me culture shock. I hadn't seen anyone in clothes this clean in months.

"I am Jonathan Price," he said, sliding a security pass card into his back pocket. He flashed a smile taken straight from one of those cheesy motivational speakers schools used to hire in the Before. "And I am, indeed, their father."

Every bit of his appearance and his attitude irritated me. Even his voice grated on my nerves. So the sum total should be instant dislike, right? But here's the thing: that's not what I felt. My gut said that this was a great guy. This was someone to trust. I simultaneously wanted to stand up straighter and trot out my best "Yes, sir!" Hell, I was kind of hoping he'd take me out into the yard and toss a football around with me. Surely someone here had a football handy, right?

"What?" I asked again, because that disconnect—that difference between what my mind told me to feel and what I was actually feeling was so profound, I reeled from it.

I didn't know if Mel and Lily felt it, too, or if they were just shocked because—holy crap—the father they'd thought was dead just popped up in the compound of humanity's greatest enemy.

Whichever it is, neither of them said anything. "I thought you said your father left when you were little."

"He did," Lily muttered, her words slurring. She sounded confused, like it wasn't just her tongue that was muddled, but her thoughts as well.

Jonathan stood there awkwardly, as if he couldn't decide what to do with his hands. He held them out as though ready to embrace either Lily or Mel. Or maybe both. "My girls. My beautiful girls."

Mel surprised me by walking over to him and slipping into his arms. She hugged him tightly, burrowing against him like a toddler might. He patted her back awkwardly. "You can't possibly know how hard it has been the past few years. Not being with you. Not knowing where you were. If you were okay. You can't imagine how we've searched."

Confused, Lily watched Mel. I could tell she was just as baffled as I was. But then Mel stepped away and ducked her head. I saw her hand slip into her pocket. She looked at her father with a kind of shy adoration that I didn't entirely buy. So why did she hug him?

When she hugged Lily and me, she'd slipped us the radios. Which she must have, in turn, stolen from the guards. So had she stolen something from her father? His passkey, maybe?

Who knew Mel was such a kleptomaniac? And she was thinking much more clearly than I was.

It took a lot of effort to shove down the eager-puppy-dog feeling I had, but I struggled to move past confusion into damage control. Maybe Mel had figured it out already or maybe she was still unnerved just by being around humans again. As for Lily, she was out of it and was only going to get worse until she got that cure.

Me, I didn't have time for emotional reunions. I needed that medic back here with the meds, asap.

I wasn't about to stand by and wait to see how this shook out. I put myself between Lily and Mel and their father. I approached him with my hands raised, looking as non-threatening as I could manage. I could imagine a lot of different ways this might go down. One of them involved about twenty armed guards deciding I was a threat, rushing in, and gunning me down. I wasn't too excited about that outcome.

So as I walked toward him I tried to look peaceful, friendly even. "Sir, could I please have a word?"

The look he gave me said he hadn't noticed me until that moment and he couldn't quite figure out who I was or why I was there.

"I'm Carter Olson. I'm with Lily. I . . ." I trailed off, not sure how to describe myself. *I'm in love with your daughter. I'm her boy-friend. I'm the guy who's going to kill you for hurting her, you gutless bastard.* This had to be a record breaker for uncomfortable first meetings. Finally, I just finished with, "I've been taking care of your daughters." He still looked unconvinced, so I added, "I really need to talk to you. Alone."

Behind me I heard Lily murmur a protest. "Carter, I can . . ."

I ignored her. There was too much at stake to let my feelings for her sway me. This sucked for her, no matter what. If there was any chance—any chance at all—that me vetting the guy would make this easier for Lily, I was going to take it.

I stepped even closer to him and said softly, "I am not exaggerating when I say that I know both your daughters better than you do. If you want any hope of actually getting through to them, I'm your best shot." I could see him waffling, so I added, "You've waited eight years. Ten more minutes isn't going to make a difference."

He didn't look at me as I talked to him; instead, he looked at

Lily and Mel. Confusion flickered in his gaze. He had walked into the room so confident, but I saw otherwise now. Something about *them* had him stumped.

I glanced over my shoulder to look at them, too, and it hit me. It had been eight years since he'd seen his daughters. Maybe he'd seen pictures of them in that time, maybe not. But he hadn't seen them in person in nearly a decade. Hell, I'd seen Mel two months ago and I was still surprised by her transformation. I'd watched Lily's rapid decline over the past day, and it shocked the hell out of me.

That was the crux of Jonathan Price's problem. He couldn't tell his daughters apart. Not because they looked so similar, but because they looked so different from what he expected. And he was a smart enough man to know that if he blundered and called them the wrong name, he'd never win them over.

And that was an advantage I was willing to use.

A moment later, he nodded to the guard, who leaped to attention and opened the door for him. Price nodded back toward the room. "Watch over them," he said softly to the guard before he led me out into the hall. Nice that he didn't trust his daughters. True, they can't be trusted, but still.

"Okay, young man, what can I do for you?"

What could he do for me? A hell of a lot, I hoped. I needed two things from him. Medical attention for Lily was still the top priority, but Mel . . . if I'd understood her correctly, Mel had a plan to get us out of here. I needed to get her alone long enough to find out what that plan was. I also needed to make sure her father wasn't around long enough to realize she wasn't autistic anymore. If I understood her rhymes, then Bob was the itsy-bitsy spider and she was going to be the rain that washed him out. Sneaking up on him would be a hell of a lot easier if everyone thought she was still autistic.

If she wanted to go after Bob, that was fine by me. One less person for me to kill later. I just needed to make sure Lily was treated before the three blind mice made their escape.

"Sir, Lily is sick." It's always best to start with the truth, right? "She needs medical attention. You know that. We came to you because we thought you could help her. Don't let her down now."

Hell, there was no reason not to lie just a little. Okay, so ten minutes ago, none of us had had any idea at all that Lily and Mel's father was still alive. But we needed him, and it was worth lying if he could get Lily the cure.

"I'm not sure I understand why you've come to me."

"You're her father. If you can help her you have to do it. Please."

"I haven't seen my daughter in eight years. You want me to have her shipped off to the clinic without even talking to her? I don't have—"

"What you don't have is time to waste." I jabbed my finger in the direction of the closed door. "She's sick. It's been nearly twelve hours since she was exposed. Whatever you're going to do to save her, you have to do it fast."

Jonathon frowned, thinking about it for longer than seemed reasonable. She was his daughter, for god's sake. What was there to think about?

Finally he nodded. He walked down the hall to where a guard was standing maybe ten feet away. While they were talking, I rapped quietly on the door. There was the click of Mel opening it from the inside with the passkey. She opened the door just a fraction and whispered, "ETA?"

"Another minute, tops," I whispered back. "I've convinced him to bring Lily to the clinic." I looked down the hall. "Actually, they're bringing the stretcher now."

"Fine. Don't let him wake me."

I wanted to ask what she meant, but Price, the guard, and the medic—still in hazmat—were almost on me.

A moment later, the second guard opened the door and they rolled the stretcher in. The medic and the guard moved quickly to get Lily onto the stretcher. It took me a moment to realize that I didn't see Mel at all. Price must have realized it about the same time, because I saw him looking around the room, too. Did Mel get out already? If she didn't where was she?

"She was exhausted, sir," the guard offered up in a voice that sounded so young, it almost cracked. No wonder the guy looked smaller than me. He couldn't be more than sixteen. "I told her she could lie down. I got her a blanket. Hope that's okay."

He nodded toward the back wall and I finally saw Mel. She was curled up on the bench facing the wall. Huddled under a blanket, all that was visible of her was her socked feet and a thick strand of dark hair, which hung out from under the hood she'd pulled up over her head.

Price looked annoyed and took a step toward her as if he was going to wake her up and make her talk to him. I remembered what Mel had said: *Don't let him wake me.*

I grabbed Price's arm to stop him. He turned to glare at me. "What?"

"She's exhausted, sir," I said. "She drove through the night to get here. She probably hasn't had a decent night's sleep in months. You can't wait another twenty minutes to let her have a catnap?"

Price glared at me, but after a few seconds, he nodded at me. "Fine. But you and I are going to have words."

"No problem."

I wasn't sure how much time Mel needed to subdue this guard and escape from the room. If "words" with Price would buy her that time, I was game to go a few rounds.

I turned back to where Lily was on the stretcher. I reached out my hand to trace a finger across her arm, but it was so hot that I instinctively jerked away. She rolled her head toward me without lifting it from the gurney. Her eyes looked cloudy and unfocused. Her lips were parched and cracked. How had she gotten so bad in just a few hours? How could she possibly pull out of this and survive? How could she not?

"Carter?" She choked out my name.

"Yeah," I murmured, "I'm here."

"Worth it," she muttered before her eyes drifted closed. My heart clenched and before I could say anything else, the medic and the guard rolled her out.

I didn't have a chance to ask what she'd meant. I could only hope that she meant that the time we'd spent together had been worth it to her. To me, it had been everything.

CHAPTER FORTY-EIGHT

CARTER

I expected him to take me right out into the hall. Instead, the guards escorted us down two hallways and up an elevator. He led me into an office—his office, if I had to guess—with a sleek, modern desk, a ton of bookshelves, and a sweeping view overlooking the town.

We were at least five stories up, which meant we weren't in the clinic anymore. One of those hallways must have been a walkway into the command building. I didn't like all the time we'd burned walking here, close to ten minutes. Lily was dying by increments and I wanted to be with her when she got treatment. On the other hand, the fact that Price had wasted the time it took to bring me to his office told me something else: he planned to intimidate me.

I knew that tactic from watching my own father do business. You want to lord over someone, you make them feel small. You show them just how powerful you are.

But I didn't doubt Jonathan Price was an extremely powerful man. And he wouldn't have needed to drive that point home if he thought I was just some punk kid beneath his notice. He'd brought me here not only to intimidate me, but because something about me intimidated him.

And that was something I could use.

He gestured me into a seat, but didn't sit down himself. Instead, he leaned against his desk, stretching his legs out in front of him.

"I'm sure you have many questions—" he began in a condescending tone.

I didn't give him a chance to finish. "Yeah, I do. For starters, the medic was in full hazmat. So were the guards. But you're not, and you're letting me wander all over. Why?"

If he was taken aback by the way I took control of the conversation, he didn't show it. Instead, he smiled benignly. "Because I've been vaccinated."

"There's a vaccine?" I couldn't help but sag against the chair. A vaccine. All these deaths. All these millions who had died due to this crazy virus. And there was a vaccine?

I was flooded with questions and they were nearly out of my mouth before I realized what he'd done. He'd distracted me and I'd eaten up too much of my ten minutes by gaping at him in shock.

"So you're safe?" I asked. "But the health of anyone else in this building doesn't matter to you?"

He shrugged like the question barely bothered him. "The vaccine is costly and rare. In due time, everyone at El Corazon will have it . . . until then, we are as careful as we can be."

"Next question," I said.

"I didn't realize I was being interviewed."

I ignored that. "Do your daughters know you're an *abductura*?" I was just making a guess, but if Price's expression was any indication, it was a good one. Why else would Price be here?

His smile practically oozed across his face. "I prefer the term *leader*."

"So did Hitler."

The charming smile froze as something like hatred flickered

across his face, but he hid it quickly. "Not all of those with the gift use it to benefit mankind. Such a shame. That power, ignored or misused, it's a tragedy, when a properly trained *abductura* is capable of such greatness."

"Wow." I didn't bother to hide the derision in my voice. "When you say it like that, manipulating and controlling all of humankind to bring about the apocalypse almost sounds like a good thing."

He looked at me for a second, his expression almost baffled. Then he smiled. "You give me too much credit. I did not end the world."

"But your master did."

"Roberto?"

"Yeah, Roberto." I was tired of him being so damn coy. I wanted to wring this guy's neck. I didn't even care if he was Lily's dad. Except I did care whether or not she got the cure, so instead, I clenched my hands tightly in my lap. I was tired of sugarcoating this crap. "The vampire who created the Tick virus that brought about the end of civilization as we know it. Sound familiar?"

But Jonathan was frowning. "It sounds like Roberto has been getting some very bad press. He is hardly the evil genius you think he is."

"And what about you? Am I supposed to believe you're a nice guy?"

"I suppose Lily's told you all sorts of horrible things about how I abandoned them when they were ten. How I disappeared from their lives without a backward glance."

Okay, sure. We would start small and work our way up to genocide.

"There are two sides to every story. Sometimes even more. Do I regret leaving them? Of course I do. Do I regret the great things I've been able to do since leaving them? No. I am sorrier than I can say that their mother didn't trust me when I asked her to send the girls to me last summer. I regret that I didn't go get them myself when the plague broke out. But at the time the vaccine hadn't been perfected yet and travel was too risky.

"And of course that Dean in Sherman was supposed to be keeping an eye on them, but he screwed that up. We've been looking for them ever since. Then a colleague of Roberto's called and said he'd found them and was sending them our way." Price's facade of easygoing charm gave way to anger. It hit me so fast and strong that I wondered how he'd kept it bottled up, but he quickly got it under control. He shook his head. "You can blame me for being too trusting. Too optimistic in my belief that other people would keep them safe, but you can't say that I never tried. I just didn't try hard enough."

Was all of that true? Had he searched for them? The Dean certainly had tried to get them back. We had assumed at the time that it was because he had guessed Lily was an *abductura*, but what if we'd read it wrong? Maybe they'd been safe all along. Maybe I hadn't saved them at all. Maybe if I'd just left them on that Farm, their father would have come for them and brought them here. To safety. To a vaccine. Maybe if I'd just minded my own damn business, Mel would never have been turned into a vampire and Lily wouldn't be slowly transforming into a Tick.

Kudos to me for being the worst boyfriend ever.

This sucked. It just effing sucked. Despair washed over me.

How many times was Lily going to be in danger because of me?

Except she wasn't in danger because of me this time. She was dying. I dropped my head into my hands. And it was my fault. All my own damn fault.

Jesus, if I'd just . . .

Before I could finish the thought, my mind sent up a warning bell. I made myself stop thinking for a moment. I just sucked air into my lungs and pushed it back out again. Slow and easy.

I took a step back, emotionally. I hit the pause button.

And I made myself think.

Yeah. I'd screwed up. A lot. But I'd have plenty of time to beat myself up about that later. When I wasn't sitting in the same room with an *abductura* powerful enough to short-circuit the emotions of the entire damn state.

I pushed myself to my feet. "Jesus, how can you even live with yourself?"

"Lily and Mel—"

"Forget Lily and Mel. Forget what you've done to them. Have you been outside these fences? Have you seen the devastation you've caused?"

"I will not be talked to like that by a child."

"I am not—"

"Whatever you are now, you were a child when this started. The world you grew up in, that's the world you need to be looking at. Do you really think that world was so great? So perfect? The American government fought wars no one could win to secure global resources to feed the economy. American consumerism was destroying the planet. Mass shootings on the rise. Social media contributing to the highest teenage suicide rates in history. We were doing everything wrong. And it was only getting worse. You think I wanted to raise my girls in that world?

"So, yes, when I had a chance to make a difference, I grabbed it. The greatest leaps in civilization that humanity has ever known have happened when a powerful *abductura* worked under the guidance of a vampire."

Shock rocked me back in my seat. Holy crap. Price wasn't just a jerk, he was a certifiable megalomaniac. "And you think that's what's happening here? A great leap in civilization? Have you seen the wrecked cities? The vacant towns? The mass graves? Have you seen any of it?"

"Yes! I have. But where you see destruction, I see a blank canvas. I see a world reborn. I see an opportunity for humanity to start afresh."

"Sure," I said. "That would be great. If there was enough humanity left. Because right now, there are a hell of a lot of Ticks, and not a hell of a lot of people."

"But here, in this compound, there are plenty of people. Individually chosen people, highly intelligent, highly educated people. More than enough to reboot humanity."

Right. I was pretty sure that if these people had been individually selected for anything it was for their susceptibility to Price's powers. Or maybe their blood type. Price was still talking with that gleam of delight in his eyes. Like this plan of his—the plan to reboot civilization—was exciting and thrilling rather than repugnant. "Surely you can see that this was the only way."

I could only shake my head. "You wanted to make the world a better place, so you decided to destroy civilization instead of just, oh I don't know, making a donation to the United Way like a normal person?"

Price leaned forward then until he and I were almost eye to eye. He smiled slowly. "But that's the point, isn't it? You and I, we're not normal people, are we?"

Something like fear skittered across my nerves and I fought the sudden urge to bolt from the room. I had nothing in common with Jonathan Price. The only thing connecting us was Lily.

But before I could ask him what he meant, the air was filled with the high pitched whine that got louder and louder. Then an explosion rent the air. The whole building shook.

Price started for the door. "Wait here," he barked.

But I was right behind him. "Yeah, right."

He whirled to face me. "Sit back down and wait right here."

I stepped toward him. He was about my height, but I had him on sheer muscle. He'd obviously spent the past eight months of the apocalypse hiding out at El Corazon, letting the guards do all the hard work, whereas I'd been out fighting Ticks. I smiled. "You want to make an issue of this now?"

"Fine," he muttered, turning to stalk down the hall. "But stay where I can see you."

"I was about to say the same thing to you."

CHAPTER FORTY-NINE

MEL

I should be planning as I wait for the perfect moment to sneak out of the room and start my search for Roberto. But instead of strategizing, all I can do is wonder: Does vampire hair grow? I have no way of knowing. Sebastian's hair is cut short. I haven't known him long enough to notice it growing, but that doesn't mean it doesn't.

If vampire hair doesn't grow, I'm going to be really annoyed that I just chopped all of mine off. I could have cut off Lily's. The state she's in, she wouldn't have even noticed. So after I knocked out the guard, swapped clothes with him, and stole his weapons, I pulled my own hair into a ponytail and sliced it off close to my head. Now my hair—my one feature that I've ever actually liked—is jagged and misshapen. Maybe it will grow out; maybe it will be like this for the rest of my life. However long that might be. I've had only a few moments of vanity ever, so I don't feel too badly about not wanting to look like Fontaine for the rest of eternity. Still, if I do, I guess it was worth it. That one little ponytail gave the illusion that it was me sleeping on that bench. I may have fooled even Carter.

When the hall outside empties, I wait another sixty seconds, then use the passkey to open the door. I have two now: the guard's and my father's. I slip them into separate pockets to keep them straight and I stride out like this is exactly what I'm supposed to be doing. As I walk down the hall, my feet clomp in my oversized combat boots loudly enough to cover the pounding of my heart. I don't know how long I'll have. From here, any number of things could go wrong.

My father could realize his key is missing. My father could decide he needs to talk to me now, nap be damned. Someone could come and check on the guard. Those were all possibilities. Remote, but possible. The more likely scenario is that there is a security camera in that room and that someone saw or heard everything I did and is on his way to retrieve me right now. If that's the case, more troops will be here any minute. My new disguise is the only thing keeping me from being identified. So I keep my glasses firmly in place, even though the mirrored lenses muck with my vampire vision. I wear the outfit like I own it. Like I was born to be a brainless, hired goon.

I move quickly down one hall and then another. I don't sneak because there are probably security cameras here, too. Still, every springy vampire muscle in my body is twitching to run. I could be anywhere on this compound in under three minutes if I let loose. But that would really blow my cover. Not just my identity, but the whole kit and caboodle. I don't want anyone knowing what I'm capable of until it's too late to stop me.

It's a strain to move like a human, but I manage it. At least, I think I do. When several minutes pass and there are no obvious signs that I'm being followed, I relax a little. I'm still sure there were security cameras in that room, but that doesn't mean someone was monitoring them.

In my mind, I try to pull up the little map that Sebastian drew for me. I know from my ride through town that it hadn't been completely accurate. He had underestimated the number of houses. Even the "Main Street" had more buildings than Sebastian's drawing. I wasn't sure where he'd gotten his intel. I assumed some sort of satellite from the Before. If the number of new buildings was any indication, El Corazon has done well in the After. Chaos rules outside these fences, but in this little swath of what is left of the United States, order reigns. Roberto's order. And my father's. The fact that he's alive shocks me, but the mystery of their connection is a puzzle box I'm not willing to play with right now. There have to be three hundred people living here. Three hundred people and one vampire. Roberto must eat well.

I step out of the clinic through one of the side doors into the late-afternoon sunlight. The temperatures are starting to drop off and there is a slight chill in the air. Directly across the street is a building that looks like a classic Texas county courthouse: four stories of impressive limestone, late-nineteenth-century architecture sitting on a neat square of trimmed grass. That's the building from which Roberto rules this little kingdom. But I'm equally sure that he isn't there now. No, it's dusk. He is definitely at home, wherever home might be for him.

I don't know enough about normal vampires—other vampires, that is—to know where he might live. Lore says vampires must sleep in the dirt of their native land, but Sebastian has never done that. So I walk along Main Street looking as I go at the buildings in either direction. I'm surprised, but grateful, that no one has come racing after me yet. To the south, I see the open plain. Longhorn cattle dot the landscape as well as active pump jacks. This doesn't surprise me. I saw the windmills on the way in. Roberto is the kind of man who would have planned this stuff out far in advance. It wouldn't even surprise me if this compound of his wasn't set for the next decade.

I walk farther down the street and don't see the house until I turn the corner and the land begins to slope gently up a hill. There it is, on the crest of the hill, overlooking the town. Actually, it's less house and more sprawling Victorian mansion: three stories of ornate, pink granite with glossy, black slate on the roof and more wrought iron than the French Quarter in New Orleans. There is a pair of massive live oaks in the front yard, shading the house from the southern sun, their branches clumped with ball moss and dipping low to the ground. It reminds me of the Haunted Mansion from Disney World.

I walk right up. There is a single guard in front and another patrolling the sides and probably the back of the house, too. I take out the patrol guard first using the tranq rifle I'd stolen with the uniform. The second guy takes a little more planning, but it is still relatively easy. I pretend to be the guard from the side of the house and call him over. I hit him with the tranq rifle. I tie them up with zip ties, like I'd seen Carter do before—then eye the back of the house looking for a window that looks vulnerable.

I return to the front, find a tree branch that's about an inch or two in diameter. I break off the branch and snap it in two and then use the knife I stole off the guard to whittle points on either end of both sticks. As stakes go, they're primitive, but they'll do.

I'm just starting to wonder why I've gotten this far without more interference, when I hear the howl of Ticks in the distance. My heart gives a little shudder of fear at the piercing yips. Even after all this time, even after I've killed so many of them, that sound still terrifies me. It's like I'm back in that parking lot, dying all over again.

I push my terror aside. I have nothing to fear. Not from them. Besides, this was what I had planned. I wanted the Ticks here. This was why I cut the tracking chip out of the neck of that girl I'd killed. This was why I'd stashed it in my pocket and carried it with me during the long drive here, despite the annoying buzzing it caused in my head. The radio frequency of those chips irritated me, but it bugged the crap out of the Ticks.

Their arrival spurs me to get moving. I turn back to consider the house. Roberto wasn't expecting an attack, certainly not from a vampire, so safety wouldn't be his first concern. This was his empire. He would want to survey it. Which means his room would be on the third floor. So I decide to scale the outside of the building and go in through the window and then search the building from the top down.

Climbing the outside of the building is slower going than I expected, even with my new vampire strength and speed. Finding the minute crevices for footholds takes time. Enough time for me to wonder whether or not anyone else lives with Roberto in this house. It's huge. There could easily be several people.

Will I have to kill them all, like that SEAL team that went after Osama Bin Laden? Or will I be able to find just him and destroy him alone?

Will I even recognize him? He's old. Older than Sebastian. Which means he'll be smart. Vicious. Heartless. Brutal. Yes, those are all the things I expect from him personally. Those are the qualities of a vampire. Sebastian's taught me that much.

As for his body, that I'm not sure about. He goes by Roberto and has lived in this part of the world for close to two thousand years. I'm picturing dark hair and high, Mayan cheekbones. Old-world manners and oozing charm. Basically, I'm picturing Ricardo Montalban, that old actor from *Fantasy Island* and *Spy Kids*.

As soon as I'm in the window, I pull off the mirrored sunglasses and tuck them into my pocket. I may need them later, but for now I'm happy to have them off. Even without turning on lights, my vampire vision allows me to see just fine. Turns out I was wrong about his bedroom being on the third floor. The window was easy enough to open, but the four bedrooms were obviously unused, elegantly appointed guest bedrooms. Creeping down the stairs, I hear voices. One pitched too softly for me to understand, the other a deep, rumbling voice that's faintly accented, like Sebastian's. And, for that matter, the voice is similar to Ricardo Montalban's.

I creep closer, back pressed against the wall, trying to catch the conversation. There's something about a security breach. No big surprise there.

The ceilings here are high and there are transom windows over the doors. This is the only room in this hall with a light on in it. From where I'm standing I can see a tiny sliver of the room. I can see a huge, four-poster bed, with a red, velvet coverlet and another piece of furniture on the opposite wall. A desk, maybe. None of that is particularly helpful. Then I catch a glimpse of a man as he walks past. He's tall with distinguished salt-and-pepper hair. And I see a phone in his hand. Not pressed to his ear, but held out in front of him like he's got the other person on speaker.

So he's alone after all.

Suddenly, my heart is racing and my throat is dry. I shift the two stakes to one hand so I can wipe my palm on my pants. Faced with the reality of killing Roberto, I'm unexpectedly nervous. Then, I hear a door open somewhere on the first floor. Reinforcements are on their way. And whether it's nervousness or excitement or what, I don't know, but I am suddenly on fire to kill him. Some primal drive inside me has kicked in and I itch with the need to destroy him. I'm alive with it. I don't question it or wonder about it. I'm out of time.

I charge through the door, stakes raised.

The man on the other side is exactly how I pictured him. Tall, stately. Dressed in a pristine suit and glossy, black shoes. He is the very picture of the debonair gentleman vampire. I expect more of a fight. I expect the kind of crazy acrobatic martial arts that Sebastian pulled. Instead, he just stands there, an expression of absolute shock on his face as I race toward him. He screams as I bring him to the ground, and I plunge the stake into his heart.

His arms flail for a second, and I jump away, passing my second stake into my right hand, just in case. I stand over him, desperately sucking air into my lungs as I watch him die. As his eyes go blank and his mouth foams with blood.

I don't know what I expect. Elation? Happiness? Joy? At the very least, I expect a release from this angry rush of adrenaline. Instead, as I stare down at his body, I feel . . .

The need to destroy. Not just him, but everything.

There are footsteps on the stairs. Someone is coming. Fast. I whirl to face the door and broaden my stance, ready to fight off the guards I expect to pour into the room.

But instead of guards, a boy runs into the room.

He's about my age, maybe younger. He's shorter than I am by at least a few inches and his build is lean. There's something delicate about him. Something youthful and unfinished. Like he hasn't quite reached his full height or grown into the man he'll become. He has hair so blond that it almost gleams in the pink light of the setting sun shining through the window. He pulses like the tinkling of a Mozart concerto. He is, quite simply, the most beautiful, most angelic boy I've ever seen.

Surprise flickers over his expression as he looks from me to Roberto's dead body on the ground. He stumbles back a step, like he might turn to flee.

Automatically, I drop the stake. Instinctively, I don't want to hurt this boy. I don't even want him to fear me. I hold up my hands in a gesture of surrender and speak slowly, calmly.

"I mean you no harm," I say. "I came here to kill Roberto. I'm not here for you."

The surprise on his face morphs into confusion as he looks from me to the body on the floor. "You're here to kill Roberto?" he asks.

I nod, trying to look non-threatening, but it's difficult because my pulse is still pounding and hate-fueled adrenaline is pumping through my veins.

He straightens, bracing his stance, as a smile creeps across his lovely face. "You came here to kill—" Then he gestures toward the man on the floor. "Roberto?"

"Yes."

The blond boy tips back his head and laughs.

It's a high-pitched, musical laugh. It's like one of Mozart's concertos: light and airy, and though the sound itself is lovely, I hate it. I hate him for making it. That furious flood of adrenaline from stabbing Roberto has not let up. My body is almost shaking with it now. With the need to kill and destroy. And somehow this boy, this boy's laughter, is making it worse. It's like the adrenaline is a fire in my blood and his laughter is a chemical accelerant. It is painful to listen to him. It's excruciating. Deep inside. Like my blood is actually boiling.

My head throbs and my knees start to buckle. I press my palms to my ears, trying to block out the sound of his laughter, but it doesn't help.

And then, the boy is walking closer to me. His laughter has mellowed to a chuckle now.

"Sebastian," he says, shaking his head as if in sympathy. He rolls his eyes. "Will you never stop trying to kill me? How many innocent young pups will you send?"

He stops in front of me, studying my face. Even though I'm taller than him, I feel smaller. Tiny. Helpless.

He reaches up, grabs me by the throat and lifts slowly until my feet dangle. I grab his wrist but his arm isn't like flesh and blood. It's like iron.

His smile broadens as he looks at me. I kick at him, but my lungs are already screaming for air and my knees feel weak.

"You came here to kill Roberto and instead you killed my valet." He glances at the body, and a frown mars his perfect beauty. "Such a shame. I liked Rodrigo. He was with me for fifty years. I was beginning to get rather attached to him. Do you have any idea how hard it is to find a good servant like that? One who's willing to dispose of bodies and overlook habits that many humans find unpalatable? You know, the more I think about it, the more annoyed I am."

The boy tosses me onto the ground. I land hard enough to rattle my bones. The impact is much less shocking than the realization that I didn't kill Roberto at all. That this boy—this beautiful, angelic boy—*is* Roberto.

Which explains why I heard no music from Rodrigo. He was as silent as his corpse is now. How stupid am I that I only now realized this.

I suck a deep breath, extinguishing the fire in my lungs. It doesn't ease my trembling or alleviate the burning need for violence.

Of course it doesn't. Because this isn't mere adrenaline. This need to launch myself at him, to destroy him, this is my vampire spidey sense kicking in. I don't know why now or why here, but this must be it.

But I feel completely unprepared for it. I thought it would make me stronger. Instead, I am crippled by it.

But of course, as I attempt to stand and Roberto looms over me practically cackling with delight, another thought slams me:

Sebastian knows Roberto. He must know what he looks like. The
angelic, blond beauty. The youth. Roberto made Sebastian, even if
it was two thousand years ago. That isn't the kind of thing you're
likely to forget. Two thousand years from now, I'll still remember
what Sebastian looks like.

And Sebastian must have known how far off my expectations
were. After all, how often had he told me that Roberto was older
even than he? That Roberto had been in this part of the world
since the early days of the Aztec empire. Surely, he must have
known what I thought. He must have. I couldn't believe that after
all the careful planning, after all he did to prep me for this, that
he would forget to mention that Roberto was sixteen and as blond
as a Nordic snowboarder. When you're talking about Aztec god-
vampires, surely that's the kind of thing that would come up.

So Sebastian deliberately misled me. He didn't send me in here
to kill Roberto. He sent me in to fail. I am not an assassin. I'm a
distraction.

After all these months, I thought I knew him. I thought I understood him. I knew I couldn't trust him, precisely, but I thought
I knew his endgame. And I thought he respected me and what I
could do. I was wrong. About everything.

I am flummoxed. And when Roberto pounces on me, I am
floored. I go down hard and together, we slide a couple of feet
across the gleaming polished wood. I swing my arms up to hit him,
but he neatly captures both my hands in his. No matter how I
buck, I can't force him off. He chuckles. Despite being whippet
thin, he's wickedly strong and he manages to hold me down with
one hand. His other hand fumbles for the stake I dropped. I see
what's coming and my terror picks up. I'd thought I was ready. I'd
thought I was willing to die to accomplish this. To avenge not just

my sister but all of humanity. But now, in this instant, with my enemy reaching for a stake, panic claws through me. I don't want to die. Not now. Not like this.

I buck and flail. My heels find purchase and I twist around, but he's seated too firmly on top of me. And then the stake is in his hands. There's a maniacal gleam in his gaze as he slams the stake down to my heart.

The impact is crushing. I feel ribs crack and break and a horrible, searing pain in my lungs that makes it impossible to catch my breath. But the stake doesn't go through.

It doesn't go through!

The wood splinters against the bulletproof vest I have under the guard's uniform. I look from the shards of wood up to Roberto's face. I don't know who's more surprised, him or me. He growls in frustration at the same time I let out a crazed laugh.

I'm harder to kill than I used to be.

"Wow. Guess you shouldn't have bought that body armor for your guards."

He snarls, his hand ripping at the collar of the vest. The tightly woven fabric of the vest bites into the flesh on the back of my neck and arms. He gives it a hard yank and I feel the fabric slice my skin before the fabric gives and the seams rip open. The buttons on the camo shirt pop as he rips the front of the vest clean off, leaving my chest bare.

He stands, pulling me up along with him. I stumble a few steps behind while I struggle to get my feet under me. He drags me over to the body of his valet. He bends down to grab the stake from Rodrigo's heart.

I won't get another chance to break free, so I duck my head and plow into him. I knock him over, and he lets go of my hands.

But he's as experienced a fighter as Sebastian and he recovers quickly, rolling with the action and popping back up onto his feet. I stumble, but before I can straighten, he swings his leg out in a roundhouse kick. I grab his ankle, but he twists in midair, forcing me off balance. He recovers before I can and he kicks me in the chest. I go down again. I roll out from under him before he can slam the stake through my heart. I scramble across the floor toward a chair by the wall. He's almost on top of me, when I grab it and swing it at him. It smashes to pieces on his head, but he's barely dazed. That's okay. I didn't expect to knock him out or anything. All I wanted was one of those spindly legs. And I'm betting the hard, polished wood of furniture will be more effective than a quickly whittled branch anyway. I grab the chair leg in both hands and bring it up between me and him just as he slams the stake in my direction. The chair leg collides with his chest, stopping his momentum, but his reach is longer than mine and I can feel the tip of the wood digging into my skin. For a second, we lay there, him poised over my body, me fighting to keep that stake out of my heart.

Roberto knows my strength is failing and that gleam is back in his gaze. He's enjoying this. Like this is the most fun he's had all day. Hell, probably all century.

I'm not going to make it. I am struggling with everything I've got, and it's not enough. This crazy damn vampire is going to kill me. Any second now.

Except it doesn't happen.

He tenses above me. Freezes completely. He's no longer looking at me, and his gaze has shifted up to the left, like he can hear something in the distance that I can't.

And then I can hear it: a piercing howl. Not the howl of a Tick, but a mechanical howl of a jet coming in too fast. It roars overhead before whining away with a Doppler effect. An instant later, there's the stupefying boom of something huge crashing to the ground.

The whole house shakes. The chandelier above me trembles and dust filters down through the air. Then the lights flicker and go out.

Roberto looks back down at me. The haze of vampire crazy-berserker clears from his eyes. He flashes me another demonic smile. "Well, now. Isn't this interesting?" He hops to his feet, pulling me with him. Again, he has my wrists in one of his hands. He plucks the chair leg neatly out of my hands. "I'll just take that, if you don't mind."

He opens the top drawer in the desk. Inside is a creepy array of instruments, the purpose for which I don't even want to consider. There are knives and picks and saws. It's like a full surgical supply cart. Along with a bundle of zip ties. He has my hands cuffed in front of me before I can even think past my horror at what I've seen in the drawer.

Then, he's dragging me out of the bedroom and down the stairs. "Let's just go see what your friend is up to, shall we?"

I stumble after him, down the grand, curving staircase, my footsteps clattering across the marble of the entrance hall. He doesn't stop until we're out on the sweeping, wide front porch. We both look out over the town. Guards are scrambling in front of the courthouse. A pair of Hummers rumble by from the direction of the barracks. Other people, civilians, are pouring out onto the street to see what has happened. And then I see it.

On the other side of town, opposite from the gatehouse, a plume of inky smoke spirals into the sky. Only then do I realize that all the lights in town are out. There are streetlights all down

Main Street. It was dusk when I went into Roberto's house and the lights were just starting to come on. Now the sun has fully set and all of the lights are dark.

Whatever crashed must have gone right into the fence and knocked out the entire electrical grid. In the distance, far beyond the edge of town, I can hear the Ticks howling at the fence. Ticks that I led here. How long will it take for them to figure out that the fences are down? How long before the innocent people of this town are overrun by monsters that I let in? But I have no time to think about that.

Roberto hooks his fingers through the zip tie and drags me along behind him down the stairs and out into the street. His presence doesn't go unnoticed. The people milling about stop to watch him with equal parts fear and awe. In this crowd, no one will come to my rescue. I am on my own.

He moves quickly down the street but I can't keep up. I stumble and hit the ground hard on one knee. I cry out, but even that doesn't stop him. He just drags me along behind him, my knees scraping the concrete. Finally he stops in the middle of the road and turns in place.

"Come out, come out wherever you are!"

He turns full circle. He's waiting. For Sebastian.

He's figured out Sebastian's plan before I did. Of course Sebastian never intended for me to kill Roberto. How was I ever stupid enough to believe that he'd be content to let me kill his nemesis? He had hunted him for hundreds of years. He's probably planned this for decades. He wasn't going to just hand this over to me. As badly as I want Roberto dead, as badly as I want this all to end, it's nothing compared to how Sebastian feels.

So of course I was nothing more than a decoy. A distraction. All this talk about how I was the only one who could do this, how I was the only one who could kill Roberto; that had all been lies. He even misled me about the vampire spidey sense, because clearly that is what I felt inside the house. That gut-deep need to kill Roberto. Or if I cannot kill him to flee his territory. That wasn't at all what I'd expected. Certainly not so soon or so powerfully. Why had it come on so suddenly?

Then it hits me. Until yesterday I hadn't been a real vampire. I had eaten, but not human blood. I had fed, but not killed. Somehow the act of taking a human life had made my transformation complete.

Sebastian had lied to and manipulated me at every turn. Was there any truth to anything he'd ever said?

And now, he's out there, watching, waiting for the right moment to come and kill my enemy. I certainly hate Roberto. I hate what he's done to the country, possibly to the world. I hate what he's done to Lily and to me. My hatred is broad, but not deep. As many reasons as I have to hate Roberto, none of them feel personal. But Sebastian? I have a lot of reasons to hate him, too. Deeply personal reasons.

Roberto marches up and down the street, dragging me behind him. "I know you're out there!"

Thankfully, he's walking more slowly now and I can keep up.

"How many times are you going to send one of your little pets in to try to kill me?" he calls out.

Wait . . . Sebastian has done this before?

"When are you going to figure out that I will always—always!—win?" He whirls in another direction. "You can't beat me! You just can't."

Across the street, I see Carter and my father dash out of the clinic only to stop on the steps when they see Roberto and me.

"For the first century or so, your pathetic assassination attempts were amusing. But I am not amused anymore. Come get your little pet"—Roberto jerks me forward and pulls me in front of him. He brings the wooden chair leg up to my neck—"before I take care of this problem myself."

The jagged edge of the splintered wood bites into my flesh, but I feel strangely disconnected from my fear. Of course it doesn't hurt that he's ripped my shirt and it's hanging open in tatters. I'm mostly covered, but I feel strangely vulnerable this way, partially naked and unable to hide myself. It's the embarrassment that stings the most. The shame of failure.

This was supposed to be my big gesture on behalf of all humanity. My great act of defiance. Some assassin I turned out to be. I murdered an unarmed valet and got myself captured.

Maybe this is how it was meant to be. I wanted to play a part in bringing Roberto down. Maybe this is simply the part I get to play. The dupe. The fool. The victim.

CHAPTER FIFTY

CARTER

I hadn't really thought about what Roberto might look like until I saw him dragging Mel out into the center of town. The guy looked younger and more delicate than any of the Elites. Hell, he looked like half the Greens back at Base Camp could beat the crap out of him. Despite appearances, he'd somehow subdued and captured Mel. Which meant he had to be pretty badass. Typically speaking, you couldn't pack that much badass into 130 pounds of scrawny kid without some serious supernatural help. Ergo, the twerp tossing Mel around like a sack of laundry had to be Roberto.

Still, I was surprised. When you think of an evil vampire over-lord, you don't automatically picture a guy who could be a member of One Direction.

Frankly, I didn't care who he was; I wasn't about to let him get away with using Mel as some kind of bargaining chip. But how the hell could I get her out of there?

I glanced at Price first. This was his daughter. Yeah, he'd skipped out on them years ago, but hadn't he just said he'd done this all for them? Surely he'd step up to save her.

But he just stood there, an expression of bemusement on his face.

"Do something," I said, grabbing his shoulder and pushing him forward. "She's your daughter. Help her!"

"That can't be Mel."

I fought the urge to slap Price upside the head. What was wrong with him? His daughter was in trouble—like, about to be staked through the heart in trouble—and he didn't seem to be able to process that at all.

Then it hit me. He didn't know what she'd become.

Besides which, other than that brief meeting at the clinic, he hadn't seen her in years. In his mind, Mel was still the barely functioning ten-year-old he'd abandoned.

Now, he couldn't reconcile that image with the one before him. This Mel had clearly overpowered a guard, cut off her own hair to complete the ruse, and done her damnedest to kill Roberto. The fact that she hadn't succeeded didn't diminish the fact that she'd tried. Price literally couldn't believe his eyes.

Great, the one man who might actually be able to help her had been struck dumb.

Which left only me to help.

I pushed past Price to walk down the steps. There were still lots of civilians milling around. They couldn't seem to figure out what to do. They were probably so used to taking direction from Price and Roberto that they couldn't think for themselves anymore. Or maybe they couldn't think past Price's confusion.

Of course, all the people on this compound had thrown in with Roberto for whatever reason. I didn't particularly have a lot of sympathy for them, but that didn't mean I thought they deserved to die. Especially since there were families here. People with kids.

I turned back to Jonathan, grabbed him by the shoulders, and gave him a shake. "Get it together. If you can't stand up to Roberto, fine. But at least get these people out of here."

He looked at me a little blankly. "Who?"

"These people! They're just standing around. Waiting for you to tell them what to do. Don't you get it? There are no lights on, so that means the electricity is out. No electricity means no fences, and that the Ticks can get in. Say something to them. You want to be this great leader? Be it now."

But he shook his head, scoffing. "The Ticks won't get in."

That's when I stopped trying to get through to him. He was obviously so out of touch he had no idea what they were dealing with. I did. The Ticks would get in and they'd eat their way through this town in a matter of hours. Sure, maybe some of these people had the vaccine. Maybe most of them did. But the vaccine only protected you from being turned into a Tick. It wouldn't do jack to protect you from having your heart ripped out.

I turned to the crowd and yelled, "The fences are down! The Ticks will get through. You're all in danger! Get your families inside. Arm yourselves with whatever you have and don't come out until well after dawn!" The people on the street looked from me to Jonathan and then to Roberto, where he stood with Mel. "They aren't going to save you! You have to save yourselves!" A murmur of disbelief and fear rippled through the crowd. "Go!"

I wanted to roar with anger. With frustration. These people had put their faith in the wrong people. They'd blindly trusted Price and Roberto to protect them. They'd thought they could pretend the rest of the world hadn't gone to hell outside their gates. They were wrong.

And it was this man's fault.

I whirled back to Jonathan Price. An *abductura* powerful enough to sway the emotions of nearly everyone in the entire state—at least. But too damn concerned with his own glory to save anyone. Not even his own daughter.

I hauled off and punched him. Not just once. I pounded him. He stumbled back, tripping over the steps to land hard on his ass.

He cowered before me, arms raised to protect his head. "No!" he cried.

The anger roiling inside of me didn't let up. I wanted to destroy. I wanted to beat him to pulp. To slam his head against the steps. Anything to break the influence he had over these defenseless lambs who were about to be slaughtered by the Ticks.

Except suddenly they didn't seem defenseless anymore. The crowd was scrambling away, scattering into buildings and houses, calling out their loved ones' names and crying for help.

Chaos hit the square hard and fast. In the distance, the Ticks howled as if in response to the panic flooding through the people in town.

Price still cowered before me, but I turned my back on him and walked down the steps to where Roberto stood in the center of the square, Mel still in his grasp.

"Let her go," I ordered.

I wasn't stupid enough to think he'd do it, but hell, I had to start somewhere.

Roberto just stared at me, his head cocked to the side, his expression vaguely baffled. "Who are you?"

"I'm the guy who's going to plunge a stake through your heart."

There was a brief second of shock in Roberto's expression. Then, slowly, he smiled. He tipped his head back and released a peal of crazed laughter.

It was the kind of cackle that would grate on anyone's nerves, but Mel seemed to flinch away from it. As if the noise was actually repugnant to her. Maybe it was.

"Oh, yes, of course," Roberto murmured as his laughter died away. "You must be Carter."

That stopped me. I hadn't expected him to even know I existed.

I'd thought the rebellion had stayed under his radar. Unsure what to say without giving anything else away, I said nothing.

That didn't seem to be a problem. Roberto was clearly the kind of guy who was vain enough that he didn't mind carrying the conversation.

"Ely was right about you."

Ely. Right. My favorite traitor. That's who had told Roberto about me.

"He said you were good. Why, for a moment there, I almost believed you myself. You, a mere human boy are going to stab me through the heart." He gave an exaggerated shiver of fear. "Scary stuff." He let loose another peal of laughter. "Absolutely terrifying."

I ignored his monologue. Frankly, I didn't have the time to listen.

I hadn't been lying to all those people about the Ticks making it through the fences. They would make it through. It was possible whatever aircraft had gone down had smashed right through the fence. In which case, they'd be here sooner rather than later.

Sure, I figured that plane going down had something to do with Sebastian, but I wasn't going to wait around for his help. I couldn't assume he'd intended to crash the plane or that he'd gotten out of it in time. I was the one who had to get us out of this. I had to get Roberto to release Mel, I had to find Lily, and then get the hell out of here. And pray there was still a Hummer left to steal, because I didn't think the Mazda had much gas left. And I had to do it all before the Ticks came streaming through town.

First up, I had to convince Roberto to let Mel go. I decided to change tactics. Clearly the whole threatening him thing wasn't working. Tipping him over the edge into crazy, maybe. Working in my favor, not so much.

I held up my hands in a gesture of surrender. "Look, we're all reasonable. This city is under attack. Let's call a truce and fight off the Ticks."

"Why would I need a truce? The Ticks can't harm me. They're an annoyance. One that I will deal with when I see fit. Sebastian, on the other hand, is an annoyance whose time has come." Roberto tipped his head back and yelled, "Se-bas-tian!" He drew out every syllable like they were separate words. "I believe your little assassin and your *abductura* are waiting for you."

What the hell? Sebastian's *abductura*?

Did Roberto know something we didn't know? Had Mel retained her powers after all?

I sent her a questioning look. We hadn't had much time in the clinic before her father had shown up, but if she still had her powers, wouldn't she have found a way to tell me?

Would she even know if she was still an *abductura*? Maybe she still had her powers and just hadn't used them.

But when I caught her eye, she shook her head like she didn't know what he was talking about, either.

I tried another tactic. "Just let us go. We'll get Lily, take the cure, and leave you alone."

"You've already said you wanted to kill me. Why would I let you go? It's completely impractical, of course. I can't have humans running around messing up my plans. It's bad enough that he's out there." Roberto whirled in a circle again. "Do you see what you've done, Sebastian? This was the last outpost of civilization, and you've destroyed it! All because of your stupid little revenge plot. You've sworn to kill me or die trying? Fine! But why kill all of humanity along with me?"

"Don't pin your crimes on Sebastian. Don't blame him for the mess you created. He's the one who's out there trying to protect people."

"You don't honestly think he ever cared about your stupid human rebellion, do you? He's never cared about that. All he's ever cared about was revenge. Two thousand years and that's all he's ever thought about. Seriously." Roberto yelled out to the courtyard, "Sebastian, you need a hobby."

Part of me knew that Roberto was right—about this, at least. Sebastian's primary motive had always been stopping Roberto. But, still, I had to argue with Roberto. "He may want revenge, but that doesn't mean he's okay with what you've done to the world."

"With what *I've* done to the world?" he asked, sounding strangely baffled. "I've protected as much of my kine as I can. I implemented the plan for the Farms. Jonathan convinced people to send their kids there to keep them safe. We've protected people."

"Obviously."

"And what has he done? He's dillydallied around, plotting out this elaborate scheme to kill me while he waited for your powers to develop. What did he really think was going to happen? That you'd just waltz in here and talk me to death?"

"The way this is going, I think talking people to death is more your style."

Roberto smiled at my joke, "You amuse me. Maybe I'll even keep you around after I've killed Sebastian. I can never have too many *abducturae*."

"The joke's on you then, because Sebastian doesn't have an *abductura*."

Roberto's smile froze. He tipped his head to the side and asked, "Do you really not know what you are?"

Icy fear hit me in the chest. Even though I didn't believe him, I felt it. "I'm not the *abductura*. Mel was."

Yet, somehow, even as I said the words, things were clicking in my mind. Pieces of a puzzle were starting to merge into a complex picture, something I hadn't seen, hadn't even dreamed until this moment.

"Of course Melanie here was an *abductura*. I figured one of Jonathan's girls would be. Why else would I have worked so hard to get them back? But no, she lost that ability when Sebastian turned her. Think about it; he wouldn't have turned his only *abductura*. He wouldn't have turned anyone, would he, unless he didn't have a choice?" Roberto pinned me with an unshakably intense stare. "It was your idea, wasn't it? To turn poor Mel here. You were the one who convinced him."

Even though I wanted to deny it, I couldn't. When Mel was dying, Lily had had the idea that Sebastian could turn her into a vampire to save her life. But I was the one who convinced him to do it. Despite the fact that he'd sworn over and over that he'd never make another vampire, he'd done it.

At the time I'd thought . . . what? That I'd just made a good argument?

Now, standing here listening to Roberto, it seemed ridiculous that I hadn't seen it before. I was the one who convinced Sebastian to turn Mel. Just like I was the one who'd convinced all the guys at Elite to start the rebellion. Just like I convinced them to search for Lily and Mel. To rescue Greens from Farms. Hell, back in the clinic I'd even convinced Jonathan to go talk with me instead of turning me over to the guards, which is what I was sure he really wanted to do. When was the last time I'd asked something of someone and hadn't gotten it?

Now, looking back on my life, it was obvious what I was. Not just what I was, but what my father before me had been. What we both were. *Abducturae*. Liars. Controllers. Manipulators.

I'd been willfully ignoring my true nature for years.

Because, hell, who would want this god-awful skill? This curse that allowed you to twist the will of others? I don't know if my father had wanted it, but he'd certainly used it to his own advantage. Jonathan had obviously wanted it. As for me, why would I want this? Why would I want to be in the company of these two losers?

Except I looked around behind and saw that Jonathan was gone. At some point in the last few minutes, he'd skittered away like the cockroach he was. The bastard.

So it was just me and Roberto. And Sebastian, if he was out there. I felt a burning wave of hatred wash over that icy disbelief. Sebastian had known what I was all along. He'd found me and nurtured my powers and used me, all without revealing what I was.

All my life, I had hated the kind of man my father was. The kind of man who used other people, who manipulated them to get what he wanted. I had despised him for as long as I could remember. And here I was, just like him.

Because in the end, I would use this supposed power of mine to get what I wanted. I would free Mel, I would get the cure for Lily, and I would get us the hell out of here.

Sebastian had always said that it took training for an *abductura* to be able to channel his powers and use them. It took focus and determination. I didn't have training. All I could draw on was the memory of the few times I knew for sure that I'd used my powers.

I remembered the fear for Mel. The sheer determination not to let her die. The need to prove myself to Lily.

I drew on all of that now and said to Roberto, "Forget Sebastian. Forget all of this crap. Let Mel go, give us the cure for Lily, and we'll just walk away. You'll never hear from us again. Or, hell, we'll stay and help you fight, for that matter. If you're pissed off that Sebastian has risked your compound, we'll stay and fight off the Ticks. I'll lead your men against them myself. But first you have to get the cure for Lily and let Mel go."

Roberto tipped his head to the side. "The cure?"

"Yes, the cure for the Tick virus. I know you have it."

Roberto gave another one of his slow, creepy smiles before dissolving into laughter. Not the crazed, maniacal laugh, but a cynical chuckle. "No, I don't. I'm not behind Genexome Corporation. I've never had anything to do with it."

"No—" I protested automatically.

"For hundreds of years, I've invested in energy, cattle, and kine," Roberto said. "Biotechnology has never interested me. I'm not the vampire with the vendetta against all our kind. I'm not the one who wants to destroy all of the vampires and wipe the slate clean. Think about it. I don't own Genexome Corporation. Sebastian does."

Shock slammed into me and I staggered back a step.

But Roberto's verbal assault kept on coming.

"When you think about it, you'll see I'm right. I'm not the villain here. He is." Then Roberto chuckled. "Well, I am a villain, just not the one you're after. And that does sting, doesn't it? Knowing that he's had the cure all this time. All this time, he could have saved humanity and he waited. He has the cure that will save your girlfriend, but instead of giving it to you, he sent you here to distract me."

"Why?" I gasped out, not meaning to, but shock had robbed me of caution.

Roberto whirled around and gazed at a point in the shadows between the buildings. "Isn't that right, Sebastian?"

A Tick howled, and the sound seemed to reverberate in the

air. The Ticks were nearer now. But before I could pinpoint a location, Sebastian stepped out of the shadows. He had his dagger in one hand and a longer, curved sword in the other.

"Sorry it took me so long." He winked at Mel. "Hiking in from the drop site and avoiding all those Ticks was a pain in the ass. Nasty business."

"Did you really think that would work? Sending in your little baby vampire as a decoy? Did you really think that I would be so distracted by her stench that I wouldn't notice you trying to sneak up on me?" Roberto flipped the stake and caught it neatly in his palm so he could use the sharper end in a stabbing motion. "Did you honestly think that would work?"

"No. I never believed that at all." Sebastian stopped a few feet away from Roberto, a mad grin stretching his mouth taut. "She was never a decoy. All these distractions, they were never for you. They were to get your people out of the way. All your guards and acolytes. I wanted them distracted. I wanted them gone. I don't need to sneak up on you to kill you. I just need to face you one on one."

Roberto nodded toward the weapons Sebastian clutched in his hands. "If you're so eager to face me on equal terms, then why do you have two swords and I have none?"

"Which do you want? I'll gladly hand one over."

"The katana, of course."

A second later, Sebastian tossed the longer of the two swords through the air. It turned end over end before plunging into the ground at Roberto's feet, swaying there for a second. Then, Roberto thrust Mel away from him and grabbed the sword. An instant later, Sebastian lunged for Roberto. The fight that followed was a flurry of movements too fast to even see. The clang of their swords was one constant clatter of metal on metal so loud I couldn't even hear the baying of the Ticks over it.

So this was what it had come to. Everything that had happened in the past year of my life had been about this one battle to the death between Sebastian and Roberto. This was never about me at all. This trip here wasn't about getting Lily the cure. It was just about revenge for Sebastian. I always knew that morality was a wavy and mysterious line for him. I always knew he couldn't be wholly trusted. Still, I didn't see this coming. I could never have imagined that he would betray us like this.

I could imagine him failing us. Out of laziness or lack of compassion or even simple hunger. But I hadn't imagined he had it in him to plan and execute a betrayal this elaborate. This well thought out.

I could accept Jonathon's role in this mess because he seemed to genuinely believe the world needed a fresh start, one guided by his twisted vision for humanity. And I could accept Roberto's role in this, because he was yet another crazed megalomaniac. No wonder the two of them got along so well. But I couldn't understand Sebastian's motivations. I couldn't imagine any thirst for revenge that would justify the murder of millions.

I watched the furious fight for a moment, but knew I couldn't stay to see the ending. That was okay. No matter how this ended, I was going to hunt down Sebastian someday. If Roberto didn't kill him, then I would.

I lunged forward and grabbed Mel, pulling her away from the fight. I found my pocketknife in my boot and sawed through the zip ties. She gave her hands a shake, cringing. Roberto had put the zip tie on tight enough that her hands were bitterly cold and already turning blue.

I grabbed her by the arm. I had to shout to be heard over the clang of the swords. "We've got to go!" I yelled. "The Ticks will be here any minute. We've got to get Lily and get out of here."

But she shook her head. "You get Lily and find some wheels. I'm not leaving Sebastian."

"Are you kidding me?" I glanced back at the fight. She was crazy if she thought she could break into that and end up anything other than dead. Besides, I couldn't believe she wasn't as pissed off as I was. "That's his shit to handle."

"No," she yelled back. Her fingers were at the buttons of her shirt, refastening the few that were left. "We can't leave without him because we still need the cure. If Roberto is right and Sebastian has the cure, then we need that for Lily. We can't leave him here."

She was right; I couldn't believe I hadn't thought of it, too.

I nodded. "I'll be back in five minutes. Get him ready to extract by then."

I jogged off in the direction of the clinic. I was nearly there when a low thrum filled the air. I looked up to see a helicopter swoop in. It stopped above the clinic, hovering in the air above the squat building. My pulse kicked up.

Of course Roberto would have a helicopter. There were only two men on El Corazon who would have the authority to call it in. One of them was out in the square, trying to slice Sebastian into shreds. The other was about to kidnap my girlfriend.

I raced to the front door. I wasn't sure how well staffed this place was or what I would encounter on the other side. As long as they were human, I could talk my way past them. It was the Ticks howling in the distance that I was most worried about. I didn't give myself much time to think it through. Right about now, I was really missing my weapons.

With the electricity off, the pair of glass sliding doors didn't open automatically, but one of them swung open when I pushed it. The entrance was empty, but I could hear sounds coming from the left. The building must have had a backup generator—I guess most hospitals do—because dim yellow emergency lights lit the hall about every ten feet. This was the opposite wing of the building from where we'd been held when we first arrived. The clinic was obviously bigger than this tiny community needed. Apparently when Roberto had built it, he'd been planning ahead. I ran down one corridor and then the next, glancing into every room, but I saw nothing. No patients. No staff.

Then I turned a corner and heard it. The faint, lulling beeps of a life support machine. I slowed to a jog. As I got closer, I realized it wasn't just one machine but several, and the noises were coming from a room beyond a pair of doors just ahead.

I slipped to the side of the doors, pressing my back against the wall so I could listen. Someone was in the room. I heard the carts rolling around. Things banging. It didn't sound like a Tick rampaging through the room, more like a human in a hurry. I peered through the window in the door and saw Price along with a woman in scrubs. Shit. And here I was. No weapon.

Still in a fight two against one, I could probably take them. Price was close to fifty. I couldn't tell about the woman, but if Roberto was right about me—if Sebastian was right—then maybe all I had to do was ask her to step aside.

I didn't want this power. I never had. No one should be able to bend others to his will. If you had asked me an hour earlier, I would have sworn that even if I had the power of an *abductura*, I wouldn't use it. And here I was, ready to abandon my morals instantly. If it meant saving Lily.

I pushed through the doors in to the room. It wasn't just a single hospital room but a whole ward, like an ICU. A dozen beds were lined up on either side of the room, each with the little privacy curtain pushed back against the wall. Four of the beds had patients tucked under the white blankets. Each had an IV bag hanging from the post above their bed. Each lay as still as a corpse.

Lily lay on the bed closest to the door on the far end of the room. Her skin looked unnaturally pale. She was as still and lifeless as the other three.

Price and the doctor stood over her. They had been talking in low voices when I came in, but both of them fell silent and turned toward me.

Thank God there wasn't a guard somewhere that I hadn't seen through the window. Faintly, in the distance, I could hear the *whump-whump-whump* of the helicopter still hovering above the building.

The doctor looked from Price to me and back again.

"Why did you let me think you had the cure?"

"I didn't."

"You said—"

"No. You said she needed medical attention. I got that for her. We don't have a cure, but we have a treatment protocol that involves inducing comas. It slows the progress of the disease. Not indefinitely, but for a while at least."

I glanced at the other patients. The one at the far end of the room was a guy with what looked like a short, military-style haircut grown out a couple of months. Had he been one of the guards? Whatever he had been in life, he wasn't quite human anymore. His jaw was too big, his brow ridge too pronounced, making his eyes look sunken. Even under the blanket, the proportion of his limbs looked all wrong. I didn't ask how long he'd been like this or how quickly he was progressing. I didn't want to know.

I barely looked at the guy on the bed next to his, but the third patient caught my eye because it was a kid. And because there was a dog asleep under the kid's bed. The chow mix slowly stretched and sat up. Chuy. Which meant the kid was Marcos. Ely's little brother. They looked enough alike—despite the four year age difference—that they could have been twins. I might have doubted myself if Chuy hadn't been there. And it made so much sense. Ely wasn't a bad guy. He was just a guy who would do anything for his family. I could understand that. Knowing his brother was in here being held by Roberto, being held in stasis—it made me hate Ely less for betraying us. That was a good thing. I had enough people to hate right now.

I looked at Lily last. I couldn't help but imagine her a few weeks or months down the road, looking like that guy at the end. How much time did she have? I didn't know; I just had to pray it was enough.

I looked back up at Price. I expected to feel that burst of hatred. Instead, I felt nothing but exhaustion.

"I'm sorry." He actually looked like he meant what he was saying. Not that I believed him. Not that it even mattered one way or the other. "I didn't know you even thought we had the cure."

I turned to the doctor. "How long can she live in stasis?"

"Dodson has been like that for two months, but we'll lose him completely at some point. There was a guard before him who turned completely at eleven weeks. The sedative must be incompatible with something in the Tick biology. He woke up and we had to—"

I nodded my understanding. So, under three months. Probably less because it had taken more than twenty-four hours to get her here and into the coma.

I had come in here determined to save her. To get her out of the clinic and drive straight to the Genexome Corporation headquarters. To rip the place to shreds until I found the cure.

But how could I know if that was the right thing for me to do?

I looked at Price again. "You've got the helicopter? Where are you going?"

"Wherever we can find that's safe. Probably one of the Farms."

"You're taking the doctor?" I looked at her. She nodded. "And you can keep her alive until I can find the cure and bring it to you?"

Pity flashed across her face. "I can try."

Price stepped forward. "Once she wakes up, she'll stay with me. I won't let her leave with you."

Now, it was my turn to feel pity. Price obviously cared about his daughters in his own twisted way, but he didn't know them. If he really thought that he could keep Lily out of this fight, then he didn't know her at all.

God knows I'd certainly tried and it hadn't worked. Not at all. When you loved someone, it wasn't always about keeping them safe. It was about caring enough to let them make their own decisions. It wasn't about control or protection. It was about respect. I'd learned that the hard way.

"You want to keep her safe with you, you're welcome to try."

Price looked at me suspiciously. "You're really just going to let me take her?"

The doctor looked at me and said, "There's room in the helicopter. You could come."

Price looked like he wanted to swallow his tongue, but then he nodded. "We could use a guy like you. With your combat experience."

For a second, I was tempted. The best way to make sure Price didn't take Lily too far away for me to find her was to go with them myself. But I'd seen the copter. It wasn't that big.

"If I came, you wouldn't have room for all of them, would you?"

Price shrugged. He obviously hadn't thought that far ahead. He was too used to thinking only of his own interests. But the doctor shook her head.

In the end, I wasn't willing to sacrifice lives, especially the life of a kid, to be with Lily.

"I'll help you load the helicopter. Lily first, then Marcos. You take as many as you can. The doctor here stays with them." I got right in Price's face. "You find the closest Farm and you let me know where you're going. As long as she's still alive when I get there, I'll let you live. But if you try to keep me away from her, I will find you and destroy you myself."

"You're so sure you could do that?"

"Yeah, I am. Don't forget, I'll have your other daughter."

Something hard and soulless lit in Price's eyes and I knew he'd been planning on snagging Mel on the way out.

"Mel won't go with you," I told him.

"She will. Mel and I have always understood each other."

"Maybe. But you're the one who said you should never under-estimate the great things a human *abductura* can accomplish when working with a vampire."

It took several seconds for Price to understand my point. I'd been right. He hadn't figured out yet that Mel had turned into a vampire. The shock on his face might have been enough to make me smile, but I was already helping the doctor wheel Lily's bed out to the helicopter.

CHAPTER FIFTY-ONE

MEL

I sneak back to the square as the fight between Roberto and Sebastian rages on. Of course, all the sneaking in the world is pointless. Neither notices me. They are completely engaged in the battle, relentlessly focused on each other. The clang of metal on metal echoes through the square, and the closer I get, the more it blocks out everything else. The howls of the approaching Ticks. The roar of the helicopter's engine. The report of rapid gunfire in the distance. All of it fades.

Roberto and Sebastian appear to be evenly matched. Roberto is smaller, of course, but the katana gives him a longer reach. Sebastian, I know, has battle experience that should give him an edge, but Roberto is fantastically good with the sword, wielding it with an easy confidence that I never managed.

As evenly matched as they are, I have no doubt this could last for hours. Days maybe, before one of them tires enough to make a mistake. They slash and swipe and parry with a grace and agility that no Hollywood special effects department could hope to match.

Their battle is a thing of beauty.

But I don't have time for this. My sister needs that cure. All I need is a few minutes alone with Sebastian to find out where the cure is, so that Carter and I can leave here to go get it.

We need to get out of here soon. There are—literally—hundreds of miles of fence around this compound, but eventually the Ticks will find their way through if they haven't already. They'll swarm over this town and when they do—if Carter is still here—he'll be torn apart. He's protected me often enough. It's time for me to return the favor.

I have to either interrupt the fight or find a way to tip the balance to end it more quickly. Neither of which I am going to be able to do unless I find some kind of weapon. I know the guard station will be well stocked, but undoubtedly there are guards there also. I'm not going to count on them handing me a crossbow so I can go murder their leader.

Instead, I sneak back around the edge of the square toward the one building I know: Roberto's mansion.

I don't know what I'll find there. My trek through the downstairs of his house was somewhat impeded by the fact that I was dragged along behind a raging maniac. I don't remember seeing anything I could use as a weapon, but even crazed vampires needed brooms, right?

Sure, Roberto doesn't seem like the type to do his own cleaning, but the cleaning staff has to keep their stuff somewhere.

I dash up the steps and in through the front door, which stands open. My eyes adjust quickly to the darkness and I stare around the foyer. There is a front parlor off to the left with a massive entertainment center and sleek, leather furniture intermixed with elegant antiques. I guess his taste is eclectic. I am about to walk on past and look for a broom closet or something when the gleam of metal on the back wall catches my attention.

I walk into the room, feeling along the wall automatically for a light switch before remembering that the electricity is off. I am most of the way across the room before my mind processes what I am seeing.

The wall is covered with weapons, from the ceiling all the way down to the display case. Swords, daggers, crossbows. Most of them look like antiques. All of them have a cross somewhere on them, everything from the crudely painted slash of red on the wooden handle of the crossbow, to the mother-of-pearl embossed on the handle of a sword. The display case is the wood-and-glass kind you'd see in a museum. It contains a series of Victorian-style boxes. The most elaborate of them is closed to show off the carving. The others are opened to reveal the contents: daggers, pistols, vials of mysterious powder, carved pieces of wood. More crosses. Crosses on everything.

That's what does it for me. That's what gives it away.

They are vampire hunting kits. Once in the Before, I'd seen a TV show about them. They'd been a curiosity item popular with paranoid Victorians after the publication of Bram Stoker's *Dracula*. And Roberto collects them. By the dozens. I look at the weapons on the wall again. All those crosses. That's what this whole display is. The tools of vampire hunters.

What kind of idiot collects weapons specifically designed to kill him?

An egomaniac with a well-equipped personal army, I guess.

I reach for a sword most like my katana. As I pull it from the wall, I notice a tiny nameplate beneath it. *Kimura 1704.* They all have labels with names and dates. So then this isn't just a collection of vampire-slaying tools. It's a personal collection. These are the tools of vampire slayers who came after him and failed.

I don't take the time to count them. I don't need to know how many have failed before me. Besides, I don't really need to kill Roberto. I only need to distract him long enough for Sebastian to do it.

Obviously, one of the bows would be my best bet in terms of

not needing to be close to Roberto to use it, but I don't have Lily's archery experience. Besides, I think I'd read somewhere that bow strings needed to be oiled regularly to be kept in working condition. Even if I could hit a target, having the string snap when I notch the arrow will do me no good.

I take the katana and a wicked-looking dagger. Then, just to be sure, I knock out the glass in the display case and grab a fistful of stakes. Maybe I am being paranoid, but I don't want my katana added to this wall.

I think for a moment, but I am not sure how I feel about Sebastian's Arkansas Toothpick. When it comes to him, I am still torn.

How am I supposed to feel? In some ways, Sebastian seems to know me better than I know myself. He understands me like no one else ever has. And he's used that knowledge against me. He's turned me into a killer.

I truly hate him. But does that mean I want him dead?

No. I don't.

Unless . . . unless everything Roberto had said was true. Unless Sebastian was responsible for the Tick virus. Unless he was the one who had destroyed the world. Unless he was the one responsible for the end of my world as I'd known it. For the death of my mother. What happened to my sister.

Then, yes. Then, I want him dead.

Once I'm armed, I sneak out the front door and slip through the darkness to the square. I stash the stakes in the pockets of my cargo pants. Then I tuck the katana under my arm as I fasten the sheath of the dagger to my belt as I walk. Confident I can reach whatever I need, I grip the handle of the katana and scrape the pad of my thumb across the blade. It's old but sharp enough. It will do what I need it to. Kimura may not have succeeded in killing Roberto, but then, he wasn't sneaking up on him in the middle of an all-out battle. Still, I couldn't help wondering if Kimura had failed because he'd underestimated Roberto. And if I was making the same mistake.

Sebastian and Roberto are still at it; I knew they would be. Roberto almost has Sebastian backed against the oak tree in the middle of the square. Sebastian sees me coming, his eyes flickering only briefly in my direction. Roberto hesitates on his next strike, and it's the window Sebastian has been looking for. With one wickedly fast movement, he lunges in and the dagger catches the katana just so. The sword flies out of his hand and goes soaring through the air.

Roberto spins away before Sebastian can skewer him, and I think he's going for the katana. But he doesn't. He jumps, flipping in midair and lands beside me. I'm not fast enough. Not vampire enough, I guess. My reflexes aren't as quick as either of theirs, because before my eyes can even process what has happened, Roberto has yanked out my dagger and has pressed it to the underside of my jaw.

His voice is hot and cloying in my ear. "Better drop the sword, love."

I toss it aside, toward Sebastian. He still has his dagger, obviously, but I figure another sword won't hurt his chances.

"I bet you're wondering"—Roberto reaches up to tuck a strand of my hair back to bare my neck—"how I'm so much faster and smarter than you. Aren't you?" He doesn't wait for me to answer. Which is just as well, since I'm not sure I could talk past the bile in my mouth. "You've been living off Ticks and wild animals because Sebastian lives like some sort of cave person. Me, I've been dining on the smartest, most content humans in the country. My dear, you really should have higher standards when it comes to picking your boyfriends."

"It's not a question of standards," I growl. "If one of you is repulsive."

The tip of the dagger bites into the tender skin of my neck and I twitch away from it. I think I've pissed him off, but then he chuckles. "Too late now, anyway. If you'd come to me earlier, I could have shown you a good time. Of course I'd still kill you right about now anyway, so I don't suppose it matters much."

Sebastian just stands there, eyeing Roberto and me. He's moved the dagger from palm to palm a couple of times. He's trying to think it through, figure out how to get me out of this.

Roberto sees it, too, and presses the blade a little deeper. "Do you want her back?" he asks. "Drop the dagger or I'll kill her. Let me end this now and I'll let her walk."

Sebastian eyes both of us, then he gives a little shrug and says, "I never intended for her to walk out of here, anyway. Go ahead and get her out of the way and you and I can keep at it. This time you won't have the advantage of the longer blade. Good luck with that."

I suck in a breath at Sebastian's words. I try to meet his gaze, but he's not even glancing at me. It's like I'm not even here.

Like I don't exist. I feel a wash of cold fury. I've spent too much of my life with people not seeing me as I really am. That's not how I'm going to die.

Roberto pulls the dagger away from my neck long enough to glance down at the handle. "Hmm . . . You picked Bagnoli's," he says in an offhand voice. "Interesting choice. I would have gone with one of the Spanish blades myself."

Before he can press the blade back to my throat, I drop down, spinning out of his grasp. I pull two wooden stakes out of my pockets as I kick out his legs. He goes down. I pounce before he even hits the ground. The stake goes all the way through his chest and sinks into the ground beneath him.

I leap back before he can move. Even staked through the heart, I know he's still dangerous. I move quickly, using the other stakes to pin his hands to the ground as well. Only then do I stand. I grab the katana and stalk over to his body.

"You may be smarter and faster than I am. But I talk less."

I raise the sword. I'm already swinging it down in a wide arc toward his neck when Sebastian grabs my arm.

There's fury and battle rage in his eyes. Emotion like I've never seen from him before. Guess he got a dose of that vampire berserker rage, too.

He just shakes his head. "He's mine."

I snarl at Sebastian, driving my elbow back into his chest. The air goes out of his lungs in a whoosh, but he doesn't release my arm. In fact, his grip tightens to the point that he's crushing the bones of my wrist.

"I've hunted him for two thousand years. You don't really think I'm going to let you kill him, do you?"

His fingertips dig the tendons in my wrist against the bone and the katana falls out of my hand. Again, I do the drop-and-kick maneuver, but Sebastian trained me and he's ready for the move. He follows me to the ground and wrestles me beneath him. We've fought enough that I can tell he's not really trying to bring me down. His heart isn't in it—either that, or the fight with Roberto has worn him down. Even I can feel the strain of being so deep in Roberto's territory. He braces one arm on the ground beside my head. His other forearm is pressed against my chest.

I look up into his eyes, trying to see past his bloodlust, but all I see is his need for revenge. There is nothing of the man I thought I knew. Nothing of the man I wanted him to be.

Maybe I just hoped that a person could still exist inside a bloodthirsty vampire.

I can't imagine why I'd want to believe that.

"Tell me something, Sebastian. Would you really have let him kill me so you could have your revenge?"

Something flickers in his eyes. "You're fully vampire now, Kit. Haven't you figured that out? You're not my responsibility anymore."

"But you would have let him kill me?"

"I would do anything to stop him. Yes."

"And Genexome? Is it really your company? Are you really responsible for the Tick virus?"

This time there's not even a flicker of emotion in his gaze. "Yes. I'm responsible."

"Why?"

"Why do you think?" he gasps.

It isn't a hard question. Why has he done anything? Because he thought it would help him kill Roberto.

It's all I need to hear.

I buck against him, rolling him under me. It's a move that would never work if he was at his full strength. If he wasn't already exhausted. It's a low blow. But no lower than what he's dealt me.

Once he's under me, I pull my arm up over my head and plunge the stake into his heart.

I do it without thinking about it. Without looking at him. Because it's the only way I can manage to do what needs to be done.

I hear him gasp in surprise, but I ignore it.

I hop up, adrenaline, vampire berserker rage, whatever it is, I'm shaking so badly I can barely hold the sword in my hand as I stalk over to where Roberto still lays, pinned to the ground. He stares up at me, shock writ clearly on his face. I swing the sword up, but I'm shaking too badly.

Tears are pouring down my cheeks and when I feel a hand on

mine, I cry out in alarm and whirl around sword at the ready. But it's Carter.

I drop the sword and scramble away. Because I almost just killed my friend. And because I just killed a man I thought was my friend.

"Let me," Carter says. He's holding out his hands, palm out in a gesture of surrender. I nod mutely and back away.

I don't look as he slices Roberto's head off. I've had enough of death for now.

Instead I move over to Sebastian, who is still alive. Barely. And gasping for breath. Suddenly, my fury, my rage, is gone. Not vanished, but fading. I look down at Sebastian, at the stake that I've driven through his heart, and something inside of me clenches.

I lean over him. "Is there really a cure?"

He's looking back at me, his expression strangely soft in a way it never has been. Death has softened him. He nods. "At Genexome. The underground storage. If Sabrina hasn't taken it yet."

"Sabrina?" I gasp. So, that's what he traded my freedom for. In exchange for letting me go, he told Sabrina that there was a cure and where it was hidden. It was a risky move on his part. Why bring me to Sabrina in the first place? Why trade his most valuable asset for my freedom? Had he really wanted me to have a choice? Or had he been setting us both up?

Whatever his intentions might have been, he came on this suicide mission knowing that at least one person on the outside knew the location of the cure.

He reaches one trembling hand up to my face and brushes back a lock of my newly short hair. He holds onto the lock and rubs it between his thumb and forefinger, looking at it like he's confused. "I liked it better long," he says. A trickle of blood seeps past his lips, making them appear bright red in the dusk. Then he meets my gaze and smiles. "I always knew you had the killer instinct, Kitten."

I choke on a sudden burst of grief that I don't even understand. Why? Why would I be sorry that I've stabbed him? Why regret killing the man who has risked everyone and everything I care about to satisfy his own lust for revenge? The man who has lied to me, tricked me, and made me a killer? The man who stole the music from me? Why would I mourn him?

But he's also the man who has given me more choices than anyone else. The man who has always respected my wishes. And who in the end, tried to do the right thing to save humanity.

My hand hovers above the stake. If I pull it out, will he survive? Will his heart start beating again, pumping out the healing powers of vampire blood?

Then Sebastian's eyes flicker closed, and a wail of grief is torn from my chest. It's not even out of my mouth when Carter grabs me by the shoulders and pulls me away.

"We gotta go!"

I look around, almost surprised to find myself in the town square. It's chaos. People are running everywhere. Ticks howl and yip, but the sound is too close. They've breached the fence. Carter is dragging me toward a car. A way out. We have to take it now because if we don't, someone else will. The Ticks are here. En masse. I could see three, four. Maybe as many as six. But there are far more than that. When I listen for them, I count more than twenty distinct sounds. Far more than I could handle.

I know Carter's right. Mindlessly, I fall into step beside him. Even though my body is aching and bruised. Even though I feel as though I've been hit by a truck. Even though I feel as though I'm leaving a chunk of myself behind.

CHAPTER FIFTY-TWO

MEL

I am alone. In a way I never have been before. Lily is lost to us. My mother is likely dead. My father has betrayed us all.

Yes, I have Carter. He's a friend. He will be my companion in the search for a cure for Lily. He is hers in a way that he could never be mine. Not that I ever wanted him that way. I'm not jealous of that. Not jealous of him, but maybe just a little bit of what they have between them. He will search for the cure, he will fight for her, no matter what. He loves her deeply in a way I will never be loved. Could never be loved.

In the Before—when I was just Mel—I was forever apart from that kind of thing. I was okay with that. I didn't yearn for it. But now, now I know what I am missing. That kind of love is something I can never have. Not with another vampire. I know that berserker vampire rage too well now. It is not something to be toyed with. But I certainly cannot have that love with a human, either. It is a strain even to be with Carter.

I am very much back where I was when I first became a vampire. Only more alone. I have no one now. Not even Sebastian.

He was never a friend, but he was a companion. I briefly consider going back to Sabrina. Throwing myself and Carter on her mercy. Perhaps she would take us in. But I am still not ready to create my own empire and to herd humans like kine. I am not ready for that. Going to her will be my last resort.

So instead, I must truly learn to be alone.

* *

For a long time, we don't say anything. Carter is concentrating on driving and I'm still shaking from my final encounter with Sebastian.

At some point, I look into the backseat. And see a dog sitting there. It's huge and fluffy and takes up most of the backseat, but it's sitting calmly with its head resting on his paws.

"We have a dog now?" I ask, hysterical laughter threatening to bubble up in my throat.

"Yeah," Carter says. "It belonged to Ely."

"Who?"

Carter is silent for a second, then he says, solemnly, "Ely was a friend. I couldn't just leave him. And I thought . . . I don't know, maybe a dog would come in handy."

I don't question his use of the past tense. I know too much about past tense friends. I nod, and let it go. "Do you think Roberto was right?" I ask.

"About what?"

"About Genexome Corporation. Do you think Sebastian really started the company? Do you think he's the one behind the Tick virus?"

Carter is silent for long enough that I think he's not going to answer me. Then he says, "I don't know. Everything that I personally know about Genexome, I heard from Sebastian. I don't know what to believe anymore."

My mind is racing. If Roberto was telling the truth, then Sebastian had knowingly and willingly murdered millions. I have spent the last couple of months living with and being trained by the most evil man in history. But that is if Roberto has told me the truth. If there's one thing I've learned it's that vampires aren't the most trustworthy sources of information. So how do I know which Sebastian I should believe in?

Under his tutelage, I'd been capable of things I'd never thought possible. Good things, yes, because I am physically stronger and emotionally more independent than I'd ever been before, but horrible things as well.

Was this how it began? The long, horrible slide into being a true vampire. Into being a creature so selfish and self-indulgent that I was willing to kill half the world to get what I wanted?

I felt Carter's hand on my leg. He looked at me, concerned, almost as if he knew exactly what I was thinking. "I don't know what's true," he said, "but I can tell you this. If there is a cure out there, we'll find it. Whether Sebastian had it or Roberto had it, we'll find it. We'll find it ourselves. As for who made the virus in the first place, who knows? If I've learned anything from this, it's that you can't ever trust a vampire to tell you the truth." A bitter laugh escapes from his lips. "You can't trust vampires at all."

His words pierce something deep inside of me. Yeah, he doesn't mean them. Not like that. I guess he doesn't really think of me as a vampire yet. But then, he doesn't know the things I've done.

For a while, neither of us speaks. Carter just drives through the seemingly endless night. After a while, I'm afraid that he does realize what he's said. That he knows how much he's hurt me and is trying to think of how to apologize. I couldn't stand that. I can't hear him say that he knows I'll be different. That he believes I'll be able to control myself. After all, vampires aren't the only ones who can lie.

To avoid that conversation, I say, "He could make it."

Carter doesn't ask who I mean. We both know that there's a good chance Sebastian is still alive.

As pissed as I am, as completely furious, as tired as I am of his endless manipulation and lies, I am strangely torn. When I stabbed him through the heart, I wanted him dead. I wanted it with every cell of my body. With my human heart and my vampire soul. I wanted him dead. Completely destroyed.

And yet . . .

And yet, some part of me misses him already. He had been a vicious teacher. He'd been brutal and hard and had never once let up on me. I had hated him for it. And loved it, too. All my life I'd been coddled. I'd been taken care of. Sebastian was the only person, ever, who had treated me like I was capable of taking care of myself. Of just functioning. And he'd done it even before he'd changed me into a vampire. As much as I wanted him dead, as much as I wanted to hate him, how could I?

Maybe he was dead. Maybe I would never see him again. But maybe he wasn't and maybe I would.

"If he is alive," I said aloud, "he's going to be pissed." Oddly, I think he'd be most angry that we killed Roberto ourselves, rather than that I'd stabbed him. "He's not the kind of man to let us walk away. He'll come after us."

Carter's eyes didn't flicker away from the road. His hand tightened slightly on the steering wheel. "Let him come. We'll be ready."